Casey's Online Diary

By

Johanna Jackson

A slightly raunchy, romantic fiction

New Generation Publishing

For Rona

enjoy i xx. Jhxx.

Dedicated to my husband Anthony, our family and dear friends

Johanna Jraeger
xxx.

Acknowledgements

It is a dream come true to be able to achieve this first publication and I would not have been able to reach this point without the love, kindness and support of my husband Anthony and our many friends and family. Thank you all for your never-ending love, support, excitement and encouragement, which kept me positive and tapping away at the keyboard.

Extra thanks also go to some of my dearest friends. To Angie, for your willingness to be a reviewer even though you were unwell, and to Jo, Gwyneth and Rachel, for your brutally honest and very helpful reviews. Each one of your valued critiques helped me to realise this book and for that I am truly grateful!

A word also to Claire; I did it and as promised, you are in it!

My final thank you goes to New Generation Publishing for their support, patience, guidance and advice, which has been truly invaluable and much appreciated.

I hope that all of you, my readers and supporters, will enjoy this first book.

Happy reading!

Contents

Chapter 1

Casey helps Tilly

Casey sat down with her laptop for the last time that day, and before she flopped into bed exhausted, she reflected on the week's events. It had certainly felt like an exciting week – if not a little scary at how fast things had moved – and was most definitely not the week she'd expected to have. Certainly not, and just as she was about to post her last entry into *Casey's Online Diary*, her stomach churned with a sensation akin to a dozen butterflies taking off inside her tummy, then madly fluttering about, crashing into each other in the confined space. Casey pondered on the questions popping into her mind. Had the last two weeks really happened? Did they not know that she really was just a regular girl, who had only ever been a full-time attendee of the University of Life? Rather than someone who had studied hard to gain an obscure journalistic degree at a top University; a degree which might – in other circumstances – suitably impress an Editor of *the* most popular women's magazine in current circulation. No, she most definitely was *not* some high-flying journalist, who would give their right arm to receive such an offer as Casey had done just two weeks ago. The truth of the matter was, that only Casey seemed to be concerned about the fact that she really *was* just a regular girl, with all the wants, hopes and dreams that a regular girl felt. Edine and Claire said that was exactly what they were looking for. But Casey was doubtful; was that actually true, or in fact, had her writing dream just been realised?

What had started out as a bit of fun and a way of escaping the everyday pressures of her day-to-day job, had somehow effortlessly morphed into Casey writing about her life in an online blog, which subsequently transformed into Casey's very own *Online Diary*. Amazingly, much to her surprise and delight, Casey's blog had become something of an addictive – yet very successful way – to express all of her fears and wants. It also enabled her to share a few naughty secrets and funny stories with her new blog-followers. Having been ever so slightly inspired by the antics of Bridget Jones and imagining that she could often be *just* as scatty and witty as Bridget, Casey had dived into that creative writing-pool head first. Although it had to be said, there was definitely no "Mark Darcy" type in Casey's circle of friends. Of course, if there had been, she would have jumped on his bones a long time ago. That went without saying really, seeing as there was probably a huge portion of the female population who had fantasised about meeting a Mark Darcy type of soul-saviour. Casey knew she definitely had, and on more than one occasion.

But, Casey's *Online Diary* was actually quite a bit different to Bridget's and truthfully, if she had supposed that anyone would seriously have been even remotely interested in her life as a normal human being, she might have been tempted to throw in some really juicy bits. You know, just to spice it up and make herself sound so much more interesting and exciting, rather than the thirty-something office worker she'd grown into. Speaking of which, *when the heck did that happen?* When did she leave her twenties to find herself smack in the middle of her thirties? Age had crept up on her surreptitiously, without as much as a hint of a warning.

Actually, if she was being totally honest, her first realisation of that dreaded event had happened one morning the previous week. Having woken up feeling quite chipper, Casey had been in the middle of her normal morning routine, casually sitting at her dressing table whilst massaging the latest skin-saving cream into her face. It was right then that she had noticed the lingering laughter lines around her eyes, which did not blend away the moment Casey stopped applying her cream. No, in fact they had begun to leave a little crease behind every time she stopped smiling. Not quite believing the reality of this previously unnoticed change in her skin, Casey remembered how she'd dismissed Amanda's warning when it had happened to her five years previously. In fact, Casey even recalled saying something like, "Don't be so ridiculous," before suggesting that her friend Amanda was imagining it. But here she was, Casey Smith, just a thirty-something girl (no, make that woman), only just realising the awful truth. Which was that her previously elastic skin had obviously saved a few creases for fun, then outrageously allowed them to take up permanent residence. How perfectly shocking. Casey cried out in an almost wailing voice, which anyone hearing would've believed she had injured herself, or was suddenly trapped under something heavy. Certainly *not* that it was just a few little creases around her eyes, which in Casey's mind, had signified the awful disaster that her groan had implied. But, and it was a BIG but to Casey, those were definitely lines that she'd not previously noticed lingering for quite so long.

A wave of despair suddenly overwhelmed Casey, as thoughts of growing old swept into her mind. So, how the heck could you stop your body from doing things like *ageing* without your permission? With a scowl on her face, Casey had inhaled deeply and given herself a good talking to, saying something like, "It's OK, Casey, calm yourself, there's no need to panic. This is the twenty-first century, which means eye and skin tightening creams really do now exist. So, all is most definitely not lost, nor anywhere near as drastic as your reaction implies."

Mentally, she then added those two items to her regular beauty regime and crossed her fingers, hoping they would work.

As her thoughts returned to the present, Casey pondered on how to end her last *Online Diary* entry. It needed to be upbeat and whilst age realisation was definitely something for her to write about on a normal day, this day was special and talking about getting old was an unwanted, albeit inevitable fact of her life, which in itself was too depressing for this day. Staring at the writing on the small screen in front of her, Casey decided that actually, it now seemed quite fitting to add a small ageing disclosure, especially as it was to be her final witty instalment in the life of Casey Smith.

Entry: 'So, have found my eyes now have permanent lines around them. Oh, and not just laughter lines either, no, these little beauties are deep enough to be mistaken for craters on Mars or Venus. Therefore my life is obviously and absolutely totally over, because no man will ever want me with such creased eyes.'

Yes, that would do, Casey chuckled to herself as she signed off and shut the lid of her laptop, recognising that this last entry was also the end of an era in terms of her *Online Diary*. From now on she had to think of her new blog as *A day in the life of Casey Smith*. "Hmmm," she mumbled to herself and repeated her own name out loud, "Casey Smith," which was not what would be described as an exciting writer's name. Perhaps now that she was going to be writing a weekly blog in her most favourite magazine, she should seriously consider a pseudonym instead of plain old Casey Smith? Even as that thought positively tripped into her head, Casey could imagine her best friends Amanda and Carole totally collapsing in a fit of giggles at the idea of her adopting a pseudonym so as to sound more interesting.

Having decided that a name change was definitely needed, after some thought, she randomly came up with the name 'Maloney', yes, *Casey Maloney*. That name sounded very grown up and sensible, maybe even a little intriguing compared to Casey Smith. Holding that thought, Casey mused on it until a little voice on her shoulder spoke up.

'Yes, very intriguing, or just like you've come straight out of a movie about the old wild west; stomping around like some kind of Calamity Jane, with people making fun and calling you Boney Maloney instead.'

Hmmm, actually no, that name wouldn't work either because Boney Maloney would be seriously un-cool. Casey had to find another more suitable name and quickly; after all, how hard could it be to choose a new surname? It had to be a simple, normal sounding name that was also easy to pronounce. She wanted to effortlessly engage with her new readers, to ensure they believed that she really was just like them; a regular girl, with no airs and graces, who was just expressing her hopes and dreams, as well as her fantasies and fears. Something her readers would probably *not* want to do themselves, at least not quite so publicly. But what name would she choose?

Who'd have thought that this would be so much harder than she'd imagined. After running through dozens of example names and racking her brains, trying to think of all the kids at school and what their names had been, Casey finally came up with Martin, that being the name of her very first boyfriend at school. Ah yes, she could still picture him now; in fact, Casey had never forgotten her very first love, with his mop of blond, curling hair, that had framed his stunning blue eyes. Oh and that gorgeous smile too! Casey chuckled to herself, how she had loved it whenever he'd smiled at her, even if they were only eight years old at the time.

As Casey indulged in the memory of Martin, she laughed to herself, thinking that he was probably going bald by now, or maybe just grey, and briefly wondered what he was actually doing with his life these days. Maybe he'd got married and was now father to 2.4 children, with a pet dog called Sammy. Of course he'd be married by now, which made her realise that she was also in her thirties – and still single!

Anyway, it seemed as good a reason as any to choose her pseudonym and she liked it. So, decision made, she would keep her own first name and be known as *Casey Martin* for her new blog, or would that be column? Calling it a column sounded a bit more *Carrie Fisher* than it just being referred to as a plain old blog. That was a label which had Casey conjuring up images of some geeky keyboard tapper, rather than – as it was in her case – being a proper grown-up and writing what was essentially *a column*. Well, in Casey's mind it had already turned into a column and was growing rapidly, sweeping up the coveted *Column of the Year* award and effortlessly winning recognition from her peers and readers alike.

Just as she was getting carried away with ideas of editorial grandeur, the front doorbell brought Casey crashing back down to earth with a bump. She glanced at her watch and was shocked to see how time had flown by and that it was already eleven o'clock at night. *Other than the police, who on earth knocks on your door that late in the evening?* she wondered. Certainly no normal person would, unless you had been playing your music too loud and disturbing them, or something similar. Imagining the worst, Casey's fantasy mind went into overdrive. She wondered if it was indeed the police coming to tell her that someone she loved dearly had been injured; having been rushed into hospital and although still alive, may not last the hour, but *yes*, they *can* drive her there on a blue light.

OK, calm down, Case, it's probably just Dolly, the old lady from downstairs asking if you've seen her cat, she thought. Casey was convinced someone else must be fussing over Freddie, which seemed like the most obvious reason that prevented the little minx from returning home to Dolly on the odd night. Of course, being a cat, Casey recognised that Freddie obviously didn't realise *quite* how much he worried his poor mistress by his absences.

Freddie had been named after Dolly's husband Frederick, who sadly passed away some thirteen years earlier. Having not been blessed with children, and after losing her husband prematurely, poor Dolly had been left behind, feeling abandoned and doomed to live out her life alone. The kind old lady had been lonely for a long time and when Freddie the cat first appeared in her life, unbeknown to him, he had arrived just in the nick of time. It was a fact nobody else knew, but Freddie's unexpected arrival had actually prevented Dolly from taking some pills to go and join the wonderful husband she still missed so terribly.

It had been a cold and frosty morning when that tiny, mewing kitten was left in a box on the front doorstep of their building. The poor little thing would have definitely died if the old woolly jumper he'd snuggled into had not been left in the box with him. Casey agreed with Dolly at the time that whoever had abandoned Freddie there, *must* have had at least a small glimmer of a heart, to have placed that old jumper in the box with him. The two women had cooed over how absolutely adorable Freddie was, such an extremely cute ball of tiny fluffy kitten, with bright blue eyes, which seemed to have only just opened to the world. Those eyes and Freddie's helpless mewing had melted Dolly's heart and she decided to take him in and adopt him, naming him Freddie in the process.

That same very cute and fluffy kitten, had long since grown into the cheeky puss he was now, who kept Dolly on her toes by disappearing every now and then for a night on the tiles. Although in reality and unbeknown to his Mistress, Freddie had long since decided that a life on the tiles was far too cold and being eight years old, he wasn't quite the catch he used to be, a fact which was proven by the local felines, who had long stopped preening for him. It was actually another human who occasionally encouraged him to stay overnight. Yes, Freddie the cat was having a cheeky deputy-owner affair with a nearby neighbour, who loved to let him stay the night, curled up on her warm cosy bed, which he wasn't allowed to do at home with Dolly. That said, Freddie loved Dolly as much as she loved him and he always came back home to her, often walking in like he owned the place, before pushing his head into Dolly's waiting hands, knowing full well he would be stroked and kissed and generally made a fuss of by his mistress. He was indeed a cheeky little minx.

More urgent knocking on the door brought Casey's straying mind back into the present and onto her feet. Now eager to see who wanted to speak to her this late at night, she rushed to peer through the spy-hole in her front door. *Aha*, she could see the top of a very familiar red-head, and on hearing low sobbing sounds emanating through from the other side of the door, Casey quickly unlocked it and swung it open. Standing in front of her like a wilting plant, was Tilly.

Tilly was Casey's friend and neighbour, whose usually immaculate shiny hair, now looked dull and unkempt. Clearly distraught, Tilly was sobbing desperately into her now scrunched up hanky. She looked at Casey with her sad eyes, swollen from hours of crying and with dried mascara stains streaked down her face. As soon as Tilly looked into Casey's eyes, which were full of sympathetic

8

kindness, she almost collapsed into her friend's extended arms.

It was the kind of look that would make any sad person fall apart, even when they were trying their hardest to hold it all together, and Tilly was no exception. Already looking like she'd been crying for days, Tilly clung to her friend. Casey wrapped her arms around Tilly's petite frame, and pushed the door shut with one foot. Trying to calm her friend down, they made their way through to the lounge.

As her story unfolded, it turned out that Tilly had been crying for the best part of two days, her unhappiness having been caused by her so-called boyfriend. It turned out that John, Tilly's latest beau, after six months of blissful happiness with Tilly (and despite having previously declared his undying love for her), had just up and left without any warning. Yes, the sad fact was, John's love for Tilly had in fact died and was now reserved for some bimbo called Gemma, who had apparently stolen his love and broken Tilly's heart.

Casey made a mental note for her new column: *Most guys blame someone else and hardly ever blame themselves for the break-up of a relationship. Is that guilt or cowardice?*

After reeling from the shock of John's betrayal, Tilly had also been trying to come to terms with the fact that apparently, John and Gemma had been dating for two whole weeks *before* he'd even had the guts to tell Tilly.

Shockingly outrageous behaviour. Casey agreed, as she established between Tilly's racking sobs, long sniffs and frequent nose blowing, that Gemma was the girl at the gym with the brown pony-tail, small neat breasts and perfectly tight butt. Also, with thighs that could crack a walnut.

Yes, it's apparently true, she can and often does that as a party trick, with the aid of two drinks coasters!

Casey revised what Tilly had told her and imagined John's version would be that it was Gemma who had lured him away, with her pretty face, perfectly toned body and big dazzling smile. However, it had to be acknowledged – even by Casey – that Gemma's body was totally the kind of sexy goddess body, which all of the guys and many of the girls, always watched, admired and envied at the gym.

Note for column (no real names to be used of course, so will substitute John and Gemma later): John, being a man of, as it turns out, less strength of character than we all thought, yes, John had eaten the apple. Meaning, both his and Gemma's fig leaves had most definitely fallen in their very own Garden of Eden, otherwise known as John's bed!

Poor Tilly was in bits and feeling totally lost, her former happiness crushed by heartbreak and helplessness.

This was most definitely one of those experiences when emotions flood over you as that special someone, whom you care deeply about, just walks away from you, easily and seemingly uncaring, without even looking back!

"Worse still," Tilly said to Casey, "is dealing with knowing that person doesn't even care about how much you love them, or how hurt and wretched you feel. No, they just up and leave. Gone. Out of your life, like they were just popping out for a pint of milk or something, uncaring that you've been left behind in bits." Tilly cried out even more fresh tears.

Casey recognised those feelings of wretchedness and reached out to her friend, hugging her firmly, offering soothing words as she gently smoothed out Tilly's hair and rubbed her back with each softly spoken word. As time ticked by and her friend's initial sobs subsided, Casey sat back to listen, as Tilly explained what had happened. Seeing fresh tears brimming with every painful word,

Casey passed Tilly tissue after tissue. She empathised and hugged her friend again, until eventually, the tears stopped, as if a pause button had been pressed, but one that could be released again at any moment.

After some deep breaths, which were encouraged by Casey, Tilly began to laugh a little as Casey tried to rubbish John, saying good riddance and that he and Gemma deserved each other. According to rumours, Gemma had a reputation as a complete bitch, who was a constant flirt and *extremely* demanding when it came to her men. So, Casey deduced, after Tilly's niceness, John would be in for the hardest ride of his life, and in more ways than one. Tilly laughed again, only to dissolve into yet more tears, as she imagined John and Gemma making love and having any kind of hard ride together.

> *Note for column: Rumour has it that Gemma is actually quite nice when you chat to her as one female to another, but boy is she high maintenance when it comes to guys! That was something her past conquests had all agreed on, as they each gave up trying to please her, usually after spending just three months of her demands having been foisted on them. Hence where the label "Complete Bitch" seems to have grown from.*

After what felt like hours later, Casey managed to calm Tilly down with soothing words and of course, the obligatory and infamous, cup of tea. Sure enough, wine swiftly followed the tea, with Casey refilling their glasses throughout the long night. They played happy music from the 1980s and danced around the living room, munching on several snacks between numerous glasses of wine, before finishing up with their favourite treat: Bailey's ice-cream with crunched up Maltesers.

Tilly's mood lifted as the hours clicked by, until finally, worn out by her own tears and their drunken state, she fell asleep on Casey's sofa. It was 4.30am when Casey threw a spare blanket over her friend. Remembering how exhausted she had been before Tilly even arrived that evening, and as the sun begun to rise, Casey collapsed into her own bed.

As the bright sunshine broke through the curtains, it was just as well it was Saturday and that neither Tilly nor Casey had to get up for work. If it had been a day earlier, neither one of them would have made it on time for work.

When Casey woke up, she reflected on the night before and how upset Tilly had been, so she got out of bed to check that her friend was OK and had not done anything silly during the night. Tip-toeing quickly but quietly through to the lounge, Casey was pleased to see that Tilly was still fast asleep on the sofa. Although she now only had half the blanket covering her, the other half having fallen to the floor.

Stirring as Casey's light footsteps filtered through her muzzy head, Tilly let out a long, low groan. Her head felt like someone was playing drums very badly on the top of it. The memory of John's infidelity pushed its way through the fuzziness of her brain and Tilly's face crumpled again. A large hot tear escaped and rolled down her cheek, splashing onto the empty wine glass, which was now lying beside her on the sofa.

Thank goodness it was white wine and not red, Casey thought, as she retrieved the glass and checked there was no wine residue to be found on the sofa or carpet. Passing Tilly the now virtually empty box of tissues, Casey knelt down beside the sofa to hold her friend's hand and tell her that she could scream, rant, cry or kick the cat if it made her feel better. Quickly, Casey clarified that she meant the stuffed cat, which was acting as a lounge door stop and not Freddie from downstairs. In spite of her misery, Tilly managed to laugh, while her friend recommended that she should do whatever she had to in order to make herself feel better. Casey reminded her that she *would* survive and John *would* fade into the past and that in time, she would most definitely be OK.

Although, thought Casey, *John fading into the past might not happen quite so quickly if he keeps dating Gemma*. Casey was very aware of the fact that Gemma also frequented their favourite bar, and *always* with her latest conquests, so that she could show them off. Casey considered Steph's leaving do at Barney's the following Wednesday, and contemplated the likelihood of them walking in together when all the girls were due to meet. Knowing what little morals John already had (reference to his dating infidelity).

Steph was one of the girl's workmates, and whilst the three of them had rubbed along nicely each day, Steph had remained a workmate and never quite escalated to the level of a close friend, not like Casey and Tilly were to each other. But both girls had felt compelled to go along to Steph's leaving drinks; after all, she had worked hard for their team and deserved a good send-off.

Tilly took a big gulp of the hot sweet tea that Casey had made, and readily accepted her offer of hot toast, with lashings of butter and English Honey. Which even though they both knew was probably *not* the healthiest of breakfast choices, it tasted absolutely delicious. Especially when accompanied by a lovely, strong cup of tea. Toast with butter and honey was most definitely one of their favourite comfort foods.

Having been in Tilly's shoes on more than one occasion (the metaphorical ones of course and not the gorgeous blue suede, killer heels she'd borrowed from Tilly for Andrew and Stacey's wedding), Casey closed the half-eaten box of chocolates, which was still lying open on the coffee table from the night before. Knowing her friend's weakness for chocolate, and given the enormous calorie intake the night before, Casey slipped the box with the remaining chocolates under the armchair.

As they ate breakfast, Tilly revisited the already open wound of John and Gemma. Once again, she walked Casey through what had happened two nights ago, when John had thrown his cowardly hand grenade into her world. Tilly could hardly believe that the man she thought she loved, had just left her a note, ending their love story with the delicacy of a sledge-hammer smashing an egg. Not only that, he'd left the note on the bed they had shared together so many times, knowing full well that Tilly would casually find it when she returned home from work (thinking it was a bedroom love note, only to find it was quite the opposite).

Tilly was ranting that John should at least have told her to her face. Feeling equally shocked at John's betrayal and downright cowardice in how he'd casually dumped Tilly, Casey joined in with the venting.

"Some kind of man he is, one who doesn't have the balls to face you, but just leaves a note...the bloody coward!"

"Yes," Tilly said, "and he wasn't afraid of sharing those same balls and other dangly bit with the walnut-cracking Gemma, was he!"

Being more of a statement than a question, both girls laughed at Tilly's come-back comment. Casey offered her own comment about John needing to be careful, or Gemma would crack his nuts too!

Tilly's braveness wilted and she began to sob again. Now feeling bad and blaming herself for the fresh tears, Casey tried to boost Tilly's positivity.

"Come on now, Til', let's take three deep breaths together and believe me, it *will* make you feel better."

Tilly, who was now willing to do *anything* to ease the heartache, eased herself upright and, sliding a foot under each knee, sat cross-legged on the sofa. With her hands gently resting on her knees and the tips of her forefingers and thumbs touching in a yoga type of pose, Tilly closed her eyes and listened to Casey.

"OK, ready, Til? Now," Casey said, "start breathing in slowly, hold it for three seconds and then let it out again very slowly...again, breathe in slowly, hold, then slowly out..."

On the third breath in, Tilly was beginning to feel a bit light-headed, but she continued to follow Casey's lead and was surprised to find she actually *did* start to feel a bit calmer. As they sat quietly for a few minutes, Tilly was feeling better and thanked Casey as she slid her feet back to the floor to sit forward and finish her tea.

Casey offered her friend the use of her shower, and then went to find her a clean T-shirt and leggings to change into.

Even though Tilly only had to go down one flight of stairs to her own apartment, Casey felt happier knowing that with her friend already being showered and freshened up, she would arrive at her own front door feeling a little bit stronger than if she'd wandered downstairs, tear-stained and still wearing last night's crumpled clothes.

Casey and Tilly often borrowed each other's clothes and shoes, both having agreed that living in the same building and being the same size in shoes and dresses was a massive bonus. The two of them quite enjoyed sharing their wardrobes; it saved them having to buy something new every week, like so many of their workmates seemed to do.

How their workmates ever managed to buy so many new clothes used to leave them both feeling a little envious at their financial freedom. That was until it dawned on them that most of the girls were either still living with their parents, or flat-sharing, which meant their outgoings were probably only half the amount that Casey and Tilly paid out each month, for their small but very much loved apartments.

Casey smiled at the thought of owning her own apartment, and was glad that she had managed to scrape together enough money to pay the required deposit on it. Both girls would be paying their mortgages for a few years to come, however, by the time they were ready to retire, they would each own their homes.

Casey had always loved the building they lived in and had nurtured some romantic notion of attracting her Mr Right by living there. That was a notion she propped up by using Feng Shui to improve the ambience and energy of each room, ever hopeful in the power of the ancient Chinese philosophical art.

With Tilly heading off downstairs, Casey resumed last night's position at her laptop to write a post-script for her last *Online Diary* entry. She wanted to share with her followers, the fact that she had been offered a dream job, which was to write her very own column for the women's magazine, *Just for You!* Casey asked that they check-out her column in the magazine and told them which week her first entry would appear in. She also decided to ask everyone at work to buy a copy of the magazine the same week. And while an extra fifteen copies wasn't going to make a huge difference to the issue ratings, Casey hoped they would enjoy reading it so much that they'd buy it every week. If they did that and her many online followers bought it too, the extra sales might influence the Editor's decision to keep her on as their new column writer.

With her one thousand-word target, Casey decided to word-count her last *Online Diary* entry, stopping at the same number of words, just to see how much space it would take up on a page of the magazine. Smiling at the thought of being given page seven for her column, she could hardly believe her luck. Being given page twenty-seven would have been as much as Casey would have expected, but to be promoted to page seven at such an early stage was absolutely thrilling. It could be said that Casey was more than a little bit chuffed, especially as seven also happened to be her lucky number. Signing off of her *Online Diary* for the absolute last time, Casey thanked her followers for helping her to realise her dream of becoming a writer, adding: "...and don't forget, you guys, this isn't the end. I shall be continuing my stories and life experiences in the new column, so make sure you reserve your copy of *Just for You!*"

Casey hoped her followers would want to keep reading about her antics, along with the many other subjects that periodically affected most women.

Chapter 2

Dominic and Jason

As she closed the lid of her laptop, Casey went to refill her mug with a fresh brew of tea. Carefully pouring the hot water from her kettle into the tea-pot, Casey imagined that she was probably the only person in the country still using an old stove-top whistling kettle. The truth was that she just could not bear to part with the old thing, which reminded her so much of her darling Nanny Em. Many of her belongings had come to live with Casey after Nanny Em had slipped away following a short illness. The unexpected speed of losing her Nan still seemed so unfair to Casey and she missed her terribly.

The familiar whistle of Nanny Em's kettle reminded Casey of her childhood days, when she would spend time with her Nan in their old kitchen, learning to cook from scratch and chatting about everything and nothing. While growing up, Casey had observed and listened to the words of wisdom, which her Nan had shared with many of her friends as they openly discussed their tales of woe with her. Most of the discussions revolved around boyfriend and husband troubles, but occasionally the worries were about their children. In the main, those discussions were about the latest scourge of nits, or where to get the best deal for their school uniform and how to cope with school bullies. Then of course, it would be the bad exam results and trying to fathom out how best to get their little twinkling's to knuckle down and study.

Casey's Nan had been a very wise lady, who'd experienced more than her fair share of love, troubles and triumphs in her younger years. Being a woman of the 1950s and then the swinging '60s, Emily Smith had truly had the time of her life, before settling down with the steady and sensible chap who'd become Casey's Grandpa. A big strong man, he eventually managed to tame the wild ways of his girl, and when he asked her to become his wife, she had kissed him passionately as she accepted his proposal. The young couple had been blessed with a beautiful daughter, who they raised and cherished as she grew from their baby girl, into a beautiful young woman. Their wonderful daughter's was name Julie and had been Casey's own darling Mum.

Thinking back and reminiscing over the stories her Nan had shared about her life with Grandpa, Casey realised her Nanny Em and Grandpa were quite the couple in their time.   Both had been party goers and yet solid family people, who had first taught their daughter (her mother), and then Casey, the rights and wrongs in life. Both grandparents had been wise enough to let their girls learn from their own mistakes, knowing it was the best way forward as they evolved into fabulous young women.

"There's no point in trying to put an old head on young shoulders," Nanny Em had often said. "It always seems like a good idea, but it never really works in practice."

True to form, there had been some first-class mistakes that Casey had made, which could have been avoided by words of warning. But the lessons learned were more effective because they were her mistakes, which meant that she had learned the hard way. Personal growth was how Casey liked to think of it now and she was glad of her Nanny Em's wisdom and direction.

Julie met and fell in love with Dave, and the two of them had already become Casey's parents, when their lives were cut short at a very young age. The two of them died together at the scene of a tragic car accident, which left Casey – their only child – orphaned and alone, to be brought up by her Nanny Em and Grandpa John. Carefree and full of love for one another, the young couple had been walking along the narrow, sunny streets in town, with their little daughter in a pushchair. Those innocent lives had been taken by a lad who was not much older than they were. Driving his car into town, he'd taken a corner too fast and too sharply. The young and inexperienced driver had panicked, over-steered to correct himself, but forgot to remove his foot from the accelerator at the same time. After narrowly avoiding a pedestrian standing on the edge of the pavement, the car had mounted the kerb on the opposite corner of the street. It wasn't even going very fast at the point it lurched towards the three of them, yet it still managed to crush Julie and Dave as they both dived forwards to protect their baby daughter in her pushchair.

The young man driving the car had also died that day, quite simply because he wasn't wearing his seat belt. The doctors said he must have hit his forehead on the steering wheel at the point of impact and stupidly, that seemingly small thing had killed him instantly, splitting open the front of his skull and causing a massive brain injury.

Losing three young people in one accident had made it all the more tragic. It had been a traumatic day for everyone involved, including the witnesses who had run to their rescue, only to be thwarted by fate. The young driver's distraught family, who were also very religious, had said at the inquest that he would not have been able to live with the guilt of killing Casey's parents, so it was probably fitting that he went with them. Not that anyone would have wished that end for him, which his parents gratefully acknowledged. It was after all, a tragic and mindless accident, which could have happened to any inexperienced driver.

Being so young at the time, Casey had no recollection of the accident. Some people had said her lack of memory was likely due to her being so young, while others had said she must have completely blocked that day out of her innocent two-year-old mind. Nanny Em and Grandpa John had been utterly devastated by the loss of their beloved daughter and son-in-law. Yet, as the years passed, with having Casey to care for, it seemed like their grief had slowly healed as she flourished under their care. From that day on, Emily and John made sure that Casey knew how much they loved her, and in time, she discovered the sacrifice her parents had made in order that she would live.

During the years that had passed since that awful day, Casey often dwelled on thoughts of how much her parents must have truly loved her. When the car mounted the kerb and careered toward them, only the love of two devoted people would have caused them to react as they had done. Sadly, that same love and devotion to Casey, also robbed their young daughter of any real memory of them. Casey only recognised them from photographs, which often left her feeling incredibly sad and wishing she could have known them for a few more years, before they were taken from her.

As their many friends looked on and supported the little family of three, they could also see that Casey's beloved Grandpa never fully recovered from the shock of losing his precious daughter. So it was that John had also died somewhat prematurely...around ten years after his daughter was taken from him, quite suddenly and without warning. That loss had been another huge life trauma for Casey and her Nanny Em to deal with, but once again, their love for each other had been the natural source of strength, which they'd drawn on daily in their recovery from that massive second loss.

Needing to stop thinking of such sad times, Casey forced her mind to the here and now as she put the milk back in the fridge. Picking up her mug of tea from the kitchen worktop, she leaned forward a little to peek out of the large window. Oh yes, there he was, the bronzed Greek God-like creature that was Dominic. As Casey stared out of the window, she felt that familiar stab of guilty pleasure on catching sight of the gorgeous hunk living in the apartment block across the road. Subconsciously, Casey smiled down at him. Dominic, who was engrossed in his usual morning workout, was oblivious to the fact that she was watching him and carried on with his daily routine. Totally unaware that he had an admirer in Casey, who could and often did watch his every move around the home gym he'd installed, Dominic stood right in front of the large double bay window of his apartment. Watching her neighbour working out, truly was Casey's guilty weekend pleasure and she often watched him for just that little bit too long. Secretly, she hoped he would peel off his very tight, vest style T-shirt, to reveal the bronzed muscular body, which he obviously took such very good care of.

For a few magical moments, Casey was lost in her weekend fantasy, as she once again imagined Dominic looking up at the building opposite his and smiling back at the blonde-haired, blue-eyed neighbour, who was watching him so intently. Leaning forward with her hair looking sufficiently ruffled in that sexy, *I've just got out of bed and why don't you pop over and take me back there,* kind of way, Casey entwined her fingers around the mug of hot sweet tea, taking a sip as her imagination ran riot.

"Oh yes, please do," she said out loud.

As she voiced those words, she closed her eyes and her stomach flipped at that imagined moment of intimacy. Other parts of her body tightened in anticipation of his touch. Those strong hands, taut muscles and gorgeous blue eyes would make her melt, as she imagined running her fingers through his soft brown hair and tracing them down his neck, then slowly moving them to lightly brush across his rippling chest. Her hands would easily travel on down towards his more than ample, hardening masculinity, which would already be pressing against her slim toned stomach, proving how aroused he was simply from her touch. His eyes would burn with desire as he moaned, "Oh Casey" and kissed her lips with a passion so strong that she would melt into his arms. As she imagined the two of them joining together, their deep and passionate wanting overtaking every muscle and bone in their bodies, he would penetrate her femininity, an urgency building with every deep and exploring thrust. Reaching that climactic height together, clinging to each other's damp bodies, the two of them would groan as each other's pleasure escaped and racked their bodies with muscle clenching tightness. *Phew!*

Casey blushed at the thought of such intense love making with Dominic, now feeling so relieved that Tilly had already left and wasn't there to witness her imagined fantasy. Yet, a wistful, dreamy look lingered on Casey's face, as her eyes half-closed at the imagined desire of it all and she wished so much for it to be real.

Looking down at his window again, Casey's pulse was still racing as Dominic jumped up suddenly and strode across the room out of her view. She supposed someone must have knocked on his door or something, but as Casey watched for just a little bit longer, she was aghast to see a tall, slim and beautiful girl stroll into Dominic's gym space. Looking very sexy in her skin tight Lycra outfit as she turned to laugh at something Dominic had obviously said to her, the woman tied up her long chestnut hair into a folded back pony-tail. Casey was stunned. "No!" Turning away, now feeling very stupid *and* embarrassed, Casey was ever more grateful that she was alone and Tilly had not witnessed her moment of crushed disbelief. *Damn, damn and double damn!*

Casey had hoped that Dominic was single and by some miraculous and unseen force, that he would one day look up and see her. She also imagined how he would invite her over with a wave of his muscular bronzed arm, whilst also holding aloft a bottle of Champagne, clearly offering for her to come over and join him in a glass or two of sparkling bubbles, before making wild passionate love to her in his gym.

No...no...no...stop now, Casey! Get a hold of yourself girl! It's obvious he's got a girlfriend and you've just got to accept it and move on. Casey was as annoyed with herself as much as the fact that Dominic obviously already had a girlfriend. Scolding herself, she forced her brain to compute the fact that he was only ever a weekend fantasy. Jees, theirs wasn't even a friendship, let alone a relationship. And Casey had never even had the opportunity to speak to Dominic, much less date him. Of course she'd wanted to speak to him and had many a time racked her brains as to how she could fabricate an event for them to meet. Well, that was all wasted effort now. *Damn that woman!* Casey sulked as she accepted the reality, which was that Dominic already has a gorgeous brunette to entertain his every desire and no, he was *never* going to look up at her window, accidentally or otherwise.

Scowling as she turned away, Casey's mood turned a little blacker until she reminded herself of how proud her Nan would have been of her wild imagined affair. After all, Nanny Em often said she was all for a bit of day-dreaming and had always encouraged Casey to believe in her dreams, no matter how ridiculously unachievable they seemed. However, this situation was beyond that stage; Dominic had a girlfriend, leaving Casey's ego feeling extremely bruised from that crushing realisation.

"Think positive," Nanny Em had always said," and don't be afraid to follow your dreams!" *Yes, think positive!*

Casey smiled at the photo of Nanny Em, which hung on the wall above Casey's own little kitchen table. "Hmmm, positive, positive, positive!" Casey thought that by repeating it, she would change her way of thinking, which worked to some extent.

Moving into the living room and throwing herself down onto the sofa, Casey picked up her latest copy of *Just for You!* in the hope it would lift her spirits again. Thumbing through the already well-read pages, Casey flicked back to page 7 and wondered where on the page her column would start. Would it be at the top or start halfway down? Meaning the reader would have to 'continue over the page'. The thought of her column spanning not one but two pages, cheered Casey's mood sufficiently. The trick was to make sure the column was riveting enough to capture her new readership. Again, she hoped that some of her *Online Diary* followers would also take up the magazine and increase the readership. After all, she did have several hundred followers for her *Online Diary* and she was sure that *some* of them would want to continue to follow her enough to buy the magazine.

It was the magazine's own Head of Marketing, Claire Anderson, who had also read *Casey's Online Diary* and recommended her to the Magazine's Editor, Ms Edine Walker. Casey was so thankful for Claire's initial contact and her subsequent encouragement and support, as Claire had tried to promote Casey to Edine. It had surprised Casey that someone like Claire would have followed her *Online Diary* for so long, having admitted that she'd been alerted to *Casey's Online Diary* after one of her friends shared a particularly funny extract on Facebook. Apparently, it was something about a date Casey had been on and how it was so awful, that when relaying the story of the disastrous date to a girlfriend, Casey had said how it had been such a total waste of make-up. Claire had resonated with that sentiment and laughed her socks off as she found herself addicted to following the antics of this aspiring new writer. After a couple of months following Casey's escapades, Claire decided the content would be a perfect fit for the readership of *Just for You!* Explaining to her Editor, Edine, how *Casey's Online Diary* had quickly become addictive for Claire, she described it as a bit like a girly gossiping session, but where you glimpse into someone else's actual, and very real life. Claire went on to explain how she'd found herself logging in every week, to catch up on the latest events and funny stories from Casey's life. Fortunately, Edine had been intrigued enough to log in herself a few times as well and soon realised that Claire was onto something and that indeed, she *would* like to speak to Casey. After all, who could deny the likeness to the everyday lives of their readership? Especially when Casey added in snippets like the one when she and her best friend had been on holiday in the Canary Islands:

...so we'd told a funny joke to the owner of the bar during the day, which went...

'What do you call a woman who can suck an orange through a hosepipe?'

Of course he didn't know and asked 'What?'

'Darling!'

We'd screamed together as we'd collapsed in fits of giggles (fuelled by far too much alcohol and sunshine). Then in the evening we'd joined the crowd in the bar for the quiz night and there was a prize for the best team name, which we won with...

'The Suckers of Seville!'

It had been an in-joke and was probably a bit unfair on the rest of the bar's customers, but naturally, we didn't worry about that at the time. As far as we were concerned, we'd won and our reward was free drinks all night! What a great holiday!

Claire's favourite diary entry so far had been after Casey met Jason and, following two months of particularly hot dates, she'd invited him to join her for a trial spa session at a new hotel that had just opened near her Nan and Grandpa's old house. The hotel had given away freebie spa evenings to the local residents, supposedly as a welcome gesture, but widely recognised as compensating local residents for the inevitable increase in traffic, which was impacting their previously quiet neighbourhood. Casey had been lucky enough to be given two passes by one of Nanny Em's old neighbours.

The luxurious private spa rooms were fabulous, containing a hot-tub big enough for four to six people, with loungers and chairs included, along with a small concession stand supporting two bottles of chilled sparkling and still water. Patrons would normally have paid a small fortune to hire the private rooms, which had to be booked in advance, so Casey knew just how lucky she was to have been given two free tickets. Spa staff were authorised to enter the private rooms, but generally, they would only disturb guests if the emergency alarm button on the side of the pool had been activated. Having a free admission pass for two people meant that Casey and Jason had their spa pool to themselves. Casey had been feeling really excited to be sharing such an intimate setting with Jason and felt like she was in seventh heaven, as he stripped down to a pair of tight fitting trunks, before stepping into the bubbling water. Unashamedly, Casey had followed suit and stripped off to reveal a skimpy pink and white polka-dot bikini, which showed off her slim toned body perfectly. Watching from the hot-tub as Casey undressed, Jason's eyes had explored every inch of her sexy body, as intense desire pulsated through his veins, threatening to burst out of his now even tighter trunks.

Jason smiled broadly as a giggling Casey, feeling slightly nervous, yet full of desire, had poured them both a drink from the bottle of sparkling wine they'd smuggled in. Casey commented how the plastic water cups were not quite as glamorous as wine glasses, but served a purpose on this occasion, and had taken a sip from hers before passing one to Jason. Casey then stepped down into the hot bubbling water, as Jason, holding his wine with his left hand, held out his right hand for her to take, ensuring she didn't slip as she joined him in the hot bubbling spa. Moving slowly through the bubbles towards him and taking another sip of the cool sparkling wine, Casey giggled again and Jason's resolve melted. The room temperature shot up with the warmth of the water and the excitement of the moment, causing them both to feel giddy with desire and wanting for each other.

What happened next was an element of the spa session that Casey didn't want to share in her diary entry. Some things had to remain sacred and whilst she enjoyed titillating her reader's imagination, she thought better than to share the whole truth of this particular occasion. But anyone with half an imagination and/or having experienced passion rise in a watery environment, would have easily guessed what had happened once Casey put down her glass. For her diary though, Casey kept it clean and just teased her followers' imaginations.

What happened was that, as Casey put down her sparkling wine on the side of the spa pool, Jason had gently pulled her down towards him, and as she sat into his lap, the hot bubbling water had splashed over her face causing her to giggle again. Jason wanted her badly, and having already put down his own glass of wine, his strong hands supported her as she gently lifted her knees to balance herself as she sat astride him. With the hot bubbling water swirling around them, Jason's hands had reached up to tug at the ties of her bikini top. Casey gasped with wanting desire as her bikini top floated away on the bubbles. As Jason's eyes admired her small pert breasts that were just visible above the bubbling water, she enjoyed his reaction and felt her nipples begin to harden. Jason's hands moved to gently caress her breasts as he lifted Casey up to expose them above the water. His firm lips caught at her nipples and gently using his teeth, he tweaked on each one, working on Casey's erotic senses. She groaned as she was taken away by sexual desire, totally uncaring if they were caught. Jason's hardening masculinity escaped, as his trunks were no longer able to restrain such desire. Tugging open the ties on Casey's bikini bottom, he'd pulled it away from her, leaving her totally naked in the bubbling water. She gasped again as she'd experienced his passion, hard and wanting. As he lifted her up and onto him, sliding deep inside her, she rose and fell onto his hardness again and again. Jason pleasured Casey like never before. Each of them lost in their overwhelming desire for each other, they both felt Casey's body clenching and tightening, with every wrenching climactic grip on Jason's equally gushing manhood. Struggling to keep their groans quiet, so as not to bring anyone bursting into their moment of passion, they'd gripped onto each other, their bodies jerking together until their joint climax subsided.

Yes, that rather tantalising diary entry had been the clincher for Claire; she was confident that this writer was able to tell a story without being crude and giving away too much information, yet with enough hinted naughtiness to keep her readers wanting more. Claire concluded that Casey would be a perfect column writer and had invited Edine to lunch, so the two of them could discuss *Casey's Online Diary*. Edine was also pleasantly surprised at the quality of Casey's writing and decided to go outside of normal protocols, by offering her an opening for the following month's weekly edition.

In her mind, Casey had already started her first column for the magazine, but was yet to put pen to paper, or in her case, fingers to the keyboard. But now due to submit her first draft for Edine's review, she'd reserved all day Sunday and Monday to review and refine her story. Close of business Monday was the deadline Edine had set Casey, and as she tapped away, moulding the story to fit the format that Edine was looking for, Casey was totally in the zone, focussed. The only planned time-out she was allowing herself was a mid-morning run, which was just to refresh her mind and keep her mood upbeat, totally motivated and yet perfectly calm. After her run she had returned to her laptop, refreshed and ready to continue perfecting her first sparkling and witty column. Yes, it was definitely a column and no longer to be thought of as a diary, or a blog.

Sunday morning's weather started out a bit misty, but soon enough the sun had burnt it off and turned the sky a gorgeous blue. Casey had arisen bright and early and was well into her story, when Tilly unexpectedly knocked on the door, calling out Casey's name as she did so. Desperate not to lose her train of thought and torn between loyalty to her friend and making sure her column was her priority, Casey decided that taking time out for a coffee would be fine. So, she invited Tilly to come in, aware that the next hour was about to be completely absorbed by Tilly's update on the "John situation".

But, it was as if a magic wand had been waved over her friend, because as Casey opened the door, she was utterly surprised to see Tilly looking remarkably bouncy and smiley, despite being so broken hearted only twenty-four hours prior. After kissing Casey hello, Tilly breezed into the kitchen, chatting away about everything (except John), whilst Casey popped the kettle on the hob. Puzzled, but happy to see her friend looking so much better than the previous day, Casey said as much to Tilly.

Not anticipating such a response, Casey was astounded, but also very pleased to hear Tilly's positive affirmation that Casey was absolutely right and that John was obviously not "The One". Of course not, he couldn't be, Tilly had reasoned, because if he had of been, then Gemma would not have been able to tempt him away so easily. Tilly began likening John to Adam (of Adam and Eve fame), adding that if she and he had truly been *in love,* then John would have remained faithful to her.

Casey was already grinning when Tilly then compared herself to a Pink Lady Apple, with John (as Adam), being tempted by the French Golden Delicious on the treadmill (Eve, a.k.a Gemma). This analogy actually made Casey laugh out loud as she commented how this was a complete turn-around on Tilly's part. Whilst she was happy to encourage her newly enthusiastic and positive thinking friend about moving on from John, Casey knew only too well, the danger of Tilly's resolve melting and this coming Wednesday would present a prime opportunity for that to happen. They were due to pile into Barney's Bar for Steph's leaving drinks, and if John and Gemma turned up, as they probably would, Tilly's now strong resolve might crash and burn. Of course, that would depend on how many glasses of wine Tilly might already have consumed when the inevitable happened. But for now, Tilly was happy, so Casey was happy, and she readily agreed to her friend's suggestion for a night out as they sipped their coffee and dunked Almond Biscotti.

Even though it was Sunday evening and effectively a school-night, the Wagon and Horses called to them. Knowing the pub always had a live band playing on Sunday evenings, the girls decided they would nip along and sink a few glasses of their favourite cider, along with sampling the evening bar food, which the Landlord generously provided. Hot roasties were always a Sunday night favourite snack which, given the chef's Marmite ingredient, always went down well with a few drinks.

Tilly retreated to her own apartment, leaving Casey to continue with her first column, but not before relaying how excited she was at her friend landing such an enviable job! As Casey sat back down and tapped away at her laptop, she acknowledged Tilly's sentiment and prayed that Edine would love her latest work enough, to let her continue writing for *Just for You!*

It was funny how – with her *Online Diary* – Casey just wrote whatever came into her head, and often with a single glass of wine to hand. However, she never wrote when she was drunk; it was her golden rule never to go online when she'd had several drinks, not since the silly mistake she had made several years before. Now she was writing for Edine and the magazine, Casey felt a little nervous. But, as she packed up for the day and having read and re-read what she'd written, Casey decided that maybe she should not spend quite so much time writing each column. Maybe she would go back to how she wrote her *Online Diary*. After all it was that spontaneity which spiced up her writing in the first place. Too much thinking and double-thinking was liable to dull down her writing and story-telling. Casey certainly didn't want her writing to be thought of as dull, or dumb even.

Picking up her empty cup, she walked into the kitchen and glanced out of the window again, just in case Dominic happened to be looking up. *No, Casey, stop it...remember the brunette? Yes, well, she has him now, so it's a no goer isn't it,* she thought. *Give it up!* Casey cursed herself for being so crazy when it came to Dominic.

Chapter 3

The Wagon, the Band and Dave's Mate

Jason was still lingering happily on the scene and Casey, remembering how much she had enjoyed the spa session a few weeks before, was feeling in the mood for some sexy fun again. So, she decided to let Jason know that both she and Tilly were going to the Wagon and Horses that evening to watch a band who were due to start playing at 9pm. Casey told Jason that most bands usually played until last orders and asked if he wanted to join them, suggesting to bring his mate Dave along.

Casey recalled that Dave was a gorgeous – if not a little raw – hunk of stuff, who Tilly had once admired, during a particularly funny evening with a bunch of friends. Casey hoped that after a glass or two of cider, that Tilly would enjoy Dave's company enough, to take her mind off John's infidelity. Also remembering when they first met Dave, they had all been watching a live band and enjoyed a fun night; so if nothing else, Casey guessed Tilly and Dave would at least enjoy an evening of music together.

Feeling like some kind of cupid, the plan was set and Casey secretly hoped it would be a great evening for them all. Dave was actually a decent chap and had himself been a little bit taken with Tilly after that one evening. Casey dared to imagine that if the two of them took the chance to get to know each other better, the evening might turn out quite nicely indeed. *Fingers crossed on that one then, Case,* she thought.

Casey told Jason about John's betrayal of Tilly when she called him about joining them that evening, and suggested that maybe he could prime Dave to step into the Tilly waters gently. Understanding Casey's motive, Jason said that whilst he felt it was really none of his business, he would go along with it and pre-warn Dave, but only because he also thought Dave and Tilly would make a good couple.

Jason had known Dave for years and regarded him as a decent bloke who, having taken a few years to recover from a previous heartbreak, needed to get out there again. It had taken him much longer than Jason thought it should, but of course, he and Dave's other mates had left him to it. Besides, none of them really knew what to say. One thing they did know, was how hurt Dave had been when his last girlfriend dumped him for being too nice, saying he needed to be a bit more of a bastard. Strange how some women thought, however, Jason suspected there were probably plenty of women who thought the same kind of thing about guys. But like Casey with Tilly, Jason was keen for his mate to find someone nice and hoped Dave and Tilly would hit it off.

Jason liked Tilly; she was funny and a little bit scatty at times, but she was perfect for Dave, at least from what he knew about her. Jason remarked on how thoughtful Casey was, to think of pre-warning Dave so he could make the best of the opportunity, adding that he would call him right away.

Still in her naughty state of mind, Casey was excited at the thought of seeing Jason again that evening and began planning what she would wear to tempt his sex buds. The two of them had agreed that theirs was a casual kind of relationship, rather than a forever thing, more like very good friends who also happened to enjoy exciting and lustful relations with each other. The type of relations which, before they had realised it, had continued for a few months since they'd first met. And however they tried to label it, they couldn't deny they were having a lot of fun and it suited them both to remain uncommitted – for now.

Having spent the rest of the day writing, Casey felt she deserved a good evening and a naughty treat. Smiling wickedly to herself as she stepped into the shower, Casey imagined how their night of music, cider and good humoured laughter, with two pretty hot guys might end up. Just as she had lathered soapy shower gel all over her naked wet body, her mobile rang. Knowing she would never make it in time before the call dropped to voicemail, Casey decided to ignore it, but finished showering more quickly than she had intended. Stepping out of the shower onto her new colourful and fluffy bathmat, she indulgently luxuriated for a few moments as she wrapped a bright pink fluffy towel around her body, then dried herself quickly, before hanging the towel back on the hook. Still naked, Casey walked into her bedroom to find her mobile and check the missed call number which, as she expected, was from Jason.

"Casey, it's me," Jason said cheerfully. "Just to let you know, I spoke to Dave and he's well up for the chance to see Tilly again. One of his mates is with him though and they've been watching the rugby all afternoon, so they've had a couple of beers already. They're just going for a quick bite to eat and will meet us at the Wagon in time for the band, hope that's OK? I'll be over at eight and we can wander down together...there's something I need to talk to you about anyway. Oh and don't worry, Dave said they've definitely only had a couple of beers so they're not trashed yet." Jason laughed before signing off. "See you in a bit, gorgeous."

Casey smiled at Jason's good humoured voicemail and felt her naked nipples harden on hearing his voice. She really was in the mood for an evening of music, cider and sexy frolicking, with the gorgeous Jason.

Both Carole and Amanda had once said to Casey that she would never be short of boyfriends and, luckily for her, that had indeed been the case. Although it was also true that none of them had led to marriage. Jason was a great guy and they'd had a lot of fun together, but Casey was quite happy with how things were between them right now. Then remembering his last point, wondered what it was he wanted to talk to her about; he seemed really upbeat anyway, so she deduced it must be good news.

Thinking about the band and the fact that her friend Carole quite liked the bass guitarist, Casey realised she probably should have called her to come on down. *Damn, it's too late now*, she thought. Besides, Carole would only think Casey was trying to set her up with Dave's mate. He'd probably think that too, so no, definitely not a good idea. *Sorry, Caz, you'll have to miss out on this one, mate*, Casey thought, but knowing how gutted her mate would be when she found out Casey had seen *Mr Guitar Man*, made her feel quite guilty. She was also aware of how much Caz would grill her for every little detail about him and what he was wearing. Casey knew Carole had a thing about him in his ripped jeans and casual white shirt and grinning at the image of him in her head, she knew Carole would verbally crucify her for not calling to tell her "Mr Guitar Man" was playing.

Carole had been single for a while, but like Casey, she also generally had a steady stream of male admirers. That was information both women tended to keep to themselves, as neither of them wanted to create an impression of being man-eaters. Whilst being very aware that men seemed to be very easily drawn to them both, those very same men would simply drift back out of their lives again, seemingly for no apparent reason. Still, it had to be said, there was a lot of fun to be had by all involved.

Neither Carole nor Casey had met their Mr Right yet and so they enjoyed their single girl-about-town lives and the freedom it gave them. They did exactly as they pleased, picking and choosing whichever invitation suited best, and loving the girlie holidays they'd shared, visiting so many different destinations. Some holidays even had gorgeous men-on-tap, fuelling their desires for hot sex on the beach, in their apartments, and sometimes in places that nobody should have been having sex in. The girls had had a lot of fun throughout their twenties and early thirties.

Just for a fleeting moment, Casey wondered how that lifestyle might change if she ever settled down and got married, knowing full well how married people always complained about not getting enough sex. At least, lots of the guys Casey had worked with over the years were like that. Whenever they moaned to her about their wives, married life and/or the lack of sex, Casey had taken to telling them to do their wives a favour and leave. That way their wives could find someone who would cherish and ravish them. Casey's comments frequently stopped the guys in their tracks and soon had the moaners back on their toes, feeling guilty at thinking so badly of their wives. No man wanted to think he'd failed his wife and Casey's comments always triggered some kind of reaction from them. Casey laughed as she reflected on the last guy she'd said that to. Jake had felt so bad about his comments after Casey's scathing response, that he bought flowers on his way home and surprised his unsuspecting wife with a mid-week session of hot passionate sex. Which as it turned out, was to her great delight, because they were trying for a baby and it looked like that session might just have clinched the deal.

As she dressed for their evening out, Casey pulled on her favourite purple top, taking care not to smudge her natural looking make-up. Smoothing the purple fabric down to the top of her dark blue jeans, Casey finished off the look with her new boots, long dangly necklace and several bangles. Checking her reflection in the mirror and ignoring the faint creases round her eyes, Casey smiled and thought, *Yep, you're looking hot girl. You'll do very nicely, that boy won't be able to resist you tonight!*

Jason buzzed the door-bell just as Casey was spraying a light mist of Beautiful-eau-de-parfum over her blonde hair and slightly exposed cleavage. Smiling at herself in the mirror, she shouted out "coming" as she walked towards the front door, and then casually swung it open to greet a grinning Jason, who was looking very smooth in his sexy hot-guy kind of way. As he stepped inside, he kissed her on both cheeks, before responding cheekily to her 'coming' comment.

"Mmmm...you will be later," he said. "Gorgeous woman of mine."

Laughing as she playfully slapped his arm, Casey grinned at his intimated promise of what was to come later – much later. Casey laughed a cheeky laugh and invited him in, and then poured them both a glass of wine. Nan's favourite saying from an old UK TV show popped into her head, and Casey repeated it out loud as she handed Jason his glass.

"Just the one, Mrs Wembley!" Jason laughed as he accepted the drink and Casey added: "Tilly text me just before you arrived to say she was running late and it's probably best not to wait for her, so she'll meet us at the pub later."

Casey smiled a cheeky and inviting smile, which prompted Jason to put his wine glass down and take the opportunity to kiss her passionately. Now knowing they would not be disturbed by Tilly, Jason pulled Casey toward him. Returning his wanting kiss, she was burning for their promised love-making session later, but as they were due to meet Dave and his mate, she resisted the temptation to bring that steamy session forward.

As they finished the last of their wine, Casey suggested they head off and picked up her jacket. Enjoying Jason's closeness as she pulled it on, she leant forward for one last kiss, before they stepped out onto the main landing, clicking the door shut behind them. When they arrived at the ground floor, Dolly opened her front door to let a meowing Freddie back in, who had finally come home after not one, but two days away. Somehow he had got back into the building via the front door, instead of his usual route, which was through Dolly's open living room window and close enough to the outside steps to allow Freddie to jump across, then clamber up and into the warmth of Dolly's homely apartment.

After passing the usual niceties with Dolly and agreeing at how naughty Freddie was becoming, Casey was relieved to see the old lady smile again; she knew how much Dolly loved Freddie and how frantic and worried she was whenever he was on one of his nights out. Even as she was scolding Freddie for staying out so long, Dolly was also telling him how much she had missed him. Casey and Jason politely said their goodbyes to Dolly and set off for the Wagon and Horses.

Seeing how excited Jason was and remembering he'd said on his message earlier that there was something he wanted to tell her, Casey gave him the opening he needed. She could see he was almost bursting to say whatever it was he wanted to tell her, so she asked him what it was that had put him in such a happy mood. But what Jason said next, left her completely flummoxed. Almost bouncing with excitement, Jason explained that he'd been offered a very privileged job in Auckland of all places. It was effectively a promotion into a very senior role and would mean a massive hike in responsibility, as well as salary. Jason was ecstatic and so lost in his own excitement, he hadn't noticed Casey's smile drop.

Casey's head spun as Jason responded to her immediate questions. Yes, he did mean *Auckland, New Zealand* and yes, *the* New Zealand, *on the other side of the world!* Not only that, but he was flying over to meet the owner of the business on Wednesday. It was for a familiarisation visit and hopefully would be the final rubber stamp, for a proposed two-year fixed contract. Jason added that unfortunately his last minute travel plans also meant that *a)* he wouldn't be at Barney's for Steph's leaving do after all, but will instead raise a glass of bubbles to her whilst at 35,000 feet, and *b)* if the visit went well, he would be leaving the UK for the foreseeable future. BUT, he babbled, it was *such* a good opportunity, could she please understand that he just *had* to give it a go?

Casey stopped walking and turned to face Jason, her mind filled with panicked repeating thoughts. *Seriously? New Zealand? The other side of the world?* What about *them*, the two of *them*? OK, they were casual, but they'd been getting on so well. Of course, he had to go, but she would miss him, she would even miss his dodgy jokes, not to mention their hot and steamy sex sessions. Casey gulped and she was sure that Jason must have heard it, because the gulp felt like a boulder dropping down her throat. Quickly putting on her brave face, she gave him the biggest hug.

"You know what, Jase," she said. "We always said that we were just casual, so you've gotta see this through. I mean, it's like a dream come true." She paused. "Wow, how amazing for you. I couldn't be happier for you."

That last part had been a fib, but Casey felt she should be generous and not at all selfish. Jason was ecstatic and picked her up, swinging her around and kissing her hard on the mouth, momentarily taking her breath away. As he gently put her down again, Jason admitted he'd been worried about telling her, but he was so relieved that she was OK with it.

At least that's what he thought, but in fact Casey was far from OK about it. Instead, she forced her brightest smile and grinned back at him as they carried on walking, Jason now talking nineteen to the dozen.

Casey's thoughts went into overdrive. She had got quite used to Jason being around and this had all been a bit unexpected, so she was feeling more than a bit gutted that he would be leaving. However, Casey wasn't surprised that Jason had been offered such an incredible job; she knew he had a strong business reputation for being an amazing Regional Sales Engineering Manager and was known as "Mr Smooth" by his workmates. Jason was an excellent and genuine sales-person, which was an unusual trait and set him apart from most sales people. All of his customers liked and trusted him because he was so different and not at all like a lot of sales people, who often came across as gushy or smarmy. Also, being an experienced Engineer meant Jason knew his stuff inside and out. His colleagues often joked that Jason could not only sell ice to the Eskimo's, he could build their igloos as well!

Casey knew it was likely that Jason would *more* than impress the owner of the business in Auckland and she acknowledged that he would be gone from her life very soon. *Damn*, just when they'd gotten used to each other too. Forcing a smile for Jason as he caught her hand and grinned at her, Casey could see his own smile full of hopes and dreams of Auckland, and the new life that beckoned him. She kept reminding herself that they were only ever supposed to be casual and silently scolded herself for not being genuinely thrilled for Jason. Feeling less than happy, she forced another dazzling smile for him, but in her heart, she felt an unexpected sadness growing.

The Wagon and Horses was having a typically busy Sunday evening. It was a warm and welcoming pub with a great landlord, who greeted Casey like a long lost friend every time she returned, and the bands that played there were always very good. The regulars said hello to the couple as they made their way to the bar, where Jason insisted on buying a round of drinks for them all, in celebration of his good news. Jason's news, and the free drinks, soon had everyone smiling. "Well done, mate," they said. "Cheers, good on ya, geez."

Casey was hugged and patted on the back too; she wasn't quite sure why, perhaps they thought she was going with him. Nobody asked, so she kept quiet and just smiled as if she was off on the big adventure too. Jason's news was enough of a shock for one night, without seeing their disappointed faces at the news that he was leaving without Casey. It dawned on her that they'd obviously been seeing each other for a lot longer than she'd previously realised. Not only that, she had grown more attached to Jason than she realised. Which probably also explained why many of the regulars thought of them as a couple, having seen them together on so many occasions. Again, Casey was not about to enlighten their pub crowd as to the casual nature of their relationship, or for that matter, how much Jason's news was truly affecting her right at that moment.

Despite asking Jason for a dry cider, he had decided to order the finest bottle of champagne so they could celebrate in style. Jason was bursting with happiness and excitement, and was eager to share his news with Dave and Tilly when they arrived. Just as Jason and Casey clinked glasses and took their first sips of the lively bubbles, Tilly appeared beside them, so Jason called for an extra glass. Despite being shocked at the news, Tilly said she was also happy for Jason and congratulated him on his good fortune, generously wishing him all the luck in the world for his familiarisation trip and meeting with the owner of the business. By now, Jason was on cloud nine with no sign of coming down. Casey let out a low sigh; she was feeling wretched, but of course had to also pretend she was as happy as everyone else, whilst secretly

42

thinking: *what on earth is the matter with you girl? You've been fantasising over Dominic for ever, so why is the fact that Jason is now leaving for New Zealand making you feel like this?* Casey asked herself the question, but didn't really know the answer. As Jason hugged her again, she just smiled back at him, silently willing the band to start playing, so as to give her a chance to turn away before a tear escaped and Jason would see how she was really feeling.

Half an hour later, just as the band walked over and picked up their instruments, the door opened again and Dave walked in followed by his mate, who was slightly obscured from their view by Dave's huge shoulders. Tilly looked at Casey and grinned as she spotted the gorgeous Dave. Now there was a man who was just what she needed, and not only that, he was looking quite sexy in his casual white shirt and brown chinos. Tilly remembered how much fun Dave was to be around. He was a natural born comedian and someone who had seemed to like her, which was very handy because she was definitely in the mood to party. Realising this encounter was likely pre-arranged, Tilly grinned a knowing smile at Casey, who winked and grinned back at her friend.

As Tilly said hello to Dave, he stepped forward to kiss her cheek and Casey drew in a gasped breath. There in the living flesh was Dominic, yes, *her Dominic*. OMG!

"Guys, this is Matt," Dave said. "Matt, this is Tilly and Casey, and of course Jason, who you already know from way back when."

Casey's heart was beating so loudly that she was sure they'd be able to hear it above the music that had just started.

"Hi, so err, not Dominic then?" Casey asked and then mentally kicked herself as Matt replied.

"What? Who's Dominic?" Matt replied.

Shaking her head, Casey cringed as she responded

"Oh no, sorry, Matt, my mistake. It's just that you look like a guy from my office. A guy who I work with; well not work with, but on the same floor."

Casey was flustered and gabbling, hoping nobody else noticed her faux pas. How the heck could she dig herself out of this hole? Oh Jees, Dominic, *the Dominic* from her weekend fantasies and who lived in the apartment across the street from her. Yes, the very same man and who was now stood right in front of her, in all his gorgeousness. Only he wasn't Dominic, he was Matt! Casey's mind was in overdrive and failing badly as she tried to explain away her mistake. Feeling herself blush, she just knew her face was redder than Matt's rather nice red top.

Praying the low lighting would rescue her from falling into the abyss of embarrassment that her feet were already cemented into, Casey smiled at Matt. As he smiled his dazzling smile back at her, Casey's knees went weak and she felt like she was going to faint. What with Jason's news and her unexpected reaction to it and now Matt...*remember, it's Matt, not Dominic, Jees, Case.* Now that Matt was stood right there in front of her, with his perfectly brilliant dazzling smile, she had to get out and get some air. She prayed to whatever spiritual power was out there, that Matt couldn't read her mind and tune into her weekend guilty pleasures and all the times she'd watched him from the window.

OMG! All of Casey's fantasies crashed into her already embarrassed state of mind as she turned to Jason and he smiled at her. Licking her dry lips at the wish and prospect of Dominic (no, Matt), from her weekend fantasies. Now with Jason and that very same person stood inside the Wagon, right here and right now! In fact, stood right in front of her and watching her intently with his gorgeous, captivating eyes. OMG! Casey couldn't cope and just when Jason had dropped his bombshell too! She needed air, the champagne was making her head spin and she had to get away, fast. Casey's knees actually buckled and she grabbed Tilly, telling her she needed some air and to come with her. RIGHT NOW!

Dragging poor Tilly behind her, Casey headed towards the exit, not able to cope with the stuffy air in the ladies' toilet. Casey needed fresh air and lots of it. As she stepped outside, she breathed in long slow breaths, trying to calm herself and her nerves. Meanwhile Tilly, who knew nothing of the drama that was unfolding in Casey's head and who had been reluctant to leave Dave, was wondering what the heck was wrong with her friend. Looking a little puzzled, Tilly asked Casey what was wrong, but realising she couldn't tell Tilly everything just yet, Casey explained about Jason leaving and how it had shocked her to her boots, because she now realised that actually, she didn't want him to go. Tilly hugged her and reminded her of the casual arrangement they'd agreed upon, to which Casey said *yes, yes, yes,* she knew all of that, which was why she was feeling so stunned.

Anticipating Tilly's next question, Casey wasn't surprised when Tilly asked her at what point she realised that her feelings had changed. Unable to speak, Casey just shook her head as she leant against the wall, gulping in more deep breaths and trying to calm her now shaking hands, whilst at the same time willing the million butterflies that had taken off in her tummy, to settle down again. Casey replied that she didn't really know exactly when her feelings had changed, but that it wasn't until Jason had said he was leaving that she'd even realised she had feelings about him. Well, feelings that were not just the sex-appeal friendship she thought they enjoyed.

With her emotions on overload, a tear escaped and rolled down Casey's now burning cheek. Reaching up to brush it away with the tips of her fingers, she looked away from Tilly momentarily before responding. Casey didn't know where to begin, but she realised she had to tell Tilly the whole story, so Tilly could at least understand why Casey was in such a state and confirm that she wasn't a complete lunatic. Tilly was studying Casey's face closely, an enquiring worried look on her own face, as she listened to what her friend was telling her, in such a rushed conversation. As realisation dawned, Tilly could understand her friend's dilemma at not being able to tell Jason how she was feeling. However, you could have knocked Tilly down with a feather when Casey told her about the effect Dave's friend Matt was having on her. That was a curved ball that even Casey didn't see coming, let alone Tilly.

Although Casey left out the more intimate details of her regular weekend guilty pleasure, she admitted to Tilly how she'd fantasised about meeting Dominic (Matt) after seeing him working out a couple of times from her window in the apartment. Then there was the appearance of his girlfriend and how gutted she'd been about that, which she admitted was essentially pretty crazy, since she'd never even met the guy. On top of that, now Jason, who Casey didn't even realise she liked so much, had said he was leaving the UK.

Jees, she felt like her life was suddenly a complete mess. Obviously, she liked Jason and the fun they'd shared, but *really liked*? That hadn't even been on her radar and all the while, she'd been convincing herself that she really liked Matt, or Dominic. *Damn*, what was his real name? Matt.

Tilly was gob-smacked.

"Jees, Case," she said. "What are you going to do?"

Tilly's question mirrored her own thoughts as Casey shrugged her shoulders and replied: "I don't know, but I know I've got to go back in there and be the life and soul of the party. Let's talk tomorrow can we, Til? Are you free after work?"

"Sure, no problem," Tilly said. "Crikey though, Case, what are you going do?"

Tilly could see what a mess Casey was, so she knew this was serious. Pulling herself together and fastening a dazzling smile in place, Casey replied a little more positively.

"I have no idea, but tonight, Tilly my girl, Dave is here for you, so we'd best get back in there and not disappoint him."

Casey managed to bolster herself enough to regain momentum for the evening ahead of them. Tilly's eyes opened wide as she gasped and then giggled.

"Really? For me? Did you organise that? Does he know? Well come on then, we'd best get back inside before they send out a search party!"

Now laughing nervously, the girls bundled back into the pub and squeezed back through the now crowded bar, to where the boys were standing. Luckily, they'd assumed the girls had gone to the ladies' toilets together and like girls do, just taken their time, so the boys didn't even question why they'd been gone for the last twenty minutes. Dave smiled and handed Tilly her drink, as she grinned back and moved to stand closer to him.

Matt watched Casey as Jason bent to kiss her lips again. Matt's own thoughts were being stirred by this gorgeous creature in front of him and he was surprised to find himself feeling jealous of Jason's kiss, even wanting to pull him off Casey. The group of friends all raised their glasses in another toast to Jason, took a drink and then turned to listen to the band's next song. Matt found himself watching Casey more than the band.

The evening went by in a blur for Casey, her heart and mind racing each other to see which would win the battle of keeping her calm, versus, allowing her to melt down. She felt like someone had just thrown a love grenade into her life, but in spite of that, it was a good night; the friends laughed and cried at Dave's jokes and Jason's stories, as they enjoyed the band and each other's company. As for Tilly and Dave, they were definitely enjoying themselves and Casey said a quiet "thank goodness" to herself, feeling happy to see Tilly laughing and smiling again, after John's betrayal. But Casey deliberately avoided Matt's eyes. She was desperate not to let him see her guilt, and as for Jason...well, he was having the time of his life. What a brilliant night it had been for him.

As the band finished up, the friends said their goodbyes, while Dave informed Tilly that he'd join her at Barney's on Wednesday, so they could have a proper chat, rather than shouting over the band like they had being doing for most of the night.

Matt said how nice it was to meet them all and kissed both girls on their cheeks as he said goodbye. Casey avoided his direct gaze, but smiled her dazzling smile, which caught Matt's heart, flipped it over and then crushed it at the same time, as he realised from her averted gaze, that he was clearly of no interest at all to this vision entwined within Jason's arms.

Tilly was on cloud nine, tripping along the road with Jason and Casey, as they made their way home, excitedly chatting all the way about how great Dave was. Jason and Casey were laughing at her exuberance, whilst ecstatic for her that she and Dave had got on so well. As they entered the apartment building, the three of them quietened down, not wanting to disturb their elderly neighbour. Reaching Tilly's apartment first, she thanked them both for a great evening and wished them goodnight.

Jason and Casey continued on upstairs, both now silent, yet with heads full of their own very different thoughts. Once Casey's apartment door was unlocked, Jason followed her inside, knowing he was desperate to make love to this woman. The curtains inside the apartment were all still open, allowing the moonlight to dust its magic, creating a very romantic, dimly lit scene. The serenity of the room added something to Jason's elation and forced a more urgent and wanting need to share his passion with Casey.

As much as she had thought she couldn't possibly make love to Jason after the evening that her heart and head had just experienced, Casey weakened as Jason's lips began that persuading and welcome journey to consume her body. Taking her into his arms and kissing her lips gently, Jason's hands ran through Casey's hair. He adored her so much. Breathing in her delicious smell and supporting the back of her head as his kisses became more urgent and deep, his lips moved across her cheek and then downwards to nuzzle into her neck. Jason was desperate and wanted her badly.

"Oh God, Casey," he said. "I want you so much."

Casey was secretly as in need of Jason as he was of her and responded willingly, if not a little huskily as her pheromones exploded.

"I want you too, Jase."

Gently nibbling her ear with his teeth, Jason's lips moved back to brush across Casey's as he kissed her harder and with more wanting, before moving down to the base of her neck. His passion was too strong to resist and as her own deliciously wicked wanting was rising, Casey's senses were on full alert. Knowing how much Jason now wanted her, she pushed him away gently and told him he could only watch and was not to touch her. Teasing him, she first removed her long necklace, before slowly sliding her top off over her head, leaving her hair to cascade down over her bare shoulders. Casey enjoyed watching Jason's expression as he caught sight of her prettiest lacy bra, which perfectly supported the pert breasts that he loved to caress so much. With her long hair now brushing across her bare skin, still not allowing

Jason to touch her, Casey told him again that he could only watch. But as she bent forward to ease off her boots, he could resist no longer and his hands reached out automatically to catch and squeeze her breasts, feeling for her hard nipples through the lacy fabric of her bra. Casey's own need for him was growing more and more quickly, as she undid her jeans then reached for his belt buckle, expertly undoing the clasp with little effort. Jason's lips began kissing her naked chest, her breasts were heaving with desire as his passionate mood intensified and she wilted as he swept her up into his arms. Carrying her through to the bedroom, Jason lay her on the bed then stood upright again as he started to peel off his clothes. She could see he was excited by his very visible hardness, which was ready to pleasure her. As he continued undressing her, tugging her jeans off and grinning at the skimpy G-string she wore underneath, she lifted herself up to allow his hands access to her bra clasp, which he unclipped with one hand, making her gasp. Jason had perfected undressing her and she was totally hot for him. All thoughts of Matt had been temporarily banished from her mind. A mind which had been overtaken by her own erotic desires as once again, Jason's hands moved back to her breasts. Pulling her bra aside to explore and expose her perfectly hard nipples before bending towards them, Jason's lips eagerly sucked them into his mouth and nibbled gently with his teeth as he drove her crazy with wanting for his hardness to enter her. Reaching down her body, his fingers exploring her femininity, he found her magic spot, and as he lightly pleasured her to the point of no return, he moved into position and thrust into her with gentle but all-consuming passion. Completely won over by this sex-god of a man, it wasn't long before Casey's own release of pleasure repeatedly climaxed and she cried out as she reached that dizzy height again and again. Hearing her cries of such repeated pleasure, instantly released

Jason's own intense wanting and he groaned with the delight he always felt, whenever their explosive love making reached that point together.

"Uhhhh. Ohhhhh, Cassseeeeyyyyy!" Jason's groan was loud and satisfying.

Lying facing each other, their hot damp bodies heaving with their spent desires, the two lovers stared into each other's eyes. Jason stroked Casey's face then pulled her towards him as he kissed her again. Snuggled together, naked and satisfied in the moonlit bedroom, Jason murmured into Casey's ear: "I think I love you, Casey."

His words were muffled. "God, I'm gonna miss you so much."

Casey smiled dreamily and pushed out thoughts of Jason leaving as they lay together. He kissed her forehead as his hand gently stroked her back. The moment was precious and as they both relaxed, feeling happy and satisfied, they fell into a deep and blissful sleep. Still snuggled together, their bodies were exhausted.

Chapter 4

New Zealand minus 2 days

The following morning, Casey remembered their passionate love-making and gulped as the memory of Jason's bombshell surfaced through the sleepy haze of her mind. Its shattering effect had been multiplied by the brief encounter of the night before when Matt had walked into the Wagon behind Dave. What on earth had happened to her, she had been blown away by Jason's news and her own unexpected reaction to it. But to then have the man of her weekend fantasies stood right in front of her and looking at her with such intensity! Well, that had blown her away and Casey had dared to imagine that Matt was having similar thoughts to her own recent daydreams. That very reason was why she had felt the need to avoid his gaze all evening, just in case he could read her mind. With a very confused mind, Casey wished someone could help her to figure out exactly what it was that she was feeling about these two men.

Jason stirred from his own deep sleep and rolled over to face Casey. Reaching out, he pulled her towards him as he slid his arm around her waist, then moving his other hand up to gently touch her cheek, his kiss was tender as he brushed her lips with his. The passion of the night before had now merged into a warmth that keeps lovers snuggling in bed for hours. Jason's mood was pensive, his excitement at the job offer was waning slightly at the realisation that like Casey, he too hadn't appreciated just how much she had come to mean to him. After all, they'd just been casual right? At least that's what his head was telling him. But his heart, well, *that* had dived into an entirely different pool of emotion, which was much deeper and had a pull to it that he'd never experienced before. What was this feeling welling up from deep within him? Did he really mumble, *I think I love you*, to Casey last night? Had she heard him say that? Jason's mind was racing and unbeknown to him, Casey's mind was doing the very same thing, albeit for very different reasons.

For Casey, there was Jason and the passionate night of loving they'd shared after arriving back at her moonlit apartment the previous night, followed with his murmured, *God, I'm gonna miss you so much, Case.* Then there was Matt, whose unexpected appearance had crashed into her reality when she had seen him with Dave. Right now she was vaguely remembering that Dave had said something about Jason already knowing Matt. What the heck was that all about? How and in what capacity did the two of them know each other?

As Casey felt a panic rising inside her, Jason was feeling something akin to blissful peace, unaware of it being the calm before the storm. Casey tried to speak enthusiastically as she chirped, "Wasn't it brilliant last night, Jase? You must be feeling so excited about the job in Auckland...it was a really good send off for you. A bit impromptu, but as it turned out, it was a really good night."

Holding her breath as she waited for his response, Casey was trying to figure out whether to ask him how he knew Matt.

"Yeah," Jason said. "It was a great night, Case, but I'm gonna miss you so much. I'm gonna miss this..." His voice caught just enough for her to hear it as his words trailed off. Had she just imagined it or had Jason said how bad he was feeling about leaving her?

Torn between the new life he would soon have in New Zealand, versus leaving behind this goddess, whom he had come to adore, Jason reiterated his thoughts. "Casey, I mean it. I'm going to miss you so much. Will you come out to visit me once I've settled into my new place over there?"

Jason waited for Casey's response, hoping and praying that she would agree. However, she lay quiet and thoughtful as she stared into his eyes, unable to answer him as quickly as he needed her to. Stunned into silence by this sudden and unexpected question, Casey's mind was frantically searching for how best to respond.

Before she could even begin to drag together any suitable words for a coherent but non-committal response, Jason repeated his question; "Casey, I think I love you. I need to see you again. I can't leave this, *us*, here, not now...not after last night. Please say you'll come and see me. I can't go off without knowing you'll come and stay for a while. Christ, I didn't expect to feel like this. I'm confused, but I know I do want you to come and see me over there and I don't just mean for a two-week holiday either. Will you come and stay for a bit longer?"

Jason's pleading words were totally out of character for him, at least for the Jason that Casey knew.

As she wondered how his mates would react if they could hear him now, the words *bit longer*, were also not lost on Casey. Instead, they raised a question in her mind; did that mean weeks, months, or was he thinking longer? Oh crikey, this was too much.

"Well, there's nothing like a bit of emotional blackmail to tug on those heartstrings," she said, her voice struggling to maintain a light-hearted tempo as she touched his chest. "I know you're only going for a short visit this time, but next time it will be forever, Jase. Well, two years for now, but it could be forever, if it goes really well, which it probably will."

Casey was feeling hot, overwhelmed by the intensity of the moment, she needed to get out of bed and distance herself slightly from Jason's tempting arms. As if sensing her reaction, he held her tighter, afraid of her reply and not wanting to let her go from his arms, in case she never came back.

"Yes, I know and once I get back from the familiarisation visit, I'll only have a month to get everything sorted before I move there permanently. Well, for the foreseeable future anyway."

Unable to quite pull away from him, Casey's gentle kiss on his lips was an automatic, almost involuntary natural response, but it also gave her time to think for a few seconds, knowing that she couldn't reply with, 'I think I love you too'. She really didn't know *what* she was feeling at that time, apart from confused, however, she did know that by adding, 'I love you too', to that state of mind, would not be a good idea.

Jason was so wrapped up in the moment that he barely noticed and kissed her passionately. Once again, she responded involuntarily to his kiss and with such equal passion, he took her physical response as being, *yes, and I love you too*, even though those words did not actually pass her lips.

As Casey's kiss returned his with such all-consuming passion, her hands explored Jason's smooth chest before reaching down and brushing over his stomach, causing him to groan with desire as his wanting increased at her touch. They made love again, the energy of the previous night's exchange had returned with an immediate urgency that they both felt, taking them both in an immediate explosion of intense, steamy desire, before collapsing again, their joint passions satiated.

They separated again and lay looking at the ceiling as their spent bodies tried to cool down; both of them heaving from the intensity of their urgent love-making, Jason's voice broke into a croak, "Oh, Casey, you are so wonderful."

Despite feeling hot, Jason pulled her into his arms again, never wanting to let her go but knowing he soon would have to.

As they both enjoyed that embrace, an abrupt and sharp rapping on the door broke through their dreamy state and they heard the familiar sound of Tilly's voice.

"Casey, are you OK?" she called out. "Are you there?"

Tilly, who should have been at work, had thrown a sickie and decided to take the day off. Well, she was feeling a bit ropey anyway and had reasoned that her ropey feeling was some kind of justification for her conscience. Being torn between going into the office and staying home, Tilly had given in to the temptation to stay home because she so desperately needed to talk to Casey about her own revelation from the previous evening. Even though she knew Jason would have stayed the night, Tilly had expected him to be long gone by now, as was his usual routine whenever he stayed at Casey's on a school night. Unbeknown to Tilly though, Jason was taking time off until he left for New Zealand, which was why he could linger in bed for so long.

As Casey reluctantly pulled away from Jason's arms and slipped her legs over the side of the bed, she curled her toes into the sheepskin rug that had belonged to her Nan. Reaching across to the wicker chair beside the bed to pick up her silky robe, she wrapped it around her body, as she wobbled across the floor, her legs still slightly jellified from their intense love-making session. Straightening up with each step forward and feeling stronger as she quickened her pace, Casey walked out of the bedroom and across the open plan living space towards her front door. Opening the door gently, she held her finger to her lips, desperate for Tilly not to blurt out something that she would find hard to explain to Jason (Casey needed to get her own head straight before saying anything to him).

Tilly realised Jason was obviously still there and said she'd been feeling ropey so had taken the day off, but could she pop in for a coffee and chat whilst Casey was writing?

Casey took her lead: "Sure, but I've only just got up so can you give me an hour to get showered?"

Casey suggested that Tilly pop back again in a bit, so they could breakfast together and catch up then. Whilst also knowing there was no way she could write her column with Tilly there, Casey was also relieved, because she really did need to spill her soul about this whole messy situation and she hoped that Tilly could help her reason it out. Breakfast together seemed like a good opportunity and besides which, Jason did have to get home and pack for his trip.

This was the same Tilly that had been so devastated about John and who Casey had thought she could help, despite her own heart and head being in such a state of shock. Even Casey thought how bizarre it was at times, that no matter how much turmoil was in your own head, quite often when it came to true friendships, it was easy to park one's own misery and despair to help a friend who was in need of emotional support. The friendship between Casey and Tilly was very much like that and Casey felt confident talking through her romantic challenges to Tilly, even though her best friends, Amanda and Carole, were her usual confidants depending on the nature of the issue. Casey felt that Tilly had to be the one for this chat. After all, she had been there and *seen* what had happened the night before. Besides which, both Amanda and Carole were working that day and Casey needed to talk to someone *right now!* That someone needed to be a friend who not only knew her well, but who also understood a little of what her current predicament was. Neither Amanda nor Carole knew the full details of what had been going on in Casey's head over the last twenty-four hours. But Tilly did, at least as close as she *could* know, after Casey's disclosure the evening before, which had been preceded by Jason and the dropping of his, "I'm leaving for New Zealand" bombshell.

Tilly, being in her own fairly emotional raw state, meant that whilst she would empathise on this one, she would probably be more pragmatic. Amanda would be a bit harsher. Whilst Carole, who was an old romantic, would be tempted to look at Casey's situation through rose-tinted glasses and then probably advise her that the best thing to do would be to run off to New Zealand with Jason. No, this needed the rawness of Tilly's current viewpoint, which would lead to a much more pragmatic discussion and decision.

With Tilly having now gone back to her apartment, Casey had time to sort herself out. As she walked back into the bedroom, Jason was emerging from the bathroom stark naked. Casey stopped in her tracks. Hmmm...always a nice view she thought, as she grinned at her very own sex-god. Telling Jason she needed to get showered, just encouraged him to pull her silky robe open and slide his arms around her waist once more; one hand travelling up her back towards her neck, whilst the other splayed across her lower back, pulling her towards him as he kissed her again, his passion still evident.

At Casey's feigned protestation, Jason reluctantly agreed that whilst he would much rather stay and make love to her all day, they both needed to crack on with their day and the stuff that needed doing. Not only that, Tilly would be back in an hour and it was probably best they weren't still in bed having hot passionate sex when she arrived. But as his arms pulled back from under the silky gown, it slowly slid off Casey's shoulders and dropped to the floor. Jason pulled away slightly to admire her gorgeously sexy body, then letting out a low sigh, he watched her turn and walk into the bathroom. He did so love her and mentally kicked himself for only just realising that most important fact. *Damn*, just when everything had seemed so simple and exciting.

It had seemed to be a reasonably straight-forward decision for him to move to Auckland, but no, he had to go and fall for the gorgeous Casey Smith who, as it happened, was soon to be known as *Casey Martin – Column Writer*, in the ever popular magazine *Just for You!* As he mused on that point, he wondered how long it would be before Casey could give up her current job and rely solely on her publishing earnings. Just for a moment, he luxuriated in his own fantasy of Casey moving to Auckland with him, where she could still write and then email her column over to the Editor of *Just for You!* As he glorified in those thoughts, Jason began gathering up his scattered clothes and absent-mindedly threw them onto the bed, ready to pull on before he left to go home.

Thinking about packing for his trip, Jason knew he only needed enough stuff for a week as it really was going to be a whirlwind trip. That said, he was still very excited, even though he knew it would probably be fairly exhausting. Lee Riley, the owner of the company, had said he wanted to show Jason around the city and had treated him to a room at the Sky-Tower Hotel. Lee went on to tell Jason that the Sky-Tower was 328 feet tall (when taking in the spire on the top), which made it the tallest building in the southern hemisphere. It was a fact that most Aucklanders, including Lee, was very proud of, which became clearer as he provided Jason with a brief Lee Riley tourist guide stint, advising him of the viewing floor at 220 feet, which offered magnificent 360° views across Auckland. Lee also told him that the viewing platform was where you could watch the bungee jumpers, as they suspended outside the windows on the fixed-line drop, so people could photograph them and witness the look of fear on their faces as they dropped suddenly, plummeting to the ground on the terrifying ride down.

The thought of that very scary ride down worried Jason because Lee Riley had also egged Jason to have a go at the daredevil bungee. Jason had been and still was, more than a little bit apprehensive. In fact, plain scared would be a better description. Doing a bungee jump had never really appealed to Jason, but not wanting to disappoint his new boss, he had agreed to *maybe* having a go at it. Now realising that actually he really *would* have to do it, or risk the ridicule of his new workmates, not to mention Lee Riley himself.

As the hot water cascaded over her head in the shower, Casey called out to Jason to pop the kettle on and help himself to tea or coffee while he waited for her to finish. After brushing her teeth and towel-drying her hair, Casey walked out of the bathroom, feeling totally refreshed and clean all over. As she bent down to retrieve her gown, she thought how there was something special about making love in the morning that she just adored.

Hang on a minute, she stopped walking and pulled her thoughts up short, *making love? Making love? What the heck happened to hot sex?* Casey really was losing it; when did morning sex with Jason turn into morning love-making? Was that *before* Jason had told her that he was leaving for Auckland, or after his declaration of, 'I think I love you', this morning?

Hurry up, Tilly, I need you, Casey thought, as she padded through to the kitchen area, telling the still naked Jason that the shower was now free, seeing as he'd only brushed his teeth earlier. Casey was very glad to see the kettle with its whistle firmly in place, slowly heating-up on the gas hob. Mmmm...yes, tea, she needed that life-saving drink to calm herself down. Jason said he'd give it a miss, seeing as Tilly was due to arrive and that he'd just take a quick shower before he shot off home. Then he asked that if Casey was going to be free, could he pop back later that evening and take her out for dinner?

Smiling broadly, Casey agreed to dinner. She was enjoying this new Jason, but was also very aware of the short time they had together, before he left for New Zealand for good. OK, so maybe for good was actually only two years, but that might as well be forever. Jason looked relieved and happy as Casey nodded a *yes* and said, "Great" before he turned to go and shower.

Following him back through to the bedroom to finish drying her hair and not even giving Matt a second thought, Casey smiled inanely at her reflection in the long wall mirror, deciding that actually, she'd let her hair dry naturally. After all, Jason had told her he liked it that way because it had a natural curl, which Casey often banished with straighteners. Hearing the shower already running and seeing steam starting to escape through the open bathroom door, Casey sat down at her dressing table. Staring into the mirror, she applied her new eye-cream and various different moisturisers before deciding that as she wasn't going out, she may as well leave her make-up until she was ready to get changed again later, to go out for her dinner date with Jason. Yes, good idea, that way she'd look and feel fresher for their date. Casey had learnt from experience that no matter how well you cleansed and reapplied evening make-up, it never looked quite as fresh as it did in the mornings. It was going to be another special evening and she wanted to feel as good as she possibly could.

Slightly surprising herself at not worrying about Jason seeing her without make-up, Casey remembered how she used to put a little on in the bathroom before he even woke up. Times sure had changed she thought, then realised that actually, she'd never had make-up on after showering before and he'd seen her plenty of times looking like that when he'd stayed the night, so why worry? Was that the slippery slope to not taking care of yourself? This love thing was clearly playing on her mind. *Oh crikey*, what was she thinking of?

Casey was dressing as Jason came out of the bathroom and she paused to admire his toned body. She also did love that whole *man-with-wet-hair* kind of look. It was a serious turn on for her and normally she would have been tempted to jump his bones again. But right now, she needed Jason to get dressed and be gone, as her mind was in turmoil and she needed more tea. Besides, she needed to talk to Tilly!

As if sensing Casey's need for him to be gone, Jason pulled on his clothes from the night before. Then kissing her full on the lips, he wished Casey good luck with her writing and promised to be on time to pick her up for dinner later.

Right on cue, Tilly was just about to knock on the door as Jason opened it to leave. Both of them laughed as they startled each other. Casey greeted Tilly once more as she leant forward to allow Jason's final goodbye kiss to land on her cheek. Then shutting the door behind her man, Casey breathed a sigh of relief and raised her eyebrows at the intrigued Tilly as she invited her in.

"Come on through to the kitchen."

Both girls were ravenous for something to eat, and more importantly, desperate for this chat...each of them having so much to talk about. As Casey put the kettle back on the hob and picked up two mugs, Tilly popped some toast in the toaster. Neither girl wanted to waste valuable chatting time by cooking anything like bacon, so breakfast was going to be toasted granary bread, with lashings of butter (the only acceptable spread for toast), topped with Marmite, Honey and/or Rose's Lime Marmalade. All three toppings were old favourites of the girls. Plus of course, the obligatory pots of tea and coffee.

Working around each other as they gathered the breakfast things, they put what they needed onto the scrubbed kitchen table, pulling out its slightly battered and well-used cushioned chairs. Tilly sat down feeling a little more relaxed than Casey, who placed their mugs, along with the coffee and tea pots on the table before joining her; she was feeling a little tenser than her friend. Tilly opened the discussion as she began buttering a slice of toast for Casey, before adding marmite to her own piece.

"So, what the heck happened to you last night, Case?" Tilly asked. "You were on melt-down. And what did you mean about Dave's mate and the guy across the road?"

Casey began the long and unwieldy task of unravelling her feelings about Jason...his news about moving to the other side of the world and how that seemed to be affecting her, particularly since his declaration of love after a night and morning of intense passionate sex. Then of course there was Matt; first, with him being Dave's mate. Casey still didn't know how he and Jason knew each other, which was something she hoped to rectify when she and Jase went out for dinner later. Second, how her secret weekend fantasies had in fact created a need and now a wanting to get to know the very gorgeous Matt.

Whilst Casey was pouring out her mixed-up feelings about Jason, along with two mugs of hot steaming tea and coffee, Tilly listened intently, crunching into her warm buttered toast and Marmite. Who understood those people who hated Marmite? It was delish' as far as Tilly was concerned. Casey explained to Tilly that she had always thought of herself and Jason as *casual*, which Tilly already knew of course. But, as soon as Jason said he was leaving, she'd felt like someone had pulled the rug out from under her feet, which had taken her completely by surprise. Then of course Jason had announced how he was feeling about Casey. Well, this was where Casey was confused, because she too was feeling something stronger when it came to her emotions and Jason, but she couldn't quite put her finger on what it was exactly.

"So, Case, are you saying you think you feel something akin to love for Jason?"

Tilly was bemused as she asked that open and honest question.

"Noooo, not love as such, but I didn't realise I liked him *quite* as much as I obviously do." The statement from Casey was firm, but then she added more. "The trouble is, Tilly, he's also leaving to move across to the other side of the world. So, even if I did love him, which I don't – *no, I really don't feel that strongly* – I couldn't possibly leave this place to go with him. I love living here. I love my friends and I love my life and, quite honestly, I don't want to give any of that up."

Casey now crunched into her own toast and just for a moment, enjoyed the homely comforting feeling that washed over her, as her taste buds caught the flavour of the Marmite and the childhood memories it triggered.

"So, really, Case, there's nothing to sort out here is there," Tilly said, "because if you don't love Jason and you don't want to leave this place, then there really is nothing to make a decision about." Tilly was being pragmatic, just as Casey had needed her to be, then she added a kicker.

"Other than, how the hell you're going to tell him that after his declaration of love this morning?"

When put like that, Casey thought that Tilly made complete sense, but then of course the bombshell of telling Jason that she didn't love him and couldn't possibly leave the UK, didn't sit well with her either. So why hadn't she realised this herself?

Tilly also knew the answer to that though: "Because, Casey dearest, you're sitting on the fence over how you feel about Jason, maybe thinking it could be something more, whilst still trying to convince yourself it really *is* just a *casual* thing."

"So how do I tell Jason I won't be going over to visit him in New Zealand then, Til?"

Casey felt her tummy tie into a knot at the thought of Jason's disappointment, when she revealed that little gem of a factoid to him. Finishing the last bite of her Marmite toast, Casey unintentionally gulped a huge mouthful of her tea and swallowed hard as she waited for Tilly to solve her dilemma.

"You've just got to be honest, Case," she said. "It's not going to be easy by any means, but you do have to tell him what you told me. You know, about not wanting to leave everything behind that you know and love. Plus, you will at least need time to think about it. Bearing in mind he's already made his decision, having already had the benefit of time to think and decide, whereas this is brand new information for you."

Casey breathed a sigh of relief. Of course, that was the perfect opening to start the conversation with Jase. Tilly felt a little smug at realising she'd just come up with the perfect excuse to help Casey tell Jason the bad news.

OK, so that's Jason sorted then...well, in theory at least. Although Casey was still wavering a little at the thought of saying goodbye, because that's what it would have to be, saying goodbye. There was no point thinking anything else, because there was no going back to what they'd had before, not after Jason's love declaration. No, this really *would* have to be a final goodbye. Casey's heart sank as she realised how gutted he was going to be about her finishing their relationship, knowing he really was leaving and inevitably their relationship had to end.

"What about Matt?"

Casey dared to say this out loud and Tilly, now on her second piece of toast – this one with honey – thought for a moment.

"Hmmm...yes Matt, or should we call him Dominic?"

Tilly's eyes were twinkling with mirth as she retorted, stating Casey needed to tell her more about this exciting, potentially romantic development.

"Oh very funny, Til. No, let's just call him Matt, shall we?"

Casey replied in a light-hearted sarcastic tone; being good friends, the two girls often used this kind of banter.

"Oh OK, boring. Well, run through it again then, Case. I mean, I remember you saying something about you *watching* him every weekend. That, incidentally, does make you sound like a bit of a stalker and a teensy bit freaky, my friend. Although, having now seen him close up myself, I can quite understand the temptation to check him out."

Tilly laughed at that thought as she waited for Casey's reply.

Casey repeated how she had watched and fantasised about meeting Dominic (who they now knew was Matt). Although again, she found herself not telling Tilly the *whole* fantasy, knowing that Tilly could fill in the blanks well enough herself. Carrying on, Casey said that seeing him standing in front of her last night, in the flesh so to speak – and him being called Matt – had taken her by complete surprise when Dave had introduced him. Plus of course, Matt had looked as good in the flesh as he had from the distance between their two apartment windows. Better in fact, because now she had seen his eyes as they'd said hello. Yes, those very sexy eyes of his, which could melt a girl with one twinkle and which she had tried to avoid for most of the evening. Not to mention that smile of his.

Tilly smiled at Casey. "Well, Case, it very much sounds to me like you should let Jason go and then somehow find a way to get to know Matt better. You've definitely got the hots for him, girl! Besides, he was a good laugh last night.

Oh, and apparently Dave's known him for quite a while too; he told me that he, Jason and Matt have been good mates for years."

Casey was tempted to throw caution to the wind and follow Tilly's advice as she remembered Matt's body from his Saturday morning workouts. Then again, Jason's love-making was still burnt into her short-term memory. He always was, and still is, really rather good at making her melt. Nevertheless, Jason was leaving and Matt was here. Although Casey didn't really know if Matt liked her, but she believed he did; especially after catching him watching her a few times the previous evening, even when Jason was holding her close to him.

Unbeknown to Casey, Matt had truly hated seeing his mate Jason touching and kissing this gorgeous woman that he wanted so badly; in fact, he had wanted to pull Jason off her and take her away with him. In Matt's mind, Jason was like a bloke shouting, "She's mine, mate, so keep your eyes off her," to any other guy who might be watching and/or thinking of trying to take her away from him. Although Jason had never *actually* said anything like that, he already knew Matt, so there was no suspicion or fear of macho in-fighting there.

"I know you're right, Tilly, but I think I need to just be on my own for a bit. At least while Jason's away on his familiarisation visit. I need time to think things through."

Casey sighed wistfully. "Sure, but I bet you'll be eyeing Matt up on Saturday again!"

Tilly giggled, which set Casey off too and they both chuckled at each other, revealing the naughty side of both their personalities.

Tilly was right of course. Casey couldn't resist checking Matt out again, especially now that she knew he had eyes and a smile that truly were as gorgeous as she'd hoped. Casey suspected her guilty pleasure of Saturday morning viewings would be taking on a whole new meaning.

"Thanks, Tilly, you've been a complete star as always. I still need to sort my head out, but you have made me look at the fact that Jason's leaving from a completely different perspective."

Casey picked up the plates and cups and then made her way over to the sink.

"I'll just clear this lot up and then crack on with some writing. Are you feeling OK yourself? You said you were feeling a bit ropey earlier?"

"Oh sure, much better now," Tilly said. "I think I just needed toast, coffee and a chat."

Tilly grinned, knowing she had also been a bit hungover from too much cider and really should be going into work. But she'd decided that as she was already home, she may as well chill out and return the next day, even though they would all give her a ribbing for being off on a Monday. Despite those thoughts, Tilly reasoned that she didn't need to feel overly guilty. After all, this was her first day off sick this year, unlike a few others she could mention from their office at work.

"OK, well, I'll be off now then, so happy writing and enjoy your dinner date tonight. I hope you manage to tell him. Just give me a knock later if you need to talk."

Tilly was already walking towards the door and truthfully, despite the banter, she felt glad not to be in Casey's shoes. Recognising how hard it was going to be for her friend to tell Jason that she wouldn't be going to Auckland to see him, plus that they would actually be saying goodbye when he flies out!

With Tilly gone and the breakfast things cleared away, Casey settled down to write her column. Re-reading what she'd already written, she decided she'd allocated far too much time and thought to it. All she really needed to do was keep mental notes and bash out something very similar to her *Online Diary*. It was best not to over-think it too much. In any case, that style is what had attracted

Claire in the first place and then encouraged Edine to offer her this amazing opportunity. Remembering that Edine had said she very much liked the rawness of Casey's writing style and felt the down-to-earth and real-life appeal of her writing would attract their readers. Casey had felt quite chuffed when Edine disclosed that compliment during their first chat.

It was just as well that writing the column wasn't going to take Casey as long as she'd first thought. Due to the need to keep her regular job going, at least for the time being, Casey had to balance her job and her writing, which she loved, whilst also leaving time for fun times with her friends and boyfriends. *Ha! Boyfriends! Plural.* Casey laughed at her own faux pas.

As much as she would have loved it to, Casey accepted that the column wasn't going to pay enough for her to live on just yet, so work had to continue. But, as always, she sent out a silent wish to become a full-time, well-paid column writer.

Chapter 5

Dinner with Jason

Having spent all afternoon writing, reading and re-editing her column, Casey was now feeling quite pleased with what she had written and emailed it to Edine. Keen to promote her reputation with Edine, Casey was very satisfied that she was submitting her first column slightly early. Also hoping that Edine would look upon her timekeeping favourably, thereby adding to Edine's already positive impression of Casey. Closing the lid of her laptop, Casey stood up and stepped away from her chair. Having been sat down for several hours, she was in need of a good stretch and reached her arms up towards the ceiling. Slowly stretching up one hand a little further, then moving the other and stretching as far as she could, Casey felt her spine releasing the tightness from every vertebrae and thought how there was nothing quite like a good old stretch. A fact that she was sure any cat worth its salt would agree to.

Casey had never liked complete silence when she was at home and always needed some kind of muted noise in the background. No matter what she was doing, even when she was writing, Casey found it calming to have music playing. Today was no exception and she'd been listening to the radio all day, but was now in need of a change of tempo. Switching off the radio in preference for one of her favourite CDs and being in the mood for something gentle and romantic to relax to, her Motown collection was the old favourite that Casey reached for, as she pulled open the smoked glass door of the storage unit that held her generous collection of CDs. Deciding random shuffle was the order of play as she slipped the disc into the open CD player tray, she waited to see what the first song would be and was not disappointed by the soothing tones of Billy Preston and Syreeta as they sang, *With You I Am Born Again*. Walking through to the kitchen, Casey paused to pour herself a glass of finest Argentinian Malbec, then, picking up a box of matches from behind an old jug on the kitchen shelf, she walked through to the bathroom to run herself a bath.

As the hot water began to flow, Casey poured a generous amount of her gorgeously scented, rich and soothing bath crème, under the running water and watched as it bubbled up quickly and easily, without needing the water to be agitated. Setting the mood further, Casey picked up the matches again and struck one alight, holding it to the already burnt wicks of her abstract collection of candles, which were already scattered randomly around the bathroom. Returning to her bedroom, Casey casually undressed, throwing her clothes onto the wicker chair, as Billy Preston sang the words, *'Come bring me your softness, comfort me through all this madness, woman don't you know with you I'm born again...'*

Feeling safe and now relaxed, Casey mused on her fantasy of Matt and imagined him watching her as she prepared for her bathing session. Standing naked in front of her dressing table, whilst pulling her hair up and then clipping it back into a mass of unruly curls, Casey's nipples hardened at the thought of Matt, as she imagined him touching her firm breasts and tweaking her nipples gently before pulling her towards him. Wanting her, needing her, Matt would kiss her fiercely, yet passionately, as they moved towards her bed and he took possession of his raging need, whilst satisfying Casey's own wanting passion.

With the bubbles of her bath-water now threatening to breach the brim, Casey suddenly remembered the water was still on and dashed back into the bathroom, relieved to have just caught it. The bubbles were inviting her to step in and as she sipped at her glass of delicious Malbec, before placing it on the ledge beside the bath, she stepped into the inviting warm water. As Casey sank down into the scented bubbles, she again imagined Matt to be there with her, his hardness wanting her as much as she imagined she wanted him. Rudely cutting across her passion, Casey's thoughts imagined Jason had just walked into the room and she was instantly racked with guilt over her fantasy about Matt. She felt so totally confused over these two men, who unknowingly, seemed to be taking over her every thought. What was wrong with her?

Now worried about how she should tell Jason the answer that he really wasn't going to want to hear, Casey laid back, closed her eyes and tried not to think about it. But she really did have to have that conversation and today was going to be that day. Now willing someone to help her with this confusion, Casey was startled when the house phone started ringing. Knowing that it would likely be Jason and that he would leave her a message, Casey decided not to drag herself out of her bubble bath. Instead, she listened as the answer-phone clicked in on the sixth ring and played her message to the caller.

'Hi this is Casey, sorry I can't get to the phone right now, I'm either on the other line or out having a good time, so do feel free to leave me a message and I'll call you back later...thanks for calling!'

Jason's voice bounced into the recorder.

'Hi, Case, I'm guessing you're probably in the bath and trying to ignore the phone, so just letting you know, I'll be over around seven-thirty. The table's booked for eight-thirty, so we can have a glass of wine at yours before we leave. See you later, gorgeous, and enjoy your bath.'

Jason sounded so perky that it made Casey feel even worse and hearing the answer-phone click again as the call ended, she drained the remainder of her already half-empty glass of wine, then regretted it, thinking that she'd best not drink too much before Jason arrived, knowing a level head on her shoulders was needed for the conversation that beckoned later that evening. Casey sighed, feeling slightly depressed. Placing her empty glass on the ledge and luxuriating in the bubbles, she smoothed the sponge down her right leg, which was now raised in the air above the water, while she inspected her red painted toenails. There was no getting away from it, Casey felt more than a little apprehensive about seeing Jason later.

Wow, what a difference to the evening before, when she'd got ready in an almost giddy mood. Indeed, but the previous night she'd had no idea that Jason's news was going to be so earth-shattering. But tonight, well, tonight she had to deal with the aftermath of that news and although he didn't yet know it, Jason would too. Knowing he was not going to be happy with her decision, Casey also knew there was no point in pretending and that she had to be honest with both herself and Jason.

After luxuriating for another twenty minutes, she stepped out of the bath and wrapped her soft warm towel around herself. But as she went to take a step forward, she paused, as the heat of the water, coupled with standing up quickly, and the wine, made her head spin for a fleeting moment. As her dizziness settled, Casey dried off and stood in front of the sink. Watching her reflection in the mirror whilst cleaning her teeth, she wondered what on earth she was going to say and did she even actually *want* to say goodbye to Jason? The answer to that question rang unexpectedly loudly in her head. *NO!* But she couldn't do a long distance relationship either and she definitely didn't want to leave the UK to live in New Zealand. No matter how fabulous it might be there, and whilst Jason had been keen to try to convince her of how wonderful it would be, she knew she couldn't give up her life in the UK. No, it was just too big a step and much too far away from the life that Casey knew. Why couldn't Jase have just gone and asked for a job in their London office, at least that would be commutable!

Blimey, Case (mentally scolding herself)*, what are you talking about? So much for it being a casual thing and besides that, how selfish are you?* Casey really was confused by the realisation of losing Jason and her very erratic thoughts of both him and Matt. But one thing she was sure of was that Jason had to do what was best for him. That was the golden rule in her Nan's book.

'Be good to others on the journey whilst you follow your heart and dreams, but do it for you and your needs, not for others.'

Glancing at the clock and realising how time had slipped by whilst she'd been bathing, Casey realised she needed to get a wriggle on and finish getting ready. So that when Jason arrived in half an hour, she would be sufficiently glammed up, with wine glasses filled and trying to maintain her enthusiasm to toast Jason's new job (again). Meanwhile, rushing to her wardrobe, she scanned the contents for a suitable outfit, feeling a little shocked that her confusion had crossed over her normal very organised self and she had no idea what to wear.

In her mind, the two of them had only been seeing each other for a relatively short time, so she had been totally surprised by Jason's unexpected love declaration. She reasoned that if it really *was* true love for him, then it sure had happened suddenly and seemed most unlike the normally super-cool Jason. Casey wondered if, rather than love, what Jason was feeling was actually a combination of several things. Perhaps it was due to all the great sex they'd had, mixed up with his fears of starting a new adventure, with maybe even a touch of nervousness thrown in. After all, he was about to leave behind his homeland for a dream life in Auckland, culminating with not wanting to leave Casey and his links back to the UK. Yes, maybe it was all of *that*, rather than true love. This unexpected flash of inspirational logic actually made Casey question her own feelings again and succeeded in helping her to accept and feel better about telling Jason her decision, which was that whilst it was an amazing idea and such a fabulous offer, it still had to be no. She just could not go to Auckland with him. Not now and not ever, because her life was here, in the UK, and she was happy with it staying that way. Casey gulped.

Jason arrived bang on time, looking very sexy and smelling so good that Casey breathed in hard, as she tried to calm the urges rising inside her. She had always been a woman that loved a man to not only look good, but to smell good too. Those two characteristics were very much a part of what had attracted Casey to Jason from the very beginning. Now seeing him standing in front of her looking and smelling as good as he always did, she found him almost too hard to resist. Jason had obviously showered again and not long before leaving home, because his hair was still damp, which was Casey's kryptonite, as again her resolve began to melt. As Jason kissed her passionately and held her to him a little more firmly than he usually did, enjoying his warmth, Casey returned his kiss with equal verve. Jason was definitely a weakness to her resolve and she had to pull herself up short. This was partly to prevent her pheromones from overwhelming him before they had even gone out for dinner, as well as preventing *his* from completely overwhelming her, as was often the case recently. As she pulled away from him, Casey took Jason's hand and walked him through to the kitchen, where she'd placed fresh wine glasses next to a bowl of mixed olives (her favourites were the black ones, which was really handy because Jason preferred the green ones). Letting go of his hand, Casey poured more of the Argentinian Malbec into their glasses and passed one to Jason.

As Casey picked up her own glass and turned to face him, Jason clinked his glass with hers and toasted their new and exciting life together in New Zealand. Smiling nervously, Casey took a small sip of her wine, which now seemed to have formed into a huge lump as it travelled down her throat. Having spent the best part of the last few hours thinking about Jason leaving and her wanting to be with him, but not wanting to leave the UK herself, Casey's bundle of thoughts were churning over and over in her mind. With nerves jangling at what she had to tell Jason, it wasn't long before he noticed her slightly distracted look and asked her what was wrong. Never sure of at which point she should tell him her thoughts, Casey decided it was best to say it before they went out. It was only fair to Jase, and besides which, she would never be able to eat with her stomach tied in knots the way it was right now. If Jason walked away from her without looking back, she wouldn't and couldn't blame him. Taking a longer slower sip this time, Casey ventured into the mire.

"Jase, I've been thinking about everything you've told me in the last twenty-four hours and churning it over and over in my mind and well...if I'm honest, it's been a lot to take on board. You've kind of hit me with a proverbial sledge-hammer and I've been a bit shell-shocked about you going..."

Jason took her hand and stroked her face gently; his voice was calm and comforting: "I know, baby, and I really do appreciate that I've kind of thrown a hand grenade into our lives."

Our lives thought Casey. Oh no, this was going to be harder than she thought.

"Jase, the thing that's hit me hardest is thinking of you leaving. Well actually, it's made me realise how much I really do care about you."

Taking another sip, Casey realised she had already managed to drink her way through most of the glass of wine, and picked up the bottle to top her glass back up, while Jason's glass was barely touched.

"I know, Case, and I'm sorry it's been a bit of a shock all round. I had no idea they would offer me this chance. I mean, they knew I wanted it. We'd talked about it months ago, before I even knew you. But, Case, I never thought it would happen, so I'm pretty stunned myself."

This was news to Casey, but also helped her understand how Jason had apparently been able to say yes to the offer so quickly and with what had seemed like to her, so little consideration of the immense decision that it was. Furthermore, it explained why she had only learned about it the night before.

"So, you've already done all the thinking about moving then?" Casey said. "Well, that makes more sense to me. I thought it was a bit quick to make such a life-changing decision."

Casey smiled a little nervously at Jason and his heart-rate quickened at seeing the expression in her beautiful eyes, but he was still positive about the move.

"Yeah, course, I totally understand this is a big shock to you Case," he said. "Although to be honest, it felt like a no-brainer for me really. What a chance, what an experience, and Auckland! Do you know it's called the City of Sails? I've always wanted to have a go at sailing and this will be like the perfect opportunity for me. It may not be forever, but it's definitely likely to be for a good while. No point going all that way for a few months. I was thinking maybe a couple of years and see how it goes."

Jason's excitement and enthusiasm was bubbling over and oozing out of every pore, that it was almost tangible.

"So you're really sold on it then?" Casey said, and then hesitated before continuing. "That's great, Jase. I mean, I'm really happy for you. It's such a fantastic opportunity and I'm sure it'll be an amazing experience for you. I can see why you want to go, and you should go, definitely, it'll be amazing for you!"

Casey was almost babbling by now and feeling even more nervous than before. This was it; she could feel the moment of truth coming. Jason smiled, happy at her enthusiasm for him, but then realisation began to dawn and he frowned slightly.

"Yeah it will, but it sounds like it's not something you'd be happy to do. What are you trying to say, Case? Don't you want to come with me?"

Suddenly Jason's smile disappeared and disappointment began to creep into his eyes as that dreaded comprehension dawned on him. All day he'd been on cloud nine thinking Casey loved him and would be up for this big adventure for the two of them. So much so, he'd already been planning how she could wangle writing her column from New Zealand. In fact, he'd been walking on air all day and had almost *skipped* along the pavement to Casey's apartment block, as he'd enjoyed the mild evening air; smiling all the way at the thought of them sitting on the plane together, excited, happy and in love. It was Jason's turn to be hit with a sledge-hammer and he looked totally gutted. Casey couldn't bear it.

"Jase, the thing is," she started to explain, "I don't actually know how I feel about you and I know you said you loved me, but I don't know if that's what I feel. I know that I really do like you; in fact, I like you a lot, more than just like actually. But I'm not sure it's love, that's a huge whole next step and if I'm honest, it scares me a bit."

Casey had avoided looking at his eyes, but now glancing at them quickly, her heart sank as she saw his bubble had burst. Worse still, it had been she who had held the pin!

"Part of me wishes you didn't have to leave right now, so we could see where this goes for a bit longer. But I know you have to go, you'd be crazy not to." Casey hesitated. "I just didn't expect *love* to be something you felt. Not yet. It feels so sudden."

Casey's eyes were searching his, desperate not to see the extreme hurt in them as Jason looked at her with an intensity that sent pleading into her very soul.

"I know. It does feel like it's happened all of a sudden. I mean the job and then us, Case. Well, me saying I love you, but when you realise you *really do* love someone, it kind of slaps you in the face and takes you by surprise. At least that's what happened for me.

"Last night (his voice broke a little)...last night you just looked so gorgeous and we'd had such a good night and, Case, well, it's *everything* about you. You make me laugh so much and making love to you is truly amazing. It's *always* amazing actually. I never want to stop making love to you Casey..."

As his voice trailed off, Jason breathed in hard and searched Casey's face for the answer he wanted to hear, whilst guessing it just wasn't going to be there. It was Casey's turn to respond, but she too found her own voice breaking with emotion. Jason had spoken beautifully, however, she knew she needed to be strong and not give in.

"Jase, I just can't go," she said. "I can't leave my life here. I love my life and with the column just taking off...well, I don't want to leave right now. Claire and Edine would think I didn't care about my column, which isn't true because I do care, very much and I want it to be a success. Plus, I really don't want to leave my friends behind. I do care about you and selfishly, when you first told me, I did wish that you weren't going, but (her voice faltered), I just can't go, Jase, I'm so sorry."

It had all come out in a rush, everything, the jumbled thoughts and words merging into one long explanation. Knowing she was stabbing at Jason's hurt with every word of rejection she had spoken, Casey cried. The tears overwhelmed her as she cried and it was not for effect, or to make Jason feel bad; it was actually because she didn't want to lose him. But Casey knew she just couldn't go and so she had to let him go, alone. She cried uncontrollably and reached for the box of tissues.

Jason sank onto the sofa, shaking his head and staring into his glass, knowing what he'd asked of her was too big. Part of him knew she would likely say no. Yet because Jason had only just realised that he actually loved her, he'd prayed that she felt the same, even though he realised it was still early days for them and that she probably wasn't *in love* with him. All the same, Jason's hopes had been strong. Now downing his wine in one go, he stood up and reached out to Casey. As Jason took her in his arms he stroked her hair, loving the feel of it as it slid through his fingers like silk.

"It's OK, Case, I know it's a really big deal," he said gently, while wiping away her tears. "I already did my thinking when they spoke to me about it all those months ago. This has all been a big shock for you and totally out of the blue. I do understand, I do, and it's OK, so shush now, please don't cry. I hate to see you cry."

Casey buried her head into his shoulder and held on to him tightly as she sobbed the words through her tears: "I'm so sorry, Jase, I'm going to miss you so much. It's been so great this past few months, but I just can't go. It's too far away."

Jason understood and again told Casey so, adding that of course he was gutted, but that he did understand, really he did. They stood hugging for a good few minutes before stepping apart and smiling at each other. Once again, Jason wiped the tears away from her beautiful cheeks and said he'd like it if they could at least still see each other when he got back from this trip and until he left for good. It was more of a question than a statement, but Casey agreed, it seemed a good way to gently finish their relationship. But she also felt some apprehension; was that really a good idea?

Jason refilled their glasses and toasted them both: "To new beginnings and happy endings!"

Then forcing a beaming smile, he took another drink before suggesting they go and eat. Genuinely wishing Jason the best of luck for his new venture, Casey said she'd just go and freshen up her make-up (which she knew must look awful after her tears). Walking through to her bedroom, Casey was feeling a mixture of sadness, relief and disappointment. But surprising herself, she held hopeful thoughts for the happy ending that Jason had toasted for them both. In her heart the weight lifted and now desperate to restore a sense of normality, Casey called out to Jason that she'd only be a few minutes and hoped Giovanni had managed to save their favourite table in the window.

Giovanni's was a small family run Italian restaurant which only had eight tables. It was in an old double fronted shop, which had two bay windows with tables big enough for four. Those tables were their favourites and they respected that Giovanni would allow the two of them to have one to themselves whenever they visited. They were actually regular and very good customers. In fact, Casey had been a customer at Giovanni's for several years and often popped in with her girlfriends, for an evening of delicious home-made pasta dishes, followed by Maria's infamous Tiramisu.

Giovanni and Maria had been married for just over thirty-six years, having raised four children during those years; two of which helped out in the restaurant, whilst the other two had pursued different careers. That is, until their only daughter had met and married a banker called Alistair. The two of them went on to provide Maria and Giovanni with two grandchildren, whom they both adored and spoilt whenever they could. Marco was their eldest son and had been an accomplished chef for several years now, running the kitchen and helping Maria, whilst his younger brother, Piero, waited on tables alongside their father. Both young men were immensely happy to be working with their parents and were very proud of their thriving family restaurant. Giovanni acted as "Front of House" but still enjoyed waiting on the tables, so he could talk to his customers and share whatever news and events were happening in their lives.

Everyone who ate at Giovanni's, loved this warm and cosy family restaurant and when Casey had first taken Jason there, he too had been entranced by the empty bottles of Chianti, with their little baskets on the bases, now holding red wax candles, which adorned each of the traditional red-check covered tables. This typical Italian style added an element of charm to the romantic ambience of Giovanni's.

Giovanni and Maria had loved seeing Casey bring a new man with her and had gushed over them both on that occasion. Since then, in their typical and traditional way, the Italian couple spoilt the young lovers every time they ate there. Casey loved Maria and Giovanni and their traditional restaurant, which was a special place of warmth and comfort to her. Mainly due to its genuinely friendly welcome from the whole of Giovanni's family, but also for the amazing home-made food they served there. Giovanni and Maria were very proud of their restaurant's valued reputation, which was constantly spread throughout the local district by everyone and anyone who ate there.

As Casey opened the glass paned door into Giovanni's restaurant, the old-fashioned bell tinkled and Giovanni appeared from the kitchen carrying two plates of Marco's delicious spaghetti bolognaise. Seeing Casey and Jason at the door, Giovanni's face lit up.

"Ciao, Bella, lovely Casey. Uno momento, Bella!"

Giovanni finished serving the hot steaming dishes to his waiting customers, before moving over to hug Casey and kiss her on each cheek and then shaking Jason's hand enthusiastically. Ever wary of kissing cheeks with male non-Italian customers, whom Giovanni never wanted to offend, he always offered a handshake to the men. However his twinkling demeanour allowed him to kiss the hands and cheeks of the women he knew and who welcomed his friendly tactile manner. Giovanni was like a trusted grandfather. Ushering them to Casey's favourite table, Giovanni again said how happy he was to see the two young lovers as he asked how they were and they responded in unison: "We're fine thanks very much, Giovanni, and it's so lovely to be back again."

Blushing slightly, Casey had not wanted to spill the beans about Jason leaving just yet. Jason then laughed a little nervously and Casey felt an embarrassed redness creep up her neck and onto her pretty face. Casey had been silently wondering how Giovanni would take their news, knowing that his high hopes for Casey to settle down and start a family would be totally crushed. Having pre-warned Jason that she would tell Giovanni and Maria the news after he had left for New Zealand, Jason had agreed that was probably best. It just seemed simpler that way. So Casey said nothing about it on this occasion and instead, gratefully took the seat that Giovanni was already holding out for her. Making herself comfy, Casey proceeded to open the pack of twin Grissini which had been placed neatly on her plate, biting the end off of the first crunchy bread-stick.

Giovanni knew Casey liked the House Red and insisted on giving both her and Jason a small glass each, whilst they perused the menu. Choosing which dish to have was often a time-consuming process for them, mainly because all of the dishes were home-made, totally traditional and so absolutely delicious. Which is what made choosing just one dish from the list all the more difficult. Casey laughed and agreed as Jason said as much again.

Having tried pretty much every dish on the menu, Casey often came back to her favourite three course choices – the Seafood Salad, which was a mixture of lots of different seafood, including her favourite mussels and prawns, served on a bed of extremely fine shredded lettuce, peppers and spring onions. Which for her, just had to be followed by Marco's fabulous Lasagne and then of course the ultimate in desserts – Maria's Tiramisu! But knowing after eating all of that, she would be complaining about being too full, on this occasion Casey decided to skip the starter and just go for the Lasagne and Tiramisu. There was no way she could go to Giovanni's and walk out with just having one course. Casey knew Giovanni would always be able to tempt her sweet tooth, so she may as well give in and go for it herself. Besides, any excuse to sample Maria's fabulous Tiramisu would do for Casey. Having decided on her choices, Casey sipped her complimentary wine and asked Jason what he was going to have.

"I think I'll go for the meatballs again," he said. "I loved those the last time I had them and then I think I'll have the Tiramisu too. Shall we just have a bottle of the house red, seeing as we both really like it?"

Casey was nodding in agreement as Giovanni reappeared at the table to take their order. Jason thanked Giovanni again for the complimentary wine and said he was looking forward to the food, which made Giovanni positively beam with Italian pride.

Despite her earlier admission of the truth to Jason, it turned out to be a good night. In fact, Casey had half expected Jason to say he wasn't up for eating after all and to just cancel their evening altogether. Not that she would have blamed him. Thankfully though, they had somehow managed to move on from the "I'm not coming with you" conversation with good grace and to Casey's very great relief. Jason meanwhile, was just happy to be with Casey and in this, their favourite restaurant. The two lovers were having such a great time that Jason suggested they should come at least one more time before he left the UK.

Final glasses of Masala finished off the evening, leaving Jason and Casey to bid farewell to both Giovanni and Maria, as they thanked them for such wonderful and delicious food. Maria blushed as she shooed them out, wishing them both a pleasant evening, as Giovanni also said goodnight to the pair.

"Come back soon, Bella, you know how we love to see you. Ciao."

Jason held Casey's hand tightly as they strolled home. They were both happy and very much enjoying each other's company, as they walked back slowly, through the mild evening air and moonlit streets. The brightness of the moon was highlighting the trees that typically lined the streets of Casey's neighbourhood and because there was little traffic this evening, it was as romantic as it could be. As they reached the steps leading up to the entrance of the apartment block, Jason paused and waited for Casey to invite him in. He was feeling cautious and didn't want to assume she would even want him to come in. At this moment in time, Jason didn't want to push Casey into anything that she wasn't happy to do, particularly knowing that he was leaving very soon anyway.

Sensing Jason's restraint, Casey questioned what was wrong and whilst bemused by his explanation, she was happy that he was being so considerate of her feelings. Albeit a little surprised by this change in his usual behaviours, which also made her silently question her own feelings again. Since he had told her that he loved her, Jason's behaviour had clearly changed and he was more reserved right now, careful even, not wanting to upset Casey or spoil the evening in any way. As Casey reflected on this change, she also thought how much she also enjoyed the passionate, spontaneous Jason and right at that moment, she wasn't sure which one she wanted most. Leaning towards him, Casey touched Jason's face and told him she would miss him and miss this, having shared such a lovely evening together. Jason caught her fingers and moving her hand to his lips, he kissed them gently.

"Me too, Casey," he said. "Me too."

He was afraid to say much more and needed to protect his heart, but Jason also knew he had to be sure that Casey knew how he truly felt, because he wanted her to miss him while he was away on his brief familiarisation visit. Maybe if she missed him a lot, she would change her mind about joining him. Jason was hoping beyond hope that Casey would change her mind and be willing to try a spell in Auckland with him.

Breaking across his train of thought, Casey whispered to him in an almost husky voice: "Let's go inside."

Stepping in front of him, Casey pushed her key into the lock. The big door opened easily, allowing them to step into the smart and very clean, tiled entrance hall. The cage style lift could be seen at the far end of the hallway, a subdued glow provided by its antique light fitting looked almost romantic and made Casey feel like they were in some old-fashioned movie scene. Although they usually took the stairs (thinking the exercise was good for them), tonight, Casey decided the lift would be a better choice. Being one of those old-fashioned types of lifts, it was very much in keeping with the old building, which had been converted decades ago and both the building and the lift were now protected by a preservation order. Casey had no idea how old it was exactly or even if theirs was the one and only cage-style lift left in the UK, but it was certainly the only one she knew of. Trying not to make too much noise, they pulled the safety door across and pressed the button for the second floor. Jason laughed when Casey said it always made her feel like there should be a bell-boy inside, dressed in a red uniform, who would greet her by name, before asking if she'd "had a nice evening ma'am".

Jason added that the lift had always made him feel a bit like James Bond and that he should do what Bond would do; turn and ravish her there and then, ignoring who might be watching as the lift travelled up through the floors to Casey's apartment at the top. That thought had them both laughing as they shushed each other, not wanting to wake any of the other five neighbours.

By the time Casey was unlocking her own front door, those thoughts of being ravished by Jason had her wanting to feel him inside her for one last time. Pushing the door open and dropping her jacket as she stepped inside, she turned to face her very own James Bond, as he closed the door gently behind them. Taking her in his arms Jason kissed her deeply and passionately. Casey responded with such urgency it made Jason sweep her up into his arms and carry her through to the bedroom.

Telling her again that he loved her, Jason whispered how much he wanted her before laying her on the bed, his own breath now quickening with excited and growing passion. As Casey began undressing herself down to her underwear, Jason pulled off his shirt and jeans. Having gone commando tonight, he had little else to remove and rarely wore socks casually anyway. Casey was wearing his favourite underwear, which looked so pretty on her beautiful sexy body. Smiling as he knelt on the bed, Jason bent down to kiss her lips, then moving to her neck as he brushed kisses across her shoulders, slowly working his way down to her breasts. Gently easing the lacy straps from Casey's shoulders, Jason pulled her bra cups down to expose her perfectly formed breasts. Taking her hardening nipples into his mouth he gently sucked them between his teeth, as he slowly moved from one breast to the other. Delighting in hearing Casey groaning with pleasure, Jason loved the way he could turn her on. As Casey ran her hands through his hair, his mouth worked on each nipple, while his hands gently moved down across her stomach, to touch and explore her most feminine parts. Jason soon had Casey writhing with ecstasy, her body arching towards him, desperately wanting him to take her completely. He loved watching Casey's face as she neared that point and he knew he had to enter her right at that very moment, so they could reach that dizzying height together.

"Oh, Casey, I want you so much."

"Jase, Jase, take me now, I need you."

As he entered her, she let out an excited, "Ohhhh…" as they both clung to each other, their bodies moved in perfect unison until their all-consuming passion exploded together, leaving them crying out in pleasure and satisfaction. Kissing her again, Jason knew only too well, how hard it was going to be for him to leave this gorgeously sexy woman.

As the two lovers pulled apart and lay beside each other, they stared into the other's eyes, but as Jason stroked Casey's face, fresh tears were brimming in her eyes. Casey whispered that she didn't think she could cope with seeing Jason again when he got back from his familiarisation trip. Almost choking on her words, Casey admitted to Jason that she thought it was going to be too hard for them both to carry on for another month and said that they would only be prolonging the agony of separation. She was also worried that Jason's love would grow and hurt him even more when he left for good and as sad as it would make them both, Casey suggested that maybe they should say their goodbyes here and now; adding that Jason should leave on this wonderfully happy note, with the memory of this amazing last evening together.

A happy memory they could both share. The words lingered in his mind as he registered the shock of what Casey had said, even though he also knew she was right. But finding it hard to speak, Jason just nodded and kissed the tip of Casey's nose as he raised himself off the bed. Now struggling to hold back his own tears, Jason dressed and smiled at Casey as he told her she looked the most beautiful that he had ever seen her and that this night would be the most amazing memory for him. With that spoken thought still lingering in the air, Jason bent to kiss Casey again and told her once more that he loved her, before then walking out of the room, gathering his jacket as he left. Casey heard the front door click shut and she closed her eyes as a tear escaped.

Lying alone in her bed, the tears rolled down her cheeks as the moonlight shone through the windows. Casey remembered their previous night of passion and the words Jason had spoken; their time at Giovanni's, and what had just been such incredibly passionate love making. Casey knew this separation was going to be hard for them both as she hugged a pillow to her, curled up in the bed and wept for what seemed like hours, before falling into a deep and dreamless sleep. Exhausted emotionally and physically, following their shared passionate love making, Casey slept until morning.

Chapter 6

Just for You!

Casey woke up early feeling warm and cosy under her duvet. She loved her bed in the mornings; there was nothing quite like waking up already warm, cosy and totally relaxed, snuggled beneath a duvet. *Especially when you turn over to snuggle into your man,* she thought.

"Oh, Jason..." she murmured.

Realising Jason wasn't in the bed with her, the memory of the previous evening and their amazing love making flooded back into Casey's mind, swiftly followed by the memory of him leaving, at her suggestion. Although she was incredibly sad at the thought of not seeing Jason again, a small part of Casey also felt slightly relieved that she had been brave enough to tell him that she just could not go with him to New Zealand. As her mind wandered and lingered on the memory of Jason's touch, she realised how much she actually would miss him and their passionate love making.

Even though her feelings for him were still uncertain, Casey realised that she wasn't truly in love with Jason. Actually, if she was absolutely honest with herself, what she had been feeling could be better described as being in *lust*, rather than in *love*. Whatever it was she felt for Jason, Casey knew that whilst it was a tempting invitation to go with him, the reality of living in New Zealand long-term was absolutely not a good option for her. Not right now anyway. She reasoned that after their incredible love making the night before, as much as she wanted it to be different, lust seemed a lot more realistic to Casey. Because surely if it was love, she would have thrown in the towel and been persuaded to go with him, not wanting to be apart from him for even a moment. *Wouldn't she?*

This was a different train of thought for Casey. The whole *lust* versus *love* comparison was not something she had really thought that much about when it came to Jason. It was only now, because of his move to New Zealand, that she was even daring to think about love. Reaching across the bed to where Jason had lay the night before, Casey closed her eyes and just for a moment, and imagined him still there. As the alarm on her clock-radio started, the annoying buzzer broke across her thoughts and Casey sighed heavily as she reached over to switch it to the radio. Feeling slightly frustrated that it was already time to get up, she was also glad that she'd beaten the alarm by waking up without it. As she had supposed was the case with most of the working population, the morning alarm clock and Casey were not good friends. Something she had always wished for was that she didn't need to have an alarm and could experience the flexibility and luxury of waking up whenever she was ready to. But sadly and just like the rest of the population, the alarm was a necessary evil for Casey, ensuring she woke up in time to get showered and suitably preened. It was important to her that she felt and looked good for work, as well as ensuring she was in plenty of time for the 9am start that her company demanded.

Thoughts of Jason now interrupted and pushed to the back of her thoughts, Casey reflected on how much she did so love the weekends. Switching the alarm off every Friday night, to allow herself that glorious luxury of waking up whenever her body was ready to, on both Saturday and Sunday mornings. That said, she often found when rolling over in bed to glance at the time displayed on her bedside clock, she had in fact woken-up around a very similar time to her mid-week alarm, which was very frustrating. Other times she'd open her eyes and roll over in bed to read with shocked surprise that 09.25 was standing out like a red beacon on the digital clock radio display. This usually triggered an immediate jumping out of bed, swiftly followed by feelings of guilt for being so late in getting-up. Casey considered anything between eight and nine to be reasonable weekend getting-up times. However, on the days that Jason was in bed with her, the time they eventually got up would be a totally different story. Thinking about those mornings, Casey smiled at memories of snuggling into Jason's open arms, as they enjoyed at least another hour in bed. Often to just lie there cuddling and chatting, whilst on other occasions the excitement of Jason's morning masculinity rising – which was always ready and standing to attention – was just too tempting. Of course, never one to resist such an open and exciting invitation, Casey always enjoyed giving in to his passion, feeling her own rise with Jason's every touch and caress until they both experienced the ultimate rush of pleasure.

Hmmm...with that thought, Casey threw back the duvet and swung her legs over the side of the bed, trying desperately to dismiss the thoughts of mornings past, which were suddenly crowding into her mind and throwing her a little off-kilter.

Picking up her mobile phone to see if any text messages had arrived, Casey's heart sank a little on seeing there were no messages from Jason. But, on the plus side, it also meant there would be no need for difficult responses either. Casey made her way into the bathroom and stood brushing her teeth hard, as if every stroke of the brush would help dismiss thoughts of Jason. Stepping into the shower she tried to do the same by washing her hair vigorously, as she forced herself to think of other things, thereby pushing the memories of Jason into the back of her mind.

Distraction 1 – The magazine – Yes! She needed to call Edine. Think diary, think writing. Basically, she told herself, think anything, except about Jason!

Distraction 2 – Skin firming lotion and eye-cream; she still needed to go shopping.

Even with the bathroom door left slightly ajar, the mirror always seemed to steam up whenever Casey used the shower and on stepping out, feeling refreshed and re-focused, she automatically looked up to the mirror and saw two love hearts with C and J in them. Casey gulped, *oh my goodness* and feeling a bit puzzled, she also smiled as she wondered when Jason had drawn that. He sure had changed a lot in the last few days and had never done anything like that before. Casey kind of liked this new Jason.

Drying her hair vigorously, she pushed herself to hurry up whilst getting ready for work, knowing it would make her feel so much more relaxed when she called Edine. Casey wanted to catch her Editor early and already feeling a little anxious, she needed to hear what Edine's thinking was about the column she'd emailed across to her the previous day. "Come on, Case, get a wriggle on," she said as she hurried herself along, hesitating briefly to rub the two hearts off the mirror before she left the bathroom. As she did do, Casey felt a bit sad but took a deep breath and finished the job; there was no need for those to upset her the next time the mirror misted over, she thought. There was absolutely no point in pining after someone who was leaving her life. No, she had to be strong and on that note, Casey pulled on the clothes she had decided to wear that day; something comfortable but smart seemed to fit the bill nicely and helped to calm her slightly anxious feelings. Finally feeling somewhat satisfied with how she looked and on checking her reflection in the mirror, Casey gave herself a little nod of approval.

Her nerves were beginning to kick in again, as Casey sat down at the kitchen table with a fresh cup of tea. She'd always found tea to be a good pick-me-up and an easy way of encouraging a relaxed mind when making an important call. So, after a few sips from her cup, and with her phone in her hand, Casey punched in the number for Edine's direct line. Even though it was early, Casey already knew from Claire that Edine would likely be in the office from around 7am.

Edine was a businesswoman through and through and completely devoted to her work. Always starting early, the Editor enjoyed seeing her night-shift team before they left for the day, knowing they'd been busy working through the night, whilst she had been sleeping. So, even though she was only able to say *good morning* to their *good night*, it made Edine feel good as a boss and her night-team valued that effort enormously, as they said hello and goodbye to her before they left for their homes and respective beds.

Putting the phone to her ear and taking another sip of tea, Casey could hear the ringing tone as it connected to Edine's direct line. Hearing a click on the line, then Edine's confident voice speaking so clearly, Casey thought how professional her voice always sounded. This morning, however, it had seemed just a little more clipped than usual, which made Casey wonder if there was something wrong. She had never been good with confident people on the telephone. Somehow they always made her feel ever so slightly on edge, but at the same time, that edginess prompted her to rise to the challenge on this occasion, speaking out as confidently as she hoped would impress Edine.

"Good morning, Edine, this is Casey Martin. How are you today?"

"Ah, Casey, hello. I'm very well thank you and very busy this morning, but I'm glad you called. I read your column last night and enjoyed it very much. I've decided to go with the raw approach and apart from a couple of punctuation changes to influence intonation, I'm leaving it exactly as it is, to see what kind of reaction we get from our readers. So you can consider it approved and we'll be sending it to print. Well done, Casey, I reckon we're off to a great start with this."

Edine's voice had changed and she now sounded full of beans, as if she had suppressed a giggle that was bubbling inside her and which was now threatening to break out into a peal of happy laughter.

"I was particularly impressed with the bit about your friend falling out of the taxi on your night out, but not letting go of her fake designer handbag, that made me laugh out loud." Edine chuckled, "I could just visualise the scene," adding, "which is perfect writing."

With that, Edine's laughter bubbled over and had Casey grinning down the telephone at her, whilst also feeling extremely relieved as her own nerves dissolved.

"That's so good to hear, Edine, and thank you. I'm really pleased that you liked it enough to go straight to print. Let's hope your readers like it as much you do. It will be good to see if we get any feedback from them."

"Absolutely, Casey," she said. "Actually, our readers do tend to email us regularly. Some even take the trouble to send in a hand written letter to let us know what they think. So, I'm sure we'll get something soon enough. Of course, I will let you know if we do. So, we'll see what happens, but meanwhile, do write your next piece and send it across to me as soon as you can. Sorry to cut you short, Casey, but I have a meeting in ten minutes and I need to gather the last papers for it, so if you have any questions, just call Claire Anderson. I've asked Claire to be your main point of contact, seeing as she was the one who found you. Take care, Casey, and I look forward to my next read!"

"OK, thanks, Edine. I'll call Claire later today. Have a good day and thanks again. Bye for now."

Casey couldn't believe how easy and well the conversation had gone.

"Have a good day yourself, too," Edine said.

Edine replaced the phone receiver and hearing the click, Casey hung up the phone at her end.

"Wow! That was easy!" Casey exclaimed.

Casey spoke out loud even though there was nobody to hear her and she laughed to herself, feeling full of excitement and renewed vigour. Quickly finishing her tea, she hurried to grab her bag and coat before dashing downstairs to share the exciting news with Tilly, whilst they walked the short journey to work together. This was something the two girls did daily; well, when they were both ready at the same time. Casey always said to Tilly, if she wasn't banging on her door by the time Tilly needed to leave, then Tilly should just set off and Casey would catch her up. But more often than not, it was Tilly who was running late.

Surprisingly, Tilly was ready early and just about to open her apartment door when she heard Casey knocking from the other side. With her coat already on, she opened the door to see a buoyant Casey bursting to tell her something and guessed it was the call with Edine that had gone well.

"Oh yes, Til, it did and I'm totally amazed that Edine has agreed to print it just as I submitted it! She hasn't even edited it. Well, just some punctuation, but not the words. Oh, Til, she must have been really happy with it, which is such great news! Edine wants to keep it raw and see what reaction she gets from the readers...isn't it amazing, I'm so thrilled!"

Casey was excited beyond belief and clearly sitting well and truly on cloud nine. Nothing could spoil her mood today; not even the grumpiest of colleagues in the office. Tilly hugged her.

"Oh, Case, I'm so thrilled for you. I knew you could do it...well done you!"

The two friends linked arms and giggled like a couple of happy schoolgirls as they continued on their way to the office. Whilst Casey was dreaming of the future and her desperate wish to be a successful writer, Tilly chattered on happily about what they would do once Casey was famous for her column writing. The sky was a brilliantly fresh blue with, small puffy white clouds and even though there was a chill in the air, it was a beautiful sunny and dry Autumnal day.

Even though it was still a work day, the girls were in such a good mood, both now feeling totally upbeat and smiley. So, on turning the corner of the home approach to the office, the two of them decided to stop at the coffee shop and pick up two skinny double shot Lattes. Also, giving in to the urge to spoil themselves, they both ordered a Cinnamon Swirl Danish Pastry to go with their coffees.

"So, Case, are you going to tell the girls in the office, or do you want to wait until the magazine is issued and show them your new column in the flesh?" Tilly was already dreaming big for Casey.

Casey had already considered this and told Tilly, that she thought it was probably a good idea to tell them now. Quite rightly thinking it would help to build up their interest in actually buying the magazine, and then if they liked her column, maybe they'd buy the magazine regularly. That way, she knew there would be at least a dozen or so, eager readers of her column. Casey had already supposed that if she could be cheeky enough to ask them to share small extracts with their Facebook friends, her readership would expand even more, thereby helping to sell lots more copies. Casey was feeling more and more confident that this really could be her big break.

"Good Point," Tilly said. "Get you, girl. "You're gonna be famous!"

At this point Casey laughed out loud and said not to be so daft; she would hardly be famous, but it would be great if there was enough interest to allow her to keep writing. Casey was excited about writing her next column and said she couldn't wait to get started. Just at that point, Tilly broke across that excitement with a question, which stopped Casey in her tracks.

"Hey, I forgot to ask...did you find out from Jase how he knew Matt?"

"What? Jase? Matt? Oh yeah, I mean no, I didn't get a chance to ask him."

Casey's thoughts of Matt had temporarily been buried at the back of her mind, what with Jason leaving the previous night and then speaking to Edine that morning. Casey already had a full mind and she looked pained as Tilly spoke again.

"Sorry, Case, I didn't mean to bring you down. I'm a total idiot. I forgot Jase would have left last night and the last thing you need is me wittering on about Matt. Listen, ignore me, let's get into work and tell the others about your column."

Tilly linked her arm through Casey's and smiled brightly at her as Casey nodded and said it was OK. It was a perfectly natural question, but Tilly would just have to ask Dave instead; after all, he'd said he was going to Barney's to catch up with Tilly at Steph's leaving do. Tilly grinned as she thought, *Oh yeah, Dave...now there's a happy thought to start the day on.* The girls walked into their office building, chomping at the bit and ready to spread the word about Casey's column to stir up interest in this week's issue of *Just for You!*

Throughout the morning Casey's mind was distracted by Tilly's question and how on earth Jason knew Matt? Depending on the *how,* made Casey feel nervous, this could easily turn into a really embarrassing situation. Luckily, common sense kicked in and Casey gave herself a silent talking to. So how about trying to keep calm and just waiting until she knew for sure; after all, Jason was leaving soon anyway, so it was all hypothetical really. But Casey still felt a little uneasy at the unknown answer to that question.

The girls in the office were in good spirits and several of them called out *hello* as the two friends walked in. Putting down their coffees and pastries as they hung up their coats, the two girls laughed as the others complained about not bringing in enough coffee and pastries for all of them. Casey and Tilly retorted.

"But you're all dieting!"

With everyone now laughing and ribbing each other, the girls sat down and started their day jobs. As the morning wore on they all joked about their previous evening's antics and wondered what the following evening would bring when they all went out for Steph's leaving bash. The whole office team had been planning how they were going to decorate Steph's desk. Every time she left the office, they'd all start whispering about who had brought what and how they could get her to leave early that evening, so they could start decorating her desk ready for her last day.

Casey found it hard to concentrate, the conversation with Edine was now buzzing through her head. She was excited about writing her column and hoped she could live up to Edine's expectations. This was such a good opportunity and Casey didn't want to blow it. Besides which, she had loved writing about what was happening in her life when she first started her *Online Diary* and this was an opportunity to keep doing that. To Casey, it was a way of down-loading all of her thoughts, feelings, dreams and wishes, including the good, the bad and the very ugly.

The fact that so many people commented on her daily stories made her realise that she was perfectly normal and just like so many of her followers, which was actually why her *Online Diary* had been so successful. Her followers could relate to her, as well as the many and varied mistakes she made. Some of them would envy the exciting dates she'd been on, whilst wincing with her at the cringe moments and disaster dates (before Jason of course). It had been such good fun to write her *Online Diary* and Casey was chuffed that it had clearly been very entertaining for her loyal followers.

As the day went on, she decided to call Claire Anderson to let her know how the call had gone with Edine, and to thank Claire again for influencing this amazing opportunity for her. Albeit one that Casey was still struggling to believe that was really and truly happening to her. Claire had been as gracious as ever when Casey called and was absolutely delighted that Edine had warmed to Casey's writing as much as she had. Claire told Casey that she was going to be a great new addition to the magazine and that she, Claire, was so glad to have been the one to stumble over *Casey's Online Diary*.

If Casey's new column was a success, Claire shared with her that it would also reflect very well on her own career with the magazine, which was a comforting thought to both women and they didn't mind admitting it. Both of them were each grateful for the recent events that had brought them together.

Chapter 7

Wednesday

Today's the day! Jason must be really excited, Casey thought, wondering what time his flight would leave, then remembering he'd said something about leaving home about 5am. In that case, she guessed his flight must be leaving around 10am, which would allow him plenty of travelling time to the airport in the morning traffic, and once he was there, he could relax and have a coffee, or something slightly stronger. Casey knew if it had been her, she would most likely have arrived at least a couple of hours earlier, just so she could wander around the duty free shops. But that was her and shopping wasn't really Jason's thing, so he'd probably just have a beer or two while he waited.

Jason had been so utterly full of excitement when he'd found out he was being picked up by a Limousine, which was apparently a standard offering when flying First Class. Just knowing he had been booked to fly that class had totally wowed him – what a massive treat it would be! Like most people, Jason had only ever flown economy in the past so he was beyond excited and 'who wouldn't be if they had been in his shoes'. The reason behind the upgraded travel was so that Jason could arrive completely fresh and be able to hit the ground running. With only a week for his familiarisation visit, Jason's new boss didn't want him to feel too jet-lagged and spoil the experience, thereby potentially impacting Jason's decision to make the move. Lee really wanted Jason to join them in Auckland, so he had pulled out all the stops to persuade him during this visit.

Jason had barely slept before leaving for the airport, having been overly excited about his new life. Yet, he also felt completely torn about leaving Casey behind. *Love* was a strange thing and Jason could now agree with and appreciate the sentiment behind those words. For the last couple of days he felt like he'd been torn in half. Part of him was listening to his head, which knew this was an amazing opportunity; whilst the other part listened to his heart and began contradicting his head, willing him not to leave Casey. So with his head being countered by his heart's desire, Jason had to forcibly remind himself that this was not a forever move, and that if the two of them were truly meant to be together, then some way, somehow, Casey would be back in his life when he returned home.

How crass you are, Jason thought scolding himself. *Yes, not only crass, but incredibly selfish too*. As his heart protested at what his head was telling him, Jason tried to convince himself that he was not expecting Casey to wait. But he definitely hoped that she would wait and would still be interested in pursuing a relationship with him, when he finally returned home from New Zealand. How long that might be once he moved over to Auckland, was anyone's guess though. With his head partly buried in the sand, Jason didn't want to linger on that thought, because he also knew it could be several months, or even a couple of years if all went well. Deep down though, he almost knew that there was no way Casey would still be free, or that she would even want to see him again, but he couldn't let go of the hope within him.

Stepping out of the Limousine into the early morning sunshine, Jason breathed in his last outdoor breaths of British air (for the next week anyway). As he turned to thank his driver, he reassured him that he was perfectly fine to carry his own bag, which was only hand luggage after all. As he walked into the airport terminal, there was a happy but nervous excitement building inside him and Jason couldn't help but smile. Finally, he was on his way!

Against her more sensible thoughts, Casey decided to send Jason a *Bon Voyage* text and added that she hoped Auckland and the familiarisation trip was everything he hoped it would be.

Crossing the concourse to the departures area, Jason's mobile phone vibrated in his shirt pocket. Whilst he was not expecting anyone to text him, he hoped it would be Casey and stopped walking as he retrieved the device from his pocket. Turning the phone over to view the screen, Jason's hopes rose expectantly in his heart. It *was* Casey. He smiled. To say Jason was happy that Casey had sent him a text message was an understatement, he was utterly thrilled. Responding immediately, Jason explained how he'd not long arrived at the airport, adding that he was just about to enter the first class check-in. Then, even though it was a bit of overkill (the text didn't need to be quite so long), he added how he only had an hour and a half to kill before his flight was due to board and that he was *really* excited and totally enjoying the whole experience. As he finished his response, he wished Casey good luck for her first column publication and signed off with: 'Love you, gorgeous. Will miss you more than you know. Jase.' xxx

The text was quite possibly the longest one Jason had ever sent to anyone.

Casey knew she probably shouldn't have sent the text to Jason. After all, they had already said goodbye, which had been at her own behest. Still, she just couldn't help herself from sending him a last message. She also recognised that if Jason did call her when he returned the following week, the chances were that she would find it incredibly hard to resist seeing him.

But, Case (she was giving herself a good talking to again), you have GOT to resist. There is no point prolonging the agony of saying goodbye, because when he

103

leaves the UK again for what could be months, years or forever, all you're going to do is cause yourself more pain!

That was Casey's dilemma, she knew what she *should* do, but it was what she *would* do that bothered her. Something to cover in her column perhaps, yes, what a good topic to touch on; the dilemma of knowing what the sensible thing to do was (listening to your head), versus what you really want to do (following your heart). Casey decided she'd save that little gem for a week when she was stuck with what to share with her new readers.

Having finished getting herself ready for work, Casey took a final glance at herself in the hallway mirror, before nipping downstairs to knock for Tilly, who was as ever, running late. A lack of perfect timing was one of Tilly's more frustrating personal traits, but one that Casey was now completely used to, so she often planned in extra time for whenever they were going out. Tilly asked Casey to come inside for a few minutes and help her decide which shoes and handbag to use with her outfit for Steph's leaving do at Barney's later. Seeing as they were all going straight from work, Tilly wanted to be sure that she was wearing something particularly special, because Dave was also going to be there. After all, he had said he wanted to have some *personal* time with her and so it was only to be expected by Casey, that Tilly would want to suitably impress him.

Knowing there would be plenty of people there, Tilly had imagined it would be easy to stand on the edge of the group and talk to Dave, whilst still being part of the celebrations for Steph. So she didn't mind hijacking the event for an opportunity to see Dave again and was, understandably, suitably keen to wear something she felt really good in. Her chosen outfit was just a little revealing on the cleavage front, which also made Tilly feel a little bit more sexy than normal, and she hoped Dave would like it too. Casey told her that she looked lovely and that Dave would *definitely* be a happy chappy when he lays eyes on her. That response had Tilly giggling again and desperately hoping Casey was right and that would absolutely be Dave's reaction when he saw her later.

Whilst Tilly was so obviously excited about seeing Dave and in a very upbeat and buoyant mood, Casey dared to broach the John subject, thinking that her friend would easily be able to cope with talking about him now.

"It's great that you and Dave are hitting it off again, Til, especially after what happened with John."

As she watched for Tilly's facial expression to change, Casey was relieved to only see a slight flicker pass over her friend's face.

"So, how are you feeling about him now?" she asked. "John I mean?"

Tilly had travelled the emotional pathway from denial and grief, to anger and was now in a kind of detached acceptance. All of which had happened surprisingly quickly over the last few days, since John had dropped his "I'm now with Gemma" bombshell. But Casey knew only too well that Tilly could, at any point in her recovery, also lose that new found strength and return randomly to one of the five stages of grief. That was of course except the bargaining stage, because that would be pretty pointless really, because John already had Gemma in his sights, and in his pants as it turned out. So subconsciously, Tilly seemed to have skipped that stage and luckily, her self-respect was strong enough not to put herself in that position.

It had been almost amusing to Casey when Tilly flipped through the anger stage in just thirty-six hours, throwing out all and any of John's belongings that she'd found in her flat. Everything went straight into the rubbish bin, and having seen the refuse collection truck in their road on Tuesday as they'd walked to work, Tilly was confident that all of John's stuff would already be languishing somewhere down at the local Council tip and totally ruined. Having cemented that wish by hoping every bit of his stuff was already covered in some nasty smelling rubbish, she thought, *Good riddance and serves you right, and I hope you rot in hell, along with all your belongings, including your favourite jumper!*

John had forgotten his favourite jumper was at Tilly's place, having left it there when they'd got back from their skiing trip two months before. Since then, with all the mild weather they'd been having, the jumper had gradually been buried underneath a pile of ironing, which seemed to forever reside on the wicker chair in Tilly's bedroom. Tilly never managed to get to the bottom of that ironing pile. Always hating it with a vengeance, she tended to pull out and iron whatever she needed, as and when she wanted it, which was something that would have horrified her mother, who had always been a stickler for ironing every weekend.

Ha! John would be totally mortified if he knew what she'd done with his precious jumper. Tilly revelled in that thought and decided that if he dropped by to ask if she'd seen it, she would just say no and then happily watch his face crumple with disappointment. Feeling ever so slightly wicked, she reflected that maybe she *would* tell him where it was and then totally enjoy her moment of revenge, as he stomped away in temper. *Ha, ha, ha,* Tilly had to laugh, as did Casey at that thought. In fact, both girls had chuckled on picturing John's jumper languishing at the tip. Jolly good riddance, it would serve him right, the total cheating swine.

The girls were well on their way to work by the time Casey plucked up the courage to admit to Tilly about the text message she'd sent to Jason. Knowing she would get grief from Tilly, Casey dutifully, albeit slightly reluctantly, accepted her friend's slightly worried warning.

"Be careful, Case, you don't want to make it harder on yourself. It's probably best for you both if you don't contact him. Otherwise, you're just creating false hopes for each other."

"Yes, you're right. I know you're right. I just need to keep reminding myself that he really is going for good." Casey was quick to change the subject. "How about a nice coffee? Shall we pop into Trina's on the way?" she asked.

"Oh yes, good idea," Tilly replied enthusiastically. "I could really do with a Flat White to give me a kick start."

As they approached Trina's Coffee Shop, both girls felt cheered and pushing open the door to find virtually no queue, was even better. Trina welcomed her now regular early morning customers and soon had them leaving again with steaming cups of coffee. Both girls always asked for the coffee to be extra hot, so as to last the final leg of their journey into the office block and up to their individual desks on the 3rd floor.

As the two of them arrived into the office, Steph was already there and babbling excitedly to everyone around her. Having arrived twenty minutes earlier than usual, Steph had found her desk beautifully decorated by the girls; covered in flowers, with pink and white balloons, curly streamers and "Good Luck" sprinkles scattered everywhere (which they'd realised they'd be finding for months afterwards). Not to mention a small mountain of cards, along with several beautifully wrapped boxes, all of them just waiting to be ripped open by the excited Steph. The mood in the office was buoyant and light-hearted as they all teased Steph about leaving them in the lurch. Casey and Tilly both thought it very unlikely that either of them would keep in close contact with Steph, once she'd finally left the company. But they were more than happy to buy her a few drinks and share in the celebrations at Barney's later that day.

With the day kicking off to a good start and everyone in a happy mood, Steph announced she had also brought in some cakes. That was a statement which always went down well in the office, and by lunchtime, they had all sampled lots of them and were now feeling totally coffee'd and cake'd out. Most of them were eating at Barney's later, before the main drinking was due to begin, so they'd decided to just grab a sandwich during the afternoon. The food at Barney's wasn't too bad – not as good as Giovanni's of course – but all the same, pretty good for a wine bar. Some people referred to Barney's Wine Bar as a Brasserie. Who knew what the difference was, except that one seemed to be more food based, while the other was more of a wine specialist. At least that's how Casey interpreted it; either way, Barney's was the perfect place to spend the kind of evening they had all planned for Steph's leaving bash.

As the clock ticked over the 5pm mark, the excited group all packed up for the day. Several of the girls helped Steph with her presents, which included a lovely Cross Pen, which she had been delighted to have received. She had been choked to think they had collected so much, and because pens were something she had a passion for, it was the perfect momento from her time of working with them all. She was absolutely thrilled with it and thanked everyone several times for making her last day so good, and for all her lovely gifts. Steph then suggested they all get off to Barney's Bar for some wine and fun! There was a lot of hurried activity as they all began packing up, closing desk drawers, grabbing bags and coats, then helping to load-up Steph's boyfriend's car with all her gifts. Finally, rushing out the door, they shouted out, "OK, see you down there," as Tilly and Casey excused themselves to stop off in the ladies' room and freshen up. Some fifteen minutes later, they hurriedly made their way over to Barney's too.

Dave had been distracted all day at work knowing he would be seeing Tilly at Barney's, so he was keen to get there as soon as he could. Especially since finding out that the girls would be going straight from work and having been pre-warned by Casey that there was a strong possibility of John and Gemma turning up. Finishing the last call of the day, Dave told his workmates he had to dash off, as he simultaneously shoved a pile of papers into his desk drawers and locked them away. Grabbing his jacket and almost sprinting out of the building, Dave set off home to quickly freshen up before he made his way to Barney's and Tilly.

The girls were eating first so Dave knew he had a bit of time to play with, but he was so concerned about John arriving and upsetting Tilly, he dived in and out of the shower quicker than he thought he'd probably ever done before. Cleaning his teeth and hurriedly running gel through his wet hair, Dave rushed into the bedroom to pull on his favourite jeans and shirt, then splashed on some after-shave and dashed out the door. Dave liked Tilly a lot and felt very protective of her, even though she wasn't technically his girl, yet. That was something he wanted to change; he really wanted Tilly to be his girl and would do *everything* he could to make that happen, so long as it was what Tilly wanted too. Dave quietly hoped it was.

Casey and Tilly had both chosen meals off the Light Bites Menu, so by the time John and Gemma walked in, the two friends had already finished eating and were sat on the high stools by the bar. Casey spotted John first and warned Tilly, who had her back to the door and hadn't seen the couple walk in. Gemma had linked her arm through John's and was looking fantastic in her tights jeans, long boots and loose white blouse, which she'd cinched in at the hip with a low slung belt, before finishing off the whole look with a long dangly hippy style necklace.

Casey gulped as she touched Tilly's arm. Gemma looked amazing and Casey knew that little fact had the power to crush her friend. Surprisingly though, John hadn't seen Casey and Tilly as he stopped at the end of the bar to order drinks for Gemma and himself, so he looked remarkably calm.

As the rest of the girls from work finished their food, they each drifted towards the bar where Steph was enjoying being centre of attention and life and soul of the group. Feeling giddy with the effect of cocktails and the happiness of the moment, Steph laughed, her laugh was loud and legendary, which made John glance over in their direction. John then caught sight of Casey and Tilly just at the very same moment that Tilly also turned and saw him. The cheating man's face was a picture. John was clearly surprised to see them there and, with a look which quickly changed to awkward embarrassment, he just nodded and smiled nervously in their direction. Then, after whispering something in Gemma's ear, John started to walk towards them.

At that very same point, Dave appeared, like Tilly's very own *Sir Galahad,* striding through the open door to seek out his woman. On seeing the two girls sat at the bar, Dave held his hand up as a hello and quickly walked over to them. Unaware of John also battling through the group of girls thronging the bar area, Dave reached Tilly first and slipped his arm around her waist and kissed her on both cheeks. Unaware that his arrival was so well timed, Dave had both girls grinning with relief and happiness at seeing him, as they both enjoyed his warm hello. Looking remarkably shocked and surprised, John stopped in his tracks. Having seen Dave's kiss, a frown crept across John's brow and he now looked ever so slightly annoyed as he walked on past them, making his way to the gent's toilet. Luckily for John, Gemma hadn't seen his reaction and so she had no idea that her new boyfriend had been so flummoxed by Dave kissing Tilly, even if it was only on her cheeks.

Dave complimented Tilly on how lovely she looked and apologised for not being there sooner, as he also offered to buy the girls a drink, which they both graciously accepted. Casey warned him that John had already arrived with Gemma and had in fact just walked past them into the gents. Shaking his head, Dave was astounded at John's thoughtlessness for bringing Gemma here tonight of all nights, knowing that Tilly would very likely be there for Steph's leaving party. *Seriously, what a complete and utter idiot,* Dave thought. And that was putting it mildly. *Oh well, his loss and my gain!* Dave relished in that thought and with a smug grin, he said as much to Tilly, which earned him a dazzling smile from the red-headed beauty in front of him.

John watched Tilly as he passed her on his way back from the gents, but she was paying no attention to him; instead, she was laughing and smiling at some guy he'd not seen before. Casey saw John's face and smiled inside, thinking *your loss, loser!* Excusing herself from the two new love-birds, Casey went to join the group surrounding Steph, who were now congratulating her loudly, with their cheers and clinking of glasses. It turned into a good night, which Steph enjoyed almost as much as Tilly and Dave.

Chapter 8

Auckland

As he walked off the plane, Jason smiled at the whole experience of being a first class passenger. Knowing that this was probably the one and only time he would ever get to experience such luxury, he'd savoured every moment and stored the memory of the whole journey in his mind. Having begun with his luggage being picked up in advance from home, to the limousine which drove him in luxury to the airport and then the first class lounge, how amazing had that been. Finally, *le piece de la resistance* was the positively huge seat and space that was all his in the front section of the plane. Being waited on hand and foot, with champagne flowing and his every need catered for, this was a luxury Jason could totally get used to. He most definitely envied those lucky creatures that got to turn left as they entered the plane and travelled in such luxurious style.

As long as the flight to New Zealand had been, travelling so comfortably and having a stopover in Singapore, meant jet-lag would not be an issue for Jason. In between enjoying several excellent in-flight movies, the wonderful meals (served on real china plates), then lying down flat (oh yes!), Jason had managed to get a good amount of sleep on both flights.

Now walking into Auckland airport's arrivals hall, Jason felt remarkably good, having been totally refreshed by the hot towels and use of the amazing bathroom facilities that first class passengers enjoyed, followed by plenty of strong filtered coffee, which he'd chosen to have with his delicious breakfast. Like most people, Jason had only ever dreamed of how much better first class travel would be, but now he could actually brag about it to all his buddies back home. Especially the luggage bit, whoever thought you could have your luggage collected from home, with all the checking in and everything done for you *and* for it then to be sent on to your final destination? *Amazing!* Of course that had meant Jason didn't have to queue or even wait to pick his bags up off the carousel. More importantly, it meant that he and his new boss, Lee, could start their tour of Auckland without the worry of dropping his bags off at the hotel first. Grinning as he walked through the airport, Jason felt a mix of elation, along with slight trepidation, at this exciting new phase of his life.

Auckland and living close to the harbour promised a perfect lifestyle for Jason and he couldn't wait to see the apartment that had been organised for him, should he choose to take the job offer (not that he doubted he would for even a nano-second). From the itinerary Lee had emailed to him, Jason knew he would also be meeting the guys in his new team the following day and truthfully, he couldn't wait, he was so enthusiastic about this new role. Today, however, Jason was just happy to meet his new boss in the flesh, having only spoken to him via a video conference call, during their previous discussions. Today though, Lee had promised to meet him personally and then take him to meet his wife Becca, before showing Jason around Auckland. Lee had warned him it would be a pretty packed agenda, but he also genuinely hoped that Jason would love his time in Auckland.

Waiting in the arrival hall for Jason, Lee was also feeling enthusiastic about meeting his new Engineering Sales Principal for the first time. Video conferencing was great, but he too knew that nothing beat a face-to-face meeting. Jason's reputation was well known to Lee and he was very aware that this was a big deal, for both Jason and his company, so he was keen for the visit to go well and for Jason to want to stay.

Moving through the bright and clean airport, Jason's walk had turned to a confident stride and he loved his first glimpses of New Zealand life, marvelling at the elaborate Maori influenced wood carved entrance, as he walked through to the arrivals hall. Yes, this was going to be an amazing trip. Jason hoped with all his heart that the visit would be a huge success, and that Lee and his team would be as suitably impressed.

As Jason walked through the opening into the arrivals hall, he expected to be greeted by a sea of faces holding up notices, with names scribbled on them, much as would be expected in any large UK airport. However, this was Auckland and whilst busy, the airport was much smaller, with a lot less people waiting for the arrivals. Scanning the faces, Jason suddenly realised Lee was actually walking towards him, smiling and holding out his hand to join Jason's firm handshake.

"Hey, Jason, it's great to meet you, mate. I hope you had a good flight and got plenty of sleep."

Jason was slightly taken aback by this warm and friendly, but fairly relaxed welcome. It was different to what he'd expected and yet at the same time, he felt very relieved and even comforted by the happy demeanour that Lee exuded.

As Jason shared Lee's firm handshake, he responded warmly: "Lee, it's great to finally meet you. I've been looking forward to this visit so much."

Relief and happiness gushed through Jason's veins and he relaxed immediately. The two men were equally impressed with each other and, as they broke their handshake, they both agreed how great it was, to finally get to meet the person behind the face and voice. Lee took charge of the moment.

"Well then, let's get out to the truck and head straight to the harbour to grab a beer before we start the day."

Jason had envisaged Lee being a typical Kiwi and it seemed he was not to be disappointed; this was an excellent start to the day and his familiarisation visit. The two men chatted easily as they walked out to Lee's truck, which turned out to be a very smart Ford Ranger. As they climbed into it, Lee explained how he used this truck for pulling his boat, because it had more pulling power than his other car.

At the mention of a boat, Jason's eyes lit up, and seeing his reaction, Lee immediately warmed to Jason. Next to his wife Becca, Lee explained how his boat and sea fishing were his two very big loves, where he spent most of his free time when he wasn't at the office. Also admitting how lucky he'd been that he'd found the perfect partner in Becca, because she loved the boat and fishing, almost as much as Lee did himself, so it worked well for them both. Jason remarked on how he too loved boats, but that where he'd been living in the UK, was a good couple of hours to reach any kind of decent expanse of water. Lee empathised with that disappointment.

As the two men drove down to the harbour, Lee shared some of the history of New Zealand with Jason, explaining how the country was so young, nothing like the age of the UK in terms of historical periods and buildings. Lee was a very proud New Zealander and always keen to share his knowledge about his beautiful country with any new visitor. Enjoying seeing how Jason was loving hearing about all the usual information that New Zealand tourists craved, Lee was also thrilled that he was eagerly anticipating seeing more of the City of Sails, the name by which most New Zealander's knew Auckland as.

As they drove into the harbour, Lee slowed down before pulling into the parking spot which came with his boat mooring. Jason couldn't fail to be impressed by the whole set-up of the harbour in Auckland; it was truly impressive and exactly how he imagined a sunny city harbour should be. Jumping out of the truck, Lee pointed out his boat, which was moored about fifty feet away from where they stood. Jason was again mightily impressed and eagerly accepted the invitation to go aboard for their first beer.

Lee was a self-made millionaire and he and Becca were now reaping the benefits of their hard work and the financial freedom the millions of New Zealand dollars had provided. As Jason stepped onto the boat he was greeted warmly by Becca, who had heard them pull up and casually appeared on deck with a cold bottle of Steinlager for each of them. *What a welcome!* Jason was blown away and grinned widely as he introduced himself to Becca, also thanking her for the beer. Lee stepped on deck and kissed his wife, telling her how he and Jason had been talking boats and cars all the way from the airport. Watching Lee and Becca together and so at ease in each other's company made Jason think of Casey. How he wished she could be there with him right now, joining in the fun and experiencing this surreal life-path he'd found himself on.

"Casey would love this."

"What's that, Jason?"

Becca's voice cut through his momentary day-dream and, not realising he'd spoken that thought out loud, Jason replied to Becca: "Oh, I was just thinking how my girlfriend Casey would have loved this."

Surprised by this disclosure, Lee spoke: "Oh, I didn't realise you had a girlfriend, Jason? Will she be moving out with you?"

"Sadly not, Lee," he said. "I did ask her, but she couldn't bear to leave her home town and the life she has there. Plus, she's been offered an amazing opportunity to write for a magazine. So it's just really bad timing for her; well, for *us* actually. I would have loved it if she could have joined me."

Jason's voice trailed away and Becca caught Lee's eye, urging him to say something to break the train of thoughts invoked by that particular conversation.

"I'm real sorry to hear that, Jason. I guess it's gonna to be tough for you both, but who knows, maybe she'll change her mind. They do say absence makes the heart grow fonder. But either way, mate, try not to let it spoil this opportunity for you."

Hearing Lee refer to him as *mate* made Jason break away from thoughts of Casey and agree with Lee. In fact, Jason declared, this was the best opportunity that had ever happened for him and he couldn't wait to get started. A good humoured laugh was shared as they all clinked bottles and swigged their beers.

Changing the subject, Jason asked Lee the name of his boat.

"We named her Sandie."

Becca and Lee's voices chimed as they replied at the same time and laughing easily, Lee went on to explain that *Sandie* had been the name of the grandmother he'd grown up with. It was a sort of homage to her. Jason was surprised at the coincidence and explained that Casey had also been brought up by her grandmother, after her parents had been killed in the accident. Both Lee and Becca were naturally saddened to hear this and said as much to Jason. To get himself out of gloomy thoughts, Jason suddenly brightened and offered a subject change by asking what they were doing next.

"We thought a tour of the town would be a good start and to check out where your new apartment is, so you can see where you'll be living when you come over. Oh and where the office is of course. Although we'll leave the staff intros until tomorrow morning because knowing my lot, they'll want to take you for lunch and suck the life-blood out of you by asking a ton of questions. You'll need to get a good night's sleep tonight, so you feel fresh for another busy day tomorrow."

Lee laughed as they all acknowledged that likelihood. Jason had already anticipated the fullness of each day and was looking forward to seeing the office the following day and meeting his new colleagues. Lee meanwhile, was keen to reiterate that there was going to be very little actual working on this trip; it really was more about checking out the city, the country and the life-style, so that Jason could be sure he wanted to make the move.

Becca had already suggested to Lee it was probably best to leave the two of them to do the apartment and office visits without her. Knowing that Lee was planning to drive around Auckland and take Jason out to One Tree Hill, Becca suggested meeting them later that afternoon at their favourite harbour restaurant for a bite to eat.

"Good idea, Becca," Lee said. He kissed Becca's cheek and turned back to Jason. "Come on then, Jason mate, let's crack on and see how we go. Maybe we could take the boat out after we've eaten so you can see the city from the water. No doubt you'll crash out tonight after a day of travel, sea air and sunshine."

Jason agreed, although at that point felt he was too excited to sleep, ever again! This was a truly amazing day and Jason couldn't believe his good fortune and how amazingly friendly and relaxed Becca and Lee were with him. Running on excitement and adrenaline, whilst hoping it would all turn out well and that he was not going to be disappointed, Jason couldn't wait to get going.

The location of his new apartment couldn't be more perfect. It had a gorgeous view over the harbour, with a balcony that had a couple of chairs and a small table. Jason pictured himself sitting out there, enjoying watching the boats in the glorious sunshine, whilst sipping a nice cold beer. Yes, just seeing the apartment, he was already mentally there and moved in. This was too easy. Jason had made his decision there and then; he was definitely coming back to Auckland and would give it at least two years, to see what future he could build.

Lee could see Jason loved the apartment and knew it would be a deal clincher, so he felt relieved that the familiarisation had started off so well, making a mental note to thank Lucy, his PA. It was thanks to Lucy's efforts that they'd been able to secure this fabulous apartment. Lee told Jason he'd organise a rental car as well; no point buying a car for two years, when they could get a great rental deal through the company. Jason couldn't believe his luck; it seemed like everything was just falling into place for him. Someone sure was looking after him up there.

The next stop was the office, which was a perfectly easy ten- to fifteen-minute walk away from his apartment, so he'd only really need a car socially. The office was in a shared building and looked very glamorous with its smoked glass exterior. As they stood outside looking up at it, Lee spoke: "OK, so that's the office and tomorrow, we'll go inside so I can introduce you to the whole gang. They're really looking forward to meeting you. In fact, they're already determined to convince you that you'll be joining the team!"

Lee was a really decent boss, who genuinely cared about the team that worked for him. With a personal philosophy that was very much like Richard Branson's, Lee looked after his staff and treated them well. In return, they worked hard and were very loyal to both Lee and the company. It was clear to Jason just how much they thought of Lee, having all clubbed together to buy him such a great present for his fiftieth birthday. Back on the boat when they were talking about the guys at work, Becca had encouraged Lee to show Jason the watch his team had bought, which was impressive and looked very expensive. Jason wasn't really a watch man, but even he could tell it was top quality. Lee was clearly very proud of his watch and more so, of how much his team thought of him.

The company was hugely successful and had grown in leaps and bounds over the past five years, hence how they could afford to splash out on upgraded travel for Jason *and* such a fabulous apartment for him. Amazingly, Lee had agreed the company would help subsidise the rental for the first nine months of his stay, so it was easily affordable for Jason and he couldn't wait to move in.

Engineering was an industry that was taking off massively in New Zealand. Retail and housing development was not only increasing across both the North and South Islands, but the whole geographical region. The Company's UK partner had joined them four years ago and since then, the market had expanded rapidly and more recently into the Australian market, which meant business was booming for Lee, and Jason's engineering design and sales skills would be invaluable to them. Business was good and life was good. Lee was rightly proud of where their company had grown from and where they were headed. More so, he was looking forward to bringing Jason into the team and truly hoped he would fall in love with the Auckland lifestyle and want to stay long term.

Having driven up to the top of One Tree Hill, Jason couldn't fail to be impressed by the amazing far reaching views, which gave him a real sense of how big Auckland truly was. Jason loved learning from Lee about the history of the Maoris and the plaques on the base of the monument; also the significance of the tree on the hill and how it had been attacked by Maori protestors twice. Sadly, despite huge efforts to try and save it, the tree finally had to be removed because of the danger of it falling down.

Breathing in the Auckland air from the top of the hill, Jason felt like he was a million miles away from home.

Even though he missed Casey, he felt comfortable here; it was like he was really *home* and just needed to familiarise himself with these new surroundings. It was a good feeling and he said as much to his new boss. Lee was chuffed that Jason was feeling so good about being in Auckland and even though it was only day one, it was a great start to this familiarisation visit. Now feeling hungry, the two of them decided it was time for food, so Lee quickly text Becca to say they were on their way and would meet her there.

As they walked from the car park towards the restaurant, Becca was already sitting outside and just about to order a drink. Spotting her approaching husband with Jason, Becca asked the waiter to hold on for their drinks order too. The restaurant specialised in fish and seafood, the quality of which was spectacular and the reason for the high rating so many patrons gave it. Jason loved seafood and couldn't fault the dish which was served to him. As he tucked in, complimenting and enjoying his food as much as Lee and Becca did theirs, Jason thanked them both again for their amazing hospitality. He still couldn't quite believe his luck.

Two hours later the three of them were climbing back into the boat and casting off to enjoy the early evening, sailing around the calm waters of the harbour. The view of Auckland from the water in the basking sunshine, was truly breath-taking. Jason was overwhelmed with everything he had seen and done that day. With Lee and Becca being so welcoming, Jason couldn't wait to begin his new life in Auckland. As he sat happily taking in the views from the boat, Jason allowed himself the luxury of imagining Casey changing her mind and coming out to join him. Those thoughts swam around his head and soon had him convincing himself that he could talk her round. As he leant back in the boat and raised a smiling face upward, Jason silently sent up his wish into the atmosphere, to anyone that might be listening. An hour later, Lee called out that he was heading the boat back towards the harbour mooring, so Jason could get off to his hotel and unpack, before crashing out for the night.

Jason raised his right arm in response and shouted back: "Great!"

As Jason smiled across to Becca, she returned his grin in her typically warm and friendly way, also feeling very happy that Lee was doing such a good job of showing Jason the benefits of life in Auckland. The sea was calm and fairly flat as they approached the mooring. Lee slowed the boat right down and said to Jason that if he'd like to, he would teach him how to handle the boat sometime. To which Jason responded eagerly and said he'd love that, again stating how he couldn't thank them enough for such an amazing opportunity and start to his visit. Feeling blown over by how fantastic Auckland was, Jason confirmed to Lee and Becca that he couldn't wait to get started and meet the team the following morning.

Leaving his hosts on the boat, Jason walked to his hotel, reflecting on the day and his hopes for this new life, which soared higher now than he could have ever imagined. All there was left to do to cement his decision, was to meet the team the next day and hope that they all bonded easily. Lee had said not to rush in too early, advising Jason to come in around ten o'clock, by which time everyone would have arrived and settled into the working day, plus the coffee would be well and truly flowing by then.

As he quickly unpacked his small bag and hung everything up, and having already showered, Jason stepped out onto the balcony to take in the evening view of the harbour while he finished his last beer. Forty minutes later, as he climbed between the freshly laundered sheets, he closed his eyes and thought *what a truly brilliant start*, as he drifted off to sleep.

Chapter 9

Girls out on the town

Back home, Casey was packing up her stuff ready to finish early. It was Friday, and she had big plans for her next submission into the magazine. The last couple of days had been a bit weird for her, what with Jason leaving, and if she was being totally honest with herself, she had definitely felt a bit out of sorts knowing he'd be gone for two weeks and then back for just a month, before he'd be gone again for, well...who knew how long?

Whatever length of time he chose to stay away though, Casey guessed Jason's decision would very much depend on whether he liked it out there, and if he made new friends easily enough. *Of course he'll make friends easily,* Casey reprimanded herself. *Jason's such a great guy; he's friendly and outgoing, very pleasant to talk to,* and in her opinion, unashamedly handsome! Of course he'd make friends easily. On top of all that, Casey acknowledged that Jason was also extremely good at his job, hence why he'd been head-hunted so strongly. So, with all that going for him, what was there not to like?

Shoving the last few things into her bag, Casey was slightly annoyed and frustrated with herself for allowing her thoughts to drift towards Jason once again. Especially after promising herself she'd be good and would just push any thoughts of him out of her mind, the very moment they tried to creep back in. Only, it wouldn't be that simple would it. *No.* How could it possibly be that simple to discard thoughts of Jason, when their relationship had taken such a turn in the last days before he'd left for New Zealand?

As she left the office alone, but still with Jason on her mind, Casey huffed before shouting out to her team: "Bye, have a great weekend everyone!"

Feeling slightly dejected and in need of a pick-me-up, Casey decided to give Carole a call and ask if she fancied going out for a few drinks at Barney's, before going for a bite to eat at their favourite Italian Restaurant. Knowing Giovanni would cheer her up and make her smile, Casey thought that plan was a good one.

Naturally Carole was well up for that idea; she'd been wondering all day what to do with her evening and quite fancied a bit of girlie banter, so Casey's suggestion was perfect timing. Besides which, Carole needed to ask Casey about a certain band member and was he still as cute as the last time she'd seen him?

Rushing home, Casey wanted to freshen up and change into something a little more in-keeping with a Friday night out. Now feeling a little happier than before, as she walked through the main door and into the warm entrance hall of her apartment block, Casey almost collided with an excited Tilly, who was just rushing out to meet up with Dave.

Tilly had taken a whole day off to prepare herself for her first proper date with the gorgeous Dave, having primped and preened her whole body to the Nth degree. Knowing it was going to be just the two of them, meant Tilly was buzzing and the moment of meeting up was imminent. Casey remarked on how happy and gorgeous Tilly looked as she generously wished her a fabulous evening. Tilly blushed slightly at the compliment and thanked Casey, before adding how excited she was. It truly was amazing to see the sparkle in Tilly's eye and to hear her giggle about Dave in that way, it made Casey's own spirits lift upwards.

Apparently, the man of the moment was taking Tilly somewhere very special, which involved an hour's train ride, so she was off to meet him at the station. Both girls laughed at the idea of Tilly meeting Dave under the station clock and wondered if there would be smoke and steam clouding their view, like in all the old movies. Of course there *wouldn't* but both girls being ever so slightly romantic, had a similar vision in their heads of Dave meeting Tilly on that smoke filled platform, with him quoting the line, *'here's looking at you, kid!'* Again, Casey wished Tilly a brilliant evening, saying to enjoy herself and just roll with whatever the evening brought. Tilly nodded and laughed as she skipped through the open door and down the front steps.

As Casey climbed the stairs to her own apartment, she truly hoped Tilly and Dave would work out. Dave seemed to be so much better for Tilly than John had ever been and Casey had certainly never seen Tilly sparkle like that whenever John had been calling for her. Glancing at the clock in the hallway as she reached the top of the stairs, Casey juggled with her bags in order to free-up her hand so she could push the door key into the lock. She stepped inside and slowly eased everything off her arms, lowering her bags and coat onto the floor around her, as she kicked off her shoes. Sighing at the relief of freeing her toes from the closed in pumps she'd been wearing all day, Casey was immensely happy to be home. Stooping to pick up her jacket again and hang it on the usual hook, she decided to leave the bags where they were for the moment.

First things first, she needed at least a half-hour to soak in the bath, to soothe away the day's stresses and remaining thoughts of Jason. Pouring her favourite lavender essence into the hot running water, Casey breathed in the warm aroma and felt instantly relaxed as she added extra bubbles and watched them froth up in the bath. Taking off her clothes, she dropped them one by one into the laundry basket behind the door, before pulling on her towelling bathrobe. Now slipping her feet into fluffy slippers, Casey padded through to the kitchen, stopping on the way to pick up her previously discarded bags. As she plopped the bags down on the table, her hands automatically reached for the fridge door and the bottle of cool Sauvignon Blanc. Always having her favourite wine glass to hand, Casey listened contentedly to the familiar glug, glug, glug, as the wine poured into the fine crystal glass. *Dartington really do make the best glasses,* she decided, and picking hers up by the stem as she swirled the wine around the glass, Casey watched the light reflect through the pale straw-coloured wine, to dance on the fine cut crystal. Momentarily sniffing the wine, she took a first pleasing sip. *Yes, that will do perfectly,* she thought. Turning around to replace the bottle in the fridge door, Casey thought of Jason once again and how much she would miss sharing her bed with him that weekend, while scolding herself for thinking of him again.

As she started back towards the bathroom, Casey decided to switch on her CD player and listen to some Jazz while she soaked in the bath. Yes, that would banish Jason from her mind she thought as she listened to the first track, which was really more Swing than traditional Jazz. Lisa Stansfield sang so well and the soundtrack from the *Swing* movie was still a favourite of Casey's.

Pulling loose the ties on her bathrobe, Casey let it drop to the floor and stepped into the warm bubbly water. With her wine glass in hand she expertly sank into the bubbly bathwater without spilling even a drop of the precious cool liquid, then carefully lay back into the warm water. Casey luxuriated in the pleasure of her bubbly lavender bath, whilst listening to Lisa Stansfield singing. The wine was nicely chilled and tasted delicious. Casey closed her eyes and revelled in just being *in the moment.*

As the second track finished, Casey opened her eyes and sipped some more wine. It had been a while since she'd enjoyed the pleasure of soaking in her bath, generally finding herself rushing around getting ready to see Jason, with only time for a shower. Today, however, the shower wasn't enough. No, today she needed a bit of self-pampering. As Lisa sang on, Casey's heart lifted and her mind livened up into a more positive state. Sitting up straight again she decided her hair needed washing and her legs needed shaving, before venturing out of the warm water. Rinsing off the last of the conditioner from her hair, Casey was humming to the music, her mind now refocused, she expertly ran the razor up her shins and smiled, thinking of Carole and the inevitable question that would come later, about that certain band member. Standing up to step out of the bath, her skin had turned slightly pink from the heat of the water, yet Casey felt surprisingly calm and relaxed, completely refreshed even. Yes, the girl was ready to take on the Friday night fun that beckoned.

Pulling on her bathrobe and leaving her body to dry naturally, rather than rubbing a towel over herself, Casey walked through to the bedroom to sit down at the lovely 1930's dressing table she'd inherited from her Nanny Em. Glancing into the mirror and unwrapping her hair from the small towel, she gently rubbed the last of the water off before picking up her hairdryer. Having decided to wear her hair curly, Casey used the diffuser to dry off the worst of the wetness before leaving her curls to naturally develop as they finished drying.

Now feeling a bit hot from the combination of a hot bath, her towelling robe and the hair-dryer, Casey needed to cool down. Slipping her arms out of the robe, she sat naked, casually looking at her reflection in the mirror, as she cooled down enough to start applying moisturiser and make-up.

What on earth is that? Was that a little dimple on her right breast? She leaned forward towards the mirror to get a closer look and then glanced down at her body. Cupping her hands underneath, Casey lifted her breast slightly upwards to get a better view of the nipple area. And her heart sank. Panic began to rise inside her; there was definitely something not right with her breast and of course her immediate thought was the worst kind. Pressing on the breast and all around the nipple area, Casey noticed that the dimple didn't move and she could feel something odd, it wasn't quite a lump, but it was definitely something. She looked up and into the mirror, watching her own facial expression develop as a scared reality crept into her mind and took up residence. Quickly pulling her robe back up around her shoulders, Casey slipped her hands through the sleeves and wrapped the gown around her body tightly, as though to comfort herself and take the worry away.

But no, her worry wasn't moving on that easily and she just stared at her reflection in the mirror, seeing only scared reality staring straight back at her. Not knowing what to think or say, she had to speak to someone sensible. Yes, Carole. Just because she worked at the hospital, Casey automatically decided her old friend would know what to do.

'It is funny isn't it, that no matter what the role of the person who works at the hospital is, we all assume they will immediately know what to do. It's as if being close to doctors and nurses somehow reflects their knowledge onto the person working there, whether they are medically trained or not.'

Luckily for Casey though, in her case, it could well be true, because Carole worked at a Private Hospital and was actually a Staff Nurse in Oncology. Dressing a little more slowly now and feeling far less enthusiastic about their girlie night, Casey was also very relieved that she would be seeing Carole tonight. Rather than blurt it out the moment she saw her, Casey decided she needed to pick her moment, knowing that whenever she started to say it out loud, it was going to be hard and she wasn't sure if she could hold it together. It was hard to voice out loud what she had found and Casey didn't want to think the worst, but speaking the words rather than just *thinking* them would make it all seem just a bit too real for her and she was afraid that by saying the words out loud, she'd be inviting fate into making it the worst kind of news. Casey was more than a bit apprehensive and didn't quite know how to even start that conversation. Damn and blast it: why did this have to happen now, when she was missing Jason *and* having to concentrate on her new column. The column was her dream and she didn't want to mess it up. No way could she be ill now, no way, it wasn't happening, she wouldn't let it! Casey's determination was kicking in, but she was scared witless and swallowed hard as she tried to calm her jangling nerves.

Pulling on her jeans and a loose white Cashmere jumper, Casey's mood had changed from the relaxed person she'd been when she first stepped out of the bath, to a frazzled mess, as her racing mind grew more scared of what might turn out to be an inevitable truth. Deciding that her make-up needed to be minimal and light, Casey just brushed on some mascara and blusher, before applying a natural tone lipstick. She was on auto-pilot, but the truth was that she *really* didn't feel like putting herself out there tonight. In fact, she didn't quite know how she was going to manage telling Carole and thought being in the noise and hubbub of Barney's Bar would help her keep a low profile, as she spoke to Carole about it. Yes, that would work, for tonight at least. Pushing her feet into her ankle boots, Casey slipped on her favourite brown jacket and cherry-red suede beret, before picking up her bag from the kitchen chair, pausing to inhale a couple of deep breaths, before walking towards her front door and stepping out onto the brightly lit landing.

Casey didn't remember much about the walk to Barney's other than it was a bit chilly. In fact, she only realised quite how chilly it'd been, as she pushed open the door to Barney's and was met by a heat-wave coming out of the place. Being Friday night, it was already busy and the chatter was picking up volume. Casey was relieved to see that Carole had beat her to it and was closely guarding a bar stool, next to the one that she herself was sat upon.

Having spent many a Friday night with Casey, Carole had guessed her usual Friday night tipple of vodka and tonic, with a slice of lime, would be the order of the day. She knew from past experience that Casey would be running at least twenty minutes late seeing she was going to have a soak in the bath before she left. Having shared a flat with Casey several years ago, Carole knew her getting ready to go out habits. Also, that "I'll just take a quick bath", always elongated far longer than Casey ever expected, so Carole had timed her arrival perfectly. Jumping up from her stool, Carole hugged her friend and then stepped back with a quizzical look on her face.

"Hey, what's with the long face, missus?" Carole said. "Come on, it's Friday night and we're here to partttayyyyy!"

Carole looked so bright and breezy that Casey really didn't want to spoil the moment, not just yet anyway. Besides which, she decided Barney's really wasn't the place to be telling Carole what she'd just found, so Casey put on her brave smile and clinked glasses with her very buoyant friend, saying: "Cheers, and here's to Friday nights!"

The crowd grew around them and their lively chatter escalated. Everyone seemed happy to be out. It was Friday and the weekend lay ahead of them, with no more work until Monday morning. Well, apart from Casey of course, who had to make a start on her column the following morning. Claire had suggested Casey could maybe write about Jason leaving and how she was feeling about it; unfortunately though, Casey wasn't too sure she could share that intimate detail just yet. It was all feeling just a bit too raw for her right now, so she'd been trying to think of something else she could chat about for her column. Claire had completely understood of course and mentally kicked herself for that clumsiness with Casey's feelings.

Joining in the buzzing atmosphere and conversation, whilst trying not to let Carole see that something really was bothering her, Casey swigged back her vodka a little too quickly. Waving her arm to the nearest bar tender, Casey had to then almost shout their order at the poor guy. The loud music was adding to the noise of the throng that filled Barney's bar. An hour or so later, the girls decided to wander down to Giovanni's and even though the outside temperature had dropped considerably, they agreed the fresh air and a walk would do them good. As they made their way to the exit from Barney's, Casey pulled the door handle just at the very same time that someone pushed the door from the outside. Jumping back, a little startled, Casey looked up to see Matt standing in front of her as large as life. *OMG!* Casey stepped back just as suddenly, almost bumping into Carole, who was standing close behind her.

"Well hello again, Casey," Matt said. "How lovely to bump into you." Matt's slightly deep and gravelly voice made Casey blush. "Are you leaving already?"

"Oh hi, Matt," she said, now feeling slightly flustered. "Err, yes we are actually. In fact, we're just off to Giovanni's for a bite to eat."

Casey could sense Carole's surprised expression, even though her friend was standing behind her and Casey couldn't actually see her face, so she turned to introduce Matt to Carole.

"This is my friend Carole and, Carole, this is Matt. He's a friend of Dave's."

Carole smiled and said hello, as Matt politely shook her hand before casting his eyes back to Casey.

"Well, I'm sorry you're leaving ladies," he said, "but I understand the pull of Giovanni's. It's one of my favourite places to eat too."

Matt's smile bedazzled Casey momentarily and she laughed a little too nervously before bidding him goodbye.

"Maybe we'll bump into each other again sometime?" he said as his eyes twinkled at her.

"Errr, yes, maybe, you never know," Casey responded.

Casey was stumbling over her words and wanted to escape before her embarrassment became too apparent.

"I do hope so, Casey."

Matt smiled again and then held open the door for the girls to walk through. As they stepped out into the cool night air, Carole was the first to speak: "Wow, Casey, who was that?"

Carole was reeling from the gorgeousness of Matt and Casey laughed at her friend's reaction.

"I told you, his name's Matt. He's a friend of Dave's. You remember Dave don't you?"

Casey was trying not to give away too much; she felt like she wasn't quite ready to share Matt yet, even though he wasn't really hers.

"Yes, yes, of course I remember Dave, but I've never seen Matt before. He's gorgeous and he's clearly got the hots for you, Case."

Carole's voice had gone up an octave or two.

"Don't be daft," Casey said. "Besides, he's got a girlfriend already."

Casey didn't dare tell Carole how she knew that little snippet of information.

"Oh damn, well that's a real shame, especially now you're a free agent eh…"

Carole winked as she took Casey's arm and linked hers through it. As they walked along the streets towards Giovanni's, their pace quickened; with their heads bowed slightly, they battled against the now cool breeze which had picked up whilst they'd been inside Barney's. By the time they had entered the cosy restaurant, both women were very glad to feel the warm air meet their faces.

"Ciao, Bella…Casey, Carolee (he always seemed to add an extended 'e' to Carole's name), come in, come in, it is so cold outside," Giovanni said enthusiastically. "Let me take your jackets."

Casey chose to keep hold of her beret.

"I have a special table for you both."

Giovanni showed them to the very same table that Casey had sat at with Jason the last time they'd shared dinner together. Gulping and pushing away the memory of her last night with Jason, Casey sat down a little edgily and picked up the menu. Carole sat down opposite stating she already knew what she wanted to eat. Both women more or less knew the menu by heart, with the exception of the specials board of course, which changed weekly. Both had their own particular favourite dishes, but neither of them was averse to trying something new, so they always looked to see what the specials were. Casey was in the mood for comfort food though and had already decided to go for the Lasagne, but she still automatically read through the specials menu.

Giovanni left them to it, returning a short while later with a complimentary bruschetta for them both, along with a glass of sparkling red wine, reasoning that he knew Casey would be missing Jason and so he wanted to buy her a drink. Having popped round a few days earlier to see

Giovanni and Maria, to briefly explain about Jason leaving, Casey was grateful for his thoughtfulness. *Bless him*, Casey did love Giovanni, it was like having a fabulous Italian uncle who doted on her. There was a mutual fondness between the two of them. Giovanni thought the world of Casey and had come to view her as if she were his own extended family. As had Maria and their two sons, all of them having known each other for such a long time now. Giovanni loved having Casey there and always found a table for her whenever she chose to drop in for a quick bite. Even if that meant a short wait with a glass of Masala on those days when the restaurant was already busy. Casey popping in was never a problem for Maria and Giovanni.

Enjoying the unexpected but welcome treat of chef Marco's bruschetta, the girls tucked in eagerly, realising the few drinks they'd consumed at Barney's were already taking effect. Agreeing that their decision to walk to Giovanni's had been well timed for them both, each of them suddenly feeling hungry.

"Mmmm...de-li-cious!"

Carole mumbled as she nodded her appreciation to Casey and raised a grateful thumbs-up to Giovanni. Casey was also enjoying the bruschetta, but was quieter than normal. It wasn't long before Carole recognised the change in her friend's mood and gently pressed her as to what was wrong, asking why she had suddenly gone all serious. As they finished off their last mouthful of food and took a sip of the sparkling red wine, Carole's mood had also now turned serious, and she was feeling increasingly worried as she noticed that Casey looked like she was about to cry.

"Whatever is it, Case? Tell me...something's wrong, I know it. I know you, come on tell me. Is it Jason?"

Carole reached across the table to touch her friend's hand, urging her to share whatever was worrying her.

Shaking her head, Casey reached into her bag with her free hand and scrabbled around for a tissue. She took another sip from her wine glass before explaining to Carole, her voice now wobbling and sounding as if it would break down at any moment.

"No. It's not Jason. Well, yes and no, but well, I found something wrong with my body, Carole." Casey hesitated before continuing: "It's my right breast actually. I was drying off after my bath and I noticed my reflection in the mirror showing I had a dimple. I've not seen it before and it's very near the nipple. When I pressed it I could feel something a bit weird...well, a bit hard in fact."

Shocked at this unexpected piece of news, Carole's reaction was a bit too loud as her voice exclaimed, "Oh no. Oh, Casey. What are you going to do?" Then lowering her voice slightly, she continued: "I can't believe it! Are you sure? What are you going to do? Oh my goodness, no, it can't be, oh, Case."

Casey's sense of unease and worry was building with every word that came out of Carole's mouth.

"I have no idea what to do, Carole," she said. "What should I do? You work at the hospital; what am I meant to do? Should I see my GP, or just wait and see if it goes on its own?"

Carole's common sense kicked in.

"No, absolutely not! You mustn't leave it and definitely don't ignore it. The best thing to do is to get it checked out, then, if it needs treatment, you've caught it early. I mean, it may be nothing, or it could just be a cyst, but the main thing is to get it checked and if your GP seems unsure, or even tries to fob you off, ask to be referred to the hospital."

Casey nodded, relieved to have been able to share this horrible thing with someone who knew what they were talking about.

"Yes, good idea, I'll make an appointment tomorrow for Monday morning."

Trying to sound calm, Casey actually felt terrified inside as Carole jumped in again: "Tell you what, make it in the afternoon and I can come with you. I'm off myself on Monday afternoon for a dental appointment. Mine's at two o'clock, so if you go for after three o'clock, I can come with you."

Carole was already planning ahead to Monday and wanted to be there for her friend.

"Oh would you, Carole, that'd be great. I know it's daft, but I am really worried and it'd be a big help to have you there."

Casey was relieved that she didn't have to do this alone, so thank goodness for Carole, she really was a true friend.

"That's settled then," Carole said. "Now, let's not worry about it tonight. There's no point worrying about what it might be, when it might also be nothing. So, let's just enjoy our food and have some more wine."

Carole was eager to distract Casey's mind from the worry of what the news might be, so she poured her another glass of wine. As keen as Carole was to push it to the back of her own mind, it was bothering her massively. Feeling concerned not to trigger any further unnecessary worry for Casey, Carole was relieved to see Giovanni walking over to their table with her special dish of seafood risotto and Casey's lasagne.

"Bueno, bon appetite!"

Giovanni smiled as he placed the food in front of the girls and took away the empty bruschetta plates. Knowing the food they had ordered were favourites of the girls, Giovanni had no doubt that they would enjoy their meals. Luckily, he did not notice the slightly sombre mood affecting them, much to Casey's relief.

As Giovanni walked away from their table, the women both breathed in the delicious aromas from their food and announced again how hungry they were before tucking in and enjoying every mouthful. The wine complimented their food and mood perfectly; neither one was a wine connoisseur, but they both enjoyed it.

The evening seemed to have flashed by as they realised it was time to head off home. Both girls were feeling nicely satisfied by the wonderful food as they walked back to Casey's apartment. Carole had previously telephoned in advance for a taxi, which she'd subsequently cancelled, deciding that she would ring for one from Casey's later, just in case her friend needed her to stay longer.

Chapter 10

Doctors Decisions

The weekend went by in a blur, and Casey, who had spent most of it at her laptop, had finished a suitably interesting column, which she had subsequently sent in to Edine, along with a note about her ideas and plans for next week's column. The worry of what the doctor would say had actually made her focus more on her column and she had not even thought about peeking at Matt through the kitchen window. That guilty pleasure had been temporarily forgotten. Also, because Jason had been so quiet since he'd been in New Zealand, Casey had no idea how things were going and just assumed everything must have been going really well for him. At least she hoped it was, then realised that he was already halfway through his visit and would be back the following week.

Monday morning dawned and Casey awoke at her usual time, again silently cursing the radio alarm clock. As she lay in bed listening to Chris Evans and his breakfast crew on the early morning show, her morning brightened and she continued listening to their happy banter for the next fifteen minutes. Whilst not being happy that the weekend was over and that it was Monday again, Casey was keen to book her doctor's appointment. Time was ticking by, so she threw back the duvet to swing her legs over the edge of the bed. Always one to sleep naked, Casey felt the coolness of the early morning air, breeze through her bedroom window and brush across her skin, causing her to shiver slightly. Stepping across the bedroom to pick up her gown, Casey continued into the bathroom. With her auto-pilot engaged, teeth were cleaned, her body showered and hair washed within twenty minutes. Having dressed and applied her make-up, she was finished in plenty of time to make the early morning call to the doctor's surgery before she leaving to go and knock for Tilly.

Luckily the receptionist at the doctor's surgery was in a good mood and said that although it was against their usual appointment booking policy, they did in fact have a cancellation for that very evening, so she offered Casey 4.45pm and wished her a good day.

"Perfect," Casey said. "Thank you very much and you have a good day yourself too."

Casey hung up the phone and quietly prayed that everything would be fine. Even though she felt very scared, she was relieved that the doctor's receptionist had not asked her what it was in connection with, which is what they often did. In fact, she had been ready to say "it's personal" with a defensive tone, but that statement hadn't been necessary. Unbeknown to Casey, the receptionist had herself sensed a tension in Casey's voice and thought better of asking that intrusive question, having become much more understanding of the patient's wishes to keep information to a minimum. This was following her own Mum's recent harrowing experience with the receptionist at her local surgery, who she had constantly complained about as being "nosey".

Unusually for Tilly, she was also ready on time and opened the door immediately as Casey knocked. Feeling a little startled by how quickly Tilly had opened the door, Casey stepped back.

"Wow, were you watching for me through the spy-hole?"

"Morning, Case, and no." Tilly laughed. "I was just putting on my jacket, which is why I was right there when you knocked." Pausing as she searched Casey's face, Tilly could see something was worrying her friend. "Are you alright, Case? You look a bit down. Is everything OK?"

Casey found herself repeating the story from the previous night about how she had found something wrong with her breast. Seeing how shocked Tilly was at her news, only added further concern to Casey's own worries, but then Tilly gripped her arm reassuringly.

"Don't worry, Case, you're bound to be fine. It'll all be fine. It'll just be a cyst or something and we're probably panicking about nothing."

Tilly was trying to be upbeat for Casey's sake, but it was more a sense of denial that came across to Casey. However, she realised her friend was trying to be supportive and thanked her for the positive thinking.

"Yes, you're probably right, Til. Best to keep positive until I know eh?"

Casey sighed slightly.

"Exactly, now come on, we'd best get off. Besides which, I'm dying for a coffee."

Tilly tried to brighten the moment for Casey, which seemed to work as Casey turned on her bright and cheery light-hearted voice. "So, how was the date with Dave then?"

"Oh it was so dreamy, Case. Dave is *such* a nice guy. I really can't believe why we haven't gotten together before now."

"That'll be because you were smitten with that lying, cheating John for so long *and* blinded by the love bug of course!" To which Tilly nodded her acceptance of the truth, with a wry smile. Casey continued.

Anyway, Dave seems like a really decent bloke. I'm glad you guys have hit it off and had a good time. I'm guessing you'll be seeing him again then?"

Casey's question, along with the accompanying chuckle, raised a bigger smile across Tilly's face.

"Oh yes, absolutely; in fact, he's calling me tonight and we're arranging to meet up again on Wednesday evening."

Tilly's voice was full of excitement and anticipation at this new development in her love life. Even after seeing John with Gemma the previous week, thanks to Dave, she was now feeling really positive and strong. This was a much better state of affairs than the battered human being she had been after John had admitted his infidelity. It amazed Tilly how quickly she had moved on from John, when an old adage popped into her head: 'The best way to get over a guy is to find a new one.' Well, even though she'd never quite believed that before, Tilly recognised her own situation was exactly like that. Knowing it was all thanks to Dave for putting the smile back on her face and the spring back in her step. It also helped her recognise that John was obviously *not* her true love and that it had been more of an infatuation rather than real love with him. Well, it had to have been, otherwise how would she have recovered so quickly? That in itself was quite surprising to Tilly, because before he had dumped her, she had been convinced that John was "The One" when she was with him. But of course, his cheating way of ending their relationship had destroyed any respect and desires she had previously felt for him.

The girls laughed and chatted easily as they made their way to the office, stopping briefly on the way to pick up their now usual early morning coffee. Both girls welcomed the warm smell of fresh coffee, which greeted them as they pushed open the door into Trina's. The place was already busy with several of the dozen or so tables taken, but luckily for them the queue was quite a small one, so Casey and Tilly just joined the end of it and continued chatting.

Suddenly, aware of the guy in front of them turning around, they were surprised when he spoke: "I thought I recognised that voice. Good morning, Casey, it's lovely to see you again. How are you?"

Matt was also a regular at Trina's but usually came in a bit later in the day, which would explain why he'd never bumped into Casey before. Startled by this sudden and unexpected encounter, Casey responded on auto-pilot: "Oh hi again, Matt. I'm fine thanks and you?"

Blushing madly, Casey turned to introduce Tilly: "Oh, sorry, this is my friend Tilly. You remember Tilly don't you?"

Feeling her face beginning to get hotter and hotter, Casey hoped Matt wouldn't notice, but he had. The pinkness in Casey's cheeks made Matt appreciate her beauty even more, and he felt flattered to have triggered such a reaction in her.

"Yes, of course. Hello, Tilly, it's nice to see you again. You've certainly put a smile on Dave's face. He's been bouncing off the walls since last week."

Tilly also blushed and grinned at this valuable insight into Dave's thoughts and feelings. "That's nice to know, Matt. Tell him I said hi when you see him, would you?"

"Sure, no problem."

Matt smiled his dazzling smile as he glanced from Tilly back to Casey. Trina asked Matt if he wanted his usual and on hearing her voice, he turned to face the coffee shop owner as he replied: "Ah, sorry, Trina, yes please. Thank you."

When Trina turned away to make the coffee, Matt turned back to Casey. "So how's Jason doing? Have you heard from him yet?"

Casey was surprised by Matt's question.

"Oh, I'm guessing he's doing OK. I've not heard anything from him actually. Well to be honest, I didn't expect to, not really, but he's almost halfway through his visit now, so he'll be back at the end of next week."

Matt immediately picked up on the fact that Casey had not heard from Jason and was himself surprised to hear that.

"So he's not called you then?"

Watching Casey's face carefully, Matt was more than a little bit pleased to hear her response. "Oh no, I wasn't expecting him to," she said. "We broke up before he left. It seemed the best thing to do seeing as he's going to be leaving for good."

Casey wasn't expecting to be having this conversation and found herself feeling a little flustered. Feeling conscious that Matt was her guilty weekend pleasure, and whilst she knew that he was totally unaware of the attentive audience watching him while he was working out, she felt as though he might at any moment be able to read her mind and be totally shocked. Worse still, he might be absolutely horrified and accuse her of voyeurism. Instead, she managed to just smile back at Matt and prayed he wouldn't suddenly turn into something akin to Derren Brown and suss out her guilty secret.

Matt's reaction was spontaneous: "Oh really?" Then he quickly added, 'Well, I guess it's for the best if he's moving out there for good.' Matt was now feeling the same fluster-burn as Casey. Both of them were relieved when Trina broke across their conversation to hand Matt his coffee. Placing the right money into Trina's open hand, Matt thanked her and wished her a good day before turning back to Casey. "Well, it was nice to bump into you again, Casey. I hope we can do it again sometime soon." Then smiling broadly, if not a little cheekily, he wished them both a good day before walking out of the coffee shop.

Tilly almost squealed as she babbled excitedly to Casey: "Oh my, Casey, did you see his face when you told him about Jason? Girl, that boy has definitely got the hots for you!"

"Don't be daft," Casey said. "He was just surprised that's all."

Casey tried to dismiss Tilly's comment, because she dared not hope it was anything more than polite surprise, although she'd also seen a flicker across Matt's face. Nevertheless, something in the pit of her stomach told her otherwise and reacted excitedly at the prospect of Matt being interested in her. *Oh Matt,* the gorgeous and very sexy Matt, whom she had definitely not expected to see in Trina's this morning, but was so very glad that she had.

As the weekend had flashed by in a blur, so the day continued surprisingly quickly and before she knew it, Casey's online calendar flashed up her doctor's appointment reminder. Quickly finishing the email she'd been writing, Casey clicked send and started logging off, whilst packing up her desk. With fraying nerves, but a sense of relief to be getting off to see the doctor, Casey hoped and prayed there would be nothing to worry about.

Tilly had offered to go with Casey to see the doctor, wanting to be there to support her friend and Casey had thanked her, but said not to worry, that she would be fine because Carole was meeting her there. But, as the day progressed, she had needed to take Tilly up on her offer when Carole unexpectedly received a call from a consultant, which meant cancelling her afternoon off. The consultant urgently needed Carole to join them for an important medical procedure, which was due to be performed on a life and death patient, and which had needed to be accelerated to that very same afternoon. Carole felt gutted, but she really needed to be at the hospital, which of course Casey understood and so she reassured Carole that it was fine because Tilly had offered to step in. To make up for letting Casey down, Carole said she would pop round after work with a couple of bottles of wine, to find out what the doctor said and to spend the evening supporting her dearest friend. Furthermore, to say thanks to Tilly for saving the day after her needing to duck out.

Casey and Tilly made good time getting to the surgery, arriving ten minutes early, which was a sure winner for keeping the receptionists happy. Amazingly, her doctor was only running over by ten minutes, so within twenty minutes Casey was sat in front of Dr Dickinson and telling her what she had found. After listening and then examining Casey, the doctor decided it would be best to refer Casey to the Breast Clinic, carefully explaining they would likely want to perform an ultrasound scan, possibly even a mammogram, but telling Casey to try her best not to worry too much, as it could just be a benign cyst, or even a fatty lump. Dr Dickinson did, however, clarify that it was always best to check these things out as soon as possible, in order to get early treatment and the very best results. Therefore, she expected that the Breast Clinic appointment would come through within two weeks.

Despite the doctor's best efforts at keeping Casey calm and explaining everything, she was feeling shell-shocked as she walked back into the waiting area where Tilly was sitting, equally anxious. Tilly could see Casey was visibly shaken and stood up to take her friend's arm as they walked out into the fresh air. As they stepped outside, Casey paused and turned to Tilly, telling her what the doctor had said. Tilly, still trying to be as positive as possible, reminded Casey that it wasn't necessarily bad news and that it could still turn out to be a simple cyst, or a fatty lump or whatever. But either way, it was best to wait until she had seen the doctor at the Breast Clinic before she started panicking and thinking the worst. Of course, although Tilly was saying this, she was hoping against hope that she was comforting Casey rather than scaring her. All the while knowing her words would likely bring little real comfort to Casey, because if it were Tilly, she would worry herself stupid until she'd had the all-clear. Casey was very much in that mind-set too, but dutifully listened to Tilly's words of advice.

As they began their journey back home, Casey felt a little sick at the thought of what might happen and was more than a little emotional, fresh tears were never far away. Thankfully, Carole arrived at Casey's flat about an hour after the girls arrived home, for which Tilly was grateful, thinking two positive heads were better than her one. Meanwhile, Tilly had already made Casey a cup of strong tea and thrown in a slug of whisky for good measure. Hoping and praying that her friend would be OK, Tilly silently wished that this lump, or whatever it was, would turn out to be nothing sinister.

Carole's arrival broke the sombre mood and as she sensibly reminded them, they shouldn't think the worst and that the best thing to do was to open the wine and eat the snacks she had brought, put on some '80s music and dance around the living room to cheer themselves up.

"Good idea, Carole. You're absolutely right, we need to keep positive. So, Casey, you put on the music and I'll go grab the glasses for the wine, while Carole sorts out the nibbles."

Tilly stood up as she took charge and walked towards the kitchen. Casey also stood up and went over to the CD player to drag out some of her favourite albums, feeling so grateful for her lovely friends. Playing an '80s dance album would make them all feel better and help to kick off their impromptu lounge dancing party. Sure enough, several CDs later, three bottles of wine, along with a selection of crisps and dips, cheese and mixed olives, they were soon giggling like a bunch of schoolgirls. The worry from earlier had temporarily dispersed as they boogied their way around the floor, trying not to spill their wine at every bump and grind.

After collapsing into a heap on the sofa for the umpteenth time, all three of them were now extremely tipsy on the wine, mainly due to only having eaten the aforementioned snacks to soak it up. But they all agreed that they felt much happier than they had a few hours earlier, *and* that they would make sure they kept upbeat for Casey. Now known as "The Three Musketeers" their new motto was to "remain positive, no matter how bad it seems". Even in their tipsy state, each girl was silently thinking that actually, the reality was too scary to even contemplate. Whatever happened, they just *had* to remain positive! Carole was in good form.

"So, onwards and upwards," Carole said. "We wait for the breast clinic appointment date and we'll all go together: 'The Three Musketeers'."

Casey said that now they really *had* had too much wine, then realised that suddenly, both Tilly and Carole had gone very serious. Realisation dawned. Casey's friends really *did* mean to support her through this awful experience. Even though none of them yet knew if it was the dreaded BIG C, the thought of it being as serious as that, was so, so, scary! As the evening came to a close, Casey thanked both of her wonderful friends again and said how much she truly appreciated their support.

Falling into her bed that night, Casey wondered if she should tell Amanda as well, but then decided against it. Until she knew what was going on, Casey didn't want to worry Amanda at this early stage, especially since Amanda's own Mum had died from breast cancer only recently. Amanda would know only too well, how awful it was to have this scary thing now happening to her dear friend Casey as well.

Chapter 11

Waiting Time

The rest of that week had been tough on Casey, but she even surprised herself when she decided that actually, she really *did* want to share this experience with her readers. There was no doubt in Casey's mind that there would be many other women going through the same random and scattered emotions that she was feeling right now. Sharing her story could end up being a good way of venting her own fears, whilst also helping others who might be in a similar position. Casey imagined they might then realise that they were not alone in their concerns.

Speaking to Edine about it, Casey was relieved when her Editor said it would certainly bring a different slant to the column. It wasn't a view Edine had previously considered, but in fact, it could engage their readers even further and awaken their realisation that Casey truly was, just like them. Being ever mindful of sales, Edine said it would also encourage readers to keep buying the magazine to see what the next stage was like.

Ever the Editor and having to think about new ideas, Edine valued the support Casey's story might offer to their readers, so she decided to back up Casey's column with an article on the subject of Breast Lumps and the worry of Cancer. The article would include guidance on how to examine your breasts and how important it was to seek help at the earliest opportunity. Edine realised they could easily cover several pages on this subject, so she was happy. It certainly would be a subject that most women would be interested in.

Edine felt for Casey and her bravery proved what an asset to the magazine Casey was going to be. Privately, Edine decided to take steps to retain her as a long-term column writer. Indeed, having been so impressed by Casey, Edine had also decided to give Claire Anderson an extra bonus for finding such a raw, yet worthy talent. Edine was more than happy with how the new column was developing and adding depth to the magazine. The new column would be called, *'From Online to Offline'* and the additional benefits it would bring to her own position, as well as the magazine's financial targets, was already evident to Edine.

Casey decided to keep up with the positive thinking and had already begun to feel the effects, from taking on a lighter approach and attitude. Besides which, focussing on illness generally made you feel worse rather than better. That was something she remembered her Nan saying as she was growing up. If only she were here now to hold Casey's hand through this period of waiting. As she mulled over that thought, Casey could almost hear Nanny Em's voice in her head, offering wise words of support and comfort. A feeling of warmth came over her and she smiled to herself. To Casey, her Nan was always there, in her heart and in her head. As well as in the many gestures and words of advice that Casey had offered to friends and work colleagues over the years, the influence of Nanny Em's wisdom had filtered through in those words and actions.

Picking up the last of the scattered magazines from their coffee area at work, Casey stacked them up neatly and automatically placed the latest copy of *Just for You!* on the top of the pile. Recently, Casey had made sure they had at least one copy of the magazine on the table, hoping to stir enough interest that would encourage her workmates into buying their own copies regularly. Not that Casey needed to worry, they were already amazed at how open and honest she was, saying how refreshing it was to have someone *real* writing about everyday stuff. Even though the girls worked with Casey, they didn't know much about her life outside of work, or all the stories, which had made them laugh, cringe and cry. So their interest was the perfect start for Casey and she was quite happy to share some of her antics and experiences, if it meant so much to her new audience.

Thinking of her original *Online Diary* and how this had all started, Casey's thoughts strayed back to Jason; she felt sure she would have continued to see him, had he not made plans to move away. The open ended questions, wandered through her mind again.

'How long would they have lasted?'

'Was the mutual attraction just because of their amazingly good sex life?'

'Would their special friendship have developed into a deeper relationship?'

Casey suspected for both of them that in the early days, it had been more about the fantastic sex, *but what about now?* These were the questions running through her mind and now she had time to reflect on things without Jason being around and tempting her with his wickedly delicious, sexy body. How did she really feel about him?

Amazingly, she still couldn't answer that final question and instead, diverted her thoughts to what Jason might be thinking or feeling. Knowing how the last few days had been before he left, Casey thought things between them had been pretty intense and not just for her, she was sure it had been the same for Jason too. But was that intensity just the *idea* of no longer having the exciting and raunchy sex that they shared together, or was it something deeper? It was true that in their last days together, Jason had seemed to think it was something more, something special, but Casey wasn't so sure.

'The truth was she didn't want to know that answer, just in case it was that she truly loves him; because the problem then would be that she'd still have to say

150

goodbye to him, once he moved over to New Zealand after his familiarisation visit.'

Besides, if that was actually the real truth and that she really was in love with him, then surely she wouldn't be dwelling on the *if...*would she? Doubts surged through Casey's mind, along with the memories of the last few days they had spent together, which even she had to admit, had been amazing. Casey had certainly enjoyed sharing her body with Jason and had always delighted in the reaction she raised in him as she explored his body with her hands and lips. As her mind drifted into thoughts of Jason's hardness, Casey felt herself growing hot and wondered how long she could live without feeling him inside her, pleasuring her into climactic explosion and delight. Yes, it really did seem to be about the sex.

As a ringing telephone cut across her thoughts, Casey hurriedly pushed away from the chair she had been sitting on and stood up. Feeling a little embarrassed at having such thoughts at work, Casey was thankful that nobody had walked in, whilst she'd been in her dream world of Jason and their sexual pleasures. *Phew!* Although still a little flustered, Casey quickly walked back out to her desk, to finish off her last piece of work for the week and before heading off home to another night out. Fridays were her favourite day of the week; she loved the open ended freedom and fun they always offered, followed by two days of no work and lots of play.

Carole had suggested another night out at Barney's, having found out that there was a great new band playing that evening. Carole told Casey the local gig guide was advertising *The Smooth Movers* as an excellent Motown covers band, whose reputation claimed them to be as close to the real thing as possible. So, feeling in the mood for a good night out, Casey readily agreed that Barney's would be perfect. Also having decided that a night of drinking, live music, loud banter and Carole's company were just what the doctor ordered.

Hurrying back home with Tilly, the two girls were in high spirits. Tilly was meeting Dave again that evening. It seemed Wednesday had been another great night and the two of them were already smitten with each other. Of course, Tilly would normally have joined Casey and Carole for a good night of dancing to a live Motown band, but the temptation of Dave was stronger and she just couldn't wait to see him again. Casey teased her about blowing out her mates, but she was secretly pleased that Tilly seemed to be so happy again.

Back home and now pinning her hair up into a *come to bed with me* kind of style, Casey decided to play one of her Motown albums whilst she was getting herself ready. Flicking through her most played albums, she selected one which started with Marvin Gaye's song, *Let's Get It On* (which was his absolute best song, in Casey's opinion). As the music started playing, Casey thought about how every time she heard it she felt ever so slightly turned on. That song was another guilty pleasure of hers and she always imagined making love with some hot guy as she listened to it.

As the song came to an end, Casey hoped the band would play it tonight and thought she might put in a request if they didn't already have it on their playlist. Pulling on her purple skinny jeans, a silky top and zipping her favourite boots up to the knee, Casey felt good and as she glanced into the mirror, she nodded in approval. *Yep, you look good, girl, you'll do...go get 'em*, she thought. Slipping on her jacket, she sprayed herself lightly with Estee Lauder's *Beautiful,* and wondered who else might be there that she and Carole would know. Stepping out into the night air, Casey imagined that maybe they would meet two completely new guys, who they didn't even know (yet!). As she hurried along the dimly lit roads towards Barney's Bar, Casey's heart and mind were filled with anticipation and excitement. Thoughts of illness and doctors were now banished from her mind and Casey was on a Friday night roll, willing and ready to have some FUN!

The band had just finished off setting-up their gear, as Casey arrived to find Carole was already at the bar, closely guarding a stool for Casey and with two rather large vodka tonics in front of her. Never having been impressed by guys who got drunk before 8pm, then tried to chat her up with crass and trashy chat-up lines, Carole was about to give short shrift to a guy who was trying his hardest to impress her, but who was actually succeeding in hassling her, with the worst chat-up lines she'd heard in ages.

"Hey, your Dad must be a Jeweller, because you've got diamonds in your eyes!"

Swiftly followed by...

"That's a gorgeous dress you're wearing, it'll look great on my bedroom floor!"

Then horror of horrors...

"Are those coming out tonight?"

'Yes boys, we've all heard them and we always groan internally as they get banged out time and time again when you're very drunk. Also, just as a word of advice, they never impress us.'

Actually, the drunken guy trying to impress Carole wasn't bad looking to be fair. But, like Casey, whilst Carole preferred her men to be good looking and with a great sense of humour, they also had to know when to be discreet, and definitely needed to have some sense of decorum in public. The drunken guy was lacking in more than one of those criteria and seemed to have no social filters whatsoever. Carole was never normally one to be rude; in fact, she usually just politely declined the offer of a drink from any guy she didn't particularly fancy. But on this occasion, she was about to berate the unfortunate guy when she spotted Casey and called over to her, hoping the drunken guy would leave of his own accord, which he duly did, having finally realised he was getting nowhere fast. Carole was majorly relieved and just groaned as Casey laughed at her.

"Who's your friend then?" Casey asked. "I take it he was a no goer?"

"Jees no, Case, the guy was so crass, he actually asked me if my boobs were coming out to play. Bloody idiot! If he hadn't of been so drunk I'd of told him what I really thought. I'm so relieved you walked in; what an utterly stupid man."

Carole was spitting feathers at the guy's rudeness and couldn't believe he would say such a thing. They both agreed he was a total jerk.

"Feel better now?"

Casey laughed at Carole's indignation, remembering how she'd also had that line said to her in the past, so she totally understood Carole's need to vent.

"Sorry, ignore me...here, have a drink."

Just as Carole passed Casey the chilled glass of vodka tonic with fresh lime, the band started their sound check, lifting the noise level in Barney's to crazy, as people tried to talk above the band's one-two, one-two. The atmosphere was great though and just what Casey needed. Loads of people had already arrived and like them, Casey couldn't wait for the band to get started. As they waited for the music to start, Carole filled her in on what had happened that day at work; it'd been a bad one, and was why she needed the large vodka and tonic she'd ordered just before Casey arrived.

Now that Carole had shaken off her unwanted admirer, the evening was off to a good start and the two friends began to thoroughly enjoy themselves as several vodka tonics were consumed.When the band stepped up to play at 9pm on the dot, everyone in the bar applauded enthusiastically, as they kicked off the first set with a

Drifters classic, which set the right vibe for the evening and did not disappoint their audience. *They really are very good*, thought Casey, as Carole voiced the same thoughts over the loud music and said they were in for a really good night. Casey nodded her agreement as she sipped on another drink.

The next five songs warmed the crowd even more, with both Carole and Casey joining the many people who were already on their feet and dancing. There was something about Motown that just worked for everyone. No matter how old or young you were, Motown music always seemed to get everyone going. Both girls were on their feet, singing along and dancing to every song the band played. The atmosphere was fantastic and everyone was happy, and the mood was electric.

Whilst the band played and the two friends danced, they hadn't noticed Matt arrive with a couple of women in tow. Dave had taken Tilly out somewhere else that night and finding himself at a loose end, Matt had called Charley to see if she was free. As it turned out, her friend Sarah was already with Charley, but they both liked the sound of joining Matt to see the band, so they accepted and came straight over to his place. Matt was more than happy to escort both Charley and her friend Sarah who, Charley informed him, was a real party girl and who also loved Motown music. It was a perfect arrangement for the evening and Matt was looking forward to seeing and listening to the band. Charley had secretly thought that Sarah would be a good match for Matt and so she had clipped on her invisible cupid wings, hoping the two of them would hit it off, which they did! Sarah was a great laugh and the three of them chatted easily, as they made their way down to Barney's. Charley was delighted and thanked her invisible cupid wings.

As they reached the Bar, Matt stopped and held open the door for the girls. Sarah walked through first, followed by Charley, who felt her friend suddenly nudging her.

"Oh wow, now he's really fit!"

Sarah had spotted a tall, well-built, muscular black guy standing near the bar who had completely grabbed her attention and Charley immediately realised her little cupid plan was not going to work. *Damn!* Charley knew only too well that Sarah had always had a thing for black men, and it had to be said, the guy really was gorgeous. He clearly worked out because his muscular frame was totally impressive to anyone looking at him. Charley noted the immediate chemistry which sparkled between the Idris Elba's lookalike and her friend Sarah. *Well, you've either got it or you haven't* and he sure did have it – in bucket-loads. You could almost touch the chemistry which had over-flowed from *Idris* towards them, immediately capturing Sarah's attention. Indeed, it would seem to have captured her heart too, from the gasp as she'd stopped in her tracks on spotting him. The two of them made eye contact and smiled broadly at each other. Matt was totally unaware of this little scene and pushing forward, he and Charley made their way towards the bar. They'd lost Sarah.

As Matt turned to ask both girls what they were drinking, his eyes scanned for Sarah. Spotting her and the guy she was smiling at, Matt laughed as he heard Charley sigh and grumble something under her breath. Ordering drinks for the three of them, Charley had suggested a white wine spritzer for Sarah, which was her usual tipple and Matt was about to hand over his cash to the barman, when 'Idris Elba' walked over and surprised them by asking if he could buy them all a drink. Having made the connection between Sarah and *Idris*, Matt accepted graciously as *Idris* winked at him, in some form of unwritten man code, which said "help me out here mate".

Matt noted the exchanged looks and smiles between *Idris* and Sarah. You could hardly miss them really as their reactions had been an instant attraction, love-at-first sight moment. Matt was happy for them both. Nothing wrong with a bit of instant attraction he thought, he'd even felt it himself the first time he'd ever met Jason's girlfriend Casey. *Hmmm*, that thought hung in the air and depressed him slightly, Jason's *girlfriend!*

Feeling a little blown away at the obvious instant attraction between *Idris* and Sarah, Charley said as much to Matt, adding that she couldn't believe how lucky Sarah was. Complaining good humouredly, how she'd never had anything like that happen to her and with a guy was so totally gorgeous! Matt laughed and lifted his glass to clink hers as they wished the now absent Sarah good luck with her 'instant attraction' man.

"Well, that's fate for you, Charley."

Just at that point, Casey turned round and saw Matt clinking glasses with the brunette she had seen in his apartment that day. The smile which had been on her face all night, suddenly faded and she felt her stomach drop like a stone. Damn it, she really didn't need to see Matt with a woman because although it seemed slightly ridiculous, she had been secretly hoping he was actually single and that the brunette was nobody special, but it would appear not. It also appeared that they were celebrating something. *Damn, damn and double damn!* Casey turned around before Matt could catch sight of her watching them.

As he glanced over towards the band, Matt noticed Carole and then realised the back of the head facing him was in fact Casey. As his heart soared, he was thankful that his hope to bump into her tonight looked like it was about to come true.

Casey was gutted, then cursed herself for thinking anything could come of her snooping on a neighbour.

Even if he *was* on the other side of the road, in a completely separate apartment block, *and* standing there completely visible, for her (or anyone) to see. As she tried to justify her guilt at watching him, Casey decided that it was Matt's fault for training in his gym in full view of the windows. *I mean, how was a girl supposed to avoid looking?* Especially when he looked sooooo freakin' fit!

Carole had not noticed Casey's expression; she was too busy watching the band and enjoying, *Amadeus*, so it was not surprising that she was totally oblivious to what had just occurred. Although to be fair, most of it was taking place inside Casey's head. Feeling her internal fright or flight mode kick in, Casey excused herself to Carole then pushed way through the crowd towards the ladies' toilets, so she could gather herself together again.

It was a good ten minutes later before Casey re-emerged, freshened up and with her brave face back in place. As she started back across the crowded bar towards Carole, Matt was also making his way towards her and raised his arm slightly to catch her attention. Pretending not to see him, Casey looked away until he was right beside her and talking in that sexy voice of his.

"Hey, Casey, it's good to bump into you again. Great band!"

"What? Oh err, hello, fancy bumping into you again. Yes, they're great. Sorry, can't stop. I've got to get back to my friend Carole. She's over there by the bar. You have a good night though!"

Casey was hot and flustered and a little embarrassed as she brushed off Matt's 'hello' and walked away from him. Trying her hardest to keep a brave face in place, Casey was pretending she didn't care one iota about the brunette he'd just been clinking glasses with.

It was Matt's turn to be gutted; he'd felt sure that Casey was interested in him. Well, she had seemed to at least *like* him when he chatted to her in Trina's Coffee

Shop the other day, but tonight she was almost dismissing him. As he made his way to the gents, Matt tried to fathom out what had happened between Trina's Coffee Shop and tonight, to make Casey cool off so much. Maybe she was just so in love with Jason that she was going to wait for him or worse still, maybe she was seeing someone else now. *No!* He hoped not.

When Matt got back to Charley she asked him if he was OK, having noticed his mood had changed.

"Sure, I'm fine thanks. Actually I just bumped into someone I met recently, she's dating Jason. Do you remember him, the smooth operator from Uni?"

Jason had gained a reputation with the ladies when he'd been at University.

"What? Jason? Sure I do. It's a small world eh? Didn't you say he'd landed an amazing job offer in New Zealand recently?"

Unbeknown to Matt, Charley still harboured a crush she'd had on Jason since Uni, but had never followed it through because Jason, Dave and Matt were such good mates. Even now, she was *always* interested to hear any news about the gorgeous Jason, the unknown owner of her unrequited teenage love.

The band started playing their next song, which was a particularly loud number, causing Matt and Charley's conversation to break off. As they listened to the song, Charley joined in, singing along with the people around her, who were also swaying to the music, which gave Matt a chance to watch Casey, whom he might add, looked amazing. Casey was everything he wanted in a woman; sexy, intelligent and beautiful, with a gorgeous smile. Matt was really gutted that she'd brushed him off so lightly.

As the band finished the song, the bar erupted into applause once again and Matt watched as Casey and Carole joined in.

Charley nudged Matt. "They're great aren't they?"

"What? Oh yeah, real good. Sorry, Charley, I'm a bit distracted."

Matt and Charley had always been close and he really wanted to tell her about Casey.

"Come on, what's bugging you, Cuz? I know when there's something playing on your mind. What is it?"

Charley nudged at his arm, her words giving him the opening he needed.

"It's Casey."

"Who's Casey?"

"The girl I just told you about: Jason's girlfriend. We met a few weeks ago and have bumped into each other a few times since then. She's, well she's totally amazing, Charley!"

That was it...it was out there and he had finally admitted to someone that he really and truly liked Casey. A hell of a lot!

"Wow, you dark horse, Matty boy, you've never said anything about Casey before. Crikey, I'd even tried to match-make you with Sarah tonight. Just as well she's been bowled over by old *Idris* over there!"

Charley grinned and nudged Matt again. In fact, Sarah and *Idris* were very much enjoying living in their own little cocoon, both of them ignoring the rest of the crowd, whilst they enjoyed the band and each other's company. It really had been an instant attraction for them both. Matt laughed at Charley's admission.

"Really? Did you? I didn't even realise."

Charley laughed back at him. "Well no wonder you didn't realise if you've got the hots for someone else, Cuz. So, come on, which one is she?"

Charley was scanning the bar trying to suss out who had captured Matt's attention so absolutely. As Matt glanced over towards Casey, she was also now facing towards the bar-tender. Charley followed Matt's gaze and could see why her cousin was smitten; he was right, Casey was pretty gorgeous.

"So, why the long face, Matt? Why don't you go over and talk to her? I mean Jason is leaving right? Presumably she's not going with him, so go for it, what have you got to lose?"

"I tried, but she kind of brushed me off."

Matt looked so dejected that as those words left his lips, Charley wanted to hug him, but thought better of it and instead tried to make him feel better, by suggesting an alternative reason for Casey's earlier reaction towards him.

"Oh right, well maybe it's just a bit too soon and she's not ready yet. It doesn't mean she won't change her mind."

"Or maybe she was really in love with Jason, in which case it could take months for her to get over him. That's if she doesn't miss him so much that she chases after him."

Matt hoped he was wrong as Charley also prayed the latter was not the case. She, however, could easily love Jason and given half the chance, would jump at the opportunity of following him across the other side of the world. Matt's gutted voice was raised just enough for Charley to make out what he was saying.

"No, I don't think it's that, loving Jason I mean. It can't be because we've bumped into each other a couple of times now and each time it felt like there was a real spark between us. But now I don't know."

Seeing Matt so dejected and with alcohol now influencing Charley's bravery, she grabbed his arm. "So don't give up, Matty boy. If you *want* her, go and talk to her and find out how the land lies."

"I don't want to blow it, Charley. I really like her."

Matt sounded almost desperate and Charley felt his pain.

"So, tell me what happened earlier then."

161

Needing to understand as much as possible, Charley questioned him as Matt explained the conversation he'd exchanged with Casey, then reiterating what had happened when they'd met on previous occasions. To Charley it stood out a mile.

"Right, so, Matt, my man, think about it; what is the difference between all of those occasions and tonight?"

Matt shook his head, "I dunno, Charley." He looked totally gutted.

"Jees, men! It's a wonder you guys ever hook up and keep a girl. Durrrr...it's *me* isn't it, and I'll bet you any money you like, that *she* thinks you're with *me*."

"You?" Matt looked perplexed.

"Yes, dimwit, she doesn't know I'm your cousin does she? I bet she thinks I'm your girlfriend!" Charley watched with slight amusement as Matt's face changed and the penny dropped.

"Oh blimey, that didn't even occur to me. Of course she doesn't know you. Wow, what an idiot I am. Well, that might explain her giving me the cold shoulder." Matt breathed a sigh of relief, but then doubt crept in again. "But what if it isn't that and she really isn't interested in me?"

Matt's brow furrowed as the latter thought penetrated his brain. Realising he needed to go and speak to Casey to find out, he decided that needed to be right now, and while he had the chance and felt brave enough to do so. It definitely couldn't be left like this; she could be thinking all sorts of wrong things, so he absolutely couldn't let her go home thinking Charley was his girlfriend. Luckily, Charley was one step ahead of him.

"Go on, cousin of mine, get your ass over there and explain who I am. In fact, no, let's both go and I'll introduce myself as your cousin, and that way it won't look so obvious, like you're chasing her or anything."

Charley laughed and playfully punched his arm, as Matt laughed as well. "Charley, you're a life-saver, that's brilliant, thank you! I could hug you, you're totally amazing."

Charley preened at such high praise from her cousin. "Best not hug me yet, Cuz, not until she knows I'm not your girlfriend anyway, eh."

Charley winked at him and Matt laughed again, thinking Charley was so brilliant. Picking up her drink, Charley winked at Matt. "Come on then, Romeo. Take me to your woman."

Matt laughed and feeling cheered, he turned around to walk over towards Casey. As he reached the two friends, Carole noticed him first and spoke with surprise in her voice: "Oh hello again, Matt. Fancy meeting you here." Then as she spotted Charley, Carole raised her eyebrows in an enquiring manner. "Is this your girlfriend?"

Casey's heart sank as Charley stepped forward and smiling widely, offered her hand.

"Hi and no, not his girlfriend. I'm actually his cousin. Our mum's are sisters. I'm Charley by the way and it's nice to finally meet some of Matt's friends."

Charley smiled warmly at them both as she shook their hands in turn. Carole was the first to react: "Oh hi, Charley, it's nice to meet you too. This is Casey."

As Casey turned to face this mystery woman of Matt's, Charley noticed Casey's face was a picture and she could tell that she was processing what she'd just heard. The stunned relief at hearing this woman in front of her was in fact Matt's cousin, and not his girlfriend, was written all over Casey's face. Carole nudged her back into reality and Casey smiled back.

"Sorry, where are my manners? Hi, Charley, it's nice to meet you, I thought you were..." her voice trailed off as the music picked up tempo again.

Charley had been right of course and winked at Matt as he smiled at Casey then asked if he and Charley could join them.

"Sure, the more the merrier."

Casey's mood suddenly lifted and she visibly blossomed as she smiled back at Matt and Charley.

"The band is really great, aren't they?"

They all nodded in agreement as the next song started. Feeling relieved at not having to make conversation right at that moment, Casey re-processed what she had just heard. *So, he really is single! Wow.* She was chuffed to bits at that little gem of information. Absent-mindedly she joined in with the smooth swaying dance moves they'd all adopted, as the music captured them all in its Motown magic. The band announced their next song as the wonderful Marvin Gaye classic, *Let's get it on.* Casey's knees buckled slightly, *oh goodness, that* song and Matt was standing so close to her, she felt her chest tighten as she drew in a breath.

Matt suddenly added, "Oh great song, let's hope they do it justice. I'm sure they will based on what we've heard so far."

Casey looked at Matt and he grinned back at her.

"Good choice eh, Casey?"

Casey's heart skipped a beat. "Err, yeah, great choice. I love this one."

As that familiar feeling stirred again in the pit of her stomach, Casey felt flustered. Matt had moved closer to Casey to allow someone to get to the bar. His very closeness, the smell of his aftershave and the accidental brush of his arm against her breast, had doubled the effect of the song on Casey. Wow, he smelt so good, he looked so good and she was instantly drunk on the happiness of the moment, as her passion began to rise.

They were all moving to the music of this sexy, wanting song and Casey had to try very hard not to just stare at

Matt. As she sneaked a glance at him, he smiled back at her and reached out his hand towards her. Taking it willingly, Casey's heart quickened pace and Matt pulled her towards him gently. The two of them danced with each other in perfect harmony, their hips and thighs gyrating gently to the rhythm of the music. Casey was lost in desire, the music, the closeness of Matt and her wanting passion, she felt like she was the only desirable woman in the world and this gorgeous man wanted her for his very own. Little did Matt know, but she was willing to give herself to him right there and then, completely and utterly. Such was the effect of his closeness and the song, both creating an all-consuming passion in that very moment.

As the song came to a close, Charley and Carole were still facing towards the band, having been oblivious to what had been going on behind them. Casey and Matt gently pulled away from each other and Matt lifted Casey's hand to his mouth, kissing her fingers, he gently whispered, "Thank you."

Casey was elated and with her heart racing, she wanted this man badly and desperately needed to feel his kisses on her lips and his arms wrap around her. Imagining how his fingers could trace every contour of her naked body, turning her on with his every touch, before entering her with a hardness that moved rhythmically and totally in tune with her. Passion and wanting was once again consuming Casey and she felt like she was out of control, yet knew that she needed to stay firmly *in* control; this *was* a public place after all.

Casey stepped back away from Matt, smiled and then leant forward to lightly brush his lips with hers. It was a spontaneous gesture, but they both felt the electricity between them and as Casey stepped back from that light kiss, they each stared into each other's eyes, searching for more.

Carole and Charley turned around asking whose round it was next. Matt said that it was his, and then turned to order drinks for them all. The moment of passion interrupted, but had left both Casey and Matt very hot under the collar, each of them smiling broadly on the inside.

As the band announced the next song was to be their last, despite the groans of disappointment from the crowd, they also received thunderous applause. It had been a brilliant night at Barney's and nobody wanted it to end, least of all Casey and Matt. As the band finished their final song and the last drinks were downed, Matt asked Casey if he could walk her home.

Casey nodded. "That'd be lovely, Matt, thanks."

Charley was catching a taxi with Sarah, and once she'd peeled her away from *Idris,* she asked Carole if she'd like to share it, seeing as they were all headed off in the same direction.

"Sure that'd be great. Thanks, Charley, although Sarah might not want to come with us."

Both of them laughed at Carole's comment, because it sure did look like Sarah might want to spend the whole night with her very own *Idris Elba.*

Knowing that for her, the night needed to continue, Casey hoped Matt felt the same way. Matt did of course, but he also had no idea where the night would end. A passionate kiss as he said goodnight to Casey was as much as he allowed himself to hope for.

As they all stepped out into the cool night air and kissed each other goodbye, Charley hugged Matt, whispering "good luck" in his ear and saying how lovely it had been meeting Casey and Carole, then flagged down a taxi and left Casey and Matt to walk home together.

Matt offered Casey his arm, and as she linked hers through his, they slowly made their way back, talking about how great the night had been and how funny it was that Casey had thought Charley was his girlfriend. Matt was on cloud nine and he didn't care who knew; he was totally besotted with Casey and wanted her to be his. His girlfriend. His lover. Just his. He was definitely smitten.

The ongoing coolness of the night air sobered the two of them up enough, that by the time they reached Casey's apartment block, they were only drunk on their chemistry and the passion developing between them. Each of them secretly wanted to explore the other's lips, as well as their thoughts and bodies. Instead, Matt decided he didn't want to blow his chances by coming on too strong and so he asked Casey if he could kiss her, and nodding, she replied a barely audible, "Yes."

Trying desperately to control her breathing, which had deepened as Matt leaned towards her, Casey accepted and returned his kiss, delighting at how surprisingly soft his lips were as they touched hers. Both Casey and Matt felt a tingling sensation sweep up their spines, as their lips met and as he moved away from them, Matt held Casey to him closely and murmured into her hair. "Oh, Casey, you are so beautiful."

Pulling away again gently, he held her head with one hand, tipping her face towards his and lightly brushed her lips again before speaking, his voice now husky with desire. "Goodnight, Casey. You sleep well and I'll see you tomorrow at eleven for that coffee."

Casey nodded and smiling broadly, she responded, her own voice also slightly husky with a similar desire. "Yes, see you outside at eleven then, Matt. It's been a great night. I'm so glad you came."

"Me too," he said. "Sweet dreams, Casey."

Matt smiled and turned to walk across the road as Casey let herself into her apartment building. Feeling surprised and really happy that Matt had been brave enough to ask her if she'd like to go for a coffee the following morning, Casey felt a warm glow inside her.

Matt had suggested they go for a walk in the park first, before sharing coffee and pastries together, at that great little coffee shop over the other side of the park. Both of them were secretly harbouring a romantic notion of strolling through the grounds, wrapped up against the cold, whilst laughing easily together. Casey had only needed to think about it for a nano-second before agreeing. After all, it was Saturday and as they were both free, there was no reason not to. Well, technically Casey wasn't entirely free because she had her column to write, but she decided that an invitation for coffee with Matt was just too good an offer to turn down, so she graciously accepted, saying she'd be ready and waiting at eleven, warm coat and scarf at the ready.

Chapter 12

A Tale of Two Men

Jason was having such an amazing time and was feeling incredibly lucky to have seen so many wonderful sights in New Zealand. Not only that, but his new colleagues were really friendly and welcomed him into the fold willingly, without any need for persuasion from the boss. The whole team had enjoyed taking it in turns to entertain Jason, ensuring he left Auckland with a good impression, as well as the desire to return for the two-year fixed contract he'd been offered. In fact Jason's last day with them all, had been totally amazing and the only thing he had wanted to change, was for Casey to have been there too.

Still hoping he would be able to persuade Casey to come back with him was Jason's biggest desire, next to the job itself. With just two more hours left until he was due to return home, he was very much looking forward to getting back to the UK. Even though he and Casey had agreed to end their relationship, Jason was determined to re-kindle it and persuade her to come back with him. The confidence he felt in that he could achieve that goal was based on their last few days together, before Jason had flown to Auckland and subsequently having convinced himself that Casey had strong feelings for him too. To help him in his quest to persuade Casey to change her mind, Jason had taken loads of pictures of his new team, the city, his new apartment, the boats and some of the sights he had seen. Including some video footage of the Maori Haka and the amazing bubbling mud pools of Rotorua, which had been fascinating to see, despite the smell of sulphur, which was somewhat less desirable.

Jason had even chosen a very precious gift for Casey. It was a beautiful Paua shell necklace, which he knew would perfectly compliment a dress he'd seen her wear, one she had worn when they'd gone out for dinner with some friends a few weeks before. Knowing her penchant for matching outfits with jewellery, Jason hoped Casey would love his gift.

It was quite remarkable how in the few days he'd been away, Jason had totally convinced himself that changing Casey's mind was going to be possible, albeit not easy. Nowhere *near* easy in fact, but he thought it would definitely be possible and that is what Jason had lived and breathed, since he'd first arrived in Auckland and spent the day with Lee and Becca on their boat. After seeing how happy his boss and Becca were together, Jason was convinced that he and Casey could achieve the same happiness. The sunshine and general atmosphere of New Zealand and its people had influenced Jason's hopes and dreams for the future, whilst also completely changing his thinking and feelings on the subject of Casey. Having mentally moved from the pure pleasure of a sexual attraction, to something akin to a serious and committed relationship, all Jason had to do now was to convince Casey. With that thought, he closed his eyes and the plane took off from Singapore, on its second leg of the journey home.

Meanwhile, Matt was thrilled at the prospect of seeing Casey again in the morning and as he slipped in between the clean sheets of his king-size bed, lying in the darkness with his eyes closed, Matt remembered every moment of the evening. First spotting Casey in the bar, her brush-off and his thoughtlessness at what she might be thinking, then Charley's brilliant rescue, which had led to some seriously sensual dancing with Casey. Matt loved her dazzling smile, in fact her very being was stirring strong passions within him, which was a sensation Matt had not felt in a long while. He was totally enthralled by Casey's beauty, her laughter, her smile and the good sense she spoke. She was perfect for him and Matt longed to hold her close to him and make slow, passionate love to her, all night.

Daring to imagine her laying in the bed next him, Matt's body reminded him of his wanting for Casey as he thought about what it would be like to caress her and to brush her nipples with his lips. He imagined kissing every inch of her beautiful body, using his fingertips to gently explore every other part of her beauty. Matt's mind was in overdrive; his senses were running riot as he imagined encouraging her sweetness until she reached that perfect climax, her body clenching his hardness with every pulse of his own exploding passion.

It was clear that Matt was totally smitten with Casey and for him there was no going back, he could only think forwards. In fact, *onwards and upwards* was what actually crossed his mind and he smiled at the sexual connotation as his hand reached for his hardness. With Casey's smile on his mind and the fantasy of making love to her, he reached that magical point. Blissful sleep followed and Matt's face was a happy one as he allowed that night-time activity to take over his body.

Now in the same time zone, Jason's plane landed on schedule and once again he was treated to the delights of upgraded travel and being transported through the airport without needing to wait for luggage. Despite the luxury of having a lie-flat bed so he could sleep during the flight, Jason had actually been too excited to sleep for the whole journey and was now feeling nervous at what Casey would say when he called round to see her on his return. Imagining that she would probably be busy writing her column for Edine, Jason wondered what Casey had been doing during the time he'd been away. So many times he'd wanted to call her, but had held back, knowing that she had been the one to suggest that it was best for them both, if they didn't see each other when he got back. The last thing he wanted to do whilst he was away was to upset or annoy her before he had even had a chance to see her again, face to face. One thing Jason was certain of was that he needed to kiss her soft lips again and to feel her in his arms. He groaned in anticipation, causing his driver to ask if he was OK.

"What, oh, err, yes, fine thanks, Anton (the driver had introduced himself as Anton James). I was just thinking of several things I need to do when I get back."

Jason bluffed his way out of that one nicely.

"No peace for the wicked, Sir."

The driver was good humoured and pleasant and normally Jason would have joined in with his small talk enthusiastically; however, on this occasion, he wanted to be alone in his thoughts of Casey, wondering how he could persuade her to move out to Auckland with him. With that in mind, Jason found a way to excuse himself from any further conversation.

"Yeah, I'm shattered though, Anton, so I think I'll just take advantage of being able to sleep until we get back to mine, if you don't mind?"

Luckily the driver was used to his clients needing sleep and reassured Jason it was fine, saying he'd wake him five minutes before they were due to arrive. Jason thanked Anton James and lay back against the seat with his eyes closed, not to sleep, just to think privately about Casey.

Matt had woken early, too excited to sleep in, so he decided to do an hours workout to calm himself down. It was ridiculous; he felt like he was a love-struck teenager again. It had taken him completely by surprise at how much Casey had affected him. Last night's thoughts of making love to Casey were burned into Matt's memory and he felt like a rampant stag, in need of sowing his seed, but cautious of the danger around him. Of course there was no real danger as such, it was just that Matt didn't want to mess things up with Casey. It was so important to him to do this right because he truly felt like they had a special connection and that this was going to be a long-term deal for them both. Matt hoped and prayed that Casey would feel the same way about him.

Having already warmed up and now reaching for his free weights, Matt took up the stance and started with a few arm curls before he did his usual dips and free-lifting reps. Proud of his developed body, Matt glanced towards the huge mirror in front of him and stood staring at his muscular, toned physique that he was just aching for Casey to touch and caress. Yes, and to love.

As Matt showered and shaved, he wondered what Casey was thinking and if she felt anything like he did this morning. He had never known himself to feel so nervous, or was it just apprehension at what the day might bring? Either way, he knew he hadn't felt like this in years, if ever, but it sure felt good...kind of wonderful in fact. Checking the clock, Matt realised he was right on time and would be ready and waiting for Casey outside her apartment building at eleven sharp. The sun was shining, which filled him with promise and hope for the enjoyable walk in the park he had planned with Casey. Pulling on a warm jacket over his thin long-sleeved, V-neck top, Matt felt good and remembering how much Casey had liked his after-shave the night before, he'd splashed some on after his shower, keen to make the best impression.

Stepping out into the glorious autumnal sunshine, Matt looked up to where he thought Casey's apartment might be and wondered if she was ready and already walking downstairs. Right on cue, the big front door opened and Casey stepped out. Matt was pleased to see that she had taken notice of his suggestion, to wrap up against the chill of the cool morning breeze. Casey looked great, dressed in her navy jacket, with the contrasting red scarf and beret, which he thought finished off her look with style and panache. The two of them stopped in their tracks and smiled at each other, then kissed each other on both cheeks. It just seemed appropriate for that moment to not kiss on the lips.

"Ready?" Matt asked.

"Yes, let's go," Casey said.

Matt's heart pace quickened slightly as Casey sub-consciously smiled her happiest and most gorgeous smile at him. The two of them linked arms and strolled down the street towards the park entrance, which was two streets down and around a corner, just a short ten-minute walk away. Priory Park was massive and had a man-made lake in the middle, which also had a delightful old wooden footbridge crossing it. When you got to the other side, you could follow the pathway along a pretty walkway which was lined with roses and which also led to an impressive fountain. This was the centre point of the park and where the four main pathways crossed. Over the years, many people had used the fountain as a wishing well, flinging their small coins into the middle as they made their wishes. The Council had positioned mesh just below the water's surface, which allowed the coins to fall through, but prevented hands from dipping in to retrieve them. The coins were collected on a regular basis and donated to the local hospice, which also held a special place in Casey's heart, being where Amanda's own Mum had spent her last precious days, attentively cared for by the wonderful staff there.

As they stood in the sunshine ready to throw their coins into the pool, Matt spoke first: "Go on and make a wish, Casey."

Casey's thoughts turned to Amanda's Mum and her own worrying situation, so her wish was going to be for the lump to be anything except cancer. In fact, she asked for it to just be a fatty lump that the doctors could easily remove without any lasting effects.

"What will you wish for?" Matt was wondering what it was that would make Casey happy, but prevented her from revealing it. "No, actually, don't tell me or it won't come true."

As he laughed, Casey just grinned back at him, relieved that he didn't press her for an answer.

"OK, I won't tell you because I really do want it to come true."

As she closed her eyes, Casey made her wish and then threw the coin into the middle of the pool. It landed safely under the fountain water and away from prying eyes, primed to ensure her wish came true. Matt threw his coin close to where Casey's had entered the water and as it splashed through the surface and quickly sank, he made his wish for Casey to fall in love with him and then turned to face her. As they grinned at each other like excited little kids, saying they couldn't possibly tell the other one what they had wished for, they glanced back to where their coins had fallen and both crossed their fingers. Turning her face back away from the water, Casey raised her eyes to look into Matt's as she wondered what he wished for, and then suggested they walk on.

"How about that coffee then?" Casey asked.

Matt replied enthusiastically and was as happy as anyone in love could be, keen to do whatever Casey wanted. "Sure, let's head over to Darcy's now and taste some of her gorgeous pastries."

Strolling through the park in the sunshine, the two of them found themselves now holding hands. Each of them loving every moment of being together, they found themselves laughing and sharing stories, finding out lots of details about each other's lives. Neither of them felt like they could have been any happier than they were at that very moment. It was the start of a journey which they were both ready for and wanted to take, equally.

As Casey looked up into Matt's eyes, they appeared so blue that she remarked on how unusual it was to have brown hair and blue eyes. Matt laughed and agreed, saying he thought it linked back to a distant relative. Apparently, his folks were both blue-eyed blondes, but his great-great grandfather had married an African lady. So he thought it must be from his great-great grandmother that he'd inherited his skin-tone and eye colour, which why he seemed to tan just by looking at the sun.

Ah, thought Casey, so that explained why his skin was a gorgeously tanned colour all year round, which made his blue eyes seem even more striking. Casey was as completely smitten with Matt as he was with her. He was gorgeous and seemed so thoughtful and kind. Listening intently as he relayed stories of his family and shared some of his hopes and dreams for the future, Casey didn't want the day to end.

As Matt spoke of his family, Casey's thoughts drifted to her own dear Nanny Em, whom she knew would definitely have approved of this young man. Matt was like your reliable boy-next-door, only far sexier and of course, *very* handsome. The two of them felt so happy being together that they totally relaxed in each other's company and chatted easily.

The morning had drifted into mid-afternoon and as they finished their coffees and pastries, they decided to stroll back through the park, still laughing and chatting as they walked hand in hand, stopping every now and then to look at something or to share a kiss.

The sun was starting to lose its brightness as the afternoon wore on and by the time they reached their road, it was almost gone. Although it was not yet dark, the day had seen the best of the sunshine and was moving into the period just before the evening dusk. As they turned into their street, Casey looked along the road and could see a familiar car parked outside her apartment block. Was that? No, it couldn't be...surely not? But it was. *OMG!* Casey couldn't believe it. Jason was back and he was obviously waiting for her.

Casey and Matt were still walking hand in hand when Jason got out of his car, full of hope for his New Zealand dream of Casey flying back there with him. Turning to walk around the back of his car, Jason's hopes and dreams were shattered in seconds when he saw the happy couple walking down the road towards him. His beloved Casey was holding hands with some guy. No, wait, that was...surely not, no, not his old mate, *Matt! Bloody hell! What on earth?* Confused thoughts raced through Jason's mind.

"Oh no...Jason," Casey said out loud.

"What did you say, Case? Jason?"

Matt followed Casey's gaze and his heart sank as he let go of her hand, feeling as shocked and surprised as she was. Neither of them had expected to see Jason today of all days. After all, he'd only landed that morning. It didn't seem possible that he was now stood there watching them as they approached. Jason's face was one of gutted realisation. Matt didn't know what to say and felt really bad because Jason was an old Uni mate, but then he reminded himself that Jason had been the one to leave. Jason had been the one to go away, and as far as Matt knew, Jason and Casey's relationship was over. Matt had assumed that much because Casey hadn't mentioned that she was still with him.

A bitter edge crept into Jason's clipped voice. "So, whilst the cat's away the mice will play eh...what's going on? Matt? Casey?"

Casey had never felt so uncomfortable in her life: "Hello, Jase," she replied nervously. "I'm surprised to see you here...when did you get back?"

Knowing full well it had been that morning, Casey had completely forgotten, following all the excitement of being with Matt. The fact was that Jason had been the very last person on her mind that morning; instead, she'd fought with the butterflies that had seemed to have taken up permanent residence whenever it came to Matt.

"I came straight from the airport; well, home first for the car of course and then here, but I can see you've already moved on."

Jason was beginning to sound angry, but it was gutted frustration that was actually overwhelming him right at that moment.

"Jase, we said we were over and it's not like that. Matt and I only just met up this morning. We bumped into each other at Barney's last night."

Casey didn't know why she felt the need to explain, but knowing the two of them had been holding hands when Jason saw them, an explanation seemed to be in order, as she didn't want Jason thinking she was boyfriend hopping. It was true that it had been a coincidence that she had met Matt again, albeit one she was very happy to have happened. While she *had* just been holding Matt's hand when they had come face to face with Jason, they had exchanged kisses on more than one occasion. Although Jason had only witnessed the hand-holding, and not the kisses.

Matt added: "Casey's right, Jase, we just bumped into each other last night and I asked Casey to go for a walk and coffee this morning..."

Matt wasn't about to leave Casey to face Jason alone, but he also didn't want to lose a long friendship in Jason. Yet he also recognised his naivety and cursed himself silently: *Don't be stupid, Matt, of course Jason would be upset you're dating Casey, even if he and Casey were over.* Matt continued: "Well, you'd already gone, Jase. I'm sorry, mate, but I thought what with you leaving, that you guys were over, and well, she's an amazing woman, Jase. We met up by accident a few times while you were away, it was pure chance, nothing was pre-planned and then last night at Barney's we bumped into each other again and well, we just clicked…"

Jason was backing off to his car and walking around it, wrenching open the driver's door, he called out to both Matt and Casey: "Well, it looks like you're very comfortable there, mate. Great!" he said sarcastically. "Thanks a lot, Case. I thought we had something special going on. How stupid of me to think that I could come here and talk you into coming back to New Zealand with me."

Jason's face was masked with distaste and contempt, as well as a deep-seated sadness. Casey looked shocked. She too had thought that something had developed between them in the last few days before Jason left. But he was going away and now, well, now Matt was here and he *was* her guilty weekend pleasure and she had *so* enjoyed that morning with him. Casey definitely wanted to see Matt again. Besides which, Jason was leaving for the other side of the world! It was Casey's turn to feel frustrated by events and what Jason had said.

"But, Jase, you already know I can't go. I don't want to leave this place, my friends, my job and now the magazine. Bloody hell, Jase, I don't *want* to leave England. You *know* that!"

Casey had wanted to add Matt to that list, but knew it would be rubbing Jason's nose in it, so she left that part out. Matt took her hand again and squeezed it, relieved to hear that there was no way Casey was leaving, even though he realised in those few moments that his friendship with Jason was badly damaged, if not totally destroyed. Matt lifted Casey's hand to his lips and gently kissed her fingers before letting it go and turning to face Jason. As he stepped forward Matt talked quietly across the car roof to Jason.

"She's incredible, Jase. I can't help myself. I think I'm falling in love with her and I know that's not what you want to hear and I know it sounds crazy to be saying this so soon after meeting her, but it's like a love at first sight thing. I can't walk away. I'm sorry mate, I didn't mean for this to happen."

Matt was strong, but he felt like he'd let his mate down badly and for that he felt gutted. But he really *was* falling for Casey and there was no way he was walking away from her, not now, not ever! Not if he had anything to do with it anyway.

Casey just looked at the two men, stunned at the fact they both wanted her so much that they were likely to lose each other's friendship because of her. This was not what she wanted, or could have even imagined would happen. Whoever could have predicted it would, knowing Jason had gone? This whole thing with Matt had hit her like a bolt out of the blue, and this little scene was certainly not what she would have ever expected to happen.

Just at that moment, Tilly appeared at the front door; she was on her way to see Dave.

"Oh hi, Case. Errr, oh crap, Jason? Matt? What's going on?"

Casey turned to Tilly and shook her head as if to say, 'don't say anything more', then in a slightly strained voice she spoke to her friend: "Leave it, Till, I'll see you later. You have a good time with Dave and I'll catch you tomorrow."

Casey's words were enough for Tilly to take the hint. "Righto, Case. Well, see ya tomorrow then. Errr, see ya later, guys."

This comment was thrown generally in the direction of the two men, who were not really listening to Tilly. Instead, they were like a pair of stags in a stand-off. Jason realised he was not going to win this one, so he just retorted sarcastically: "Whatever, Matt. See ya later, Case."

Then slipping back into the driving seat, Jason started up and revved the engine just a little more than was needed, but he didn't care, he just needed to get away from this whole mess and quickly. As he pulled away and sped off down the road, Jason left a bewildered Casey and his mate Matt watching the car as it disappeared around the corner, tyres screeching in protest.

Tilly was already walking down the road and luckily was far enough away from the two of them not to hear Matt's words as he turned to Casey and took her in his arms. Hugging her tightly, he said, "I'm so sorry, Casey. I just didn't expect this to happen."

"No, me either."

Casey's voice had lost its sparkle and as Matt held her away from him again, he looked into her eyes; she looked so terribly sad that Matt wondered if things with Jason really were over for her, or if she was just fooling herself.

"I think I'll just go upstairs now and maybe see you tomorrow if you're around?" she said softly.

Matt was gutted as those words came from Casey's lips; the fun and pleasure of the last few hours had been blown apart by the last ten minutes with Jason. *Bloody Jason! Why did he have to come back, today of all days?*

Matt wanted to curse, but managed to hold his cool as he replied: "Sure, of course, Casey, I totally understand. I'll pop over tomorrow around midday and see how you're doing."

With that, Matt kissed Casey's cheek and turned to cross over the road. As Casey watched him walk away, she felt sad for Matt as well as for Jason. What a complete mess this had gotten them all into. With a slightly heavy heart, Casey turned and walked up the steps to the front door, sliding her key into the old lock, she pushed open the big door. As the warmth of the entrance hall welcomed her, Casey closed the door again and then wept uncontrollably. Casey struggled to know whether they were tears of sadness for Jason, or for Matt, because of the way their time together had just ended. She wondered how Matt must be feeling right now about Jason, who was also his mate, as well as about her, his *what? Girlfriend?* No, it was too early to think that way. Feeling emotional and not wanting to speak to anyone, Casey ran upstairs. Letting herself into her apartment, she flung her bag down and walked through to her bedroom then collapsed onto the bed. Crying out all the tears that she'd been storing up at losing Jason and him leaving for New Zealand at such short notice, she also cried with sad frustration at how this unexpected encounter had messed up the start of something special with Matt.

In spite of her feelings for Jason, Casey was drawn to Matt, yet she also felt like an emotional wreck right now. Doubts crept into her mind as she worried about what both men thought of her right now. Not that any of what had happened was wrong; after all, she and Jason *had* agreed to end things, which was why it wasn't necessary for her to worry so much. Casey knew now that she and Jason were definitely over. Not that she hadn't already made that perfectly clear, before he left for his familiarisation trip. So actually, there was no reason why she shouldn't have accepted Matt's offer of a date and certainly no reason for her to be feeling this guilty about it. But she couldn't help herself; she did feel guilty and she couldn't explain why she did, just that she did and that it made her feel incredibly sad.

After what seemed like hours of crying, Casey got up from her bed and went into the bathroom to splash her face with water and take off the remainder of her already running mascara. Staring at her reflection, Casey sarcastically thought, *how attractive*, as her running mascara had turned her into a panda lookalike, with big black puffy eyes and a white face.

Making herself a big cup of coffee, Casey added a dash of Morgan's Spiced Rum to it, as she needed a pick-me-up and Jason's rum was all she had to hand, which would also work with her coffee. Sitting down on the sofa and flicking on her laptop, Casey decided to write down her feelings. Having used her *Online Diary* as a way to release pent up feelings before, she decided to write down exactly how she was feeling. She could go back and edit it later, when she was less emotional. Writing seemed to always help her when she needed to get something off her chest and as she wrote, Casey felt calmer. Thinking how she could add this experience to a future entry for her column, she decided that whilst she *would* do that, it would definitely have to wait for quite a while. This was all too raw for her to share right now, but later, once her own feelings had recovered, she could tell the whole gut-wrenching story to her readers, which would include her worries over the lump she had found.

Thinking about her column as she started to tap away at the keyboard, Casey distracted herself from what had just happened and she was off on a roll. Before she knew it, three hours had passed by and she'd written more than enough for one month's entry. After reading and re-reading what she had spent the last three hours writing, Casey closed the lid of her laptop and felt quite a bit happier than when she had first sat down. Although, she acknowledged that her mood probably had a lot to do with the rum, as well as downloading her sad feelings into the written word, either way, she was happier now.

Having found that her online readers related to her stories, Casey had been spurred on to continue writing regularly and had soon found that it was something she loved to do. In fact, it was an activity which often calmed her state of mind. Writing had always made Casey feel better, which is why she had started her *Online Diary* in the first place.

Deciding that this evening needed to be a cosy and comforting one, Casey curled up on the sofa, eating crisps and dipping them into the pink Taramasalata that she loved. A nice dry Sauvignon Blanc was the drink Casey had chosen to accompany her snacks, as she also picked up one of her favourite rom-com movies then flicked on the TV. With remote control in hand and now dressed in her comfy leggings and baggy top, Casey lay back into the cushions and stared at her fluffy socks in between flicking through the TV channels, searching for something to watch that might suit her mood better than the rom-com she had in her hand. *Something's Gotta Give* won. Casey pressed play and snuggled back into the cushions.

It was around 9.30pm when Casey's mobile sounded the text message ringtone. The brightness of its screen lit up the darkened room to reveal a short text from Jason, simply saying: '*I'm sorry, it was my fault for leaving. I will miss you. Take care of yourself. J' x*

Casey sighed as she stared at the words on the screen and imagined Jason sitting at home, feeling sad and alone. Whilst her emotions stirred at that thought, her tears didn't come, just a sadness that the time had now come for them to say goodbye. Today had not been the way she would have ever imagined that would happen.

Throwing her phone to the other end of the sofa, Casey sipped the last of her wine and decided to make herself a mug of hot chocolate. Standing watching and waiting for the milk to boil, Casey glanced down to Matt's window, but he was nowhere to be seen. Turning round and feeling a little glum, she whisked the cocoa flavoured powder into the now steaming milk, frothing it slightly before pouring it into her mug, then adding a generous dollop of squirty cream, along with some pink and white marshmallows.

Now sat back on the sofa, Casey sucked in a pink marshmallow before turning back to the TV and picking up the remote control, to increase the volume just a little more, as she tried to drown out her thoughts of Jason and Matt.

Chapter 13

Matt

The following morning was a bright and crisp autumn day. As Casey stood in the kitchen making her porridge, she glanced out at the bright blue sky and instantly felt better than she had since the car-crash-event of yesterday afternoon's encounter with Jason. Matt had remained remarkably calm and thinking about it now, she was sure she had heard him say something to Jason that sounded suspiciously like, *I think she's amazing, Jase.* Had he really said that? Casey had been stunned by the very fact that Jason was even there, let alone the exchange of words they'd all had. Being so stunned, she'd been staring at Jason and not concentrating at all on what Matt was saying, as he spoke quietly over the car roof to his friend. Yet the very idea of Matt thinking she was amazing (if she had heard right and that *was* what he had said), brought a smile to her face. Remembering how good she had felt during their walk through the park and how they'd laughed and chatted so easily together, Casey was sure Matt had enjoyed it as much as she had.

Stirring sultana's and cinnamon into the hot porridge in her dish, Casey was tempted to lean forward and look out of the window to see if she could catch a glimpse of Matt working out. Hesitating for a brief guilty moment, the temptation proved too strong and she weakened all too easily. Sure enough, there he was and looking oh so good. Casey warmed to the thought of seeing Matt again as she watched him working out. Suddenly, leaning back away from the window, Casey's guilt stepped back in, making her feel bad about secretly watching Matt, now that she knew him. Deciding that she really must tell him she could see his apartment from her kitchen window,

Casey wondered when to mention it. Maybe not today, maybe some other time, when they were better acquainted. Casey wasn't sure how well Matt would react to the knowledge that she frequently watched him at the weekends. After all, some would call it voyeurism, which didn't seem quite as innocent as her weekend viewings seemed to her.

Matt had been up for hours, unable to sleep, he too was disturbed by the encounter with Jason the day before and wondered if things really *were* over between him and Casey. Clearly, that was not the case for Jason, he'd obviously wanted more from her, but what about Casey, what did *she* really want? Remembering how Casey had looked as stunned as he'd felt on seeing Jason getting out of his car, gave Matt a little reassurance that things really were over between Casey and Jason. It was an assumption which had been reiterated when he saw Jason's face change with his realisation that Casey appeared to have already moved on. Not only that, but she had moved on with Jason's very own mate!

What neither Matt nor Jason knew was that Casey had been drawn to Matt the moment she had clapped eyes on him from her kitchen window. But Jason, well, Jason had been very exciting for the time that they had been seeing each other. Casey had to admit that fact and there was no doubt in her mind that they'd shared some amazing sex and many lovely evenings together. Some were quite romantic, while others were filled with pure lust, which often felt like both of them were just satisfying their passionate desires with a sexy and willing partner. Casey had never really felt totally convinced that their relationship would go on for more than a few more months. Mainly that was because to her, they never truly felt like a boyfriend and girlfriend *in love*. They were more like two people who liked each other a lot, went to some nice places, enjoyed some delicious meals together and *definitely* fancied the pants off each other, but that was all. What had never seemed to really develop between them had been a deep and meaningful love. At least, that's how Casey viewed it and now, in the cold light of day, she wondered what Jason's thoughts would be on that very same subject.

Matt had been taking out his frustrations over Jason whilst using his gym equipment and had worked himself into a heavy sweat. Needing to shower and sort himself out, he searched his closet to find something suitable to wear for the local wine bar and his date with Casey. Matt was planning to take Casey there for a bite to eat *and* to chat about what had happened the day before. He needed to be sure Jason was no longer on Casey's romantic radar. The wine bar seemed to be a more suitable venue for chatting quietly, with its comfortable sofas and soft squashy chairs, which were scattered randomly throughout the rustic building. The boarded floor and two open fireplaces added to the ambience of the popular wine bar. Matt knew it had only been a couple of weeks since Casey and Jason had split up and realised that if she *had* been in love with Jason, that meant he wouldn't stand a chance with her. Not for a long while yet, she would need to recover from that heartbreak.

Standing under the hot running water, as he washed his hair and rubbed shower gel over his body, Matt was pleased with how pumped-up his muscles looked and felt following his workout. He hoped they would suitably impress Casey (little did he know she'd already seen most of them, from her window across the street). Matt rinsed off the foamy gel from his body, watching as the bubbles washing down his abdomen and legs, as he imagined what Casey's naked body would look like if she were stood under the water with him right now. His mind wandered to how pert her breasts would be, with their two perfectly formed nipples that he imagined she would have. As Matt's fantasy ran into over-drive, his passion also began to rise and almost urgently and whilst groaning Casey's name, his hand gripped around where he wished her hands could be. As he worked faster and faster, his pent-up passion exploded, causing him to call out her name even louder, temporarily releasing the frustration he felt at wanting her so desperately. Matt knew he needed to hold back and be cool with Casey. He knew he had to wait patiently and allow her to feel sure of him, before he breached that precious barrier and tempted Casey to share her body with his.

Washing his spent passion from his taut muscular body, Matt stepped out of the shower and towel dried himself, before liberally spraying his entire body with his favourite Lynx spray. Knowing that Casey liked a man to smell nice, he smiled to himself as he finished off with enough hair gel to maintain a wet look, then got dressed quickly. Having already checked the clock on his bedside table, Matt knew he had ten minutes before midday. Deep slow breaths calmed his nervous excitement before he stepped out of his front door to go downstairs and across the road to Casey's apartment block.

Casey was in a slight panic and not quite ready when Matt rang the main doorbell and speaking through the intercom, she invited him to come in. As he made his way upstairs, Casey was rushing around like a mad woman and tidying things away, until she heard him at her front door, then, first checking her appearance in the mirror, she opened the door with a flourish and beamed at Matt. As they were saying hello to each other, Matt leaned forward to kiss Casey on both cheeks; he couldn't quite believe how gorgeous she looked and his heart swelled with admiration. Meanwhile, Casey's own head had filled with the gorgeous smell that wafted over her as Matt's kiss

189

touched her cheeks. *Oh boy, does he smell and look good*, she thought.

"Come in a sec, Matt, I'm almost ready. Where are we going? Is what I'm wearing OK or do I need to change?"

Casey actually felt and looked amazing and there was no way she really wanted to have to change. So she hoped Matt hadn't planned some crazy wild adventure for them, which would need a change of clothing, or shoes at the very least.

"You look amazing, Casey." Matt took in a breath to slow his pounding heart before continuing: "I thought we could go to the wine bar and grab a bite to eat and chat. Maybe take a taxi?"

His voice trailed off as Casey replied, feeling very relieved at not having to change clothes. "Oh that sounds lovely, Matt but, if you don't mind, could we just walk there rather than take a taxi? I've been stuck indoors all day and I really could do with some fresh air to clear my head."

Matt wasn't sure if that was a good or a bad sign, but he remained upbeat as he replied: "Sure, no problem, I'm happy to walk there. We could cut through the park."

"Oh yes, good idea, let's do that. It's such a lovely day. I love walking through the park when it's so bright and sunny."

Despite her very calm exterior, which took all her strength to maintain, Casey felt overwhelmed with excitement. The butterflies were back, but this time she welcomed them because she knew this happy feeling that she was drunk on, was the best feeling in the world. Slipping on her navy beret, which went perfectly with the outfit she'd chosen for their date, Casey thought she looked very chic as she took a final glance at her appearance in the mirror, mentally approving the reflection. Turning to Matt, Casey smiled again.

"OK, I'm ready."

Her eyes twinkled with delight as she noted Matt's obvious approval. Whilst his stomach flipped with nervous excitement and the potential outcome of the conversation he was expecting to have, Matt felt a little overwhelmed. He so wanted this to go the right way and yet Casey looked so incredibly sexy, he could barely contain himself. Wanting her badly Matt managed to reply calmly, "Sure, let's go."

The two of them walked downstairs and stepped out into the sunshine. Matt offered his arm to Casey and slipping hers through his, they both enjoyed the closeness of their bodies. Casey thought how perfect the day was going to be. The two of them were so blissfully happy as they strolled along together arm-in-arm, basking in the autumnal sunshine as it warmed their faces.

"So, Case..."

Matt had to start the conversation about Jason; it was playing on his mind and he just couldn't wait until they reached the wine bar. As they were crossing the little wooden bridge, he paused to face her and suddenly looked serious as he searched for the right words to ask the question he was so desperate to ask, while afraid of the answer he might hear.

"I need to ask you this question and sorry if it seems a bit forward, but after yesterday I just need to know what is happening with you and Jason. Is it really over? Because it looked like Jason didn't want it to be yesterday."

Matt almost winced as he added the last part.

"It's fine, Matt, of course you need to ask and the answer is yes, for me it is most definitely over. There's really no point in us carrying on seeing each other is there, not if he's going to be on the other side of the world. When Jason told me about the new job and everything, we agreed that what with him going away, it made sense to end things there."

Casey hesitated, having spoken so matter-of-factly about Jason that she was now wondering what Matt was thinking and if his friendship with Jason would over-ride his feelings for her.

"The thing is and if I'm honest, I probably would have carried on seeing Jason if he wasn't planning on flying off to New Zealand. He wanted me to go with him, but I couldn't because I just don't *want* to leave the UK, not really. Besides which, we weren't in a long-term relationship. It was still actually quite new and truthfully, I didn't feel strongly enough about Jason to run off to the other side of the world with him."

As her voice dwindled slightly, Casey looked at Matt, wondering what he was thinking, but she had said it now.

"So, you wouldn't have split up if he hadn't been off to New Zealand?"

"Well, no, I suppose we probably wouldn't have, well not right now. But we did and things changed and well, now that I've met *you*, it's all different again."

Casey's almost *helpless female* reaction was involuntary and she was in fact feeling more than a little daunted at not being able to manage this conversation as well as she would have wanted.

"Well, that's good to know then."

Matt smiled at Casey and saw a look of relief cross her face, which pleased him even more, because what he read into *that* was, that she did in fact seem to like him as much as he liked her. At least that's what he hoped for as he followed up on that comment.

"I was worried that maybe, with Jase being back and him coming to see you the moment he landed, it would mean you might want to pick up from where you left off with him."

Almost making that a question, Matt now searched Casey's face looking for any kind of clue as to what she was feeling. As a half-smile crossed her face, Casey glanced down at the water before looking back at him.

"No, Matt, there really isn't any future in me and Jason. It was best for us to have left it where it was. I don't think I would want to go back to that now anyway. To Jason I mean."

Smiling at Matt, Casey moved her hand to touch his arm.

"I'm kind of hoping that you and I will be seeing each other again and well, who knows where we'll go from here but..."

Casey paused as Matt interrupted her.

"Casey, I was so hoping that is what you would say. I really do want to see you again because I think you're amazing and..."

It was Matt's turn to be interrupted.

"Matt, would you just kiss me?"

Casey looked up into Matt's eyes and from under her lashes he could see hers were sparkling with happy tears. Taking her into his strong arms and pulling her close to him, Matt reached up to Casey's face and brushed away a strand of hair before kissing her lips. Holding her to him, Matt's hand moved down to press against the small of her back, pulling her even closer into him, as his kiss became more passionate and wanting.

As Matt explored Casey's mouth, she returned his passion and encircled her arms around him, holding onto him as his kisses continued, exploring and caressing this gorgeous woman that he adored.

"Oh, Matt..."

Casey's breathing was low and heavy as Matt's kisses slowed down. Feeling overcome with passion, Matt knew he needed to stop, or he would take her right there and make wild passionate, wanting love to her. But the bridge over the park lake was not the place for such an occasion, even though there was nobody around and the park seemed unusually deserted. As tempting as it would be in that moment to find a secluded spot and take things further, Matt wanted their first time to be perfect and very special. Knowing he was falling in love with this gorgeous woman, he wanted her to give him permission to make love to her and he wanted it to be right for them both. Pulling away from her suddenly as his passionate need was evident, Matt was slightly embarrassed, knowing that Casey must have felt it too. He wanted her so badly.

Casey had most certainly felt Matt's surging need, which had tripled her own passionate desires, which were now exploding inside her like a fireworks display. Desperately needing Matt to make love to her, Casey wanted him to kiss and caress every inch of her and to plunge his hard passion into her wanting body, so they could reach those dizzy heights of oneness together. But that togetherness would have to wait for another time. For now, the passion of their kisses was powerful enough. Casey had never felt quite like this before. There was something about Matt that captivated her very being and it was something more than just his hardness, which she had felt growing with every one of their kisses.

As the two of them parted, their heartbeats reduced and their breathing slowed as they smiled at each other; Casey flicked her tongue along her lips, a subtle gesture that was not lost on Matt. Wow, she was just so gorgeous and she tasted delicious. Matt wanted her badly, but he also wanted her freely and for her to want him this much too. After that kiss, he was fairly certain they were on the same track.

Matt laughed: "Shall we carry on to the wine bar?" he said.

Casey looked into Matt's twinkling eyes and giggled: "Yes, I think maybe we should," she said, "before we get ourselves into trouble."

Taking his arm once again and this time snuggling into him just a little bit more closely than before, Casey relished Matt's desire for her, because she already adored him.

Matt felt like he was ten feet tall, this woman, and this goddess was with *him* and not only that, she had just kissed him back with a passion that was truly undeniable. He was *totally* smitten.

The wine bar was quite busy when they arrived and had a happy buzz about it as they took a small table by the front window. It seemed the two of them were lucky to have arrived when they did, because the tables all looked pretty full, with happy smiling groups of couples and friends. This was definitely one of those places which friends rather than families used, and whilst Matt had expected it to be a bit quieter than Barney's, today it had a happy buzz which was not overly loud.

Matt ordered a bottle of the house Rioja for which this wine bar was famously known and the two of them scanned the light bites menu, neither of them wanting or needing a heavy meal.

Looking around the bar, Casey remarked at how much she liked this place and its quirky eclectic collection of artefacts and interesting décor. It really was one of those places that wherever you looked, there was something different to see and often something you'd not noticed before. One of her particularly favourite things was the scrolled writing along the top of a huge archway which simply said, *'There are no strangers here, only the friends that you haven't yet had the pleasure to meet, so don't be afraid to say hello!'*

Perfect, the place was perfect for this moment and following *that* kiss, shared on such a stunning autumn day in such a romantic location. Both of them felt they would never forget it. As they sat and chatted, the two of them soon found themselves totally engrossed in conversation about each other's lives, their families and mutual friends. In particular, they talked about Dave and Tilly, who had seen each other almost every day that week. This news had pleased both Matt and Casey, because it seemed to them that Tilly and Dave were totally made for each other. Love was definitely in the air and they were happy to revel in it.

Casey was surprised by the fact that both she and Tilly seemed to have recovered so quickly from their individual heart-breaks, which had been unexpected. Yet, Casey was so happy that they each seemed to have met such genuinely great guys, which made it pretty obvious to Casey that for both Tilly and herself, John and Jason had *not* been their Mr Rights. Instead, she hoped that Dave and Matt were about to step into those happy shoes.

Just at that point, Dave and Tilly walked right past the window. Startled by the uncanny coincidence, Casey jumped slightly in surprise, as she lifted her hand automatically to wave hello. Matt followed her gaze and seeing their two friends looking in at him and Casey, he grinned and beckoned for them to come in and join their table. The fact that Matt reacted in the same generous way that she had, was not lost on Casey and she felt a warm glow as she realised they both felt a similar instinct when bumping into mutual friends.

"Hey, you two, fancy bumping into you over here."

Dave gave Matt a nudge and winked at him as Tilly leant forward to kiss Casey's cheek.

"Oh, Case, I feel like I haven't seen you in ages and I can see why. Hi there, Matt, how nice to see you two together, are you sure you want us to join you?"

Tilly was smiling an infectiously teasing smile and was thrilled with Matt's reply: "Don't be daft, Tilly, of course we do. Pull up a chair, you guys, and I'll ask the waiter for a couple more glasses."

Matt indicated as much to the very attentive waiter, who having seen the two new arrivals, immediately understood the requirement and raised his hand in acknowledgment of Matt's request. Minutes later, two fresh glasses arrived, and Tilly and Dave took off their hats and coats and settled down with their friends. The waiter offered to pour the wine for them, which they acknowledged and thanked him for. Luckily, they were all great fans of the infamous Rioja and so were eagerly raising their glasses in a toast, as a second waiter appeared beside the first, carrying the mezze board that Casey and Matt had previously ordered. Although there was enough for the four friends to share, to be sure and not wanting to eat all of Matt and Casey's food, Dave asked the waiter to add a couple more side dishes to the order.

It seemed they'd all subconsciously decided to stay and enjoy the whole afternoon in the wine bar together. Two or three bottles of Rioja later, having told Tilly and Dave about the shock of Jason turning up, the four friends briefly pondered over his future as they cleaned the mezze board of all crumbs. They were thoroughly enjoying their afternoon together and as the boys moved on to a brief discussion about the latest club rugby match they'd been to, Tilly took the opportunity to ask Casey if she'd told Matt about the lump.

"No, no, not yet, I thought I'd wait until after the...you know...I'd rather wait and make sure there's nothing to worry about first."

Tilly looked surprised. "So you guys haven't done it yet then?"

Casey almost hissed as she said a little too loudly, "Tilly!" and then had to explain that it was 'nothing' when both men looked at her, enquiring as to what it was that Tilly had said.

"Oh ignore us," Tilly said. "It's just girls stuff; we're just messing about."

Tilly saved the day as she managed to fob off their inquisitiveness by laughing off the conversation, not wanting to be the one to leak the news to Matt about Casey's lump. But thanks to Tilly's untimely question, Casey had just been reminded of the fact that this week would be when she was due to attend the Breast Clinic. She would be finding out whether the lump she had found was something to worry about, or not. Tilly meanwhile, was gutted at having spoilt the mood by her thoughtlessness. Well, not so much thoughtless, just a badly timed question and although it wasn't the best timing, Casey actually appreciated that Tilly cared so much that it was on her friend's mind. One thing for sure was, that there was no way Matt needed to know about the lump until it had been sorted it out, of that Casey was certain.

As the afternoon drew to a close and with darkness upon them, the friends paid their bill and wrapped up against the now considerably chilly early evening air, before then setting off for their respective homes. As the four of them stood outside saying their goodbyes and hugging each other, Tilly said she was staying over at Dave's, so would see Casey at work the following day. The two of them looked so happy that Casey's heart swelled and she nodded at Tilly, wishing them both a good evening, before turning to link arms with Matt, as they both hurried back home to the warmth of their apartments.

Chapter 14

The Clinic

The next two working days passed without too much bother, until Casey received a brief call from Jason, who was still desperate to change Casey's mind. After listening to his plea, Casey reiterated that it really "*is* best for them to end things now". Jason of course tried his best to change her mind, but as she explained again, what with him going to New Zealand and, knowing she absolutely did *not* want to do that, there really was no future for them. Still then, Casey had to repeat the words that it really "*is* over between them" and that no, it was probably best if he didn't pop round to talk and that it was time for them to go their separate ways. Casey could see no purpose in dragging on a pointless discussion, as she tried to end the conversation. But Jason didn't take this outcome well and began to sound frustrated and angry on the phone. In an effort to vent his frustration and make Casey feel as badly as he did, Jason started digging at Casey about her seeing Matt so soon after Jason's plane had left the tarmac.

Casey was beginning to find it hard to remain calm and sighed as she gently but firmly told Jason that it had been a pure coincidence that she and Matt had bumped into each other. Also, that the two of them had only been out for a walk and coffee, on the morning that Jason had returned and seen them together outside her apartment.

Jason expressed how he found it hard to believe that she and Matt had only had coffee. Mainly due to what Matt had told Jason about how he (Matt) now felt about Casey and so Jason said as much to her. However, following Casey's repeated and determined explanation, Jason reluctantly accepted that as ironic as it had turned out to be, he had in fact introduced the two of them himself, when Matt had turned up with Dave at Jason's leaving bash. So he also had to accept that Casey was right, in that she *had* only just met Matt that night. Knowing what his mate was usually like when it came to dating, Jason realised that Matt must have been thinking about Casey well before he'd invited her out for coffee, so realistically she couldn't have planned anything herself.

How flaming ironic that he himself had been the catalyst for them meeting, Jason cursed under his breath. Although, feeling crestfallen and dejected, he calmed down and actually apologised to Casey. He explained to her how he was just so completely gutted that she wouldn't consider going to New Zealand with him and that no, he wouldn't have a go at Matt again and yes, that they should all still try to remain friends. Although how he would be able to be hers and Matt's friend he really didn't know, at least not right now. But even Jason could recognise that he would probably feel differently after two years away and yes, as Casey said, he too would probably have met someone else by then.

Later that same day, Casey received a call from the Breast Clinic. As she recovered from the shock of it being the call she was dreading, Casey listened carefully to the efficient voice on the other end of the line. The caller stated that there had been a late cancellation, due to ill health, and would Casey be able to attend an appointment on Friday morning? The efficient voice went on to explain that they would examine her and if it was deemed necessary, also use ultrasound to take a needle biopsy under a local anaesthetic. Casey was beginning to wobble. The efficient voice added that there was nothing to worry about at this stage and that it should all be relatively painless. But in her mind Casey thought, *That's easy for you to say, you're not the one about to have a huge great big needle stuck in you to find out if you have the dreaded 'C' or not!* Oh and there would be no need for an overnight stay, but that she might like a friend to accompany her during the visit and to take her home, as she may feel some discomfort and feel unable to drive herself. As well as being stunned by it being the call she'd been dreading, Casey was not only surprised by the friendly efficiency of the person on the other end of the line, but also the immediacy of the appointment. The gentle voice also carefully explained that seeing as there had been a cancellation, it was obviously best to accept it and get the process over and done with as quickly as possible. At least, that was the common sense part of it. The less straightforward part was Casey worrying what the lump could turn out to be. Dreading the worst news, she absent-mindedly crossed her fingers and prayed a silent prayer, hoping and begging that it would not be the 'C' thing.

Casey couldn't even bring herself to *think* the word in full, let alone say it out loud, because that made it seem all too realistic and it could still turn out to be the 'C' thing. So instead, she was hoping and praying that it would just be a fatty lump and nothing too much to worry about, anything in fact that could be more easily dealt with and be non-life threatening. The trouble was that it did look pretty obvious, even to Casey's untrained eye, that something definitely wasn't right. One thing Casey *was* sure of was, that although she didn't really want to have to live with her breast looking the way it currently did, she would rather do that than have to lose it to the 'Big C'. So many women had had their breasts removed and were so brave, but Casey really didn't think she could be as brave as them; in fact, she was scared stiff of that being the outcome for her.

Sighing heavily, it was all too much to think about and after explaining to Tilly what the Clinic had told her, Casey then quietly asked her manager if she could leave work early. Already having shared her concerns with her privately earlier that day, Casey had been so relieved that her boss had been completely supportive, telling Casey to take the time she needed to prepare herself for the procedure. So, yes, it was fine for her to leave work early, also adding that Casey was not to worry about any future treatment and that they would work out how to manage things once she knew the outcome of the tests.

As well as mentally preparing herself for the visit to the clinic and now thinking about Matt and the fact that she was due to be seeing him later that evening, Casey felt like she also needed to relax and calm herself down by the time he called for her. There was no way she wanted to create any sign of there being something wrong and knowing Matt would likely pick up on her mood, Casey had to make sure she was feeling upbeat by the time she saw him.

Once out of the office and being forever grateful for having such a lovely and easy going, understanding boss, Casey went home to call Carole and ask her if she could come with her to the hospital. She couldn't ask Amanda, not with her having lost her own Mum to Breast Cancer so recently. Not only that, Carole had medical experience and seemed to be the best friend for Casey to lean on during this ordeal.

Seeing Casey's number ringing on her mobile phone and not expecting a daytime call from her friend, Carole was understandably surprised at Casey's news. More so, that Casey had managed to get such an urgent appointment at the breast clinic, knowing how stretched they usually were. Casey explained that the timing was due to another patient cancellation and on hearing slight panic in Casey's voice, Carole quickly reassured her that the short notice appointment was actually good news. Also, that of course she would book the day off to go with

Casey to the hospital, she could even pop over after work that day, if Casey wanted her to.

Thanking Carole for being such a great support, Casey explained that Matt was calling round later, so she would be fine. She then also told Carole not to say anything about it to Matt just yet. Casey thought it was kind of useful that Matt was taking her to the cinema, because it meant less talking than if the two of them had just gone for a drink, which Carole totally understood.

"Well the good thing is, you will likely know by the end of next week exactly what the lump is. Also, what the next steps are, if any, I mean it could be nothing to worry about at all."

Truly hoping that it would turn out to be nothing and Casey would be fine. Carole was understandably worried for her friend, but was trying very hard to remain positive and bright for her, knowing only too well the importance of keeping Casey as upbeat as possible, in case it did turn out to be cancer.

"Well OK then, Case, I'll come over on Friday morning and we can drive over there together."

Casey thanked Carole as they agreed a suitable time for Friday, both ensuring that they had allowed plenty of time for the journey. Partly so they didn't have to rush about, but also to prevent Casey from feeling any more stressed about the test than she already was.

The cinema date with Matt was great and just what Casey needed. They watched the movie whilst eating their way through a family sized box of popcorn, which was actually the medium sized one, but was big enough to feed a whole family and the people next door. The movie was a romantic comedy which had enough laughter and frivolity, to keep both Matt and Casey amused throughout the entire two-hour showing. After the film ended, Matt started to feel guilty, although also slightly impressed by how much popcorn they had consumed between them, he remarked on how many calories they must have just eaten, adding that he would likely have to burn it off in his gym the following morning. Casey beamed back at him and agreed, stating that maybe she should jog to work to burn it off. Secretly feeling fairly certain there was no way she would ever jog to work, unless someone was chasing her, and then laughed at her own joke. The impromptu conversation about popcorn and burning the extra calories off, led them into discussing working out. This was a prime opportunity for Casey to tell Matt about her guilty pleasure of having sneaked a peak at him working out (on more than one occasion), from her kitchen window. But not wanting to spoil the evening, Casey decided she would wait a bit longer and make sure she could judge how Matt would react to that little fact, in case he thought she was some kind of crazy stalker or something.

Friday came around much quicker than Casey expected and she had found herself unable to sleep much on Thursday night. Waking up really early, she had worried herself into a stew by the time Carole arrived. Casey was almost frantic as she charged around her apartment, changing into various different outfits because she still wasn't sure what to wear. Not that it mattered, knowing she would have to change into a gown at the hospital anyway, but it was more to do with her self-esteem rather than trying to impress anyone. Seeing her friend in such a state had Carole swinging into life-saver mode and she boosted Casey with some witty banter to help relieve the tension, somehow managing to get her laughing before they'd even left for the clinic.

Having allowed enough time to get to the clinic, the two friends still had to wait before being called through to the treatment room. It was now their turn. As they followed, the clinician spoke calmly with a confident manner but seemed really nice, suggesting that Carole could stay with Casey during the first part of the

204

examination, if that's what Casey wanted. Both women were very grateful that the clinician was clearly used to keeping her patients and their attending family member/friend, as relaxed as possible.

As she sat next to Casey, Carole watched her friend closely as Casey concentrated on watching the clinician's face. As her records displayed on screen the clinician referred to the GP's notes. It was always unnerving watching doctors read someone else's notes and Casey watched intently for any change of expression, which might give away some information that one would expect a doctor to normally hold back. Carole now glanced at the clinician herself, sub-consciously thinking the same as Casey.

After discussing the lump and going through her relevant medical history, Casey was asked to step behind the curtain, strip off the top half of her clothing, then to sit on the edge of the couch for the initial examination. This was to check the lump and so the clinician could view both breasts as a comparison. Casey felt embarrassed at first, but the female clinician examining her was so normal, it made her feel like this was almost an everyday activity. By the time the examination was finished, Casey was almost as relaxed as the clinician seemed to be and even cracked a joke, which made them both laugh. Carole, who had remained on the other side of the curtain, could hear what was being said and was relieved that the clinician was so good at her job. It made both her and Casey feel confident that she would be able to fix whatever the problem was.

The adjoining room housed the equipment for the needle biopsy and the ultrasound machine. After the initial examination, Casey was asked to leave her top clothes off and pop a gown on, then walk through to the couch in the adjoining room, whilst a nurse was called to assist. The clinician told Casey that whilst she felt fairly sure the lump was just a cyst, she would feel happier taking a biopsy to rule out anything sinister. Carole was asked to remain in the first examination room whilst the biopsy was being taken, but was assured the whole procedure would be done very quickly. Carole explained that she wasn't worried how long it took or how long she would have to wait, it was more that she wanted Casey to be OK. To reassure her friend, Carole squeezed Casey's hand as she walked into the treatment room and whispered, "Good luck" to her.

Lying on the couch, Casey felt her stomach knotting and tried to calm herself, as the clinician prepared her working area. The equipment was all wrapped in plastic, which seemed a bit odd to Casey, but she guessed it must be for protection against germs and stared across the room, focussing on another strange looking piece of equipment. This was less about her interest in medical paraphernalia and more about using it as a distraction to avoid looking at the needle that was going to be inserted into her breast. Casey had never been great with needles and said she was glad to be lying down in case she fainted. Even though it was minutes, it felt to Casey like she'd been lying on the couch for ages and she was beginning to feel clammy and tense as the clinician started examining her using the ultrasound machine.

Asking her patient to try and relax, as she ran the ultrasound pad across Casey's breast, the clinician confirmed that she would need to take the biopsy and began preparing the skin so she could insert the needle. As she chatted to Casey, trying to relax her whilst the anaesthetic began to work, she then very gently inserted the needle and took the biopsy. Gripping the side of the couch in an involuntary gesture as the fear of being probed took hold of her senses, Casey surprised herself and did not faint. However, once it was all over, she did feel extremely uncomfortable. The clinician told her that the results would take between seven to ten days and they would be reported to Casey's GP, as well as being confirmed in writing to Casey herself. The letter would also include notification of what the next steps would be, which of course were dependant on what the lump turned out to be. The clinician very calmly explained the likely scenarios and despite Casey's questions, managed to side-step answering the burning question of whether it could be cancer. Because she was so calm in her explanations, Casey couldn't guess anything more from trying to read the clinician's facial expressions, so her immediate reaction was one of pessimistic optimism.

Getting dressed again was a little more delicate, due to the medical dressing and feeling sore, so Casey was grateful that Carole was there to help her. But not wearing a bra felt very weird to Casey and today it felt wrong somehow, to be bra-less in a public place that wasn't a beach. It surprised Casey at how uneasy being bra-less made her feel today, which also seemed crazy, because she'd gone out plenty of times before without wearing a bra, particularly under some of her more skimpy tops. But now, having had this test, Casey suddenly felt vulnerable and as if the whole world would be watching her.

Having got dressed, Casey thanked the clinician once again, who tried to encourage her not to worry before they knew what it was. Casey nodded to Carole that she was ready to go, agreeing that there was no point in blowing it up into something it may not even be. But her mind was now in overdrive and not quite as calm as before, leaving her secretly thinking, *That's fine for you to say, you're not the one facing a possible lumpectomy or even worse, mastectomy!*

Even though Casey knew mastectomy was the extreme view, in her mind it was still a *very* real possibility, until she had the results of the biopsy back. Carole took Casey's arm and they walked slowly down the corridor and out of the clinic, towards the car. As Carole helped Casey into the passenger seat, she glanced up and noticed Matt on the other side of the car park.

"Oh, there's Matt. I wonder what he's doing here. Aren't you seeing him tonight?"

Casey was horrified and asked Carole to get into the car quickly before he saw them, which she duly did and then reassured Casey that there was no need to worry, Matt hadn't even been looking over their way. As they set off home, Casey leant her head back and closed her eyes, thankful that Matt hadn't seen them, while wondering what the result of the biopsy would be. As Carole turned out of the end of the road where the hospital was, she tried again to console her friend.

"It might be best if you go and lie down when you get back, Case," she said. "You'll be sore from today and if you like, I can stay and make you something to eat for later."

"Thanks, Carole, you're a star...that'd be lovely. Oh and to answer your question, no, I'm not seeing Matt tonight. I already told him we were having a girly evening so he wouldn't ask any questions, so dinner together would make that the true answer. Thanks, mate, that'd be great!"

Casey closed her eyes and dozed as Carole drove her back home. Just as they arrived back at the apartment and walked through the main front door, Dolly opened her own door to let Freddie out. On seeing the two girls so unexpectedly, the older lady greeted them with a surprised hello. She wasn't used to seeing the girls in the middle of the day; well, not on a week day, because they were generally at work, so Dolly asked after them both in a slightly concerned voice, but then smiled at their unified chirpy responses.

"We're very good thanks, Dolly," Casey said. "And how are you and Freddie?"

Dolly was as fit as a fiddle and told them she too was fine, but that Freddie was being a little tinker today and she wouldn't be at all surprised if he was planning another night on the tiles. Bless Dolly, she did so love little Freddie and talked about him as if he were human rather than feline. The girls laughed along with her and wished her a pleasant evening, adding that they hoped Freddie would not stay out all night.

Taking the lift, they continued on up to Casey's apartment and the relaxed evening they had planned. Casey was still feeling a little uncomfortable and decided to take two more paracetamol, before changing into her favourite PJs. Carole had turned into 'Nurse Carole' and took care of her friend in the best possible way, by busying herself with tea-making and preparing a light supper for them both (after ordering Casey to rest and take a nap if she could). Doing precisely that, Casey was thankful for having such a lovely friend as Carole and swinging her legs onto her comfy bed, she lay propped up on the pillows and closed her eyes.

As the day wore on, Casey moved from the bedroom to the sofa and Carole insisted on bringing her pillow and duvet through for her, in spite of Casey's protestations at being able to manage. But the two of them agreed it was definitely a perfect excuse for a duvet evening as they settled down with plates of food and something funny to watch on TV to lighten the mood. Carole had decided to stay the night, so the friends both snuggled under the duvet and watched *Love Actually*, laughing and crying at all their favourite parts. Casey was so grateful to have a friend like Carole, she really was her all time rock and she squeezed her friend's arm a little tighter as a gesture of thanks. Nothing more needed to be said between the two of them as they carried on with their movie fest late into the night.

The following morning, Carole checked that Casey was feeling OK before making them both a heart-warming breakfast of crispy bacon sandwiches, along with the traditional must-have, HP sauce. Such a yummy breakfast accompanied by two pots of good old English breakfast tea, soon had both of them feeling relaxed and loving that easy Saturday morning feeling, as they both enjoyed their kitchen chatter.

But Carole was concerned about Casey; it was not so much about how she was feeling physically following the procedure, but what the result might bring that worried Carole and she knew full well how worried Casey was. Not daring to broach the subject of Casey telling Matt, Carole suggested Casey could maybe just call Matt to arrange to see him later that day and to help take her mind off things.

Casey nodded and said that she would, after writing some more of her column, saying she wanted to get some thoughts down before they left her. Telling Carole there was another movie she fancied seeing at the cinema, Casey said she would ask Matt if he fancied going again that evening. That would also prevent her from risking having to tell him where she had been the day before.

Relieved that her friend seemed in pretty good spirits, Carole decided she would slip off and leave Casey to write, confirming that she'd call her later, to check that Casey was OK. Thanking her friend again, Casey hugged Carole and said she'd be fine and yes, she would call if she needed her.

Settling down to write, Casey planned to review what she had written following Jason's unexpected appearance the other day. Then, using artistic licence, she made up a scenario, which meant it wouldn't be directly linked to her present life. Edine had, after all, offered her a wider scope and she *was* quite good at writing just enough to keep her readers hooked, whilst still keeping the story as real and normal as possible.

Chapter 15

News

Exactly a week and one day later, Casey received the letter from the clinic. Nervously holding it her hand, she stared down at the window envelope, willing herself to turn it over and slide her letter opener along the folded edge, which was glued so perfectly. Casey felt relieved and at the same time, scared that the letter had finally arrived. Now that it was in her hand, she was feeling pensive about what result it would contain, and worried, in case it was the bad news she had been dreading. A moment later Casey decided she couldn't open the letter alone and instead, holding the sealed envelope in her hand, she opened her front door and walked downstairs to Tilly's apartment.

Finding herself knocking a little too fiercely when she reached her friend's front door, Casey stopped her rapping as she heard Tilly unlocking the door from the other side. Opening it with the chain on, partly because she was only half-dressed and partly because she was worried at who could be knocking so urgently, Tilly peered out through the gap and was surprised to see Casey standing there, still in her PJs. Tilly hurriedly slipped off the chain and opened the door properly.

"Case, what's wrong, honey, you're a white as a sheet?"

Casey just held out the envelope and looked at her friend like a frightened child might look at its mother.

"It's from the clinic," Casey said.

"Oh golly, is that it, the letter, the results?"

Tilly gabbled her questions in one sentence and knew she was talking way too fast and in a voice, which could easily be described as shrill. But she just couldn't help herself, having been taken completely by surprise to see Casey stood outside her door so early. Now ushering Casey in, Tilly told her to sit down on the sofa and asked what the letter said. Casey sat down and just looked blankly at Tilly as she held out her arm, thrusting the still unopened letter towards her friend and asking her in a hushed voice to please open it for her. Tilly was shocked to see Casey looking so fearful. The girls just looked at each other and Casey held her breath as Tilly picked up a knife and gently slid it along the length of the envelope, exposing the contents for Casey to take out. Holding the now open envelope towards Casey and then seeing her friend shaking her head, Tilly realised Casey was serious and wanted her to actually read the letter for her.

Taking the folded notepaper out between her thumb and forefinger, Tilly pulled it from the envelope slowly. As she did so and without even realising it, Tilly was holding her own breath, whilst unfolding the paper. With the letter unfolded and Tilly having composed herself, she breathed out slowly as she read the contents to Casey. It started with 'Dear Ms Smith', of course, Casey's real name was Smith, and Martin was just her pen-name.

Tilly continued: "With reference to the breast biopsy undertaken'...blah, blah, blah...'unfortunately, we must inform you that the biopsy results indicated the presence of abnormal cells, which will require further investigation. We therefore ask you to telephone the clinic to arrange an appointment to have the cell excised."

Tilly stared at the paper as Casey slumped back in her chair, tears beginning to roll down her face. Looking from the letter and then back to Casey, Tilly moved to hug her friend, as she tried to soothe her fears by reminding her that it had just said *abnormal cells* and didn't say *cancer*, so she didn't need to worry quite so much, she would be fine. Of course, Tilly had no idea if her friend would actually be fine at all, but this was her best attempt at a pragmatic calming approach.

Casey felt like the bottom of her world had just dropped out of her life and her face was ashen. As Tilly hugged her even tighter, she grabbed tissues from the box on the coffee table and handed several of them to Casey. As her friend quietly sobbed, Tilly tried her best to comfort her and in the end, resorted to the very British approach to a crisis, saying she would put the kettle on and make Casey a cup of hot, strong, sweet tea. Good old tea, it was the answer to everything whenever anyone was upset or had experienced a shock.

Tilly slugged a large Scotch Whisky into the mug of tea before handing it back to Casey. Then returning to sit beside her friend, Tilly asked Casey if she should maybe tell Matt now and that he would surely want to know. Tilly still couldn't believe Casey was trying to deal with this by herself. Well, with Tilly's and Carole's support of course, but it was never quite the same as having that special person there to hold her hand.

But Casey was still being stubborn, she reminded Tilly that she and Matt had only been seeing each for a short while and this was far too much of a burden to put on him. Besides which, he probably didn't want some invalid girlfriend, to which Tilly scolded her friend, saying she was being too harsh and not giving Matt the credit he deserved. After all, he hadn't pressured her into sex or anything yet, so he must care about her, massively! Casey thought on Tilly's words and reluctantly agreed that she probably *was* being reactionary and yes, Matt might be OK about it, but she still felt like it was just too weird to tell him yet. Tilly shook her head and said she thought Casey was wrong and that Matt was the kindest, sweetest person (well, next to her wonderful Dave of course), and that Casey should give him credit and at least *think* about telling him. Realising her friend was probably right, Casey said yes, that she *would* think about it and then drank her laced tea, embracing its potency. Half an hour later, Casey was feeling a little better. It was so true, tea really was good at making one calm down and feel better, especially when laced with a slug of Scotch Whisky. In fact, both women felt a little brighter, although at that precise moment, Casey didn't think she would ever feel quite the same again, but thanked Tilly for being there and for listening. To which Tilly raised her eyebrows and playfully slapped her friend's arm.

"Don't be daft, of course I'm here, you old bat. That's what friends are for isn't it? Besides, you know me, never one to miss out on being a hero."

Casey laughed and then hugged the quietly relieved Tilly, who was now much happier, having made her friend smile again. Thanking Tilly again, Casey then disappeared back upstairs, hoping nobody would see her in her PJs as she reached her own landing and opened the door to her apartment. But as she walked in, a small doubt crept back into her mind. Casey walked through to the kitchen to look out of the window and see if she could see Matt. Yes, there he was, still looking as fabulous as ever. Casey knew she probably *should* tell him about her lump and how worried she was, but something was holding her back. Instead, she text Carole to tell her that the letter had arrived, then asked if she would like to meet for a coffee and browse the shopping centre. Casey felt like a bit of retail therapy was needed and would make her feel better before she met up with Matt later that day.

Immediately, Carole called to check Casey was OK and hearing her friend's voice, she said she'd be right over and would only be about twenty minutes, because she was already out and about anyway. Casey said not to worry about coming to the apartment, but to meet her at Trina's and they could sit in and have coffee. Carole agreed to meet her there in about an hour. After all, Casey needed to shower and dress first and Carole knew that was not a five-minute job.

Within the hour, the friends had met and ordered two skinny double shot lattes, along with an almond biscotti each. As they sat down and sorted themselves out, Carole was like a cat on a hot tin roof and wanted to know what the letter from the clinic had said, whilst being almost too afraid to ask. Casey passed the letter to Carole and took a sip of the caffeine rich latte before opening her small packet of almond biscotti. Dipping the hard biscuit into the hot liquid, then hastily eating the delicious coffee soaked softness, Casey couldn't bear to watch as Carole read the hospital letter. Instead, she savoured the richness of the coffee with the yummy flavour of almonds, taking another couple of sips to wash down the remainder of the biscotti. Carole had read the letter twice and was now looking at Casey to see what reaction Casey was showing in her face.

"Tilly said that because it just says abnormal cells and doesn't say cancer, that I wasn't to worry too much and that it would be fine. So I'm trying to keep positive and be strong."

Casey tried to smile, but it was apparent that she was struggling to keep up with the positive attitude. Whilst Carole was relieved about it only being *abnormal cells*, but she felt concerned about Casey, knowing she would bounce between strength and despair on this one, as would anyone in her position.

"Tilly's absolutely right, Case, it's not the worst news. Even though it does mean a small operation, you'll be fine, they'll just whip it out and that will be it, gone. We've got to keep upbeat and stay positive."

Carole smiled at her friend and asked, "So, are you going to call them on Monday?"

Casey said she would and that yes, of course, she would let Carole know when the date was, again gratefully accepting Carole's offer to be at the hospital on the day of the op. Casey was so lucky to have such good friends in Carole and Tilly.

"OMG! Amanda, I haven't told Amanda!"

Casey suddenly stopped drinking her latte as Carole reminded her Amanda was away.

"Don't forget she's on holiday from tomorrow, Case. Maybe wait until she gets back, no point having her worrying herself silly whilst she's away and can't do anything, especially as it's not the worst news. Besides, there's not much she can do right now anyway."

Carole talked sense and Casey nodded, agreeing completely. "You're right, I'll let her know when she gets back, I don't want to spoil her holiday and have her worrying about me when she should be enjoying herself. Besides, I might have even had the operation by then anyway."

Casey was again trying to keep herself upbeat. After finishing their coffee, the friends decided to wander through the new shopping centre and check out the windows, to see which shop would be the first to put up their Christmas decorations. Usually it was the bigger department stores, but since they'd had a few smaller shops open up in town, they both guessed that it was anyone's game to be first this year. Sure enough, the jewellers had tinsel and baubles already decorating the trays of rings, watches, bracelets and necklaces. They were obviously hoping to catch the eye of anyone passing, most likely aiming for the husband or boyfriend market, hoping they would be keen to impress a girlfriend or partner with something shiny and sparkly. It did look very festive, but as it was only the first week of October, both women agreed that it was just a tad too early.

As they passed the new handbag shop, Casey and Carole were still feeling strong and resisted the temptation to browse, deciding they were not going in because they both had more than enough handbags. However, that didn't stop them from being drawn into the shoe shop though. Ah yes, shoes, they were always a good pick-me-up when you were feeling a bit down, because generally they always fitted, no matter what your size or shape, unlike clothes. Furthermore, as most girls would say: 'You can never have too many shoes!' Casey wanted a pair of black suede boots. She loved suede and always found herself drawn to suede rather than leather. The brown suede boots she had bought the previous year from Jane Shilton were amazing and she loved wearing them, so she was hoping to find a similar pair in black.

"Here you go, size seven, Case. Try them on."

Carole had found a gorgeous pair of boots, which were about forty pounds more than Casey really wanted to pay, but they both agreed that with boots, you truly got what you paid for (and what's another forty pounds if they *were* the perfect boot). Laughing at their spending naughtiness, the girls had a great time, trying on several pairs of boots and shoes, before then moving on to Debenhams and the hat department. Since they had first known each other, they had *always* tried on the hats whenever they went shopping together. Both cracking up with laughter at each other, as they tried on the ugly ones as well as the finest ones and hiding from the assistants whenever they walked anywhere near the hat stands. It seemed to both Casey and Carole that retail therapy, particularly hat retail therapy, was certainly one very positive way of making you feel better.

After the two friends had walked their feet off and treated themselves to lunch and more coffee, they started off back home to prepare for their respective nights out. As they were walking back to their cars, Carole told Casey she was meeting a guy that one of her workmates had set her up with, to which Casey immediately responded with the whole twenty questions scenario:

1. What's his name?
2. Where does he work?
3. How tall is he?
4. What colour is his hair?
5. What colour are his eyes?
6. What type of build is he? Skinny, chunky, muscular?
7. How does your friend know him?
8. What star-sign is he?
9. Where is he from?
10. Does he have any brothers?

At number ten, both girls started giggling; it was just the standard thing Carole normally asked Casey whenever she met a new man. This time the tables were turned and Casey loved the fun of asking all the questions, whilst also feeling really chuffed about Carole's date; telling her she wanted a full report the next day.

As always, she reminded Carole that if she needed to escape the date and wanted the 'rescue phone call', she should just make a missed call to Casey and she would call her back twenty minutes later. Discussing this arrangement had them both chuckling again and hoping that there would be no need for the rescue phone call and that Carole's date would turn out to be some gorgeous hunk. Mind you, he had to be taller than Carole because she really didn't like dating men smaller than her. He also had to smile a lot, be very sexy, make her laugh and have a good job, or at least be financially independent.

Not too tall an order then!

"He sounds really nice but you never do know, not until you meet someone face-to-face, to see if the chemistry is there!"

Carole was in optimistic mode despite her nerves jangling at meeting someone new.

"Yep, fingers crossed he fits the bill, Carole," Casey said. "It's about time you got hooked up again and had some fun."

Casey knew Carole had lived through a hard few years since her husband Tom had died so young. Losing Tom had been a great loss to everyone who had known him. He'd had such a magnetic personality and seemed to draw people to him no matter what the situation. Best of all, he had doted on Carole, who had blown him away with her dazzling smile when they were both just twenty-five years old. Tom's sudden and unexpected death had devastated Carole and it took her a long time to come to terms with the finality of him dying. It had seemed so unfair to have been killed by a brain haemorrhage at such a young age and even the doctors had said that nobody could have predicted what had happened. Sadly, it was just one of those rare occurrences when healthy looking people seem to die for no reason. Despite being told that, Carole had still somehow felt responsible for not noticing any warning signs and the only consolation for her was that Tom knew nothing about it. One minute he was playing football and the next he was gone; it was that quick, totally painless, but so very immediate!

Casey hugged Carole and wished her good luck for her date, as well as thanking her for being so available at the drop of a hat, to help Casey deal with her own drama today. Setting off for home, Casey was in an upbeat mood and looking forward to her own date with Matt, the worries of her procedure pushed to the back of her mind for the time being.

Chapter 16

Next Steps

In the build up to the day of her op, Casey had grown closer to Matt and so two nights before she was due to have the surgery, she decided to tell him all about it. The two of them were enjoying an evening in and had planned on cooking a meal together, followed by a movie and accompanied by the obligatory bucket of popcorn. Matt had already resigned himself to the fact that as Casey loved popcorn and he was too tempted to resist, he was going to have to work a little harder in the gym to burn off the extra calories he was now consuming on a regular basis.

Having decided on a delicious fish dish for dinner and knowing that Matt was actually a very good cook, Casey was looking forward to their food. A boyfriend who could cook was always a bonus in Casey's book and Matt loved the idea of cooking with Casey, even if that had actually been just Casey preparing a few veggies, then drinking the glass of wine he poured for her, whilst *she* watched *him* cook. Casey decided to wait until after their meal for the planned big speech.

But as Matt picked up their plates to clear the table, her pre-planned speech went out the window and she just ad-libbed it whilst she too helped clear the dishes.

"So, Matt, there's something I need to tell you."

Casey almost blurted it out and hearing her voice sound suddenly urgent, Matt stopped in his tracks and turned around, concerned as he searched her serious face, trying to second guess what she was about to say. Casey had gone from laughing to looking very worried. Matt was immediately concerned, thinking she was about to dump him or something.

"What is it, Case?"

"Well, I guess you've been wondering why I've not jumped your bones yet?"

Casey had to make light of it, as it was the only way she could tell him about her fears, without it sounding too dramatic. Matt breathed a sigh of relief, clearly *not* being dumped then he thought and responded as honestly as he could.

"Well, to be honest, I've wanted to make love to you ever since I first met you, Casey. You're so beautiful it's hard to resist you, but I wanted you to be ready and well, I guessed that when you were, you'd let me know."

Matt was desperate to make love to Casey because he truly had fallen for her in a big way, but he was afraid to tell her in case he frightened her off. Casey smiled happily at his reply and he reflected that smile back, thinking *It can't be too bad then*, as he waited patiently for Casey to elaborate. Reaching out to take his hand, Casey had wanted him to make love to her, but she had been afraid to let him see her breasts and so that was how she explained it.

"I have so wanted you to make love to me, Matt, on several occasions actually," she said. "But I found a lump in my breast recently and I've been having tests, then waiting for the results and well...basically, I have to have an op to remove it and that's going to be the day after tomorrow."

There, she had said it, albeit having barely drawn a second breath as she spoke, and now searching Matt's face for a reaction, she was fearful of it being one of shock and horror and not wanting to be any part of this situation. Matt automatically reached out for her though and pulled her into his arms, holding her close and almost whispering his reply.

"Oh, Casey, that's not what I expected you to say. I thought you were going to dump me, Jees. Is it serious?

Sorry, stupid question. It must be if they're operating. Are you OK?"

Matt was shocked and didn't really know what to say, but on hearing those words, Casey pulled back a little so she could look up at Matt's face. *Bless him*, Casey thought, he looked so concerned that she felt a little tug of love for him as she went on to explain further.

"They said it's a collection of abnormal cells; apparently, it's not yet showing up as cancerous, but they want to take them out before anything more sinister develops."

Casey actually voiced the word 'cancer', which was the first time she had done so. Yet, having said it to Matt in a manner that was so matter-of-fact, she realised there was nothing more to worry about. If the doctors were right, she would be absolutely fine after they'd excised the collection of cells, which were basically forming some kind of lump.

Matt heaved a sigh of utter relief, telling Casey that he had total faith in the doctors at that hospital, having worked there on and off for the last five years.

Casey was naturally surprised to hear that Matt worked at the hospital. She hadn't known that his work as a Personal Trainer extended beyond the gym, because he rarely spoke about it, which had been due to client and patient confidentiality. But Matt's connection to the hospital required further explanation for Casey. So he explained that he was qualified to work with people who had medical conditions, like heart problems, and that he had been aligned to the Physiotherapy Department on an ad-hoc basis for some years now. As he continued, Matt explained that he was not fully employed by the hospital as such, but was called in as and when he was needed, usually to work with specific patients. The length of time depended on their medical condition and rehabilitation requirements.

"Ah, that explains why Carole saw you at the hospital the other day then."

Realisation dawned on Casey and she felt much better about telling Matt about her own condition. Also, because he had been so sweet in his reaction to her news, Casey leaned forward to kiss him without even thinking about it. Matt's heart leapt and he gently pulled Casey toward him, kissing her passionately and saying her name over and over in between his kisses. "Oh Casey, Casey, Casey."

The passion between them was growing and although both of them could feel it, they each held back, not wanting to rush into anything. Feeling nervous about hurting Casey, even Matt's embrace was a little more relaxed than it would usually be. Sensing his concern for her, Casey reassured him that she was fine and that she wouldn't break, then said she wanted him to make love to her. To convince him of that fact she slipped off the thin straps of her dress from her shoulders and let it slide to the floor, revealing scanty lace panties and her naked breasts.

Matt's response was to briefly pause and take in the vision of the beauty standing in front of him, before sweeping Casey up into his arms and carrying her through to the bedroom, where he laid her on the bed very gently. Pulling off his jumper and unbuckling his jeans, Matt stood beside the bed in his bright red and white jocks with his masculinity very obviously wanting and ready to take Casey. While his fingers slid his jocks down, Matt watched excitedly as Casey's nipples hardened, gasping lightly as she took in the sight of his expanded manhood. Matt knew he was well endowed and for once, he was thankful that he could please this woman with whom he was so in love with. Wanting Casey to feel every inch of his hardness, as she reached out to touch him, Matt groaned and knelt down on the bed to slip off her panties, exposing every womanly part of her. As Matt knelt astride her legs, he took in the beauty of her and leaned forward to kiss her tummy before working up her body. His lips explored and kissed every part of both breasts before taking a nipple into his mouth and sucking on the hardness of it. Exciting anticipation was swelling within him as Casey, now groaning with pleasure, reached her hands down to touch him. She loved the muscles bulging in his arms as he supported himself so as not to lay on her fully. The ripped tautness of his abdomen made Casey's own stomach flip and she felt that familiar wanting beginning to grow wildly inside her. Casey was ready for him and she wanted Matt badly. But he was lingering on her nipples, savouring every part of her, driving her wild with desire before moving up to kiss her throat, her face, her lips, and as his tongue explored her mouth, she returned his passionate kiss. Casey's body was aching for Matt and she arched up towards him, encouraging Matt to bring his own passion to join with hers. As their rhythmic movements conjoined and they explored and enjoyed every part of each other's bodies, their joint passion escalated into an explosion of pure ecstasy, love and completeness, as their ultimate joint climax was reached.

Breathing heavily, they parted and lay next to each other on the bed, as it took a good few moments for their breathing to calm down to a slight panting. The soft lamplight was comforting yet romantic and the two of them turned their heads to face each other for a few extended moments. Matt rolled onto his side and kissed Casey's lips gently, before pulling his head back just enough to focus on her face. His gaze became intense as he admired in her beauty and said the words he had wanted to say since the first moment he saw her.

"You truly are a very sexy woman, Casey, that's obvious to any guy looking at you. But there is so much more about you than any other woman I have ever met. Since I first saw you, I've not been able to stop thinking about you and I knew from that moment, until right now, that I have been madly in love with you. As crazy and as stupid as it may seem, I love you, Casey, very much."

Matt's voice faltered as he hoped she would respond with the words he was so desperate to hear. Casey smiled and touched her fingers to his lips as she caressed his face.

"Oh, Matt, I never expected to feel this way and I've wanted you for so long, but now, having you here and making love with you...I know it's true. I haven't imagined it, I love you too, and I want to make love with you every day and to be held in your arms..."

Before she could finish, Matt's mouth was upon hers and kissing her passionately, he was ecstatic that she loved him too and he pulled her towards him, gently rolling onto his back until she was laid on top of him. Wanting to feel the closeness of her, to make sure she was real and that he wasn't dreaming, Matt just held her, then reached up to cup her face as he pushed her hair back so he could look into her eyes.

"I love you, Casey, and this feels like we are truly meant to be together."

Casey kissed him and again their joint passion stirred from within, both of them consumed by the intensity of the moment. Their love for each other and the animalistic intent for repeated consummation was growing by the second. Casey moved down Matt's body, kissing his chest and abdomen, teasing him to the point of him being ready to enter her again. As she sat astride his ample manhood, she worked them both to the dizzy heights of pure pleasure once again, both crying out each other's name as they reached their climactic peaks.

With Casey still astride him, Matt sat up and holding her to him, he kissed her again. The two lovers were completely oblivious to everyone and everything else going on in their lives, because right then, at that very point, they were consumed by each other.

Much later, the two lovers fell asleep in each other's arms, snuggled together under the duvet and at peace with everything and everyone around them.

The following morning, Casey awoke before Matt and after freshening up, decided to make them both a drink. Whilst waiting for the kettle to boil, Casey thought about the previous night, their love-making had been better than she could have ever imagined. Casey could scarcely believe how happy and relaxed she felt. Particularly after explaining to Matt about everything the doctor had said, and now feeling incredibly relieved at no longer having to keep that news a secret from him. As she pondered that thought, Casey remembered that actually, she *did* have one secret and the time had come to tell Matt. Just at that point and taking her completely by surprise, Matt's arms slid around Casey's waist and he kissed the back of her head.

"Good Morning, gorgeous. Last night was wonderful; *you* were wonderful."

Matt murmured into Casey's hair before turning her around to face him and kiss her good morning. Feeling guilty, Casey found it hard to kiss Matt back with the same passion, which made him pull away, worried that something was wrong. Reassuring him that she was fine, Casey finally admitted her secret to him.

"But there is something I really need to tell you, Matt."

"Oh, what's that?"

For a moment, Matt was worried, not knowing what Casey was about to say.

"Well, actually, if you just stand there" – she moved him to the right spot – "and now lean forward to look out of the window."

Casey was nervous but hopeful that Matt wouldn't freak out.

"OK, what am I looking at?"

Matt was puzzled by this request but being in a playful mood, he did as Casey asked.

"Look down to your apartment."

Casey was really nervous now. "I have a confession, Matt," she paused. "Before I knew you, I was looking out of the window one day and saw you working out and well, after that, I would watch you every now and then. Not *every* day, but quite a lot."

Her voice trailed off as she looked at him, worried about how he would react to this news of her guilty pleasure. Matt burst out laughing.

"Ha, ha, ha, ha, ha. So, I have my own cheeky voyeur do I?" As he laughed out loud, he pulled her towards him. "If I'd known, I could have popped over sooner and had my wicked way with you."

Matt was ready to do that very thing again and so instead, he picked her up and almost ran back to the bedroom, still laughing as he threw her on the bed and tickled her as her punishment. Casey was screeching and wriggling to get away from his tickles, giggling like crazy and totally relieved at Matt's reaction to her little confession. Her giggles turned back into high pitched screeches as he tickled her relentlessly and the only way she could stop him was to reach out and grab his hardness. Matt sure was impressive and Casey wanted to experience him again. As Matt felt Casey's hand touching him, he stopped in his tracks and groaned with pleasure. Casey laughed, knowing she had the power to own him right there and then.

"Ha! I'm getting my own back now, Matthew Truman."

Whilst taking full pleasure in watching Matt's reaction to her touch, just at that very point the kettle whistled as the water boiled. But not one to be put off, Matt jumped off the bed to switch off the gas and then returned, standing to attention and ready to service his wildly naughty woman once again.

As they showered and dressed after their morning love making session, Matt told Casey he was actually really glad that she had told him about her op. He also said that he wanted to be there with her, so that when she woke up, she would see him sitting beside her. In fact, he had already decided to reschedule all his personal training appointments, to free up his time for a couple of weeks, so he could help her during the recovery days after surgery. In his mind he was thinking that if it did turn out to be bad news, he wanted to be with Casey, from the get-go.

Casey smiled at him from the shower and told him she was really happy that he wanted to be there. She also felt very relieved too, knowing that Matt must really care about her if he was prepared to do all of that for her.

It was two days later and Casey was now lying on the bed in the hospital's Day Care Centre, waiting for the anaesthetist to arrive with her pre-meds. Matt was by her side. Carole and Tilly were both extremely pleased that Casey had finally told Matt. Both of her friends had agreed that it was very decent of him to want to be the one to stay with her *and* to be there for her when she came around from the op.

The truth of it was that Matt had been a complete rock for the last couple of days and had reassured Casey that he would call both Carole and Tilly as soon as she was awake. Carole told Matt that Amanda was due back from holiday on the day of Casey's op, so they'd agreed that Carole would call Amanda after she'd landed, but would also tell her not to rush over to the hospital because visiting was restricted anyway. Also, seeing as Casey would likely be home within two days, Amanda could visit her there much easier; meanwhile, she could recover from her jet-lag.

Casey was expecting her apartment to be busy for quite a few days once she was back home again, what with all the anticipated visitors coming and going.

As Matt kissed Casey, he wished her good luck for the last time before she was taken down to theatre, adding that he would be waiting for her when she came back in a couple of hours. Feeling slightly apprehensive, but equally hopeful for a good outcome, Matt walked along the hospital corridors to the cafeteria to get a coffee, also thinking he would take the opportunity to text Carole and Tilly, to tell them Casey was in theatre.

The canteen staff knew Matt well and what type of coffee he drank, so they chatted easily with him as they prepared his drink and wished his girlfriend a speedy recovery. Picking up his cup and an almond biscotti (Casey had got him hooked on those too), Matt walked over to the sofa area and choosing one of the new tub chairs to settle into for the next couple of hours, he picked up a newspaper to help distract his thoughts, whilst he waited for Casey to come back from surgery. Matt sent his text messages to the girls and then turned straight to the sport pages of the newspaper. The staff nurse had told him to pop back in three hours, to give them time to settle Casey back into the ward once she came back up from recovery.

Those three hours felt like the longest time to Matt and for the last hour, he had paced the floor like an expectant father waiting for news of the birth of a child. The newspaper had barely distracted him; he couldn't really concentrate on anything for more than a minute and even the sports news wasn't grabbing his attention for long. Whilst he'd been pacing, one of the team from the Physiotherapy Department had popped into the cafeteria to pick up a sandwich. On seeing Matt, Tim asked if he was OK. Without giving away too much detail about Casey, Matt replied that he was waiting for his girlfriend to come out of surgery; he then swiftly turned the conversation around to enquire after a mutual patient the two men had both worked on the previous week. After a brief update, Matt's colleague made his farewells and said he hoped Casey's surgery went well. Matt thanked Tim and agreed the same thoughts, that Casey would be fine.

Time seemed to drag for Matt and he became more and more tense. The clock hands seemed to move slower as he watched them move around to the time that the staff nurse had instructed him to wait, before he could return to the ward. With every painful tick, that time finally arrived and Matt almost ran back to the ward, stopping at the nurses' station to check it was OK to go into the side room that Casey was in previously. But he was surprised when the staff nurse responded: "Oh hello, Matt. I'm sorry but she's not back from theatre yet. I'll put a call into recovery and see when they expect her to be coming back up."

Staff nurse Mary Clark already knew Matt from the Physiotherapy Department, when he'd been brought in to look after one of the hospital's long-term patients, who also happened to be Mary's cousin, Lucy.

A serious car accident had left Lucy badly hurt, which resulted in a long recovery period for her. Yet despite her injuries, Lucy had been amazing and surprised everyone with how determined she was. She had been so totally focussed on making a full recovery, in spite of the reduced capability of her left arm and leg. Matt could not fail to be impressed by her gutsiness. Lucy had certainly been dealt a tough blow, but she was such an optimist and was not about to let a car accident affect the rest of her life. Having seen injured soldiers recover from the most horrific of injuries, during their shared physiotherapy sessions, Lucy had decided that she could manage exercising an arm and a leg to get them working again. At least she still had her arm and leg. Matt had been impressed by Lucy's positive attitude and had supported and encouraged her, getting her moving again to the point that she was strong enough to leave the hospital. The aim was for Lucy to manage living back in her own home, without the need for additional carers. Staff nurse Mary Clark would be eternally grateful to Matt for the effort and care he had put into Lucy's treatment. Mary and Lucy were really close, like sisters really, so to see how far Lucy had come and how effective her rehabilitation had been, thanks to Matt, swelled Mary's heart with sibling-like love for this extraordinary man.

Now looking up at Matt with a concerned expression on her face, Mary listened to the person on the end of the phone. Matt knew something was wrong and that it must be serious for Mary to be on the line for so long. Mary thanked the person speaking and put the phone down gently before looking back up to Matt with what he could only describe as an incredible sadness in her eyes.

"Mary, what is it? Something's wrong. What is it, please...?"

Matt's voice was desperate and his face drawn by the worried expression which had developed as he'd watched Mary on the phone.

"Oh, Matt, I'm so sorry...it seems Casey has had a reaction to the anaesthetic and her heart stopped and well..."

Mary couldn't help it and she knew it wasn't professional, but she cared about Matt and couldn't control the tears in her eyes. Matt's voice interrupted her words; he was reeling with shock.

"No, no, Mary, no!"

Matt's voice broke and he staggered back, hitting the wall behind him. Mary rushed to take his arm.

"Matt, listen to me," she said. "They managed to re-start her heart, but now they can't bring her round. She just won't wake up. All her vital signs are OK, but she just won't wake up. They're working on her right now."

Matt couldn't take it in. "You mean she's OK? You mean, she's not dead?"

Relief was creeping into Matt's voice as he hoped for better news. As Mary responded, her own tears were under control again and her professional front had kicked back in. "No, Matt, she's not dead, she's *alive,* but they just can't wake her up."

Mary repeated what the Recovery Team had told her and watched to see that Matt had understood what she was telling him.

"Oh, Mary, I thought when you said her heart had stopped that she'd died. I can't believe it. No. No. It can't be true. I love her Mary, she has to wake up, she has to..."

Matt's voice was full of despair and desperation. Mary's heart reached out for him, hating to see his pain and willing that Casey would pull through and wake up soon.

"Will they bring her back to this ward?"

Matt was struggling to stay calm, but he knew he needed to pull himself together, so he could be ready for Casey.

"I expect she will be taken either to the High Dependency Unit or to Intensive Care, Matt, until they can determine why she's not waking up. They will call back in half an hour to confirm. Why don't you sit down and I'll fetch you a cup of tea."

"Thanks, Mary."

Matt needed a stronger drink than tea.

"It's no problem," Mary said. "Now sit yourself down, you've had a shock. I'll be back in a few minutes."

Mary went off to the staff-room to make them both a drink.

What seemed like hours later but was in fact only forty-five minutes (slightly longer than the thirty minutes she had previously been told though), Mary took another call and confirmed to Matt that Casey would indeed be taken straight to the High Dependency Unit (HDU). So, if he would like to gather her things, he could go and see her there. Visiting would be restricted to one person and only close family. Mary knew that Casey was an orphan and had no family, so Matt would be the only person allowed to see her to begin with. Mary went on to explain that once Casey was stable, the doctor would likely allow two people to visit, but timing would be restricted and they would probably be told what to do.

Even though he was listening to Mary, Matt wasn't really taking it in properly. All he could think about was Casey and how much he loved her and wanted her to wake up. He had to tell her how important she was to him; he needed her, she couldn't leave, she couldn't die! Overcome by the worry that was consuming him, Matt thanked Mary and walked over to the empty space where Casey's bed had stood before she had been taken down to theatre. Picking up her bag, Matt carefully placed her few belongings into it before zipping it up and turning back towards the nurses' station. Matt stopped to thank Mary again and then walked towards the High Dependency Unit waiting area. Desperation for Casey's recovery caused Matt's shoulders to slump as he walked along the familiar corridors.

Chapter 17

Casey

As he sat in the waiting area of the High Dependency Ward with Casey's bag of belongings on the chair next to him, Matt realised for the first time in his life, how scary it was to have someone you love so desperately, hanging on to life by a thread. There were so many people who lived with life and death situations as part of their everyday life, and Matt could now totally empathise with their worries and concerns.

The coffee machine in the corner of the room was Matt's only respite, as he recharged with a caffeine shot and thought about what and how he was going to tell Carole and Tilly the awful news. In fact, would it be good news or would there be no change? Would Casey miraculously awaken when they brought her back, or would she still be unconscious and in a coma? Matt's head was spinning, fuelled by caffeine, which he knew wasn't good for him, but he just didn't care about himself right now, all he cared about was Casey. Matt knew Casey's friends all loved her so much and were as close as family to her. How on earth was he going to tell them all and how could he live without her if she never woke up again? That thought did not even bear thinking about and yet it had Matt on the brink of tears.

Leaning back in the waiting room chair, Matt closed his eyes. Remembering when just two nights before, they had made such wonderful love together. It had been amazing and he had known then, how deep and true his love for her was. A tear finally escaped and ran down his face, brushing it away, Matt heard the lift doors opening and as his head snapped round, he could see Casey being wheeled out of the lift and into the unit. Watching as they wheeled her past him, Matt was shocked at how pale Casey looked. There was a drip hooked up to her, as well as several bags hanging from her bed and a portable heart monitor resting at the bottom of the bed. She looked like she had already gone from him. Matt gasped and struggled to hold it together.

The Surgeon, Steve Morgan, followed Casey out of the lift and knowing Matt would be waiting for them to arrive, he stopped to speak to him briefly. Steve Morgan explained to Matt that all had gone well until they were closing her up and then something, which they could only guess was linked to the anaesthetic, had reacted with her and totally unexpectedly, Casey's heart had stopped. The surgeon went on to say that whilst they had managed to re-start her heart, they still couldn't bring her around from the anaesthetic. Casey just wouldn't wake up. All that could be done now was to monitor her closely to ensure she remained stable and then re-check her brain function the following day.

Steve Morgan touched Matt's arm. "I'm so sorry, Matt, there's nothing more I can tell you at this time."

"What? Brain function? Oh no…" Matt was mentally reeling in shock.

Steve Morgan sat him down and asked a nurse to fetch some water. Continuing, Steve Morgan said he would settle Casey in and come back to talk to Matt again shortly. Nodding but unable to speak, Matt lifted his hand slightly in acknowledgement, his mind now in overdrive. Of course, they would need to check brain function, because her heart had stopped and she wouldn't wake up. Of course they would check brain function. Matt kept repeating the words in his head and couldn't quite believe this was really happening. How could his beautiful Casey be lying there unconscious and with possible brain damage?

What felt like an hour later, Steve Morgan returned to where Matt was sitting, anxiously waiting for good news. On seeing the greyness of his face as Matt stood up to speak to him, Steve Morgan encouraged his colleague to sit back down and took the chair beside him. Carefully explaining to Matt that whilst this was a very rare and unexpected outcome, Casey's vitals all seemed good and so long as the brain scan showed normal function, they would just have to wait and see how she responded in the next twenty-four hours. The best any of them could do in this situation was to hope and pray that Casey would wake up soon. Steve Morgan was as anxious as Matt and added that there seemed to be no real reason as to why Casey had not woken up; it just seemed as though she was that one in a million person that this sort of thing might happen to.

Steve Morgan had recognised Matt when he first saw him, having seen him around the hospital quite regularly and when asked, Matt explained what his role was. The Consultant Surgeon nodded his understanding, feeling encouraged to know that Matt would likely kick into medical mode sooner rather than later and would then feel more useful knowing he could help. If the coma extended, Matt's skills would be needed to exercise Casey's limbs to ensure blood flow was maintained and to reduce stiffening and/or deterioration of her joints and muscle tissue. Whilst that would help Casey, Steve Morgan also knew it would help Matt to cope, knowing he was able to do something to help, whilst they were in this unknown territory of when exactly, Casey might wake up.

Matt felt drained as he walked slowly out of the ward into the corridor to call Carole and Tilly. Still shaking with shock, he just wanted to be with Casey, but Steve Morgan had asked him to wait until she was properly settled. The nursing team needed to perform their first observations following Casey's arrival on the ward and it was easier to do that without loved ones present.

Matt's stomach was churning as Carole answered the phone with a chirpy voice: "Hi, Matt, so how's our girl doing...did it all go alright?"

Almost unable to speak, Matt began the dreaded conversation: "Hi, Carole, they just brought her up from recovery, but there was a problem..."

Matt's voice was cracking. On hearing this, Carole immediately knew it was serious and gripped the phone tighter, as she asked the inevitable question: "Matt, what is it? Is she OK? What happened?"

Hearing Carole's voice taking on such a sense of urgency broke through Matt's resolve even more and he struggled to croak out the words: "She hasn't come round, Carole. They said her heart stopped, a reaction to the anaesthetic or something...they don't really know, but she won't wake up."

Matt's voice trailed off, not knowing what else to say, but knowing that Carole would be as distraught as he was right now. At the other end of the line, Carole sank into the chair beside her.

"No! But she's going to be OK isn't she, Matt? I mean she's still alive isn't she? She just hasn't woken up right? Do they know when she will? Oh, Matt, what are we going to do?"

Carole's voice sounded as desperate as Matt felt.

"I honestly don't know, Carole. There's not much we can do right now; she's in the high-dependency ward and only allowed two visitors at a time. You could come down, but there's nothing we can do other than sit and wait. I'm going back in as soon as I get off the phone."

"Of course," she said. "I'll come right away. Have you called Tilly yet?"

Carole was beginning to think logically again, moving into auto-pilot as she felt compelled to support Matt and Casey by being the strong one.

"No, not yet. I rang you first. Could you call Amanda and I'll call Tilly?"

Matt was suddenly exhausted. His brain had gone into some kind of overload; at least that's what it felt like, but he had to hold it together. He had to be there for Casey and he knew her friends loved her as much as he did, so he had to be strong for them too.

"Yes, of course, yes, of course I will."

Carole was responding with a repeated answer, but she needed to feel super-efficient to help her cope with the fear that was creeping into her bones.

"I'll get a message to Edine too."

"Oh yeah, of course, I forgot about Edine…thanks, Carole. I'll see you soon. I need to call Tilly so I can get back to Casey. Bye for now."

Matt was anxious to get back to Casey's bedside and felt he needed to get all the calls done as soon as he could.

"OK and, Matt, I'm glad Casey's got you there."

Carole genuinely meant every word. She had seen how happy Matt was making Casey and hoped it was the real thing for them both. What a tragedy if they lost her now, just when she was at her happiest. No, that thought didn't need to be in her head, so Carole pushed it back out again and slammed the door shut on it, determined and knowing she needed to keep as positive as possible.

Matt dialled Dave first and told him the news, then said he was going to call Tilly, so Dave had better get over there because she would likely need him. Dave couldn't believe it and was devastated for Casey, but also for Matt. Like Carole, Dave had also seen how happy the two of them had been since they'd started dating and couldn't believe this had happened to them. Dave told Matt not to worry about calling Tilly and that he would go straight over and be the one to tell her face-to-face. Then they would both come to the hospital straight away and sit in the waiting area for him, in case there was any news, or until they could see Casey.

Feeling relieved at not having to say the words again, Matt thanked Dave and said he'd see them later, then hung up and walked back to the ward. Waiting to be buzzed back into the secure unit and being an old hand in the hospital, Matt knew the drill, so as he walked towards Casey's room, he hesitated at the nurse station to confirm who he was and that he was there for Casey. Steve Morgan had already pre-warned the staff nurse on duty who Matt was and had instructed them to allow him to also help with Casey's care, by exercising her limbs, as and when it was needed. However, for today, Casey was to be left to rest, so Matt could just talk to her and hold her hand, but nothing more than that at this stage.

This is what the nurses relayed to Matt and nodding his understanding, he thanked them then turned towards Casey's room. As he walked into the clinical space, the sunshine was streaming in through the window and throwing a brilliant light into the room, which lifted his spirits slightly. Matt knew that if Casey were awake she would love lying there in the sunshine. However, she wasn't awake. Instead, she was lying motionless, her complexion looking paler than he had ever seen and even worse, she wasn't just sleeping, she was still unconscious, and in a coma.

Despite her paleness and lack of expression, Matt could still see such beauty in Casey's face and he bent over to lightly brush her lips with a delicate kiss.

"Hello, Casey, my love," he said softly. "You look beautiful lying there in the sunshine. The surgery went really well; so come on now, my love, it's time to wake up."

Matt watched Casey's eyes, hoping she would stir, but no, there was nothing, no response, no flicker of her eyelids, nothing. Matt was gutted as his beautiful Casey remained unconscious. It was as if she was quietly sleeping, in a deep and dreamless state without a care in the world. As he sat down, Matt took Casey's hand and leaning towards her he whispered quietly: "I love you, Casey. Please come back to me. Come on now, wake up my precious beautiful girl. It's time to wake up, we all love you and we need you here with us."

Still no reaction, Matt kissed Casey's hand so tenderly and just sat holding it, as he stroked the soft skin of her face with his other hand. His touch was gentle and loving and so perfectly wonderful that, had Casey been watching him herself, she would have cried at the tenderness Matt displayed. It was obvious to anyone watching, that this man very much loved his sleeping beauty.

It was this scene that Carole witnessed as she arrived an hour later, with flowers and chocolates, lemon barley water, tissues, wet-wipes, deodorant, a toothbrush and toothpaste, magazines and various other bits of paraphernalia. Even though Carole knew that Casey could not see or use any of what she had brought, she felt she just had to bring it, in case her friend woke up and needed *anything*, anything at all. Carole was worried sick, but on seeing Matt holding Casey's hand and gently stroking her face as he quietly spoke to her, Carole's own heart melted and she just said, "Oh, Matt," as a tear escaped and ran down her cheek before splashing onto the floor.

Hearing Carole's voice break through his own words, Matt looked up. Carole could see that even through his usual tan, he looked drawn and had lost his usual sparkle. His face was pale and carried a worried expression.

"Carole, thank goodness you're here. I keep talking to her, but I'm just not getting through, I don't know if she can hear me or not. I'm hoping she can; apparently, some people can still hear you even when they can't respond, or so the nurses told me."

Matt was willing to do anything to encourage Casey to wake up and would talk to her for as long as the Medical Team allowed him to.

The consultant surgeon and the nurses had told him to keep talking to Casey, because coma patients often claim when they wake up that they've heard conversations which had taken place in the room, whilst they were still unconscious. This was something the medical profession had varying opinions on, but it had given Matt some hope and so he had confirmed to them that he would keep talking to Casey and encourage her to wake up.

The nursing team had also instructed him that the talking could only be in between the breaks that they had insisted Casey must have, so she could completely rest with no sound. Carole now joined Matt on the opposite side of Casey's beside and quietly sat in the visitor's chair, trying not to drag it and make a noise as she took Casey's other hand.

"Casey, it's me, Carole...are you going to wake up for us now, honey. We're dying to know how the op went. Matt's here too; we both are. We're here for you, Casey. Come on now, honey, it's time for tea. Shall I pop the kettle on?"

Carole thought that if she spoke as though nothing was wrong, if Casey could hear her, she wouldn't be worried and would wake up. But no, still nothing. Carole looked at Matt and asked him if he was OK? It seemed a silly question because of course he wasn't OK, but Carole then whispered very quietly to Matt that if they spoke normally, Casey might just hear them and wake up. He agreed it was worth a try and answered her as best he could.

"I'm fine, Carole, just waiting for sleeping beauty here to wake up. You know some people will do *anything* for a lie in."

Matt tried to crack a joke even though laughing was the very last thing he felt like doing right now. Carole joined in and between them they continued chatting in a light-hearted manner, talking about the weather, their work and what they were doing that evening (or at least what they had *originally* planned to be doing, which had now changed dramatically with Casey's condition).

Matt explained to Carole that the surgeon's name was Steve Morgan and that Steve had told him the surgery went very well, and they think they had managed to get all of the abnormal cells out and so Casey should recover well. That was if she woke up ever again, thought Matt. Although he didn't say it, he knew that if the worst scenario were to come true, he didn't know if he would be able to live without Casey.

Carole continued to talk to Matt about everything she could think of, both she and Matt hoping their conversations would trigger something in Casey's mind, telling her to wake up. The two of them could only stay for one hour before they had to leave for two hours to let Casey rest again. They decided to keep talking for the rest of their time in the room with her, before leaving for the two-hour rest period, by which time both of them were in need of a coffee, or water, anything in fact. The stress and constant chatting had left them parched. They would also catch up with Tilly and Dave, who, unbeknown to them, had both arrived in the hospital and were already on their way up to the floor where the High Dependency Ward was located.

As Matt and Carole were walking back along the corridor with their double shot lattes from the hospital café, Matt told Carole he was willing to stay 24/7 if he could. Whatever it took was OK by him. But he also knew it was more sensible and fairer for them to arrange a rota, so that there was always one of them on hand to be with Casey, should she wake up suddenly during the visiting times. Carole was about to respond as the two of them rounded the corner leading towards the HDU waiting area, when she and Matt both noticed Tilly and Dave walking out of the lift.

"Tilly. Dave." Matt spoke their names loudly enough for them to hear and turn around. Tilly rushed towards Matt and Carole with a dozen questions spilling out of her. Matt could see Tilly had been crying and hugged her to him. With Casey bringing them all together over such a crisis, the friends were immediately bonded by their joint concern for her and they united together as if they were indeed her family.

When Tilly finally pulled away from Matt's hug, she just looked at him, scared to hear the answers to her questions. As the four of them walked into the waiting area and sat down, Matt explained everything to them again, every little detail that had happened since Casey came back from recovery, including what the consultant surgeon had said.

Steve Morgan had been so brilliant with Matt, that he felt totally confident that Casey's best interests really were at the forefront of Steve's concerns. Despite many years of experience, this was apparently not something the consultant surgeon had ever encountered himself, but he had reassured Matt by telling him he had been researching it ever since Casey had been brought into the HDU from recovery. Steve Morgan also told Matt that he had spoken to a colleague at another hospital to ensure their plan of care was correct and would help stimulate Casey's brain into waking up. This piece of news was a pleasant surprise to Matt and he felt like Steve was really *owning* Casey's situation. The man was definitely doing everything in his power to help.

Matt also told the group of friends that Steve Morgan had booked a brain scan for the following morning, which was to check Casey's brain functionality. At this piece of news, the others gasped, shocked at the prospect that Casey might have brain damage, which subsequently launched them into a discussion about how bad it might be.

Matt stopped them. "Guys, let's not panic or fear the worst. I know it sounds bad, but we've got to keep as positive and upbeat as possible for Casey's sake. Just in case she *can* hear us and senses something is wrong."

This was a point to which they all agreed and they decided that as it was unclear as to whether Casey could hear them or not, they must all make a pact to keep positive and upbeat whilst they were in her room and talk as if she *definitely* could hear them. Each of them would try not to say or do anything that might worry or upset Casey, which included no crying. They agreed that they had to save their tears for the waiting area, or even when they got home. The pact was agreed and they reminded each other to also tell Amanda, at which point, Carole said she would try to call her again.

The four friends then took it in turns to go in to see Casey, each speaking to her as if she could hear them and all of them trying hard not to show any sign of concern, or speak of any worries, whilst they were in the room with her. All of them were hoping and praying that Casey could hear them and wanted everything she heard to be positive, to keep her upbeat, so that she would know all was well and that it was OK for her to wake up. As they each came out and returned to the waiting area, they cried, hugged and comforted one another, as Casey stayed the same.

Although the visiting time for the high dependency ward was fairly open, the nursing staff did ask visitors to leave by 7pm so they could settle patients for the night. At this point the friends thanked the ward staff for looking after Casey so well and then left together, comforting each other as they walked out. All of them now exhausted by the worry of what was wrong and why Casey still wasn't waking up.

As it was too late to be going home and then worrying about cooking dinner, the group of friends decided to go for something to eat together and to agree a visiting plan for Casey. Carole said she'd still not been able to reach Amanda and would call her again when she got back home, but that they should count Amanda in on the visiting plan. Carole knew Amanda would definitely want to help and be involved.

Matt asked Carole if she'd managed to speak to Edine, to which she replied no, unfortunately not, and that she'd had to leave a message with Edine's Personal Assistant, Sally, who was herself really concerned for Casey and she asked Carole to please pass on all of their good wishes. Sally also confirmed that of course she would tell Edine as soon as she was out of her Board Meeting and offered to be the point of contact for Edine. Knowing that Casey would be glad her Editor was being kept in the loop meant that even if that was all Carole could do for her friend, then it was no trouble at all for her to keep Edine informed of her progress.

The friends decided on a restaurant close to the hospital and ended up chatting together for a good couple of hours whilst they also agreed their visiting rota. When their much welcomed food arrived, each of them realised how ravenous they were and silence fell as they all ate. As they finished their meal and said their goodbyes, they hugged each other just a little tighter and for a little bit longer than they normally would have done. Every one of them feeling all the more emotional because of their friend and wishing that she would wake up and come back to them, whole and well.

The following morning, just before Matt arrived, Casey was wheeled down for her brain scan, which, to Steve Morgan's delight, showed no signs of damage. This was good news indeed, although it also seemed all the more puzzling as to why Casey wasn't waking up. But it was actually the news that the consultant surgeon was massively relieved to hear and lifted the spirits of each member of the medical team who was looking after Casey.

When Matt first arrived at the hospital in the morning, the nurse station was lacking in nurses, so he was stood outside the ward anxiously waiting to be let in to see Casey, at the same time that Steve Morgan returned for his daily rounds. Both men were relieved to share the fantastic news that there was no sign of brain damage, and as Matt stepped forward to man-hug Steve, the consultant surgeon totally understood the emotion of the moment and took the hug. Adding how relieved he was himself, that to all intents and purposes, Casey seemed to be OK and that as far as he could tell, there was no reason for her not to wake up. This made both men feel more optimistic about Casey recovering, but also left them puzzled as to why she wasn't waking up. The caveat was that if Casey didn't wake up soon though, other complications could kick in. So the latest advice was to try and stimulate Casey in the mornings, allow her to rest in the afternoon and then stimulate her again in the early evening, before leaving her to rest for the night, then start the whole regime again the next day.

Today's rota was for Matt and Tilly in the morning, followed by Carole and Amanda in the evening. The next day would be Tilly and Dave in the morning, with Matt and Amanda in the evening. This would be the first time that Matt would meet Amanda and he wished that it could have been on a happier occasion with Casey at his side, instead of lying comatose in bed. Tilly was also bringing in some music so they could play some of Casey's favourite tunes.

Luckily, the HDU was arranged as a collection of single rooms rather than a multi-bedded ward. This was to ensure patients could rest quietly, as well as receive visitors, which maintained that all important connection to home and often meant the patient recovered quicker.

It was lucky that Casey had her own room, because the following day a massive bouquet of very expensive looking, beautiful flowers arrived from the magazine, along with two, *Get Well Soon* helium filled balloons and all accompanied by a lovely card, which simply said: *'We are all thinking of you, Casey, get well soon. Much love, Edine & the Staff at Just for You!'*

Kisses had been added to the bottom of the card and as Tilly read it to Casey, she looked at Matt, while silent tears rolled down her own face. Matt squeezed Tilly's hand and said how lovely it was that Edine should send such beautiful flowers and how much they obviously thought of Casey to have sent them so quickly too. Matt and Tilly nodded in understanding to each other, knowing they had to keep upbeat and positive, which had been their joint pact. Tilly brushed away her tears and smiled at Casey. Now squeezing her sleeping friend's hand, Tilly talked about the flowers, describing the colours and scents in such wonderful detail that Matt was impressed by her artistic descriptions. The two of them talked all morning and Tilly played some of Casey's music. Three songs into the collection was *Let's get it on,* the song that, unbeknown to Tilly, held such a special meaning for Casey, but which Matt also remembered. After all, it had been the song he and Casey had danced to that night at Barney's. Matt gulped as it started, not sure he would hold it together. It was around thirty seconds into the track that Casey sighed and her right hand twitched.

Matt and Tilly had both heard the sigh and Matt had felt Casey's hand twitch as he held it in his own hand. Looking at Tilly, then back at Casey, this was the first sign they'd seen of any kind of reaction. Both Tilly and Matt's hopes soared.

"Casey, sweetheart, can you hear me? Can you hear the music? Do you remember us dancing to it? Casey?"

Matt sounded desperate as he tried to break through Casey's comatose state and Tilly chipped in brightly: "Case, it's me Tilly, can you hear us, honey? Can you hear the song?"

But there was no further response and feeling utterly helpless, Matt and Tilly just stared at Casey, willing her to wake up and desperate that she had seemed to be so close, but had then disappeared back into her comatose state just as quickly.

The afternoon came along all too quickly and they had to kiss Casey goodbye, both telling her they would be back the next day and that Amanda and Carole would be in to see her later. Of course, they had also told the nursing staff what had happened and felt encouraged by the reaction of the ward staff nurse at the news. This was a good sign she had said and meant Casey might be slowly waking up, but that they would also need to be patient because she may still stay asleep for a while yet. But in any case, the staff nurse reiterated that it was a good sign and that she would let Steve Morgan know, then went off to check on Casey's again. Matt and Tilly were cautiously optimistic though and because they were so desperate for Casey to wake up, both took the better scenario as being what *would* happen, neither of them wanting to think about the alternative.

As soon as they left the ward, Matt and Tilly rang the others to tell them the news, knowing just how relieved and encouraged they would all be, whilst acknowledging that their hopes might still be dashed. At the end of the day, it all depended on Casey herself and when she was able to wake up, or chose to wake up.

Chapter 18

In her head

Casey felt like she was walking through treacle. She could hear someone calling to her and could hear voices, but couldn't quite make out what they were saying. One was female and one was male; they sounded familiar, but she couldn't quite remember who they were. There was a mist descending, but even though she knew she was alone, Casey felt safe and wasn't at all worried. Casey wanted to reach out to the voices, to hear what they were saying, but she couldn't move. Why did it feel like she had lead boots on? Who was holding her back? For that matter, what was holding her back? She could hear music. Casey recognised the song; it was one of her favourites and she remembered dancing with Matt to it. At least Casey thought it was Matt, or was it Jason, she couldn't quite remember. Jason, yes, Jason, that name seemed more familiar to her, but who the heck was Dominic? Why was Dominic suddenly in her head? She couldn't quite fathom it out; what was wrong with her? She felt weird; her chest hurt and her tummy wasn't right, she felt sick, but couldn't move and she couldn't be sick. The music! That song! Casey loved that song and reached out towards it with her right hand, but, but, dammit, she couldn't quite reach it. What the heck was wrong with her?

'Nanny Em! You're there! Oh I've missed you so much! Nan, Nan. Oh, my darling Nanny Em.' As Casey was calling out to her, her Nanny Em stood still and just smiled. It was such a wonderful happy smile, but there was no reaching out of arms, just a peaceful calmness and such pure love, that it made Casey also stand still. As she could feel her Nan's love wrapping around her, Casey felt an intensely

249

blissful peace holding her and loving her. Casey's Nanny Em told her how wonderful it was to see her again, that she was so proud of her and was so happy to have this moment with her, but that it wasn't her time yet. As Casey reached out to touch her, Nanny Em told her not to and said that she had to go now, again stating that it wasn't Casey's time and that she must stay and be happy. *'What do you mean it's not my time, Nanny Em? What are you talking about?'* Casey was puzzled, she couldn't make out what was happening, she was slipping and falling. Nanny Em's arms were no longer holding her. No, not her arms, they were never *holding* her, but she had felt like they were. Casey felt her Nan's love, stronger than ever before, and she could feel her nearby, but she couldn't see her. *'Nan! What is that? What's happening?'* Casey was frowning and felt worried; she was upset. Why was Nanny Em leaving her? *'Nan!'* Casey was calling out, but there was no sound. The voices, there were those voices again…who were they and where had the guy's voice gone, she could only hear female voices now. Why couldn't she hear them properly? They sounded excited about something, and she wondered what that was, but why couldn't she hear them properly though?

Carole and Amanda had arrived to find Casey frowning and feeling excited at seeing some kind of movement in Casey's face, the two women started calling for a nurse to come in. As the staff nurse rushed into the room, Amanda spoke first: "Look at her, something's happening! Is she waking up?"

Desperate for answers and for Casey to wake up, the two friends stood watching, as the staff nurse checked Casey over.

"It does look like she's waking slowly, but she's not out of it yet. Do keep talking to her, she might respond to your voices. Her vitals are all fine and there is brain activity, so that is a very good sign."

The staff nurse had checked all the equipment surrounding Casey, including the machine attached to the pads that were stuck on Casey's scalp.

"This is such good news. I will call the consultant surgeon immediately," the staff nurse said brightly as she left the room to go and record this new development on Casey's records, and to call Steve Morgan.

"Oh, Carole, do you think we could get her to come back to us?" Amanda asked.

Amanda was begging for the right answer, which of course, Carole couldn't give, but just agreed that she hoped so. Amanda had been horrified to hear the news about Casey, on arriving home from her holiday and had raced around to Carole's to hear exactly what had happened. Although gutted at only just having been told about the lump, Amanda also totally understood and appreciated their kindness in keeping it from her, thinking she should enjoy her holiday. Deep down though, Amanda would still have preferred to have flown back early, to be there at the hospital with Casey, however, aware there was not much she could have done, especially since Matt had been there for Casey while she waited to go down to theatre. But then having heard the terrible news, Amanda was desperate to see her friend and was so relieved to have been counted in for the next visit.

Carole said that they should keep talking and perhaps Amanda could tell them both about her holiday adventures? She signalled to Amanda to carry on talking. Amanda appreciated Carole's generosity in letting her start off the chatter and launched in with what had happened at the airport and how she had bumped into Jason in Singapore. This had Carole raising her eyebrows, but then of course she remembered that Jason was travelling to New Zealand via Singapore, on his outbound flight.

Jason had decided to stop over for one night and on visiting a famous bar in the city, had bumped into Amanda, who only had a few days left of her holiday before she returned to the UK. Amanda had already heard about the encounter outside Casey's apartment and was surprised to hear Jason admit that Matt was probably better suited for Casey. In fact, Jason had admitted to Amanda that if he was being honest with himself, even though he was totally hacked off that Matt had won Casey's heart over him, Matt was a really decent bloke and would be good for Casey.

Just as Amanda reached that point of her story and relayed Jason's admission about Matt, Casey smiled. Amanda missed it but Carole saw it.

"Amanda, Amanda, look, she smiled, she actually just smiled, and it was exactly at the point you said that about Matt!"

Carole was suddenly excited and talking so fast that Amanda jumped up at her reaction and leaned in closer to Casey. "Case, can you hear us? It's us, Amanda and Carole. Come on, old girl, wake up, you're keeping us all on tenterhooks now."

Amanda was trying to talk normally, but unintentionally her tone crossed over into pleading, as she was willing Casey to wake up and to be OK.

Casey could hear those voices again and there was something familiar about them. Who were they? Casey couldn't figure it out. She smiled and hoped they could see her smile, but she had such a fog in her head; why wouldn't it go and what did it mean? Matt, Jason, who were they, and why did she know their names? She was tired and had a cracking headache. Why wouldn't it go? Where was she? Where had Nanny Em gone? Casey sighed again. Her chest felt like something had been pressing on it and then suddenly released again. What was that? She was confused.

Amanda and Carole were now both on their feet leaning in towards Casey and holding her hands whilst calling to her gently, asking her to wake up. But all Casey did was sigh. The women sat down again...she had felt so close. It felt like Casey was almost with them, but had then gone again, just as quickly. Both of them were close to tears and were now struggling not to let them fall. They *had* to be strong and keep the pact to stay positive, whilst they were in Casey's room.

Carole stood up and said she was just popping down for a coffee and did Amanda and Casey fancy a latte? Of course she knew Casey couldn't drink one, but Carole wanted to keep trying to drag Casey back to the real world and back with them, so she talked to her as if she were already awake.

Amanda said she'd love one and looked at Casey as she asked, "What about you, Case. Fancy a Latte? Carole's treat!"

Casey smiled again. That voice, she knew that voice so well. Who was it? Why were they asking her about coffee? She tried to nod, but she couldn't move...this was so frustrating, why couldn't she move? Jason, Jason, she kept hearing that name. There was a mist again. Who was that? There was a figure in the mist; she couldn't see who it was, the face was hidden, covered by the mist and a really bright light seemed to be pulling him towards it. Yes, it was a man. Was it...? Jason? Yes it was Jason. A tear rolled down Casey's face and splashed onto her pillow. He was saying goodbye. Why? Where was he going? Why was he so sad? The light was pulling him. He was saying goodbye.

'Casey, you're so special to me, be happy my love, I won't forget you.'

Casey felt anxious, she needed to reach out to Jason, she wanted to touch him, but he was being pulled away, such love, such immense love. It was like nothing Casey had ever felt as the love reached out for Jason, wrapping him in its arms.

'It's OK, Casey, I'm ok, I'm happy, you be happy too.'

Jason's voice was speaking to Casey, but she could no longer see him. He was part of the light; she could still feel the love, and she knew he was safe, but she felt sad. Another tear rolled down her face.

Amanda and Carole had seen the tears and looking at Casey they wondered what was causing her to cry. Both of them were disturbed by this emotion from their sleeping friend, which made them even more desperate to wake her and hold her and tell her everything was fine. That she *would* be fine, that all was well in her world, in this world, the one they occupied too. But they couldn't tell her because she wasn't hearing them. It was all so frustrating and they wanted to cry too.

Casey felt incredibly peaceful. A sense of calmness had washed over her. It was a feeling she had never before experienced; she sighed again, her tears had now gone and blissful peace was upon her once more. Casey felt sleep wafting over her and allowed herself to drift into the waves, and as they came over her, she could hear music again and relaxed as it played a song she knew well. She drifted again and was gone; there was nothing to wake up for yet, and she felt like she could sleep forever.

Carole and Amanda had reached the end of their visiting time and on leaving their friend for the evening, they each kissed her goodbye and told her they would see her the following day. Eager to share what had happened with the others, Carole and Amanda called them immediately after they'd left the ward. As Carole explained what had happened to Matt, Amanda repeated the same story to Tilly and Dave, who were together for the evening and waiting to hear the latest report.

Matt was slightly encouraged and very relieved to hear that Casey was experiencing more brain activity. He was, however, also gutted that he had not been there to witness it himself. Not only that, Matt had some news of his own, which he needed to share with Carole. It was not good news and certainly not news that would make Casey happy when she finally woke up. Matt was troubled by what he was going to have to tell Casey when she did finally wake up. Of all the things to happen, and at such a horrible time in all of their lives and for it to be Jason too. Matt felt so sad.

As he told Carole about the call he'd taken that very evening, Matt could barely believe it was true. The call had come from Jason's brother. "Apparently, Jason had arrived back in New Zealand and all had been well. The day after he arrived, Jason had gone out on a boat with his new work colleagues; most of the team were diving, but Jason had sensibly stayed in the boat with one of the women, who was pregnant and couldn't dive. Jason was keen to learn to dive, but had taken heed of his workmates' suggestions, to take an instructed course in diving, *safety first* being the key.

"The day out on the boat was supposed to be a 'Welcome to New Zealand' celebration for Jason and had started out really well. The weather was fantastic and they were all having a brilliant day. Everyone was excited about the dive, especially following their siting of a piece of treasure, which they had all dived back down to check out. The spot had happened right at the end of the dive session and they were almost out of air, so they'd marked the point on a map and headed back inland." Matt took a deep breath as he continued the story.

"As Jason was getting off the boat back onto the jetty, he had somehow slipped, which caused him to bang his head quite badly and he fell into the water, quickly going under. Two of his new colleagues immediately dived in after him and they managed to get him back to the surface and out of the water fairly quickly, but he was already unconscious and had stopped breathing. Luckily, a paramedic had been at the marina and he'd rushed over to help. Thank goodness he was there! It had taken a good while for the guy to resuscitate Jason. At the hospital, they confirmed he'd suffered a serious head injury, which they believed had triggered his heart to stop while he was in the water."

Jason was now in Auckland Hospital in a medically induced coma, which his brother Michael had told Matt, was to allow Jason's brain time to heal and for the swelling to go down.

Matt could barely believe it. Jason and Casey both in a coma and both at the same time, albeit for different reasons, but how freaky was that when they were on the other side of the world from each other! Carole couldn't believe it either and was as shocked as Matt, agreeing with him at how weird it was that the two of them should be so desperately ill, right at the same time. Carole and Matt ended their conversation so that Matt could call Dave and tell him about Jason, while Carole also relayed the sad news to Amanda.

Nobody could believe what had happened to Jason, especially with Casey being the way she was. The girls decided they were in need of a strong drink and as neither one had eaten, they decided to meet up and go to Giovanni's comforting restaurant. It would also give them the opportunity to let Giovanni know about Casey and now Jason too. Both girls knew of Giovanni's fondness for his 'adopted daughter' and guessed that Giovanni would feel as desperate as they did, for Casey to recover quickly and of course now, Jason too.

The air outside was decidedly cool and definitely had a wintery feel to it, so much so that both Carole and Amanda shivered as they stepped out from the warmth of the hospital. Wrapping their coats around themselves just that little bit tighter, they folded their arms as they both hurried back to their cars. The plan was to take Amanda's car home and Carole would then drive them both to Giovanni's. They were planning to have a very large drink and knew they'd be getting a taxi home, so as it was the weekend, there was no rush to get back to pick up Carole's car the next day.

Over in Auckland Hospital, Jason was stable and being well looked after. Lee and Becca were by Jason's bedside. The couple were totally gutted about the accident and were doing everything they could to keep Jason's parents up to date with his condition. Lee was paying for Jason's dad and brother to fly out to Auckland the next day, so they could be with Jason. Unfortunately, Jason's mum was unable to go with them, because of a heart and blood condition, which prevented her from travelling that far. Doctors had advised her that flying was not a good idea for her, besides which, she would not be strong enough to make the long journey to New Zealand. Reluctantly, Gloria had agreed to stay home and hold the fort. But she was worried sick about Jason, so Gloria had also given her husband strict instructions to call her, the moment he arrived at the hospital, to let her know how Jason was. Don had hugged his wife, knowing how hard it was going to be for her to be left waiting at home and knowing how much he would miss her. But he had to be strong and not let his beloved Gloria know how disappointed he was, to be leaving without her. He didn't want to upset her more than she already was.

"Of course I will, pet, and don't you worry now, we'll soon have our lad up and about. At least he's got Lee and Becca looking out for him, he'll be fine. Now, try not to fret too much, you know Jason would tell you that himself."

Of course Don knew that telling his wife not to worry when their son was lying in a coma, was like asking her not to breathe, but he didn't really know what else to say and truthfully, he was as worried as she was. Don and Gloria hugged each other tightly and sent up a little prayer for their son, begging for him to survive and to be well again.

Carole and Amanda were sat at Giovanni's front window table. Giovanni stood at their table, unable to believe what he had been told, turning around, he called out to Maria. Giovanni wanted to help, and asked what he could do. It was Maria's turn to be devastated by the news and she echoed Giovanni in asking what they could do to help. Carole and Amanda told them how the hospital had said playing sounds of familiar music and noises can often help, so they suggested that maybe Giovanni and Maria could make a recording of the restaurant, during the evening service period, so they could then play it to Casey. The Italian couple eagerly agreed, adding that perhaps they could each speak on the recording and call Casey's name, asking her to come in and sit down and that her favourite meal was waiting for her. Maria suggested bringing some of the food to the hospital, so Casey could smell it when the tape was playing, saying they would include some garlic bread and waft spoonfuls of her favourite lasagne and tiramisu under her nose.

Carole and Amanda laughed at their inventiveness, but agreed that anything could help. So they welcomed the idea and suggested two days' time, so that Giovanni and Maria had time to make a recording and to prepare the food. They were all excited by this latest idea and agreed to meet up at the restaurant and go to the hospital together. Of course they would have to wrap the food up well to keep it hot and would warn the nursing team of their plans. Carole said she would call Matt later and tell him.

As the four of them firmed up the plan, they all relaxed and laughed at the prospect of it being food that awakened their sleeping beauty. Maria insisted the two women have a meal on the house that evening and wouldn't hear their protestations, insisting that the gesture was for Casey, with them being her friends. Carole and Amanda both accepted graciously and thanked Maria and Giovanni for their kindness and generosity.

Matt thought it was a great idea, having also laughed at their inventiveness. Anything that might wake Casey up was absolutely fine by him, so he told the girls he would meet the four of them at the hospital. The plan was for Giovanni and Maria to go into Casey's room first with the recording already playing and taking the lasagne and tiramisu with them, all the while talking to Casey, whilst tempting her memory with wafts of food smells. The others would all be in the waiting area and would swap around every twenty minutes.

"Bellissimo, Bella, Casey, how are you?" Giovanni made a big entrance with his warm welcome, just as he would at the restaurant, but it was clear he was shocked at how pale and small Casey looked in her hospital bed. True to their promise, both he and Maria chattered on to Casey and wafted lasagne and then tiramisu under her nostrils, asking if she would wake up and try her favourite dish. They both crossed their chests and kissed their rosary beads as they spoke to Casey in turn.

Casey thought she could hear Giovanni. Was it him? Where was she? Was she at the restaurant? No, not the restaurant, but she decided that yes, it must be Giovanni because she could smell her favourite dish. Where was she though? It was really bugging her. She didn't feel like she was at the restaurant. She felt like she was lying down, her head was fuzzy, and she couldn't think, couldn't speak. What was wrong? Struggling to make sense of the noises and smells, Casey could still feel a pain in her chest: what happened? She remembered going to the hospital. Did she die? Was that it, was she dead? Was that why she couldn't move? Nothing made sense, but Casey kept fighting to understand, and then she heard another voice, it was softer, female, but it sounded foreign. Giovanni? No, not him, Maria! Of course, Maria, but why were they here? Where was she? Casey was becoming agitated at not being able to make sense of everything and tried to lift her hand to her head, but it wouldn't move.

Giovanni and Maria were watching Casey intently as they spoke to her and were excited to see her eyes moving beneath her eyelids, so they called to her; "Come on, Casey. Wake up, Bella, we miss you."

But to their great disappointment, Casey did not wake up; instead, they saw her hand lift off the bed and drop down again. Giovanni sent Maria to tell the others and a few moments later Matt burst into the room and took Casey's hand as Giovanni looked on. Now silent and scared that Casey might be dying, Giovanni couldn't bear to lose her and was making the sign of the cross multiple times across his chest, as he kissed his rosary beads again, praying for Casey to wake up.

Matt held Casey's hand in his and spoke to her gently, encouraging her to wake up, to open her eyes and to know they were all there, willing her to get better. Matt felt Casey squeeze his hand back and immediately brought her fingers to his lips and kissed them hard, holding her hand to his face, before saying her name over and over again. Meanwhile, Giovanni had finished his prayer and opening his eyes again, he gently kissed his Rosary once more, before placing it on top of the bedding that lay across Casey's chest.

Casey felt someone take her hand and as she squeezed it, she felt stronger and could hear a familiar voice, which sounded like Matt. She recognised his voice and remembered watching him from her kitchen window and then making love to him. It was magical. Her dream of making love to him had come true! Casey remembered Matt telling her that he loved her. She told him that she loved him too.

Those words were barely audible, but they were words. *Yes!* Casey had spoken! Matt's heart soared with hope and he asked Giovanni to fetch a nurse; he was sure Casey was about to wake up. Sure enough, as Giovanni left the room, Casey's eyes opened slowly. Frowning as she tried to focus on the person she could just about make out sitting next to her.

Matt froze for a split second before speaking: "Casey, my love..." Then in a whispered prayer he added: "Thank you, thank you, thank you."

Not really knowing who or what he was thanking, but he just sent it out there, not caring about anything except Casey waking up.

"My darling, we've all been so worried about you," he said.

Matt leaned forward to kiss her forehead, and then the nurse arrived and began checking the monitors beside Casey's bed, nodding to Matt, signalling that Casey was indeed waking up.

"Welcome back, Casey," she said. "You gave us all quite a scare."

The nurse spoke quietly and gently, so as not to alarm Casey and then told Matt that Giovanni had gone to tell the others. Matt just nodded, unable to speak, he was just thankful that Casey was awake and checked again with the nurse that all was well with the readings on the array of monitors around Casey's bed.

Casey had been silent as the mist slowly lifted from her mind. Now she was able to focus on Matt's face and she smiled at him, then squeezed his hand weakly.

"Hello you," she whispered quietly to Matt, and then asked for some water, as her mouth was so dry she could barely speak.

The nurse said they needed to continue to monitor her, but she was thrilled to hear Casey respond so lucidly and said the consultant surgeon would be in to see her very soon. The nurse then rushed from the room to call Steve Morgan and tell him the good news.

Suddenly, Carole appeared at the door and almost ran over to the bed, then checked herself and she took Casey's other hand, quietly saying hello and telling her how she had scared them all. The nurse had told Carole not to expect too much and that Casey may be slow to respond, so to be gentle with her. Remembering this, Carole just held Casey's hand for a brief moment and said she was so happy that Casey was awake and that she would see her later.

Leaving Matt alone again with Casey, Carole slipped out of the room quietly. Amanda had already said she would wait and let Casey adjust before she too went in to see her dearest friend, but she was on tenterhooks, desperate to see her awake.

Matt couldn't take his eyes off Casey and told her again and again that he loved her and couldn't wait to get her home. Casey asked him what had happened and so he slowly explained about the operation. As he said the words, Casey's memory began to return and she asked about the lump.

"Did they get it all out?"

Matt was about to reply when the consultant surgeon walked in, so he just nodded and stepped back away from the bed, to allow Steve Morgan full access to examine her.

"I'll be back in a few minutes, my darling, after the doctor has finished."

Matt left Steve Morgan to do his checks and examine Casey and although he didn't want to leave her side for a moment, Matt knew that his leaving the room would be required, as well as appreciated. It would also give Casey some privacy to discuss her surgery with her doctor, including what had happened to her during the procedure.

Walking back into the waiting area, Matt was visibly relieved as the others turned to him. Each one of them was ecstatic and began happily clapping him on the back, kissing and hugging him, saying how relieved they were. Maria was still wringing her hanky, having not stopped crying since the news broke that Casey was awake. Giovanni was like a father who had just been told his baby was born and was fit and well. The energy in the room had rocketed at the good news. The emotion of the moment had overtaken them all and raised the elation in the room to ceiling height, as they all cried and chattered, and finally let out their relieved emotions and laughter.

Knowing they would have to let Casey rest before they all visited her, the group of friends decided it was best to leave Matt to it. Even Amanda, who had yet to see Casey – but was just so relieved her friend was awake and OK – said she would return tomorrow and see her then, but could Matt pass on her love and call her later with an update? The others seconded Amanda's words before they prepared themselves to leave.

Thankful that they were leaving him to have some quiet time with Casey, mainly for her to get used to being awake again and to understand what had happened to her, Matt assured them all he would call later. Hugging each of them in turn, he thanked Giovanni and Maria from the bottom of his heart, for he truly believed that they had been the final trigger to waking Casey up. Both Giovanni and Maria swelled with pride at Matt's suggestion that they had been the key to her waking up and said they were relieved to have been able to help their beautiful Casey. Again promising calls and updates later, Matt waved as they all left and he turned around to walk back into the ward. Punching in the code that the nursing staff had given to him, to save him buzzing each time he needed to enter the HDU, Matt's stance was just a little bit taller than it had been when he'd arrived earlier that morning.

Steve Morgan was beside the nurse station as Matt walked back in and so he explained to Matt that Casey was still a little bit confused, which was to be expected. But essentially, there seemed to be no long-term effects following the coma, other than it would probably be a few weeks before she was back to full strength. It was very common to feel exhausted after a coma and she would no doubt feel a bit under the weather for a while, but so long as nothing abnormal occurred and all tests were clear, Casey should be fine to go home in a couple of days. He also explained that Casey must rest to allow her body to heal properly and that she should have somebody with her at all times during the first seventy-two hours. The consultant surgeon also confirmed that he had explained to Casey that the surgery was otherwise a complete success, and that she was clear of the abnormal cells. There seemed no need for further worry and he would arrange for a routine out-patient appointment for Casey, which would likely be one week after she was discharged from hospital, just to check all was well. Naturally if there were any concerns at all, Matt was to call the hospital immediately and get a message to Steve Morgan.

"Thank you so much, Steve. I don't know what to say except, *thank you*, which hardly seems enough." Matt was just so relieved and shook his hand vigorously, before walking back into Casey's room. Already beaming from ear to ear, Matt's smile spread even wider, when he saw that Casey was now propped up a little further in the bed. Casey smiled back at him, albeit a little weakly, but a smile all the same and to Matt. She was a vision, his vision, the woman he loved!

The next couple of days were filled by a range of medical tests to ensure Casey was not experiencing any issues, or after-effects of her unexpected coma. Which, when coupled with visits from Matt and her friends, had left Casey totally exhausted and she couldn't understand why that was. It made no sense to her because in her mind she felt fine. However, she did admit to feeling a little foggy in her head, which she said was similar to having a heavy head cold and having her sinuses clogged up. Her chest felt sore, but otherwise she felt reasonably OK.

Not having had surgery before, Casey had expected that she would feel perfectly fine straight afterwards, a bit sore maybe, but with no other after-effects. So when she had first awoken and felt totally confused, it had thrown her completely and her head had felt really weird. But of course, at that point, Casey had no idea that she had been in a coma for the last few days. Steve Morgan explained that the way she was feeling, was not only a result of the intended surgery, but the heart trauma that had occurred during surgery, followed by the resulting coma. Taking all that into consideration, it was to be expected that she would feel confused and very tired. In fact, it was considered perfectly normal under the circumstances. When Steve explained what had happened, Casey had felt a great sense of disbelief, which was quickly replaced by a mix of emotions and feelings which totally overwhelmed her. The nursing team were used to these types of reactions in patients like Casey and were quick to reassure her again, that how she was feeling was to be expected, and in fact was perfectly normal for someone who had been through what she had, in the last few days. The staff nurse advised Casey to try not to worry and just to rest, eat healthily and sleep. If she did exactly that, they said she would feel much better within a couple of weeks or so.

Carole, Amanda, Tilly and Dave had all popped by at various times, each laden with gifts of grapes, chocolates, more flowers and several cards. The huge bouquet of flowers from Edine and the Team at *Just for You!* had been sat on the table at the foot of Casey's bed ever since they'd arrived. Still looking absolutely gorgeous and smelling so fragrant, Casey felt compelled to gaze at the flowers whenever she was left alone in her room, which so far, had not actually been that often. This was mainly because the nurses were keen to keep checking on Casey whenever her steady stream of visitors had left.

Two days before Casey's operation, Claire Anderson had popped over to New York for a magazine promotions visit and had been very shocked to receive a call from Edine telling her about Casey. Since then, Claire had been calling the hospital daily, to check how Casey was doing, but each time being told that as she was not family, they could only give her a high level update for Casey. Claire had understood, recognising it as normal practice, but she also felt a little frustrated at the restricted messaging. Although at least with them advising her that Casey was comfortable, or that there had been no change, it had given Claire some indication of how she was doing. But she wanted to know the real truth and more importantly she wanted to be there for Casey. However, today there had been excellent news passed to her from Edine, being that Casey had finally woken up! *Phew!* What a complete relief and having rearranged her schedule to finish a day earlier, Claire was able to change her flexible ticket to a different flight. Never before had she been so keen to get back to the UK, or anxious to get there as soon as was physically possible. Claire was planning to go straight to the hospital from the airport.

As a patient, Casey was genuinely grateful to Steve Morgan and his team of nursing staff for looking after her so well, but she was anxious to get home and to get back to normal life as soon as possible. This was something the medical team were used to their patients feeling and luckily they already recognised that the sooner patients could return home, generally the faster they recovered. Being ill in hospital was not something Casey had ever experienced before and it was something she never wanted to live through again. So, when Steve Morgan approved her discharge, she was elated, as was Matt and all of their friends.

Giovanni and Maria had even popped back to see her and had invited Casey, Matt and all of her friends, for a private meal with their family. Giovanni had explained that because Monday's were usually quiet nights for them, they would close the restaurant completely and use it for their private dinner party. The Italian couple wanted it to be an uninterrupted celebration of Casey's recovery, but also for it to be as relaxing as possible for her. The whole of Giovanni's family had been saddened to hear of her being in the coma and each of them had prayed hard, begging for her to recover completely. So, to their religious little family, having Casey back safe and well, was like a gift from God and they felt the need to be thankful and to celebrate her return to them.

Casey was staggered by this generous gesture from Maria and Giovanni, as well as all the love and support from all of her friends. She realised how incredibly lucky she was to have such wonderful people in her life and recognised how much they all cherished her. Remembering Nanny Em's wise advice from years back, those words once again ran through Casey's mind.

'Riches do not always come in the form of money. It is the love of our family and our friendships that truly enrich our lives. These are the important aspects of our life that truly matter, whenever life throws us a challenge.'

The day Casey went home was also going to be the day Matt broke the news about Jason's accident. Having discussed it with Steve Morgan and their friends, they had decided it was best to wait until Casey was well enough to go home and then Matt could break the sad news to her himself. Now that Jason's recovery was being impeded by the head injury and resulting swelling on his brain, such news would come as a massive shock for Casey. Jason's head injury was, at that precise moment in time, unpredictable and the doctors treating him could give no firm timeframe as to how long Jason would have to be kept under sedation.

Chapter 19

Jason

As Matt opened the front door to her apartment, Casey felt an overwhelming sense of relief and happiness to finally be home again. The whole experience at the hospital had been completely surreal to her, whilst for Matt and the girls, it had been so incredibly scary and worrying. The fact that the surgery had gone well was an immense relief to them all, but for Casey, having been told the story of what had happened to her during the operation and in the days following it, she could hardly believe it. It all just felt like it must have happened to somebody else.

The hospital staff had been unable to offer any real explanation for the way the anaesthetic had impacted Casey, saying it was just one of those things that sometimes happened and nobody really knew why it affected a small minority of people. Nevertheless, the so-called dangers with general anaesthetics was something they discussed before every procedure. When this was explained to her, Casey had reflected on how nobody ever truly thinks, or believes, that it will happen to them. Which was exactly how she felt. Yet it had happened. It was weird, like an impossible dream.

What had been carefully explained to her was that, due to Casey's abnormal reaction to the anaesthetic, any future surgery she may need would have to be very carefully managed. Steve Morgan would be writing to her GP and red warning labels would be added on the front cover of her hospital records. Most importantly, Casey was advised to ensure her family and friends knew and to always remind doctors and relevant hospital staff of her condition, should she need further surgery. Steve Morgan had been clear to ensure Casey was aware that this included when giving birth. That very comment had made her almost choke at the prospect of babies, *her babies!* Wow, that was a thought which had not even entered her head, but of course was now a very important consideration for her, given the risk to her health which could be caused by anaesthetic. Something to think about for later though, if ever, she thought, having never even considered having a baby.

As they walked through to the living room, Matt suggested Casey sit down immediately and put her feet up, whilst he went to make her a cup of tea. Already feeling surprisingly exhausted by the journey home, Casey was extremely grateful for Matt's caring kindness and did as he suggested. Listening to Matt clattering around in her kitchen and hearing the familiar whistle of her Nan's kettle as it came to the boil, comforted her somewhat.

Feeling the need to make light of the moment, before he revealed the latest news, Matt called out to her: "Wow, who has a whistling kettle these days?"

It was more of a fun statement than a true question so Casey just laughed back. Once the tea was made, Matt knew the conversation he now had to have with Casey was going to make her very sad and whilst he knew he *had* to tell her, he was dreading it at the same time. The last thing he wanted was to be the bearer of news that would hurt and make her cry and even more so since it was about Jason.

Taking a deep breath, Matt came back into the room with the tea and sat down on the sofa beside Casey. He glanced around to see where the box of tissues was and then moved them closer so she could reach them easily. Appreciating his thoughtfulness, whilst not knowing the reason for it right at that moment, Casey thanked Matt again for making her a cup of tea and placed her hand over his as he sat down beside her. Still pleasantly surprised at how caring this gorgeous man was, Casey felt so lucky to have Matt in her life and she smiled at him as he started to speak. Casey leant forward to pick up her mug of tea and sip the hot liquid, whilst she listened to what Matt was saying.

"Casey, it's brilliant to have you home, we've all been so worried about you. It's such a relief that you're back with us and feeling OK. Steve Morgan said we needed to make sure you were really OK before we shared some bad news..."

Matt's voice trailed off as he watched for her reaction, needing to make sure she was really listening to what he was about to say. Looking at him over the top of her mug of tea as she took a sip, Casey paused at Matt's *bad news*.

"The girls thought it best if I tell you, seeing as we're both close to Jason..."

"What about Jason?"

The mug of tea was suddenly lowered into her lap as Casey stared at Matt, feeling immediately concerned at seeing him frown; she knew by the expression on his face that he wasn't messing about and that it really must be bad news.

"Matt, what is it? What about Jason? Tell me please!"

Matt continued explaining as Casey's worried response sunk in through his brain. "I had a call from Jason's brother a few days ago, when you were still unconscious." Matt was watching carefully, he had no idea how to break the news gently, so he took her hand and continued: "Jason had a boating accident in New Zealand, Casey. In fact it, happened as he was stepping off the boat, onto the jetty. They don't really know how he slipped because the deck was dry, but somehow he did and he banged his head, quite badly..."

Casey interrupted Matt's words with a shocked gasp, as tears instantly sprang into her eyes and she begged the answer to her question: "But he is OK isn't he, Matt? I mean, it was just a slip wasn't it, he's not badly hurt or anything?"

It broke Matt's heart to see how upset Casey already was and worrying that she would burn herself with the hot liquid, he took the mug of tea from her and placed it on the coffee table as he responded to her questions: "No, Casey, it's more serious than that. Jason fell into the water and he stopped breathing. Although they managed to resuscitate him, the bang to his head caused some swelling in his brain, so they've put him in a medically induced coma to allow his brain to recover."

There, he had said it and now he watched his beloved Casey crumble.

"No, I can't believe it, is it really true? Oh, Matt, he will be OK though?"

Casey's voice was faltering as tears sprang into her eyes and she started to cry as she desperately repeated her question: "He *will* be OK, won't he?"

Tears were now running down her pale cheeks. This couldn't be true, it was freaky. How could they have both been in a coma at the same time? It just didn't make any kind of sense. The questions were asked, but of course, neither Matt nor Casey knew the answers. Matt did explain, however, that Jason's dad and brother had flown over to be with him and that his mum, Gloria, was now waiting on news from them. Matt also explained how Jason's mum had been devastated that she was unable to fly out to be with Jason, due to her own health issues. Matt went on to explain that Lee and Becca had paid for and organised it, so that Don and Michael could fly out to be with Jason. Lee and Becca's kindness and generosity, was something they would all be eternally grateful for.

Matt had explained it all as calmly as he could to Casey, but he too felt the desperation of Jason's situation and of Gloria's too. With her eldest son lying badly injured and needing his mum, it seemed cruel to her that she was unable to fly over to be by his side.

What seemed like an age later and feeling shocked by the news, Casey had fallen strangely silent, her tea now abandoned as she stared in bewilderment across the room. Matt watched her closely. Seeing Casey so shocked and quiet and not particularly looking at anything, worried him even more. Luckily, Steve Morgan had prepared Matt for Casey's most likely reaction and said to allow her time to process what he had told her. Also, that she may suddenly go quiet *whilst* processing that information. Matt was watching her face intently. What he didn't yet realise was that Casey *was* remembering something, yet she couldn't quite recall it clearly and was staring across the room, as she tried to drag the memory to the forefront of her mind. Suddenly it was there, it was a memory from her time in the coma, at least that's what she thought it was, but something about it was puzzling her.

Casey snapped out of her trance and spoke quietly, in a puzzling way, as though she was trying to make sense of the memory. "You know, Matt, something really weird happened to me while I was out of it. You know, when I was sleeping, I mean; well, in the coma I suppose. What I mean is I saw him, Jason that is. Yes that's right, I remember that I saw Jason and he was talking to me, saying he was sorry and that I should be happy. He was saying goodbye."

Tears began to run down Casey's face as she struggled to remember the whole memory. Whilst Matt – who was understandably surprised and a little shocked – listened intently to Casey's slightly confused recollections. She *was* remembering and because she knew it wasn't real, Casey reasoned that it must have been a dream she'd had whilst she was unconscious. At least she had thought it was a dream, but it felt weird because she knew she had seen

Jason and it felt like he really *was* with her. But he couldn't have been because she knew he was in New Zealand. Not only that, Jason was saying goodbye, like it was forever.

Just recalling that part of her dream made Casey cry even more and reaching for a tissue, she looked up at Matt, her eyes brimming with tears, hoping he would suddenly tell her everything was fine and that Jason was OK. But he couldn't say that because it wasn't OK, was it.

Feeling helpless at this point, all Matt could do was to hold Casey's hand whilst she continued telling him her story. As she became ever more tearful, he tried to comfort her, whilst actually feeling quite shocked at what she was telling him. To Matt it sounded very bizarre, yet intriguing. Although, he'd never been particularly religious, he had always felt like there was *something* out there. Something bigger than all of us, not a God exactly, but something spiritual, which also felt like it was a *good* something.

Matt had been feeling really bad about Jason's accident. Although he recognised it *was* just a tragic and terrible mishap, Matt also knew that Jason had felt hacked off with him when he'd left for New Zealand. The fact that the two friends hadn't really sorted it out before Jason had left, meant that Matt was feeling twice as guilty.

As the dream returned to Casey's memory stronger and in more detail, she knew and now believed, that Jason had definitely said goodbye and that she should be happy. Remembering the bright white light and the immense sensation of love that was with her so strongly, she was unable to explain why the memory of it now scared her, because she was feeling really worried for Jason.

"What if he dies, Matt? What if he has already died and they don't know yet? What if that was his spirit coming to say goodbye to me?"

Casey was becoming frantic at that thought as Matt tried to comfort her.

"Hush now, my darling, it was just a dream; as far as we know he is still with us and we can only hope he pulls through. You know we're all willing him to pull through don't you, but we just have to hope and pray that he does."

Matt hugged Casey and stroked her hair, trying to soothe her tears and her fears, whilst knowing how much his own fears had grown with each day that had passed and now more so with Casey's recollection of her dream. He was now worried more than ever about Jason, but he tried to hide it from Casey, knowing Jason's condition was extremely critical and that it could go either way at any time. It was not looking good for their friend and in truth, all they could do was just hope and pray for Jason to keep fighting and pull through. Not knowing how to handle his own feelings and worries about Jason, Matt got up to make them both some fresh tea, needing to pull himself together and restrain the emotion he was feeling. He didn't want Casey to see him break down, he wanted to stay strong for her. He needed to help Casey and to keep her as calm as possible, yet he wondered how he could possibly achieve that, when he didn't have the answers she wanted.

Feeling drained and emotional, Casey needed to feel Matt's arms wrapped around her, to comfort and reassure her. She would be glad to snuggle into them later, when they shared her bed.

As he made their tea and recovered his composure, Matt realised how much he also needed the comfort of holding Casey in his arms when they lay together later. For he too was feeling as though he'd been put through an emotional wringer whilst Casey had been unconscious, and now he was revisiting those very same feelings with the worry over Jason.

Needing each other so much, Matt returned to the sofa so they could snuggle up together. He was grateful for the comfort their togetherness offered and as Casey relaxed against him, Matt kissed the top of her head, telling her again that he loved her and how scared he had been, knowing that he might have lost her. Feeling deeply touched by what Matt was saying, Casey truly believed him and in that moment she felt utterly loved by this wonderful man, who had happily walked into her life and swept her off her feet. For a few short moments, thoughts of Jason slipped from both of their minds, as they enjoyed a loving embrace in the silence of Casey's home.

Much later, as they lay together in bed, snuggling in the warmth their bodies created, Matt kissed Casey very gently. After telling him that she was fine and wouldn't break, he kissed her again, this time more passionately, and although she was very tired, Casey welcomed Matt's kisses and responded with as much love and passion as he had shown her. Desperately wanting Matt to make love to her, Casey found it hard to resist him, but she knew her energy levels were low and that she had no stamina for love making. Furthermore, Steve Morgan had advised her to rest completely and there was no way Matt would go against those orders. So, she happily settled for Matt's arms and spooned her body to fit perfectly with his, as they drifted off to sleep together, both exhausted from the events of the last few days.

The following days passed by in a blur for Casey, as she drifted in and out of sleep. In between eating and resting, she was grateful for and very much enjoyed having Matt around to look after her. After all, what was not to like about watching his naked athletic body walking around her bedroom every day, his masculinity clearly displayed and enjoyed by Casey's watching eyes. It was a perfect world for Casey, the two of them together, Matt's loving and sensuous ways, as well as cooking healthy meals and helping her to exercise.

Steve Morgan had explained everything to Matt very clearly, so that he was completely au fait with how to look after Casey and encouraged her with gentle exercises to help rebuild her strength. Luckily Casey had not been unconscious long enough for her muscles to deteriorate to any great degree. But the trauma of her heart stopping during surgery and the subsequent coma, had totally affected her energy levels.

As Matt helped her with each exercise, Casey's mind strayed and she imagined making love with him; feeling his gentle touch and passionate kisses, as they explored every part of her body, working up to his perfect placement of virile hardness and penetrating her femininity with ease, pleasuring her as they reached that point of intense passionate union together.

Although enjoying helping Casey with her exercises, Matt's mind was also straying as he too imagined making love to her. As Matt's hand brushed Casey's shoulder whilst he demonstrated a particular exercise, right at that very moment, he could have easily kissed that bare skin and pulled her towards him. Casey was close enough for him to stroke her breasts and he imagined taking one into his hand, gently feeling its fullness as her nipples would harden at his touch; she would sigh deeply, as her hormones raged, causing her femininity to ache for him. Oh yes, Matt wanted Casey as much as she wanted him and more than ever, he *needed* her. With his whole body he ached for her, his desperate wanting, and his love, burned ever stronger with each passing day that he was in her presence. Casey was bewitching, compelling, and Matt wanted her to be with him forever.

Reality returned and Matt forced his passionate wanting thoughts to the side-lines. But as he continued to encourage Casey, a growing hardness affected his masculine needs and his thoughts drifted between intense fantasy and this very moment. Casey was like no other woman he had ever loved and Matt was more in love with her than he could have ever imagined was true.

Thankfully, having had been able to rearrange his appointments for that whole week, Matt could focus completely on Casey and her recovery. Only leaving her whenever the girls visited, Matt would take the opportunity of them sitting with Casey, whilst he nipped back across the road to his own apartment to check his mail and have a quick gym session. Knowing how these women liked to talk, Matt knew that him leaving would also give Casey and her friends some precious and private time to talk girl stuff. Not only that, it also gave the two of them a healthy break from each other, particularly as they were not used to being together quite so much as they had been over the past few days.

As he exercised, Matt considered how very fortunate he was that his work had allowed him to be so flexible. Still marvelling at how his regular clients had been so very understanding, when he'd told them what had happened with Casey, he could scarcely believe their kindness. It was amazing how each one of them had encouraged him to help Casey and not to worry about their appointments. Matt had felt honoured to have such fantastic clients and had thanked each one of them for their warmth and generous understanding.

In the days after Casey had returned home, Giovanni and Maria sent one of their sons along with a meal for Casey and Matt. In typical Italian style, the two of them wanted to continue to help. Knowing how much effort Matt had put in, they insisted it was nothing for them to provide a meal, besides which, it would save Matt the bother of cooking, so he could focus on Casey for that day. Both Casey and Matt appreciated the genuine loveliness of Giovanni and Maria and said they couldn't thank them enough.

As the days ticked by, Casey grew stronger; although she still needed a short nap during the day and was dozing on the sofa when Matt's mobile suddenly rang. Absorbed by the book he was reading, Matt was startled by the unexpected call. Quickly grabbing at his phone to prevent the ringing from disturbing Casey, he noticed the caller was Jason's brother. Standing up quickly and swiping the screen to accept the call, he walked through to the kitchen so as not to disturb Casey.

Knowing that this was a long distance call for Michael and being aware of the time difference at his end, Matt spoke quickly: "Hi, mate, how's Jase doing? Is he awake yet?"

Hearing the tiredness and sadness in Michael's voice as he responded, made Matt's heart go out to him.

"Hi, Matt, no he's not awake. In fact, it's not looking good at all, mate, he's in a bad way. They said he'd ingested water, so he must have been semi-conscious when he fell in after hitting his head. The consultant said that his heart stopping could've just been the shock of falling, but it could also have been caused by him losing consciousness *after* inhaling the water. To be honest, they can't really tell us anything yet because they don't know what will happen, other than another brain scan, which will be done once the swelling has reduced a bit more."

Michael sounded exhausted and totally drained from the emotional turmoil that both he and Don had suffered since they took the phone call from Jason's boss, on the day of the accident. Matt knew exactly how Michael felt, having been in the very same position with Casey just a few days ago. After hearing the update on Jason and passing on their best wishes for his speedy recovery, Matt told Michael about what had happened to Casey following her surgery. He hoped that somehow it might give his friend some comfort, as well as some kind of *hope* that Jason might do the same. A relieved Matt told Michael that Casey had since woken up and was on the mend, so not to give up hope for Jason.

Shocked to hear about Casey, Michael too, was amazed by the coincidence. Having met Casey when she'd dated Jason, Michael had taken to her bubbly personality and liked her very much. In fact, he'd felt gutted for his brother when the relationship had been forced to end, because of Jason's move to New Zealand. Like his brother though, Michael had also hoped that Jason would be able to convince Casey to go with him. But Michael totally understood why she could not, because he knew himself that as tempting as it would be, he could not leave his parents back in England and live on the other side of the world. Now though and very graciously, Michael said to Matt that he was really pleased to hear Casey was recovering well, hopeful he would be able to report the same about Jason soon. Michael also asked Matt to tell Casey that he said hello and that he was glad to hear she was OK. In answer to Michael's next question, Matt confirmed that he had of course told her about Jason and how upset Casey had been, adding that Casey had asked him to post a letter she'd written for Gloria, saying how very sorry she was to hear the awful news. Michael was grateful for Casey's kind gesture and asked Matt to thank her from him and Don.

Unbeknown to Casey, Jason's mum, Gloria, had received Casey's note that very day and was extremely thankful for her support. It had been so hard for Gloria, having to wait at home and she'd been feeling the distance from her boys. With them all being so far away and having to rely on phone calls or Skype to see them, for Gloria, just knowing that someone else in England truly cared about Jason's welfare, meant a huge amount to her. Thankfully, Jason's boss, Lee, had left an iPhone with Michael and Don so they could 'Face-time' with Gloria and at least show her Jason in his hospital bed, even if her beloved son was unable to respond yet. For that kind gesture, Gloria was eternally grateful.

Michael had found that small connection to be such a massive boost for both his mum and his dad. As a family, they all needed each other so much right now and being apart and on opposite sides of the world from each other, had been really tough for them all. So just being able to see each other's faces, even though it was only via a small screen, had offered some comfort for them all.

Several of Jason's colleagues had also dropped by Auckland Hospital, to provide support to Jason's family, plus of course, there had been daily calls from the office to enquire after him. Jason's work colleagues had been shocked and devastated by what had happened and seeing such concern in Jason's workmates had brought great comfort to both Michael and Don. If they were honest, it actually surprised them a little, especially with the guys having only just met Jason. But Don and Michael quickly realised that their friendliness was a big part of what had attracted Jason to the warmth of these people in the first place.

Knowing how important it was for Jason's family to be close to him, Lee and Becca had arranged to take Don and Michael to Jason's apartment from the airport, thinking it would be much nicer for them to stay there, rather than a hotel, particularly as it was next to the harbour as well. Then each day, either Lee or Becca had taken Don and Michael back and forth between Jason's apartment and the hospital, each of them checking on his progress during every journey.

Knowing that Don and Michael would be spending most of their time at the hospital, Lee and Becca were keen to try and give them a break from the intense worrying, so on alternate days they would also take them for dinner and spend the time between visiting hours, showing them some of what had drawn Jason to Auckland.

The whole company were hoping and praying that Jason would recover fully and that it would just be a matter of days before he was awake and regaling them with a detailed recollection of how he had lost his footing. Lee and Becca had themselves been devastated by Jason's accident and both felt completely responsible for his current condition. But, even though Jason's family were generous in not blaming them, instead acknowledging that it was just a terribly tragic accident, the couple felt compelled to take care of Jason's father and brother, for as long as they needed to be there with him.

Back in the UK, Matt knew only too well what the pain was like for Don and Michael, having experienced the same whilst he waited for Casey to wake up and not really knowing if she ever would, or if she would even be OK when she finally did. So, Matt's heart again went out to Jason's family, as he wished with every positive thought that he had for Jason to pull through, saying as much to Michael every time he spoke to him.

Lying in a private room in Auckland Hospital, Jason was motionless and with limited brain activity showing on the scans, which wasn't a good sign. In spite of the induced coma, the medical team had expected more activity than they were seeing, which was concerning them greatly. But having Jason's brother and father arrive from the UK, had been encouraging for the whole medical team, knowing that once they started to bring Jason out of the medically induced coma, it would be so much better for him to hear the familiar voices of people he loved and was close to. Furthermore, those voices would be far more likely to trigger a reaction in him than any of the medical team, or Lee and Becca and his workmates could ever hope to do.

Understandably, Don and Michael were beyond worried sick and despite the momentary distractions of dinner conversations with Lee and Becca, or admiring the amazing view of Auckland Harbour from Jason's apartment balcony, they soon returned to discussing Jason and what they should do next. Don was expecting to speak to the consultant in charge of neurology in the morning, to have an open and honest conversation about the reality of Jason's injury. Up until now, everyone had been hopeful, but Don knew himself that every passing day was a day too long for his boy to be unconscious; it was not looking good and he knew it.

Michael's relationship with Jason was precious to him; they always had been and still were a close family and he just couldn't believe what had happened to his brother. This whole situation was so surreal that Michael was struggling to remain positive. But, like his father, he kept trying to stay upbeat, whilst feeling totally afraid of the worst possible outcome, which would be to lose his brother forever.

"Dad..?"

Michael stood in the doorway of the balcony, watching his father's back as Don stood by the railing, looking out over the moonlit view of the harbour. He was absent-mindedly watching the lights on the many boats and yachts, gently bobbing on the calm harbour waters, whilst his thoughts were still back at the hospital with Jason. Turning to Michael, he looked tired. "Yes, boy, what is it?"

Don's voice was gentle as he spoke, knowing Michael was as worried about Jason as he was himself.

"What if Jason doesn't recover; what are we going to do?" Michael's voice was low and slightly faltering at that unwanted thought.

"We'll need to arrange to take him back with us son, so that your mother has him back home. But let's not think the worst just yet eh. Let's try to keep upbeat and positive."

Don was so choked with emotion that he could barely speak and instead, he stepped forward to embrace his son. The two of them stood hugging each other for the longest time; both needing to feel comforted by each other, whilst equally scared of the grim realities facing their little family.

The next few days were much the same for Don and Michael. Jason was improving slightly, in that the swelling on his brain was reducing, but he remained unconscious. This seemed less of a worry to the doctors, who had in fact said that if Jason continued with this improvement, they would expect to be waking him up in a few more days. Obviously, they couldn't be specific, or promise them a particular day when they could wake Jason up, because that part was dependent on Jason himself, but they would reduce the sedation once they were sure his recovery was continuing.

Sitting on the visitors' chairs on either side of Jason's bed, like Casey's friends had done with her, Don and Michael talked to Jason as if he were already awake. Encouraged by the doctors to speak as normally as possible, the two men relayed everything they had seen in Auckland, what they'd had for dinner and how good it was; in fact, anything and everything they could think of, as well as telling him that his mum was calling every day to see how he was and begging for him to get better. So, could he now just wake up and come back to them safe and well?

Unbeknown to Don and Michael, Jason could hear their familiar voices because he was looking down on his father and brother, which he was certain meant that he was already gone. He had to be, why else was he outside of his body? Jason longed to comfort them both, but he knew he couldn't because the body lying on the bed was just a shell. His soul, his spirit, was now free and he no longer felt trapped by the physical body he'd left lying in the bed below him. Jason felt an intense love comforting him and whilst he knew this was meant to be, he just wished it had been less painful for the family he was now leaving behind.

Remembering that he had already said goodbye to Casey, Jason was about to send part of himself to say goodbye to his mother. Gloria, his darling mum, who had nurtured him whilst his dad had worked to support the family and give them everything he could. Jason's parents had opened up so many opportunities in his life, that he felt lucky to have had them as parents. It was their sacrifices and encouragement, which had enabled him to have the chance of the future he had dreamt of and this opportunity of a wonderful new life in New Zealand. Only he'd just gone and ruined it hadn't he; that small mistake of missing his footing had cost him dearly. Jason found it a hard wrench to leave and so he waited, watching over his father and brother, wishing that he could reach out to them and talk to them, just to reassure them that there was no need to worry and that he was fine now.

Desperately wanting to relieve their pain and anguish, Jason felt frustrated that he couldn't find the way back into his body. But as he continued to watch his family and seeing their raw emotions spilling over, he was aware of a presence beside him and looking around he saw his granddad. The older man was smiling and looked so very happy to see his grandson. As he spoke, Jason's granddad sounded calm, his voice was smooth and unruffled.

'Jason, my boy, I'm so happy to see you. I've been watching you grow over the years and I'm so proud of you, you've done well my boy. I've seen that you've made some mistakes, but you've learnt from them, as you were meant to do. Well done, my boy!'

Jason told his granddad that he loved his 'Gramps' and missed him, very much, as they all had since he'd passed.

'I know, but it's OK. I'm fine now, so don't you worry, my boy, we'll see each other again sometime. Now, go on with you, get back there...they still need you. I'll see you later.'

With that, Jason's granddad smiled and waved to him as his reflection faded to nothing and he was gone once more. Without even trying, Jason found himself being pulled back into his body and turned his face towards his dad ever so slightly. Jason could hear his dad speaking, but he was still unable to respond.

Right at that moment, the consultant came into the room and told Jason's father and brother that they'd held a case discussion and because of the improvements they'd seen with Jason, they had decided to start the process of waking him up. The two men were excited and alarmed all at the same time and having expressed their understanding of what they'd been told, the two of them then watched anxiously as the drug that would wake Jason up, was injected into his drip. To give the doctor full access to Jason, both men had moved to one side of his bed where they found themselves standing close together and grasping each other's hands. As they gripped the other tightly, the two of them pleaded encouragement to the sleeping patient.

"Come on now, Jase."

Whilst watching his brother's face intently, Michael spoke first, closely followed by Don.

"Come on, boy, it's time to wake up now, we need you to open your eyes, son."

Don was now encouraging Jason to come around in a pleading voice.

Jason was becoming aware of his legs, they felt heavy, but boy did his head feel weird! He could hear his dad and...yes, Michael. His brother Michael was there as well and the two of them were talking to him. Jason half-expected to hear Casey, but then he remembered he had said goodbye to her, which seemed so long ago and in a faraway place. He couldn't quite remember. His head was muzzy. Was he underwater when he had said goodbye to her? How did that happen? He remembered tripping and falling; did he go underwater? Jason's mind was confused, but he could hear his dad telling him to wake up. He was struggling; something wasn't right. Where was he? Why did he feel so weird? As Jason tried to lift his hand to his head, it wouldn't work properly and just flopped back down. Was he in bed? Now trying desperately to wake up, Jason was struggling inside to move his arms and his legs; he had no energy, and wondered what was going on?

"Dad, did you see that, his hand moved!"

Michael and Don were excited. They wanted to reach out and shake him awake, but instead they stood back, and along with the medical team, were willing Jason to wake up properly.

"Come on, Jase, you can do it...come on, wake up!"

Both of them were talking at him together and almost frantically, desperate for Jason to open his eyes and speak to them.

The muzzy feeling was clearing and Jason could hear Michael, although he couldn't quite make out what his brother had said, because he sounded so excited. Jason needed to wake up and to see what was going on, as he didn't want to be missing out on anything.

Watching the scene in front of him, the consultant was as anxious as Michael and Don, but managed to keep his reactions professional. However, the young nurse beside him was just as excited as Jason's family. Maia had been looking after Jason ever since he'd arrived and had grown attached to both her patient and his family. Whilst it was not usual for her to get attached to patients and without having spoken a single word to him, Maia had somehow fallen in love with this one and desperately wanted Jason to wake up and to be OK.

As the four of them watched Jason, they also glanced at each other momentarily, each one of them anxious, but happy and smiling. There was something special about this moment that they were all sharing, none of them said anything, but they all sensed an immense feeling of love in the room. Somehow they knew that Jason was going to wake up any moment and more importantly, they were sure he was going to be fine. As they all looked back to Jason, his eyes moved beneath his eyelids and slowly they began to open.

"Jason, my boy…"

Don was so relieved he could hardly speak. The consultant stepped in: "Hello, Jason, welcome back. Can you hear me? How do you feel?"

As Jason glanced towards him, his eyes struggled to focus on this face he'd never seen before. The voice spoke to him again: "You had a little accident on the quayside, do you remember? You're in hospital in Auckland and your dad and brother are here too."

As Jason followed the consultant's eyes, he looked towards his dad and brother, who were stood on the other side of his bed. The two of them were smiling at him and hugging each other, both laughing with relief and happiness to see Jason awake. Although he felt incredibly tired, Jason smiled back at them as his voice rasped a question: "What are you guys doing here?"

"Jees, Jase, you gave us a fright," Michael said. "We've been here ever since your accident. Do you remember falling from the boat?"

Michael was ecstatic that Jason was awake and responsive, but like the consultant, he needed to know if Jason had any recollection of the accident.

"Boat? Whose boat?" Jason said confused.

Jason was puzzled. Why were they asking about a boat and why were the two of them here in New Zealand? Don answered Jason and explained what had happened, as the consultant listened and watched Jason's reactions. Yes, his responses seemed fine; there seemed to be no brain damage affecting his mind, except that he had absolutely no recollection of the accident itself. Jason could not remember falling into the water, or that he had even been out on Lee and Becca's boat. Thankfully though, he did remember that he was in New Zealand, having recently moved there for work and that Lee was his new boss and Becca was married to Lee.

Such recall was more than the consultant had expected, so he was more than satisfied for now that Jason appeared to have no lasting damage mentally. All that was needed for the moment was to check that Jason could move his arms and legs, and that his reflexes were as expected. Then leaving Jason to rest with his father and brother, the consultant said they would try and sit him up later and run some further tests. Before leaving the room, the consultant asked Nurse Maia to stay with Jason and check on him every five minutes, adding that if anything seemed abnormal she should page him immediately, otherwise he'd be back in an hour.

Don and Michael thanked the consultant, both of them still ecstatic that Jason was awake and seemed OK. Needing to call Gloria, despite the fact it was the middle of the night in the UK, Don knew his wife would be as overjoyed as they were that Jason was awake and seemed fine. Calling her in the middle of the night was no issue at all. In fact, Don joked he'd be in trouble if he *didn't* call her immediately. Dialling the international call, they waited for Gloria to answer the landline and as her sleepy hello rang out across the line, Don told his wife to switch on the mobile phone so they could 'Face-time' her.

Realising something important must have happened, Gloria questioned them as she turned on the iPhone with her now shaking hands. As soon as the handset sprang to life, Don rang and Gloria accepted the call, then, as she saw the face that was looking back at her, she cried out loud: "Jason! Is that really you? Oh my God I can't believe it. Oh, Jason, you're alive, you're awake. Oh, my boy, I can't believe it. Oh thank you, God, thank you!"

Gloria was sobbing with relief as she stared at the screen. Don's face appeared and he smiled at her. "Gloria, you won't believe it, but he's OK! Our boy is back with us and he's doing fine so you can rest well now, my darling. As expected, he *is* very tired and because they only brought him round an hour ago and he'll be drifting in and out of sleep for a while yet, but he's fine and he can wiggle his toes and everything."

The relief in Don's voice and the news he was now sharing with Gloria was all she needed to know, and even though the tears kept flowing, she was just so incredibly happy and thankful that her son had been given back to them.

"Oh, Don, I don't know what I would have done if we'd lost him."

Gloria was smiling through her tears, wanting to reach into the phone and hug her husband and both sons.

"I know my love, but we didn't lose him, we have a lot to be thankful for. He seems fine and just needs to rest for now. Nurse Maia is checking him every five minutes to make sure he's OK and the consultant will be back soon. We'll be here for the rest of the day so don't you worry. Try and go back to sleep now and I'll call you later today, when you're up and about. I love you, Glor' and always will my love. I can't wait to see you."

Don winked at his wife and blew her a kiss before passing the phone to Michael to say hello to his mother and share his relief that Jason was awake and back with them.

As she hung up the phone from her boys, Gloria sat back against her pillows and said a prayer of thanks. Snuggling back down into bed, she cuddled the Teddy she had retrieved from Jason's childhood bedroom, the day Don and Michael had flown out to New Zealand. Gloria smiled, kissed the bear and closed her eyes, completely exhausted by the worry of the last week and the relief she had just experienced.

The boy's mother slept properly for the first time in days; a deeply relaxed and dreamless sleep, comforted by the knowledge that her boys were all alive and well, and more importantly, together. As Gloria slept through the hours, so her father appeared beside her bed. He smiled down at her frail sleeping form and told her that he had seen Jason, and that he was going to be fine and that he had sent him back to be with Michael and Don. As the sleeping Gloria sighed, her father gently lifted his daughter into his arms once more and as the room filled with pure and intense love, he told her not to worry and that Don would be joining them both soon.

Chapter 20

The Next Chapter

Casey sat down to have a stab at writing a new column; her plan was to start with her recent relationship experiences, but also to use a certain amount of artistic licence when describing the episode involving Jason and the day he had turned up at her apartment so unexpectedly. Yes, she decided, she would definitely rewrite the part where Jason had vented at Matt, most especially now that Jason was still lying in a coma (or so she thought).

Edine had said to Casey that if she ever felt like telling the full story about her hospital experience, the magazine would run it as an extended column. This meant pretty much offering Casey two whole pages for her story, if she could fill them. Being the successful Editor that she was, Edine thought it was a great opportunity to put a positive spin on things. Casey had such a lot to share with their readers, what with the cancer scare, her reaction to the anaesthetic *and* then recovering from the coma. It seemed like a no-brainer to Edine. Knowing that the headline alone would push sales up, Edine encouraged Casey to link up with Doctor Kate, who also wrote for the magazine. All three women thought it would be a great idea to share Casey's story, but they also agreed to leave it for a few weeks, until Casey was fully recovered and less fragile about the whole topic, confident that Casey would still be close enough to the whole episode, to be able to relay her very real feelings and experiences.

It was because of Edine's suggestion that Casey decided to actually start writing her story now. Because even though it would not be printed for some time yet, Casey could capture all of her current emotions and thoughts, whilst it was all so fresh and raw. Whilst her story needed to be as close to the truth as possible, Casey also wanted to put a more positive spin on it, to encourage women to check themselves thoroughly and speak to their GP about anything which seemed odd or out of the ordinary. Doing that as soon as they found anything odd, rather than waiting too long, was so important and Casey wanted to encourage women not to delay seeking medical help. This was also where Doctor Kate could assist in providing guidance and accurate medical advice, to ensure that it was a responsible article.

Casey had been feeling so much better over the last few days that she managed to assure Matt she was well enough to be left alone. She encouraged him to go and train two of his regular clients, who had been patiently waiting for him to start working again. So, after making Casey promise to call him if she felt at all unwell, Matt agreed to leave her to her writing and rang two of his clients, whom he knew would be able to do a gym session at short notice. Like them, he too was keen to get back into his normal workouts and daily routines.

Matt hadn't been working with his client for more than twenty minutes when Michael's number flashed on his mobile screen once again. Having pre-warned his client he may have to take a call, Matt picked up the phone. His heart seemed to skip a beat as he answered with a worried voice, knowing it was the middle of the night over in New Zealand.

"Hi, Michael, how are you doing?"

"Oh, mate, I'm just great, fantastic in fact!"

Matt was relieved to hear Michael reply with a much happier voice than the previous call. In fact, he was exuberant in telling Matt that Jason had finally woken up and yes, that he seemed to be OK and had even managed to 'Face-time' with their Mum during the night. Michael was clearly relieved and went on to say the medical team were monitoring Jason, but that he was awake and talking and so far, seemed unaffected by the accident, other than the fact that he had no recollection of it. Apparently, the nursing staff had told him that was perfectly normal and almost to be expected in these types of circumstances. Michael also mentioned Nurse Maia and how she had been looking after Jason so well, and that he thought something might develop between the two of them because he could see how much Maia thought of Jason.

"Yeeessssss!" Matt shouted out loud and punched the air, making his client, Bob, jump out of his skin, at which Matt apologised for scaring him. Listening to Michael's happier voice and the good news, Matt felt like a huge weight had been lifted from his shoulders. Suddenly the whole weight of his sense of guilt and responsibility for Jason's accident was gone and he felt totally free from it. Matt was ecstatic to hear that Jason was OK. Punching the air again with relief, he thanked Michael for letting him know and said he would tell Casey as soon as he was finished with Bob. After finishing the conversation with Michael and hanging up the call, Matt immediately turned to Bob and almost bursting with relief, relayed the bones of the story about Jason's accident to him. The rest of the training session flew by with both men benefitting from the power and energy of Matt's euphoria, which had released the burden of guilt that Matt had been carrying since the awful day, when Jason had challenged him outside Casey's apartment.

As Matt let himself in through Casey's front door, he called out to her that he was back. Standing up to greet him as he strode across the floor towards her, Casey was surprised when Matt picked her up and swung her around, hugging and kissing her. As he explained the fantastic news, Casey broke down, this time with tears of joy and happiness that Jason was awake and seemed to be fine. Matt said the only negative was that Jason had amnesia about the accident, which they both agreed, wasn't surprising considering the trauma he'd suffered and besides, it could all come back to him any day, but so far he was fine and that was all that mattered. Casey couldn't quite believe it, but she was as relieved as Matt and totally thrilled that Jason was going to be fine. Hugging her to him again, this time Matt kissed Casey passionately; both of them felt so utterly relieved and thankful that Jason was awake.

The two of them couldn't stop hugging as relieved happiness seemed to exude from every pore of their being. This truly was the best news they could have wished for, since Casey herself had come out of her own coma. The two of them were both keen to pass on the great news to Carole, Amanda, Tilly and Dave, as well as Matt's cousin Charley.

Knowing that very evening, they were all due to be eating with Giovanni and Maria, Casey suggested they could all celebrate the good news of Jason's recovery with their hosts, to which Matt happily agreed.

"Good idea, it's going to be an even better night now!"

Although he did call Charley straight away, now aware of her long-term crush on Jason, Matt knew she would be desperate for the news and as ecstatic as they were to hear that Jason was OK. As he expected, Charley was over the moon and couldn't stop thanking Matt for calling her with such good news.

The fact that they all had such a lot to be grateful for was not lost on Matt or Casey, with the whole experience of the last few weeks feeling completely unreal to them both. Whoever would have thought that what had happened to them all in the last few weeks, could have ever happened to one small group of friends. It really *was* like they had stepped into and then back out of some kind of parallel universe; but thankfully, one with such a happy result for both Casey *and* Jason, with both of them now on the road to recovery.

Giovanni and Maria could hardly believe their ears when Casey and Matt told them the brilliant news about Jason. The Italian couple were amazed that both Casey *and* Jason, whilst on opposite sides of the world and due to different causes, had both been in a coma, more or less at the same time. It was totally bizarre and whilst they struggled to comprehend the news, both of them were also extremely happy to hear that Jason was also now recovering. Giovanni and Maria reactively drew their hands across their chests in the sign of the cross and kissed their rosary beads, as a gesture of thanks for the safe return of both Casey and Jason. This action caused Matt to again recognise what lovely people Giovanni and Maria were, and completely understood how Casey had come to look upon them like they were her extended family.

As the others began to arrive at the restaurant, Maria dashed back into the kitchen to ensure all the food was ready, so that Marco and Piero could also join in with this very special dining occasion. Carole and Amanda were just as excited and so very grateful to Giovanni and Maria for the invitation, as were Tilly and Dave. Their small group had truly bonded during the time that Casey was in hospital and this evening, they were all bubbling with enthusiastic excitement and warmth, as well as much love for each other *and* their generous hosts. This promised to be a night to remember for them all, as glasses were clinked, along with calls of *Bon Appetito* amid much laughter and exclamations.

As always, the truly wholesome Italian food that Giovanni's family created was of the highest quality and everyone enjoyed sharing and eating. So, as the wine flowed, the small group ate, drank and were having the best of evenings that any of them had experienced in a very long time.

Looking around the table at this bunch of amazing people who now meant so much to him, as well as to Casey, Matt picked up his knife and gently tapped his glass, causing them all to pause and look towards him. As Matt stood up to speak, he stated that he had three toasts for them all that evening and looking directly at their hosts, he began.

"Maria and Giovanni," he said. "Thank you both for arranging this wonderful evening, and to be able to share this moment with you both, as well as all of our dear friends, makes me very happy. Everyone, could I please ask you to raise your glasses to Maria and Giovanni, our wonderful hosts."

As everyone responded with raised glasses, nods of appreciation and excited calls of 'Salute' and 'Grazie', Maria and Giovanni visibly blushed, but took the thanks with great pride, as Matt also thanked their sons for the delicious food.

"Now, whilst you still have your glasses in your hands, folks, let's also raise a toast to Jason and give thanks that he's awake! We all wish him a speedy recovery, as well as much happiness with his Nurse Maia!" Matt said with his glass raised.

"To Jason and Maia!"

Everyone chimed in together and laughed as they happily clinked glasses again, took another sip and with smiles all around, looked back to Matt for his third toast. With their glasses rattling as everyone set them down between the cutlery and plates, Matt said his most important toast involved a question first. Turning to face Casey who was sat beside him, Matt pushed back his chair and slowly bent down on one knee. Everyone around the table gasped, including Casey, as Matt took her left hand in his and looked into her eyes.

"Casey, my darling, you are the most beautiful woman and person that I have ever met. I cannot believe how you have affected my life in such a short time and when I thought I would lose you, I just couldn't bear it. I promised myself that if I was lucky enough for you to be given back to me, I would waste no more time and ask you this very important question."

A hushed silence fell across the table as everyone held their breath and Matt continued: "My darling, Casey, every day I look at you, I cannot believe how beautiful you are both inside and out, and how very lucky I am to have found you. So, will you now do me the very great honour of becoming my wife?"

As the group looked on, still holding their breath, Matt's stomach did a back-flip with nerves at what Casey's reply would be. Smiles spread across the sea of faces watching the two of them, as anticipation filled the hearts and eyes of their friends, as along with Matt, they awaited Casey's reply.

"Oh, Matt..."

Casey leant forward and hugged Matt as she nodded, unable to speak as happy tears rolled down her face and she kissed him before whispering her answer: "Yes, yes, I will marry you! Oh, Matt..."

As the words left Casey's lips, the table erupted into thunderous applause as banging hands thumped down on the table, causing the glasses, plates and cutlery to bounce and clatter. With tears rolling down their faces, Maria and Giovanni hugged each other, their happiness flowing over as they then stood up to embrace and congratulate the happy couple. Cheers and whoops of delight were made as every other person around the table also stood up to hug them both. The men were slapping Matt's back with congratulations, hugging them both and kissing Casey's face, as the girls joined in with more hugs and more kisses. Each of them encouraging the two young lovers to enjoy all of the worthy congratulations and good wishes, now being showered upon them.

Casey felt amazing and gobsmacked at this totally unexpected proposal, but she was so very happy. She was going to be married to her gorgeous Matt and here now, with this group of friends, who truly were her real family, she couldn't be happier and she loved them all dearly. Even Tilly's Dave, being a relative newcomer to this little group, had earned his way into Casey's affections.

But it was Matt himself that Casey now admired, as with shining eyes, she watched him interacting with her friends. Her gorgeous man was confident, handsome and totally engaging. Casey felt truly blessed, as she also sent a prayer out to her Nanny Em and granddad, whom she felt sure would be happily watching over their celebrations tonight. Casey was happier than she had ever been since her beloved grandparents had left her and she just knew they would both be thrilled for the two of them.

Matt and Casey had been incredibly lucky and were reaping the benefits of their loving friendships, as their lives transpired in a way that others looking in from the outside might only envy. For Casey, Matt and all of their friends, this was a night to remember. The champagne corks popped and bubbles flowed into their glasses over and over again, as the music was turned up and they danced and partied into the early hours, each of them drunk on happiness and their love for each other.

Epilogue

One Year Later

Don and Michael were unable to reach Gloria when they tried to call her again on the day that Jason woke up. After receiving a worried call from Don and using her spare key, Gloria's best friend and neighbour had entered the house to find Gloria still in bed, the Teddy in her arms and a smile on her forever sleeping face. Gloria had indeed joined her own parents and would see her husband Don again just three months later, when he would join her, happy that his boys were doing well, but no longer able to live without his adored Gloria.

Jason made a full recovery, with the exception of the memory loss from the day of his accident. When he was finally discharged from hospital, Jason and Maia did start seeing each other. As the months passed and he fell more deeply in love with her, Jason decided he would stay in New Zealand to create his future with Maia and asked his brother Michael to join him.

Although Michael had not wanted to leave England previously, with their parents now gone and Jason on the other side of the world, he decided to take up his brother's invitation. Michael now worked for a guy that Lee and Becca knew, running tourist boat-cruises from Auckland Harbour around the coastline and was having the time of his life, enjoying the single dating scene in sunny Auckland.

Nine months into their love affair, Maia and Jason got engaged, and planned to get married on the beach at Christmas, having already discussed how many children they would have. Jason wanted two children, while Maia had been thinking three. Therefore, Michael informed his brother that meant they'd be having at least three...then laughing, had said maybe even four children, particularly since Maia had twins in her family tree.

Giovanni and Maria's son Marco (the Chef), took a shine to Carole the same evening that Matt proposed to Casey. They have been dating ever since, much to the delight of Marco's parents - who are already asking them when they plan to marry? Luckily Marco knows his parents well and is not fazed by their early encouragement. Carole on the other hand blushes every time they mention it, but secretly, is also quite open to the idea, should Marco choose to propose.

Amanda is travelling again and is not ready to change her single lifestyle, which takes her to so many interesting places across the world, and which she loves.

Having moved in together, Tilly and Dave announced they were to become parents; it wasn't planned, but they were both thrilled to bits and Tilly is growing bigger by the day. Dave is already planning for the mad dash to the hospital and is convinced Tilly will have twins because her tummy is so big. Everyone thinks Dave secretly wants that to be true and they all agree that the couple will make great parents.

As for John, well the inevitable happened and Gemma dumped him the moment a new fitness instructor started at her gym; which left John single and heartbroken at losing Gemma.

Giovanni and Maria are still running the restaurant and see all of the friends on a regular basis, treating them all as part of their own family. The next big gathering is already being planned.

Claire Anderson got promoted by Edine and is now a very close friend of Casey's and has been supporting her throughout Casey's induction into the world of writing for the magazine.

Edine has seen Casey's column go from strength to strength and ever since Casey shared her recent medical and romantic experiences, Edine has been delighted by the dramatic increase in the number of copies sold and loves having Casey on the writing team at *Just for You!*

Casey and Matt got married in the spring and as the blossom trees showered their pale pink petals over the happy couple, their friends congratulated them and photographed the happy event. On the eve of their wedding, Matt carried his bride across the threshold of their recently built colonial styled house. Swiftly making his way into the master bedroom, the two of them consummated their love and their vows, hoping for the sound of tiny feet to be joining them both soon.

The End

Lightning Source UK Ltd.
Milton Keynes UK
UKOW02f2203140716

278396UK00002B/23/P